Who Said Dying Was Easy?

JACQUELINE WILDEN

JACQUELINE WILDEN

About the Author

As she came to the end of a nursing career spanning 46 years, Jacqueline was increasingly inspired to develop her spiritual side. She is also a complementary therapist, Reiki Master and practicing Medium.

At this time in her life she found herself becoming inspired to write poetry, much of which is devoted to spiritual and environmental issues. This resulted in publication of an anthology of her poems, *Angels Ink: A Collection of Poetry Inspired by Spirits and Angels,* which is also available on Amazon Books.

Who Said Dying Was Easy? is Jacqueline's first novel.

A second anthology of poems is also close to completion, and she has a second novel in the pipe line.

JACQUELINE WILDEN

Acknowledgments

My heart felt gratitude and thanks go to my patient, understanding and knowledgeable husband, Dave, without whom I wouldn't have been able to publish this book.

Likewise, my attitude of gratitude goes to my Inspirer Guides, Angels and Spirit team, who have inspired and guided me in writing this novel.

This novel is also dedicated to all those who have awoken, and to all those who eventually will.

Namasté

"Be like a sunflower — always turn towards the light"

JACQUELINE WILDEN

Foreword

Apart from indigenous populations, much of humanity has forgotten that we are spiritual beings. We are all connected, not only to a higher consciousness, but also to each other, to all animals and to all flora on this planet. We are not a mortal body with a spirit, but rather a spirit in a mortal body. When we exist in the physical, we are mortal yet also immortal.

As Spirit we exist as a vibration of light energy, and each time we decide to reincarnate back into a mortal body, we contract to learn an important lesson, gained by having the physical experience. Energy cannot be extinguished or destroyed, only changed — therefore as Spirit we are eternal.

Our soul too resonates as a light energy but is also omnipresent. Our soul is a part of us, yet apart from us. It resonates with our spirit essence, yet is, and has, independent vibrational consciousness.

Every spirit's goal is to achieve enlightenment by way of learning and experiencing all of the universal lessons, so that eventually it will ascend to a higher dimension of love consciousness. In turn, a soul's destiny is to bring about the means by which that spirit can ascend, as it too seeks to exist within the higher echelons of unconditional love ubiquitous to the universe. As human beings, how we choose to accomplish enlightenment is entirely up to each and every one of us, for we all have choices and free will. Eventually, when our spirit's purpose is achieved and our soul's destiny is fulfilled, together they ascend and come to know that which is Divine consciousness — a consciousness that is all-consuming, unquestionable and immeasurable, and is the total expression of the Divine's unconditional Love.

Prologue

<***>

It came as quite a surprise to Gerard Elliot when he suddenly became aware of a distortion within his energy field. Although it was barely perceptible, he knew that something had changed and it was so unexpected that it almost stopped him dead in his tracks. The feeling was very strange and quite unnerving, and having never experienced anything like it before, he was intrigued to find out why it was happening.

Instinctively, he knew that he had to make his way to the Halls of Wisdom, and as he entered through the expansive opening and headed down a brightly lit corridor towards the even brighter reception area, he felt a little unnerved. The reception was vibrant and lively and held an imposing position at the very centre of the majestic building. Because it served as the main meeting place for all returnees, it was a very busy area. Ged was amazed at the amount of hustle and bustle which was taking place around him, as he recognised the differing energy prints and vibrations which were being emitted from a variety of Ethereals who were congregating there.

Feeling a little perplexed and unsure, he looked around for somewhere to escape the crowds and decided to elevate himself up into a corner recess. From this vantage point he could observe the comings and goings from a measured distance. Settling into the recess, he could tell that some of the Ethereals were angels and archangels, as he sensed that they were resonating at a higher frequency and emitting a light vibration unlike his own. Looking across the reception area, Ged suddenly realised that some monumental disaster must have happened or be happening within the earth realm to account for the huge influx of returnee spirits and their guides.

Intuitively he knew that some of the guides were teachers, enablers or inspirers, as he sensed that they were wise and worldly. He recognised that many of the energy auras belonged to life guides, but it was apparent that there was also quite a large number of healer guides there as well, as not only were their vibrations different but they also emitted a glowing energy field of blue, oscillating light.

Ged gave a chuckle to himself at the recollection of what being in a crowd had been like, back on earth. The reception area reminded him of a very busy train station or airport terminal, as spirit who had returned home went about their quest to be where they knew they needed to be, and their guides, who were getting re-acquainted with each other, joked and conversed and rambunctious laughter intermittently filled the air. The comings and goings amused him, as despite the apparent chaos of the place, the atmosphere was one of great jollity and happiness

His thoughts were suddenly interrupted as he again became aware of a strange tingling sensation and he began to ponder why he had been summoned. Above the noise and banter, his attention was drawn to an opening door from which a figure dressed in a flowing white robe emerged and beckoned him to come forward. Floating down towards the figure, he eagerly crossed the threshold of the doorway, as his impatience to learn why he had been called become all-consuming.

Shyly glancing at the ethereal figure, Ged noticed how tall and willowy she was. Smiling, she gestured for him to follow her. She was graceful and serene and moved effortlessly but at speed down a long, wide corridor. Ged hurriedly followed, trying to keep pace with her. Nearing the end of the corridor, the robed figure stopped abruptly in front of a large, wooden door and turning the handle, indicated for Ged to go in. Doing as she asked, he entered a small ante-room.

"Wait here," the figure said in a soft, lilting voice as she retreated and quietly closed the door behind her.

Ged was alone and looked around expectantly. He realised that the room was incredibly bright yet had a tranquillity about it, quite unlike the hustle and bustle which he had just experienced in the reception area. His attention was drawn to the quartz floor which glistened and sparkled with bursts of blue and silver flickers of light. The spectacular phenomenon was hypnotic to watch, and Ged felt comforted as he remembered that this was what it was like to float weightless in the vastness of space, surrounded by a million galaxies, stars and planets. Looking at the walls and the ceiling, he noticed that they were shimmering as though he was looking through a heat haze, and he became aware of how serene he felt. It reminded him that he, himself, was part of this amazing, expansive Universe.

Lost in thought, Ged suddenly noticed a movement in front of him, as a door which appeared to be made of quartz crystal swung open, effortlessly and silently. The robed figure appeared again and sombrely nodded her acknowledgement to him. Transfixed, he noticed her porcelain beauty and delicate features. She gestured for him to follow her once more and Ged found himself entering a chamber which held an air of unquestioning importance. Becoming abruptly aware that he was surrounded by a kaleidoscope of beautiful hues which bounced around the room, he felt like he was being immersed in an immense rainbow, and instantly felt a great sense of bliss and tranquillity flow over and through him. Realising that the chamber was made of the most exquisite crystals, he yielded to the magnificent power which enveloped him and started to absorb the healing energies while he waited for further instructions. Silently the robed figure appeared at his side again and telepathically told him to make his way to the centre of the vast, windowless chamber. Looking behind him, he realised that the entity was now retreating towards the crystal door. She then turned towards him, briefly exchanged a tender glance and graciously nodding her head in a farewell gesture, vanished.

As instructed, Ged approached the centre of the opaque, crystal floor and noticed two figures standing close together a little way in front of him. They were in muted conversation, with their heads bowed in mutual respect, and didn't seem to have noticed that he was in their presence. Giving a nervous cough as a means of attracting the two entities attention, Ged smiled as they abruptly stopped their discussion and simultaneously looked over in his direction.

"Ah, good, you're here! Welcome," said the smaller of the two figures.

Ged respectfully lowered his gaze and stared at the crystal floor. He suddenly became disorientated, almost hypnotised, as he noticed a turbulent, broiling mass of swirling, fluid energy ebbing and flowing beneath him. Enthralled at what he was seeing, many moments passed before he became aware that the two entities were still looking over in his direction, studying him. The taller one gracefully approached him and holding out her hand, touched the centre of Ged's heart channel and instantly connected with his energy field.

Ged felt a slight tug and stared mesmerised at the kindly face with its serene features, before realising that she was speaking to him telepathically.

"Ah, welcome most Beloved, although it is with much dismay that we have need to bring you before us," she said forlornly as she withdrew her hand. "I am Kyah, Keeper of the Akasha, and this is Hamneth, Chief Elder of the Adjusters."

Ged glanced over in Hamneth's direction and nodded respectfully in acknowledgement.

"Beloved one, it is with heavy hearts that we have to inform you of an unfortunate matter," Kyah said remorsefully.

"What matter? I don't understand," Ged replied, somewhat puzzled.

"The matter of our Beloved, the one known to you as Molly," replied Hamneth, somewhat impatiently. "This is a matter which is in much need of your urgent intervention and assistance."

Ged felt confused and bewildered as he struggled to make sense of why he was there.

"Beloved, we have the unenviable task of informing you that the Beloved One known to you as Molly is currently trapped within the dimensional structure of the astral plane, unaware that she has left her physical body," Hamneth continued. "Obviously, being where she is makes her quite vulnerable, so this situation has unprecedented urgency, which is why we are asking that you go and assist in her transition back here to the spiritual realm."

Ged was visibly shaken as he tried to comprehend what Hamneth had just told him. "I'm sorry, I still don't understand. What do you mean Molly is trapped within the astral plane? How can she be?" he asked, hesitantly. "How can she... unless you're saying that she's dead?"

"Yes, that is exactly what we are saying. For heaven's sake, do we have to spell it out?"

Hamneth was perplexed at Ged's lack of comprehension. "Yea, faeries in higher realms! Yes, her physical body's dead, the problem is that her spirit is stuck in limbo in the astral plane."

Ged looked back and forth between the two entities and feeling somewhat foolish, wished that he didn't feel so inept and powerless.

"It is with great consternation and much dismay that we have learned that our Beloved has been rendered virtually inert — so inert that we fear she will be unable to find her own way back to the spiritual realm," Hamneth continued.

Finding it hard to comprehend what he was hearing, Ged began to pace back and forth, as his mind began to swim with numerous questions and his mounting anguish couldn't be contained. "Oh, my goodness! This is terrible. How long has she been there for? Will she be all right? Is she safe? What can we do?"

Hamneth raised his hand trying to calm Ged down. "Yes, it is terrible, but as far as we are aware, she hasn't... Oh, just a moment... Good, I have just had clarification from Pettruf, Chief of the Council of Elders, that she is unseen at present. Fortunately, she hasn't been confined to the astral plane long enough to have attracted the attention of the shadowers, or any unpleasant transitional beings or other similar negative energies, if that is what you are concerned about."

Ged let out a sigh of relief. "Oh, thank goodness," he said, reassured. "You had me worried there for a minute. I knew that eventually I would be the one to meet her, I just hadn't reckoned on it being this soon and certainly not in this way."

"No, I'm sure you hadn't," Kyah interrupted, giving Ged a reassuring smile.

Ged let a grin cross his face as he suddenly recalled some of Molly's childhood antics. "Ha! I was just remembering when she was a kid. Always up to mischief she was, always wandering off, doing her own thing. She could be a right little madam too. Drove us mad most of the time, she did, well at least her mother," he said ruefully. "Always had to do things her way. Always had to have the last word, that one."

"Yes, Ged, we are aware of all that but now isn't the time to be having a trip down memory lane, I'm sure you'll agree," Hamneth said abruptly, interrupting Ged's train of thought.

Ged was irritated and a little put out by Hamneth's brisk manner. "No, of course not," he stammered, "I was just…"

Kyah smiled once again before intervening in the conversation. "Now, now, no matter. Blessed One, you will have plenty of time and an abundance of opportunities to reminisce with her upon your return."

Eagerly nodding in agreement with Kyah and rubbing his hands together Hamneth smiled encouragingly at Ged. "Right then, that's settled. We will see how things are when you get back. I trust that you know what to do, don't you?"

Ged nodded vaguely. "Erm… yes, I think I do. Isn't it just a case of locating her spirit light?"

Hamneth looked incredulously at Kyah and raising his eyes and arms simultaneously, shook his head in disbelief.

Kyah glared at Hamneth and telepathically told him to stop being so petulant, before turning to Ged and nodding encouragingly.

"Yes, Ged, exactly that. But I would also advise that prior to your departure you seek the wisdom of re-attachment from the Tree of Knowledge, just in case her cord has been severed. And don't forget that Molly may be a little disorientated. I think it would be prudent to also remind you that once you are within the Astral plane, you'll need to completely open your heart channel so that your spirit light will shine brightly and become a beacon of unconditional love for all to see."

Ged nodded his understanding as Kyah continued, "Also just to remind you that when you do return, Molly will be in your charge, for you are now her designated custodian, at least that is, until the Elders and Wise Ones receive further instructions from the twelfth dimension as to the course of any interventions which may be required."

Ged winced as he realised the enormous responsibility which had been bestowed on him.

Hamneth gravitated to Ged's side. "So, are you up for the job?" he asked, looking him up and down.

"What? of course I am, what do you take me for? I'd better get a move on; she mustn't stay there a minute longer than she has to."

"No, exactly," smiled Kyah reassuringly.

Ged hurriedly left the Halls of Wisdom and made his way to the Gardens of Tranquillity. He headed straight towards the Tree of Knowledge, which was firmly planted in the centre of the Gardens on a slightly raised, grassy embankment. He knew about the knowledge tree and had passed it on many occasions, but had never needed to access its wisdom or teachings. It stood tall and majestic, with its boughs and branches reaching high into the ether. It always had a full canopy of gold and silver-coloured leaves which never shed, faded or died and the bark on its trunk glowed with a mixture of iridescent blue, pink and silver hues.

Bowing his head in reverence, he approached the ancient tree and noticed that it had begun to pulse and quiver. Telepathically he asked if he could proceed with his intended intimacy and the tree's trunk began to pulsate and glow brightly, consenting to his request. Expanding his radius of energy and encircling the trunk in an embrace of loving intent, Ged allowed the tree's wisdom cortex to meld with his vibration. Feeling a pulsing surge of energy as the tree's vigour mingled and blended with his, he began to feel soporific and almost drunk as the tree's heady exchange of vim blended with his own. Revelling in the purity and honesty of the tree's energy, he now knew exactly what he needed to do if he were to successfully bring Molly home, and he reluctantly released his connection.

Scanning the expansive space of the garden and peering into the distance, he recognised an energy light which was radiating from a tall, muscular figure. It was Molly's spirit guide, Orick. Ged telepathically connected to the energy light and instantaneously he was at Orick's side.

Studying the tall form of the beguiling entity, Ged sensed that Orick had shoulder-length, brown hair and gentle, smiling, green eyes, the corners of which were creased with laughter lines. He wore a short, green tunic and a long cloak made of brown hessian cloth which was fastened at his throat with a gold brooch, fashioned into the shape of an acorn. In his hand he carried a wooden staff made of oak. It was highly polished and seemed to gleam and shimmer, while the embellished animal carvings which ran down its length appeared to leap and dart, taking on a life-like appearance of their own. Ged also noticed its top was carved into the shape of an acorn which was sitting in its cup.

"Hello, Beloved. I believe that it is you who has been tasked with rescuing Molly. I'm so sorry that you find yourself having to do this, truly I am. We did not anticipate this turn of events," said Orick awkwardly.

Ged stiffened slightly. "No, I don't expect you did. I was just about to leave actually so if you'll excuse me, I have to go — time being of the essence and all, well certainly in cases like this, that is. I'll see you when we return, I expect," he said more belligerently than he had intended.

"Of course," nodded Orick, as he stepped aside. "Blessings to you. I eagerly await both yours and Molly's safe return."

Ged strode off without looking back. He knew what he had to do to accomplish his task. The tree had told him that the Astral plane dimension would be easier to access on the furthest side of the Gardens of Tranquillity, as the energy there was somewhat thinner and more permeable. Ged hurried to the far side as he had been instructed and condensing his energy into a spherical orb, drifted along the length of the perimeter, searching for a portal. After a while he sensed an area where the energy was thinner and more translucent and floated towards it. Sizing it up, he braced himself for what he knew would be an unpleasant experience. Thrusting his energy forwards, he penetrated the slightly resistant force.

Adjusting his vibration Ged sensed the murky, swirling greyness which now surrounded him and he became alarmed as he began to sense the presence of all manner of malevolent and unpleasant, regressed energies. With another powerful thrust he propelled himself downwards going deeper and deeper into the seemingly endless lagoon of dense, gooey greyness, he struggled to suppress his mounting fear. It took all of his strength to stop himself becoming overwhelmed with feelings of foreboding and despair, and he knew that he could quite easily succumb to the negative energies of the greyness, as he felt his vigour slowly being sucked out of him.

Ged fought hard and gathering what remaining resolve he had, drove himself forwards, intuitively floating into a quadrant of dense, white mist. Remembering Kyah's advice, he swelled his heart channel and expanded his spirit light, searching for any sign as to where Molly might be. Suddenly he became aware of a fading energy shadow. Peering into the mist, he scanned the depths below and could just make out a dull, fading flicker of an energy print and a long, silver-coloured cord flailing in the distance. Increasing his energy output, he pushed himself towards the flailing cord. As he got nearer, he felt a gentle tug as his energy field connected to it, and he could feel it pulsing and contracting weakly. Ged felt a wave of anxiety crash over him as he realised that the situation was worse than he had initially feared. It was about as bad as it could get.

Grabbing hold of the frayed end of the cord as it whipped past him, he gripped it tightly and began to descend down its length. Ged began to feel disorientated as he slowly inched his way down the length of cord into the murky depths. Becoming even more fearful and anxious, all sorts of negative thoughts began to run through his mind as he feared the worst. He wasn't sure how long he had been there. Was it minutes, hours, days even? He couldn't tell, but it felt like an eternity had passed. Suddenly a surge of relief swept over him as he realised that he could feel some resistance, as the cord had become taught. An unexpected swell of unconditional love washed over him and his joy and utter delight was all-consuming, causing him to let out a cry of elation.

Looking around, he began to notice that the white mist which had enveloped him was becoming brighter and less dense. He continued to grasp and follow the cord and felt certain that he must be getting closer to Molly, until suddenly he glimpsed her a little way beneath him. She was sitting up, gazing around, looking very bewildered. Hanging back a little, Ged watched for a while, needing to be sure that no negative entities had become attached to her while she had been in an altered state of transition. He also had to decide what the best approach would be. He couldn't just go up to her and expect her to know him — after all, he had been absent from her life for quite a while and had also missed a great deal of her childhood, what with one thing and another.

With a sudden flash of inspiration, he knew exactly what he needed to do. Swiftly changing his orb energy into spirit form, he projected onto himself how he would have looked when she had last seen him as a child. As he slowly walked towards her, he hoped that she would remember and recognise him.

The Halls of Wisdom had taken on a sombre atmosphere as Kyah and Hamneth waited expectantly for news of Ged and Molly's return. They paced the vast expanse of the inner chamber and in hushed tones discussed the seriousness of what had befallen Molly.

"It beggars belief! It has all the hallmarks, I'm telling you! I don't know what he thinks he's playing at, but one thing's for certain, this won't be tolerated. Mark my words, he's gone too far this time."

Kyah looked gravely at Hamneth as he continued his tirade. "And another thing… this just won't do. It causes no end of problems with my timetables, you know. Causes no end of a nuisance, it does," he said grumpily.

Kyah nodded in agreement. "Yes, I'm sure it does, Hamneth, I'm sure it does. I'll tell you something, though — I wouldn't want to be him when he's eventually taken to task about this one. His behaviour is becoming truly disgraceful — so arrogant and unpleasant. Why he's always trying to upset the balance of things, why he just can't let things be, is beyond me. I've often thought that it's such a pity that he can't be held accountable to karma, just like Spirit are but I suppose with him being an angel, being different and all… "

Hamneth scoffed, "I know what you mean and I couldn't agree with you more."

Kyah smiled contritely. "I find it quite difficult to utter his name, let alone bring myself to speak about him, if I'm entirely honest. Forgive me for my truthfulness, but as you know I have a hard time being as forgiving and loving as the Great Spirit is towards him. But then, I take it personally, I suppose. I know I shouldn't — it's just that when he manages to mar and maim an Akasha of one of our Beloved, he makes me and the other Elders so cross. And as much as he may be an angel — well an ousted one, — he is still a creation of the Great Spirit, more's the pity."

Hamneth nodded and grunted in agreement.

"And another thing," Kyah continued. "As an instigator of malady and maker of wretchedness, he has a right old attitude and a big chip on his wings to boot. So yes, you are absolutely right, I cannot bear to speak his name for fear his malevolent energy will taint and blend with my own."

Hamneth nodded once again. "Yes, I know what you mean, Kyah. He thinks he's being clever. He thinks he's gaining the upper hand, but as long as we and the Great Spirit have unconditional love for our charges, it doesn't matter what he gets up to — he'll never be powerful enough to win. If only he'd realise that! Thank goodness for the Great Spirit is all I can say. And don't worry for yourself, you are much too pure to be of any interest to him."

Kyah smiled fondly. "I only hope that our Great Spirit knows what's going on."

"Huh, you and me both, Kyah. You and me, both."

Chapter One: There Is No Future In What's Passed

<***>

N ancy Elliot shuffled into the hallway from the small kitchen and standing at the foot of the stairs, raised her eyes as if by doing so meant she wouldn't have to exert herself as much. Steeling herself and drawing in as deep a breath as she could manage, she shouted up the stairs.

"Molly! Molly! Are you done in the bathroom yet?"

Nan's gravelly voice faltered with the exertion and needing to steady herself, she held onto the newel post as the effort made her go into a paroxysm of coughing.

Molly heard but didn't answer; instead she carefully reached for the volume dial on her CD player and turned it up as high as it would go before returning to what she had been doing. Sitting on the edge of her bed, she carried on blowing her fingernails dry. Nan shook her head in dismay and taking out the tissue which was tucked inside the sleeve of her cardigan, dabbed away the spittle from her chin. Swearing under her breath, she started her ascent up the flight of stairs.

Molly examined her manicure efforts; she had filed and buffed each nail perfectly and then painted and given them a final top coat of clear varnish, and she was becoming impatient for them to dry and harden. She loved the deep cerise tones and the girly, purple colours which were currently all the fashion, and she went to a great deal of trouble to match them with her lipsticks. She was pleased with her latest purchase of 'Coral Rock'.

At twenty years of age, Molly Roberts was naive and young for her years. She was a petite, size eight brunette and stood all of four foot eight in her bare feet. Although she wasn't strikingly beautiful, she was considered to be attractive, having elfin features, steely blue eyes and high cheekbones. She was also an only child. Molly was also considered to be a waste of space; she knew this because her Nan repeatedly told her so. Nan also told her that she was a lazy, bone-idle, good-for-nothing lay-about who would more than likely 'amount to nowt, just like her useless father had done'.

Throughout her childhood and into her teens Molly had tried to hang on to the memories which she had of her father. When she was around ten years of age, she found a colour Polaroid photograph of him while rummaging through the sideboard cupboard. She had kept it hidden with other treasures and trinkets in a shoe box which was secreted under a pile of clothes at the bottom of her wardrobe. When she was alone or felt sad, she would retrieve the box and sitting on her bed, longingly gaze at the handsome man in the crumpled photograph. It had been taken when he was posing by a car he must have bought at some time. He was sticking his thumb up in the air and looked very pleased with himself. He was tall and slim with collar-length, brown hair and a neat moustache and he was smiling back at her, but the sun must have been shining in his eyes because he was squinting at the camera.

Molly would daydream and remember the times when her father had taken her and her mother, Annie, to the seaside on day trips. They would enjoy picnics in the sand dunes together and he had treated her to candyfloss and ice cream and held her hand at the water's edge as the ripples of the rolling waves tickled her toes and lapped around her ankles, playfully washing away her small footprints from the damp sand. She could still remember the feeling of exhilaration when he swung her up to sit on his shoulders to play 'Who's the king of the castle' — she'd loved it when he did that. She recalled memories of him taking her out and getting the bus into town for the matinee session at the local pictures on a Saturday afternoon, when she would be allowed to stuff herself to the point of feeling sick with popcorn and fizzy drinks. Then there were the visits to the zoo, when he and her mother had laughed together at the antics of the monkeys and the stink of the elephant house. Molly would smile knowingly to herself as the memories came flooding back, even though they were bitter-sweet. She hadn't told her mam or Nan that she had the photograph; it was her secret and she wasn't going to share it. Besides which no one appeared to have missed it anyway.

Sadly, with the happy memories also came tainted ones. During her early childhood she remembered hearing raised, angry voices and arguments, usually while she was tucked up in bed. Lying in the darkness of her bedroom, she would listen, hardly daring to breath. She vividly remembered the feelings of being helpless and scared, and she would bury her head under the pillow and silently plead for the rows to stop before crying herself to sleep. In the morning her mother would act as though nothing had happened and would be bright and breezy, pretending that everything was okay and that things were back to normal. Yet as young as she was, she had come to notice that her Dad was never there for breakfast after the rows.

Then one day it happened; her Dad left them. The awfulness of it all was still etched deep in her memory. She hadn't been home from school very long and was sitting at the kitchen table reading her school books when she heard raised, angry voices coming from upstairs and knew that the shouting and banging was coming from their bedroom. Her mother was crying and pleading with him to stay, and she could hear him swearing and ranting, shouting that he had had enough and was leaving and never coming back.

Molly had run to the lounge door just in time to see him come storming down the stairs, his face livid with rage. He'd flung the front door open so hard that it had bounced back off the wall and caught the back of his heel, causing him to stumble. In his anger he had stomped off down the garden path, nearly taking the wooden gate off its hinges. Standing on the doorstep, she had watched, lost and bewildered, as her Dad threw a small suitcase into the boot of the car, slammed the door shut and drove off with a spin and screech of tyres. To this day she remembered the confusion and the hot, stinging tears rolling down her cheeks and her mother sitting in a crumpled heap on the bottom stair, sobbing and pleading, "Don't go, Daniel, please don't leave." But he hadn't even looked back and that had been the last either of them saw of him.

Annie didn't get a wink of sleep that night. She spent it instead in turmoil, tossing and turning, ranting and crying, recounting the awful scene of Daniel's departure over and over in her mind and asking herself what had gone wrong with her marriage. Was she really that bad a wife and mother? Was she too needy? Was she a nag? Wasn't she pretty enough anymore? Why… why… why…?

The following dawn broke all too soon, and knowing that she would have to tell Nan that Daniel had up and left made her feel all the more wretched; she knew she would have to endure her withering looks and the smug 'I told you so' lecture. Reticently and with a broken heart, Annie had called round at Nan's house after she'd taken Molly to school. Dreading what she knew was to come, she'd fumbled for her key and let herself into the hallway of the small terraced house. Hesitantly she'd gone through to the kitchen to find Nan standing at the sink, up to her elbows in soap suds. Taking off her coat and tentatively pulling out one of the kitchen chairs, she perched on its edge and braced herself for the venomous onslaught of stinging words. The tears welled in her red, stinging eyes as she incoherently babbled and blubbered her way through her heartache.

Without a word Nan had slowly dried her hands on her apron, filled up the kettle, and set it to boil on the gas stove. Lighting a cigarette, she'd sat opposite Annie, flicking her ash into an old saucer which she reserved for that purpose. She waited for Annie to finish her torrent of howls, sobs and sniffs before stubbing out the cigarette. Looking at Annie with a disparaging stare, she shook her head and without passing any comment, went over to one of the cupboards and took out a packet of biscuits, while Annie fumbled with a screwed-up tissue which was now the worst for wear.

Blowing her nose and dabbing her eyes, Annie had eventually managed to compose herself. "Well, say something,"

Annie had implored when she'd finally finished her sorrowful tale.

Drawing in a deep breath and shaking her head, Nan got on with making a fresh pot of tea while Annie, again choking on sobs and incoherence attempted to make sense of the situation that she now found herself in. Nan placed the freshly made pot of tea on the mat in the middle of the table and sitting down, lit another cigarette. Inhaling deeply on it, she sized Annie up before launching into a full verbal tirade. She didn't hold back and told Annie exactly what she thought of Daniel. Covering her ears, Annie had tried to block out what Nan was saying, but to no avail. She hadn't expected anything less; she just wished that the verbal assault would finish. Nan always took great satisfaction and delight in being able to speak her mind and revelled in her attack, even if it did reduce her daughter to tears again. She didn't even attempt to hide the smirk which marched all over her face as she told Annie in no uncertain terms that she was better off without the 'great pillock'. And then the expected 'and I told you so' tumbled from Nan's mouth in a tone rivalling Angostura bitters. She was delighted that Annie was now free of Daniel, as in her mind, her daughter deserved better, deserved much more.

Nan had never liked Daniel from the moment she first clapped eyes on him. She didn't trust him and had taken an instant dislike to the lad which soon turned to loathing. He was cocky and arrogant, and Nan had made her opinion of him well known. Even when Annie and Daniel had got married, Nan hadn't stayed any longer than was necessary after the wedding ceremony. She'd made the usual excuse to leave early by claiming to have 'one of her heads coming on'. It was the same when Annie announced that she was pregnant — Nan hadn't even bothered to hide her disapproval. Annie couldn't understand how Nan could dislike a child so much before it was even born, and hoped that once the baby had arrived. she would feel different. Unfortunately. that hadn't been the case. because as

Molly got older, the resemblance to Daniel had in itself been a constant reminder and bugbear for Nan.

At that time Annie couldn't see any faults in Daniel; she was in love and that's all that had mattered to her. Yes, he came home late from work and had weekend conferences to attend, but that was because he was working hard and hoping for a promotion. And yes, he flirted with her friends and other women, but so what!

Annie knew that Nan was an angry woman but had never dared question her as to why that was. In fact. most of Nan's life had been spent being angry. She was angry at the world, angry at the hardship and many injustices that she had had to endure in her life, and she was particularly irritated that her youngest daughter, in her eyes still her baby, had been wasting her life with a bloody idiot. Annie hated the rows and the slanging matches that seemed to happen on a daily basis, and could never understand why Nan had taken against Daniel so readily.

Of course, Nan could never ever tell Annie the truth — never tell her that many years ago she had had a brief extra-marital affair with Daniel's father, Sam, and that she had got herself pregnant as a result. Nan knew in her heart that there was no future in the relationship — being the other woman there never could be. Then when she miscarried, her grief and the shame of having been made a fool of was so very hard to bear. It had almost broken her, and the only way for her to deal with it and save face was to always go on the attack, to avoid ever having to deal with the consequences of what had happened or what she had done.

And so, over the years Nan had become increasingly antagonistic in an attempt to push people away and hide her guilty conscience. The way Nan saw it, it was inevitable that Daniel would follow suit and do the same to Annie. After all, what was that old adage, 'like father, like son'? Nan had borne the guilt and shame of her secret and would take that secret with her to the grave but she had been proven right after all, and it was hard not to gloat. She also instigated many a heated argument with Annie about Molly and Annie would argue back, leaping to Molly's defence and wishing that Nan would keep her bitterness and resentment to herself. Yet even though Nan knew that her cutting remarks about Molly were hurtful and harsh, she just couldn't seem to help herself; the spiteful, malicious words just seemed to tumble from her mouth.

Now that she was older, Molly really didn't care what Nan thought or said about her. She had her memories and her 'little secret'. From a young age she'd heard Nan constantly telling her that she was a waste of space. Not knowing any different, Molly assumed that Nan was probably right, so why should she try and prove otherwise? Molly had reasoned that her dad had left them because of Nan's nasty tongue; it was her fault that he was gone, and to a six-year-old that had been unforgivable. Yet even now Molly only knew the gist of what had happened; her mother had never volunteered any details and having been so young, Molly had never pressed her for the full story. But she did remember how ill her mother had been and how she would hear her sobbing into the early hours every night for months afterwards. As the years passed Molly had often wondered what it would have been like to be a 'proper family', and she would fantasise about the relationship she could now never have, imagining how different things might have been if Dad was still part of their lives.

Chapter Two: The Follies Of Youth

<***>

Molly Roberts and Debbie Travis had been firm friends since they first met at infant school. They were inseparable and would have sleepovers in the holidays and at the weekends, and would take it in turns to have tea at one another's houses after school. Molly loved going around to Debbie's house, as to Molly's way of thinking the Travis's were a real family. Molly idolised Debbie's father and she loved tucking into Debbie's mum's home-made cooking and baking.

At the age of eleven they had both started at the local comprehensive school and would often play truant together. Once a week or so they would skip lessons after lunch and walk the mile to the local bus terminus, where they would sneak into the toilets and get out of their school uniforms and into a change of clothes which they had hidden inside their P.E kits. Then they would catch the number 23 bus into the next town. where they would spend hours window shopping or browsing round the big department stores, trying on the latest fashions and giggling together in the changing rooms. They were nearly found out a couple of times but managed to blag their way out of trouble with the usual excuse that it was a free study period.

When they were both nearly sixteen, they finished school at the end of the Easter term. Waiting nervously for the exam results to drop through the letter box with the morning post, Molly was amazed that she had done as well as she had. Sitting five exams and passing them had been no easy feat and having got a couple of B's and the rest C's, she was quite pleased with herself. Now that she was out in the big, wide world, she knew things would change dramatically, and the thought of being at home all day with Nan going on at her was enough to spur her into action to start looking for a job. Trawling through the classified ads in the local newspapers, she spotted a job advert for a full-time, trainee receptionist at a local engineering firm.

Molly applied and got an interview, and much to her relief she succeeded in getting the job. And she had been there ever since.

Molly had slotted right in to the job and quickly got to know most of the regular customers. She got on well with her workmates and had even had a fling with the boss's eldest son, Adrian. He had taken her out a few times — dancing, to the pictures, and to the local restaurant for a couple of meals. Annie had been delighted that her daughter had 'gone and landed the boss's son'. She encouraged the friendship as he seemed like a nice lad and to her mind it was a step up the social ladder, which meant that Molly was going places. After all, she reasoned, the boss's son had to be a quite a catch and the fact that Molly was going out with him must mean she was on to a good thing. But six months on it had become apparent to Molly that he was as boring as her job was and she ended the relationship. For eight weeks she never heard the end of it.

Although Molly found her job boring, she did enjoy the banter and flirting, especially with the apprentices and even with some of the customers. Occasionally though, she would get flustered and embarrassed if the intimations were a bit too near the knuckle. She would try and give as good as she got, but as she had only just turned seventeen, she was sometimes way out of her depth, and would feel herself blushing before quickly having to make an excuse to disappear into the back office. She remembered on one occasion being propositioned by a particular customer who had commented on her short skirt, and had suggested she bend over and give him a flash of her knickers. He had been old enough to be her grandfather, never mind her father, and the thought of it still made her shudder.

Then one day a company rep asked her out on a date. She had seen him many times, usually when he came into the office to have his invoices dealt with. He was polite and charming and although significantly older than her, she'd eagerly accepted the invitation. All of that week she was like a scalded cat as the butterflies in her stomach made her excited and flustered, and by Friday she was hardly able to concentrate on anything at all. She wished the day away and couldn't wait for five o'clock. Yet although she was elated and filled with excitement, she was also a little apprehensive, as she nervously waited for him to pick her up after she had finished work.

He'd showed up at her house driving a flash red sports car and her eyes nearly popped out of her head when she saw it. He was polite and was the perfect gentleman at first, opening the car door for her, making sure that she was comfortable and flattering her on how gorgeous she looked. But Molly began to feel uncomfortable when she noticed that his hand constantly brushed against her thigh as he changed gears and he questioned her as to how many boys she had been with and joked about whether she had brought her toothbrush with her. Molly had thought that they were going to a restaurant, so when he turned into the car park of a hotel just on the outskirts of town, she became nervous and unsure. He parked the car on the far side of the hotel car park and leaning towards her, tried to grope and kiss her. Molly was shocked at his level of nerve and somewhat affronted, she lashed out, accidently scratching him on his top lip with a ring she was wearing. He had flown into a rage and making a grab for her, called her a prick teaser and a stupid little cow. Molly had almost fallen out of the car in her hurry to escape and ran as fast and as far as she could before flagging down a taxi.

The experience had shaken her, and the only person she had ever told about it had been her best friend, Debbie. A couple of weeks afterwards Molly heard through office gossip that the creep was married and already had a kid, with another one on the way. She dreaded the prospect of seeing him again, and the thought of him coming into the office and having to be nice to him turned her stomach. Molly would daydream and play out a scenario in her head in which she would take revenge - should he ever show his face again, he'd best get his own bloody coffee because, given the chance, she would spit in it and pour it over his head. Much to her relief she never did see him again and she made a pact with herself that she would stick to lads her own age

— that way at least she would avoid a repeat of the 'dirty old man' scenario.

Molly's life was generally dull. The daily routine of checking invoices, answering the phone, and making coffee for her boss and customers bored her rigid. Yet it had never entered her head to apply for another job or even to seek a promotion. Nan was right; Molly Roberts was a waste of space, just like her father had been.

Molly couldn't wait for the weekends to come around — Friday and Saturday nights just couldn't come quick enough. They were fun and full-on, and in Molly's book that meant having a bloody good time, which ideally consisted of going out to the town centre clubbing, getting pissed as fast as she could for as little money as she could, and dancing like it was going out of style. Molly and Debbie had their favourite discotheques in town and would club crawl, going from one venue to another. Because they were under age they would flirt with and chat up the bouncers in order to get in, but once inside the various clubs they would make a bee line for the bar, latch onto some lad who thought he was on a promise, and get as many free drinks as they could. Molly loved the deep thump, thump beat of the music — the louder the better — and she would dance as near to the speakers as she could, to feel the vibration of the music reverberating in her rib cage.

She would spend hours getting ready to go out and was meticulous with her hair, nails, make-up and false eyelashes, transforming herself into what Nan disparagingly called a 'common tart'. Being a fashionista, she read any and every fashion magazine she could get her hands on, not that she ever bought any of them. Instead she would stand in a quiet corner at the back of the newsagent shop and read them from cover to cover, mesmerised by the glossy adverts. Molly knew all the products which enhanced this, and lengthened that, and she also knew how to 'flaunt it if you've got it.' She wished she could afford to buy all the latest beauty products, fashionable clothes, handbags and shoes, but the reality was that on her meagre weekly wage all she could do was look longingly and dream. In Molly's fantasy world she would imagine that she was a top model for a designer fashion house. In her dreams she was rich and famous and got to travel the world, and her mother was so proud of her. Unfortunately, Molly had got into many a row with Nan about the way she dressed. Usually Nan would complain that her dress was too short, or that she had too much 'muck' on her face, or that her top was too low. Molly eventually learnt to ignore the remarks and would just flounce out of the door, muttering under her breath, "Whatever! Silly old bag!" Annie would raise her eyes to the ceiling with a flick of her head and tut under her breath.

Molly's favourite weekday night out was Wednesday, when she and Debbie would go to the local pub, the Horse and Jockey. The pub held a karaoke night every week and Molly and Debbie would always perform, singing to their heart's content under the illusion that they had talent. And so, on this particular Wednesday evening Molly made sure that her nails were properly dry before standing in front of the wardrobe mirror holding an assortment of dresses up to herself, and finally deciding on a particularly cute and girly pink number. Out of the three pink dresses that she owned, this was her favourite. It was quite short with a plunging scoop neckline, black piping around the hem and capped sleeves. Putting on her new, padded, push-up bra, she teamed the dress with a wide, black, patent leather belt which accentuated her already small waist, before carefully hitching up a new pair of skin-toned tights. She pushed her tiny feet into a pair of black, stiletto-heeled shoes; she loved the shoes as much as the dress. Squirting her favourite perfume on to her neck and wrists, she smiled at herself as she gave one last look in the mirror before applying another layer of lipstick to the already perfect pout. Sashaying down the stairs, she loved to exaggerate her sexy walk, although balancing on heels took a lot of practice.

Annie was ironing and eyed her daughter as she entered the kitchen. "You off out to the karaoke with Debbie then?"

"Hmm," Molly nodded, as she gave a final twiddle to her flicked hair and made sure that her earrings were secured in place.

Annie stood admiring her daughter as she slipped her black jacket on. For all her faults, Annie felt a heart-swelling gush of love and sense of pride as she pressed a five-pound note into Molly's hand. "Here, love — enjoy yourself."

Molly smiled before giving her mother a big hug.

"And be careful — watch out for the idiots. Have you got your key?"

"Yeah, yeah, thanks Mam. Stop fussing… I will. And yes… I have. Don't wait up. Got to go, I'm meeting Debs at the bus stop. We're gonna catch the 8.15. Love you! Byeeee…"

With the remnants of her perfume hanging in the air and a slam of the front door, she was gone.

Chapter Three: Those You Trust

<***>

The Horse and Jockey was a popular pub on the local council housing estate. Its design was a typical 1970's architectural eyesore with a flat roof, peeling paintwork and pebble-dash exterior. It looked unkempt and scruffy, even though part of it had been renovated following a fire a couple of years before. Inside, the decor wasn't any better; the wallpaper was ripped in places, the paintwork was scuffed and chipped, the carpets needed a good scrub, and a stale smell of cigarettes and beer clung to the furnishings. Debbie's father had once commented that the only good thing about the place was the price of the beer.

Pushing open the double swing doors which led into the public bar, Molly and Debbie looked around the room, eyeing up the potential for a couple of free drinks. They walked towards the stage at the front of the room and staked their claim on a table which looked relatively clean. Leaving their jackets on the back of the chairs, they headed off to the toilets.

"Do you think this shade of lippy suits me?" Molly asked as she eyed herself in the cracked wall mirror.

Debbie gave a cursory glance in Molly's direction. "Yeah, it's nice on you, Mol. You gonna be much longer? Hurry up will you — I'm gagging for a drink."

"Yeah, give us a minute, I've got to look gorgeous for my public," she joked.

Returning to their table, Debbie said, "Usual?" and went over to the bar without waiting for a reply. Molly checked out the competition. The pub wasn't too busy yet, probably because it was still quite early. If it stayed quiet, she or Debbie would be in with a chance of winning the karaoke hands down, she thought.

Returning with two Bacardi and Cokes, Debbie took a large gulp of her drink. "Quiet isn't it? Oh, I forgot to ask, do you want crisps or nuts? Oh blimey! Don't look now but there's two lads at the bar looking over and drooling! Don't fancy yours much though," she giggled.

"What? No ta, I'm not hungry. Where? Where're you looking?"

Rummaging in her handbag, Debbie found her lipstick and compact mirror and Molly watched her apply another even layer of colour to her lips, while using her mirror to check out what was going on behind her.

"At the bar — the two who are looking over. Tell you what, let's play hard to get and give 'em a run for their money," she said as Debbie slipped the compact back into her bag.

"Yeah, they're all right, I suppose. The one on the right obviously fancies himself — thinks he's God's gift all right."

Molly sighed, "Wish they'd hurry up and start the karaoke."

She loved the anticipation of performing on stage and craved the adrenalin rush and the feeling of butterflies in her tummy as her excitement began to rise. She was sassy and confident, and held the microphone like a professional; God knows she had practiced enough at home with her hair brush. Molly considered herself to be quite talented and secretly thought that she was miles better than Debbie. Having won the competition a couple of times, along with the crummy first prize — usually a cheap bottle of house plonk — Molly had failed to realise that without many other contestants to compete against, it was inevitable that she would win on occasion. This particular Wednesday she sang her usual favourite songs which she thought suited her voice, and as it turned out, she did indeed win a bottle of the said house plonk. Molly was pleased with herself as there had been another four acts on in addition to her and Debbie.

Oozing confidence, she sauntered over to the bar to collect her prize. Out of the corner of her eye she could see the two lads ogling and looking at her. She glanced over in their direction and gave them a coy, cheeky smile before returning to where Debbie was sitting. She could feel their eyes following her so she did her best to walk with a hip-swinging, sexy sway.

Sitting down at the table, Debbie eyed the bottle. "You opening that now, or what?" she asked, nodding her head in its direction.

"What do you think?" laughed Molly, as she picked at the wrapper. "Crap! I forgot we need a cork screw and some glasses."

Just then the two lads who had been at the bar came over to join them. "Anyone sitting here, love?" one of them asked.

"Duh! Like you know there isn't," replied Debbie sarcastically as she winked at Molly, giving her a knowing look.

"Mind if we join you then? I'm Gareth and this is me mate Tony. Eh, you've got a crackin' voice by the way," he said to Molly, ignoring Debbie's brash remark. "Can I get you and your friend here a drink?"

Molly forced a smile and wrinkling her nose replied, "Erm, thanks. We've been here best part of the night and now you decide to come over. Pair of cheap skates! Or were you figuring on just helping us drink the wine?" she mocked, picking up the bottle and pretending to read the label. "Tell you what, seeing as you're asking, mine's a rum and Coke. What you having, Debs?"

"Hmmm… same, thanks, but make 'em doubles and I'll have a bag of salt and vinegar as well. Oh, and get some glasses and a cork screw while you're at it. This wine won't open itself."

Gareth went over to the bar to get the drinks, while Tony sat down and chatted up the girls. "So, you come in here every week, don't you?" he asked.

"Yeah, pretty much. It's okay s'pose. It's a bit of a dump really. We only come for the karaoke," replied Molly.

Tony nodded in agreement. "Yeah I know. My dad and mum used to run the place. Now it's just my mum who works here as a barmaid."

Debbie raised her eyebrows. "Wow, that means you must get loads of free drinks, you lucky sod."

Tony shook his head. "Nah, no such bleedin' luck, the old bag would lose her bleedin' job. I've seen you both around and about a few times though. How come you know each other?"

Molly and Debbie looked at one another and together burst out giggling. "Oh, me and Debs go way back — school and all that. I suppose you could say we're joined at the hip. My mam says we should have been Siamese twins. What about you two? Molly nodded in Gareth's direction. "Been friends long?"

Tony looked over towards the bar. "Nah, we're just mates. We met at the probation office." Tony lifted his trouser leg up to show off the tag which was fastened around his ankle.

"Oh, that's bloody marvellous!" Debbie said snootily. "We've just got saddled with a couple of deadbeats — just our luck. Any road, how come you're still out at this time? Thought you had to be tucked up in bed for seven o'clock on a curfew or summat."

Tony winked. "You're a right cheeky mare. Nah, the daft sods never bleedin' check. Any road, I don't think it's even working. It'll be off in a couple of weeks, anyway."

"Oh, so who's been a naughty boy then? What have you been up to, or dare I ask?" asked Molly, wagging her finger as though to chastise him.

"Nowt big. Just got bleedin' caught by the bizzies with a bit of weed on us."

Debbie feigned a shocked expression. "Not drugs! Oh my God, you're not a common drug dealer, are you?" she said in a pretentious posh voice. "My good man, I don't suppose one could see oneself to letting us partake of a joint or two, does one?"

"Debs, you don't even smoke," Molly said, rolling her eyes.

"Oh, shut your gob! I've always wanted to try it and one won't hurt. Don't be such a goody two-shoes. Live a little, for God's sake."

Debbie giggled and turning to Tony began playfully walking her fingers up his thigh. "Well, can you?" she asked teasingly.

Tony felt in his pocket. "Yeah, I can roll you one up. Tell you what, for a snog I'll even put a roach in as well. What'd ya say?"

"A roach?"

"Yeah, a filter to the uninitiated," Tony smirked.

"I know what a roach is. Anyway, I don't make a habit of snogging strangers, so it better be worth it. And just for the record, I think you're a cheeky buggar," said Debbie, stiffening her back indignantly.

"Ouch, that's a bit harsh. What about you, Molly? You'd give us a kiss, wouldn't you?"

"No! Like she said, you're a cheeky buggar."

"Well you can't blame a bloke for trying. Though seriously Molly, I quite fancy you. You could be me bird. What d'ya say?"

"Sod off is what I'd say, if that's your idea of asking us out! Jesus, who said romance was dead? Tell you what… I'll think about it," she said, blushing as Tony slipped his arm around her shoulders and started to kiss and nuzzle her neck.

Gareth returned with a tray loaded with drinks and packets of crisps and nuts. Setting it down on the table, he handed round the drinks. "So, what've I missed, apart from you two lovebirds obviously getting all cosy? Who've you been bitching about?"

Molly looked him up and down. "Well, certainly no one you'd know. Cheers for this," she said cheekily as she accepted the drink from him. Taking a large gulp of her rum and Coke, she settled back into her chair, allowing Tony to put his arm around her again.

"Your mate here's been showing us his tag. Have you got one as well?" she asked curiously,

"His tag! I ain't never heard it called that before."

Molly blushed. "You know full well what I'm talking about. You've got a filthy mind."

Gareth smirked. "Me? Nah! I'm a very good boy. Tony here, he's the rebel. Damn, I forgot to get the wine glasses and cork screw. Pass us the bottle over and I'll ask them to open it at the bar. Won't be a sec."

Reaching across the table, Molly passed him the bottle. As she did so his hand purposefully brushed against hers and he gave her a cheeky wink. A shiver ran down her spine as she watched his retreating back, and she instantly decided that she didn't like him. She couldn't quite put her finger on why not — he just gave her the creeps. Watching him as he stood at the bar, she had a gut feeling that he was a wrong-un and she felt on edge and a little unnerved. Joining in with the conversation again, she decided to enjoy the attention which Tony was giving her and snuggled up to him again as the moment passed.

Gareth returned with four wine glasses, the opened bottle of wine and another round of drinks. Molly eagerly accepted the proffered drinks and gulped down the double rum and Coke. Gareth knew that the alcohol was beginning to relax her and that he was winning her over, gradually gaining her trust as he complimented and smooth-talked her. He was intentionally being very attentive and considerate, and when it was time to leave, he helped Molly put on her jacket before putting his arm protectively around her waist, helping to support her so that she wouldn't stumble. Gareth was acting the perfect gentleman and Molly was giddy and intoxicated, laughing at his corny jokes and silliness. But when she stepped out into the night air, she felt her head spin and her legs wobble as she staggered towards the taxi. And that was pretty much the last thing Molly remembered…

Chapter Four: When Systems Fail

<***>

Gareth Shaw was what many people would call a loner. He had always found it difficult to make friends because of some strange habits and a very weird and warped sense of humour. He had never known who his father was, and his father had never known of Gareth's existence, as his conception had been the result of a very brief fumble behind the swimming baths one Saturday afternoon.

His mother, Rachel, had been fourteen years old when unexpected, searing pains had her screaming in the early hours of a Monday morning and woke the sleeping household. She was rushed to the local hospital in the back of an ambulance where the reason for her absent periods and distended belly soon became all too apparent. After Rachel had the surprise delivery, it was agreed that with help from her family she would keep the baby. Gareth turned out not to be the model baby which everybody had initially cooed over. He screamed relentlessly for the first three months of his life, and as he neared his first birthday, he began to fly into uncontrollable temper tantrums, the severity of which even unsettled the family doctor and health visitor. Motherhood hadn't turned out the way Rachel thought that it would; the sleepless nights and endless crying had taken its toll on the young mother, who soon realised that having a kid at fourteen kind of cramped your style. Taking the advice of one of her best friends, Rachel gladly handed Gareth over to her social worker when he was a little over fourteen months of age.

And so it was that all of Gareth's early life came to be spent in the social care system, going from one foster home to another, as none of the foster carers were able to cope with his violent outbursts and disruptive behaviour for very long. The decision to take him off the foster register came when he was eight years old, after he had drowned a foster carer's family cat and set fire to one of the other children's teddy bears. Over the years he was psychologically profiled and assessed more times than he'd had hot dinners, and his case had been discussed by numerous doctors, social workers and paediatric psychiatrists, all of whom were at a loss as to how to treat him or what to do with him. Gareth was described as being a 'very disturbed child' — a child who could no longer be fostered, and in fact who would never even be considered for adoption.

Proving to be one of the most disruptive children in the entire local education system, Gareth was often excluded from school for weeks at a time. When he wasn't excluded, he played truant. And on the days that he was in school, he spent most of them standing in the corridor outside the headmaster's office or in detention. He was the child who stood alone in the playground because none of the other kids would play with him, sensing that he was 'different'.

From the very beginning Gareth's childhood had been fraught with problems, and by the time he was in his early teens the authorities had explored and exhausted every council-run children's home in the local borough. Following numerous meetings, it was eventually decided that children's homes in the surrounding boroughs should take their turn in caring for and managing him. Regrettably each placement failed to cope with Gareth's behaviour as he became increasingly challenging; Gareth Shaw had become quite a problem.

When he turned fourteen, he ran away from the latest children's home and lived in a squat until it was raided by the police a couple of months later. Secretly he was glad that he was returned to the home because he had been scared and afraid at times., although he would never admit it to anyone. It was during his time in the squat that he became addicted to alcohol and soft drugs, eventually getting hooked on heroin and cocaine. Sometimes the drugs were the only thing which could release him from his torment, making him sufficiently numb to cope with ever-emerging memories from his past which continued to haunt and hold him prisoner. For Gareth drugs had become a necessity which needed constant funding, and the only way he knew how to maintain his habit was through thieving, usually in the form of burglaries or shop-lifting. He craved the highs that the drugs gave him, and the feeling of invincibility made him cocky and indifferent, especially when they were coupled with a few cans of lager. In Gareth's mind he was always right and the rest of the world was wrong. Very few people ever said "No" to Gareth, and those who did were sorry that they'd ever opened their mouths, as the full fury of his temper and torrent of verbal and vile threats rained down on them, leaving them quaking with fear.

Now aged twenty-one and considered to be an adult, he was given a place to live. It was a squalid bedsit which was damp and overrun with vermin but what the hell, it got Gareth out of the system which meant that he was one less problem that the authorities had to worry about. All he had to do was pay the monthly rent.

Gareth had first seen Molly in the Horse and Jockey through getting to know Tony. He would deliberately sit on the other side of the mahogany bar or play the one-armed bandit fruit machine, so that he could watch and study her without it being obvious. He couldn't wait for the middle of the week to come around, knowing that she would be up on the stage, teasing him with her pert breasts, sexy legs and swaying hips — God, he fancied the arse off her.

And so, it was on that particular Wednesday night that he and Tony had met at the Horse and Jockey. Standing at the bar and waiting expectantly for the two girls to arrive, he caught sight of her and felt the familiar excited flutter of anticipation. He watched as they picked one of the tables near to the stage but was slightly disappointed when they disappeared off to the toilets together. He laughed to himself at how girls always went to the toilets in twos — like Jehovah witnesses, he mused, always knocking on doors in pairs as if they needed moral support, whatever that was supposed to mean. The thrill of the chase had started to build as Gareth began to feel a familiar stirring. He had already decided that tonight he would make his move on the brunette.

Both he and Tony had enjoyed watching the girls perform on stage, and clapped and wolf-whistled as they returned to their table. "Bit of all right them two, especially the brunette. Do you fancy having a pop at the blonde?" mused Gareth.

"Sure, I'm game. They can only tell us to piss off but you never know, tonight could be our lucky night," said Tony, smirking.

Having won the karaoke competition, Molly made her way over to the bar, flashing a smile at the lads as she collected her bottle of wine. They both smiled back and watched as she returned to her friend.

Downing their pints, Gareth rubbed his hands together in glee. "Right then, game on," he said as he winked at Tony. Trying to look cool, they sauntered over to where the girls were sitting. Gareth couldn't believe his luck when they accepted his offer of drinks. He desperately wanted to get off with Molly, but it became increasingly obvious that Molly fancied Tony rather than himself. She was flirting and being very girly with him and Gareth was becoming increasingly jealous and disappointed at the way things were panning out. She was making a fool out of him and he couldn't have that now, could he?

In actual fact even before meeting the girls in the pub, Gareth had made up his mind to have Molly any way he could. For a couple of extra quid, he had bought some Rohypnol from his dealer when he got his supply of weed and cocaine the previous week. Checking the inside pocket of his jacket, he made sure that the small plastic bag was still there. While getting the rounds in, he discreetly dropped a small white tablet into one of Molly's drinks, making sure that he handed the doctored one to her. As the night wore on, he'd watched, fascinated, as she succumbed, appearing to become tipsy at first and then seeming to become quite drunk. Her words had become increasingly slurred and her inhibitions lessened, yet neither of the others seemed to suspect a thing. Gareth was careful to judge the right moment to take matters in hand and make his move on Molly. Then he flashed Tony a look which told him in no uncertain terms to back off, Molly was his.

Just after last orders Gareth rang for a taxi, expecting Debbie and Tony to go off together, but Debbie wasn't having any of it. She'd tried to get Molly to go home with her but Gareth managed to steer Molly into the taxi, and after a bit of an argument Debbie had stormed off in a huff. Tony was the worse for wear too, so when Gareth ordered him to get into the taxi he had obediently complied.

After the brief journey Gareth instructed the taxi driver where to drop them all off near his place, and paid the fare before roughly manhandling Molly out of the taxi and into his bedsit. Tony was very drunk and less than useless, so Gareth half carried, half dragged Molly by himself, before dropping her heavily into the armchair — petite as she was, she was still a dead weight. Slouching in the chair, she was laughing, giggling and slurring her words, oblivious to where she was. Continuing to play the perfect host, Gareth seized the opportunity to ply Molly and Tony with vodka shots and slipped another pill into Molly's vodka and another into Tony's drink for good measure. He was surprised at how effective the 'roofies' were, as Molly soon passed out, closely followed by Tony. Gareth was banking on Tony being clueless as to what was about to happen. As for Molly, she wouldn't remember a damn thing anyway; he'd made sure of that. Rubbing his hands together and feeling very pleased with himself, he scooped her up into his arms and carried her over to the bed. 'God, it had been so easy," he sniggered to himself.

Slowly and carefully he began to undress her motionless body, savouring and caressing the perfect form which lay inert before him. As each part of her exquisite body was revealed to him his excitement increased, and his want and desire became overwhelming. Gareth was consumed with lust as he twisted and contorted her limp body. She was like a compliant rag doll as she gave herself over to his every demand, and allowed him to fulfil all of his sexual perversions and desires. Managing to drag Tony onto the bed as well, he fondled and coaxed Tony's unconscious body into a state of unreciprocated arousal while Gareth fantasised that they were having a threesome and became lost in his perverted fantasy. When he was spent, he revelled in the glow of what had been the most fantastic sex he had ever experienced. It was undeniably the best yet. God, he loved it when they gave into him like that. "What a slag!" he thought to himself.

Molly began to groan and moan as he continued to kiss and nuzzle her slender neck and pert breasts and in Gareth's imagination she was moaning and sighing with pleasure, obviously wanting more. Suddenly she opened her eyes and as confusion and panic consumed her, feebly lashed out. Catching him unawares she kicked out and struggled, trying to push him away, mumbling for him to get off her. In the confusion his flailing hand grabbed the bedside lamp and without thinking he hit her with it. He heard the muffled thud of metal on skull and watched as her body went limp. He reasoned that he had taken the necessary action to shut her up and quieten her. Staring at her in a state of disbelief, he pinned her down by her shoulders as he fully expected her to start struggling again.

Incensed, he angrily shouted at her, "You fucking stupid bitch! What did you do that for?" He was enraged that she had tried to fight him off and shook her roughly. After dropping her flaccid body back onto the bed, he looked at Tony, checking that he hadn't stirred during the commotion. Gareth realised that he needed to pee, and after checking that the coast was clear in the corridor, left the two of them and went to the bathroom which was opposite his room. Returning to the semi gloom of the bedsit, he stumbled over Tony's trainers in his haste, and swore under his breath as he made his way back to the bed. Picking up the lamp, he stood it upright on the bedside table again and made sure that Molly and Tony were still unconscious.

Climbing back onto the bed, he lay down next to Molly and began to fondle her again, soon becoming fully aroused once more. Straddling her, he forced himself into her again but this time she was unresponsive and completely motionless. Shaking her again to get a response, he now became aware of the pool of blood that was seeping into the pillow. As if in a dream, he watched fascinated as her head lolled from side to side and her unseeing eyes stared blankly back at him. Suddenly reality hit him; she was dead and he had killed her. Gareth felt a surge of rising panic and fought to suppress a rush of vomit which threatened to rise up into his mouth. Pacing the floor, he became more and more agitated, uncertain of what to do next. Lighting a spliff, he inhaled deeply and beginning to feel calm again, a plan started to form in his deranged mind.

Hurriedly getting dressed, he sat on the edge of the bed. He couldn't take his eyes off her motionless body and his gaze kept being drawn to the bright red pool of her life force soaking into the grubby, grey pillow. He slapped himself to snap himself out of the dream-like trance he was in. Clumsily attempting to get her dressed, he tried to sit her up, but as he swung her legs over the edge of the bed, he knocked her handbag off the table. The handbag was unzipped, and its contents spilled out over the floor. Swearing at his own carelessness, he hurriedly shoved everything back into the bag. The rush of adrenaline had affected his co-ordination and he was becoming increasingly clumsy and agitated.

Suddenly frantic and irate, he hissed through gritted teeth, "Fuck, this wasn't supposed to happen. This is all your own, stupid fault. Why did you do that? You shouldn't have struggled; you were supposed to be enjoying it. None of the others struggled. You're an ungrateful, silly bitch."

Leaving Tony unconscious on the bed, he roughly man-handled Molly's limp body and wrapped her, her handbag and the blood-soaked pillow inside the duvet. Checking that there was no one about, he dragged the duvet into the deserted hallway. He quietly locked the door of his bedsit behind him and with his legs nearly buckling beneath him, part carried, part dragged the rolled-up duvet and its contents round to the back alley, where he hid it behind some loose fence panels. He ran to the row of garages opposite where he knew that a car used by a local gang of drug dealers was parked. Guessing that the car would not be locked, he tried a door handle and let out a sigh of relief as it opened. Loose wires were already dangling from the ignition and he twisted them together. They sparked and crackled and the car engine roared into life. Hurriedly looking around, he made sure that no one had seen him before driving the car back to where he had dumped the body. Nerves were getting the better of him as he bundled it into the boot of the car. Realising that he would need something to dig with, he began to frantically scramble around in the semi gloom until his fingers fell upon a piece of broken roof tile. Throwing it on top of the duvet, he quietly closed the boot lid and double-checked that no one was around to witness what he had just done.

A mixture of nervous excitement and adrenaline continued to course through him as he drove to a local beauty spot. Parking as close as he could to the start of the bridle trail, he checked that the place was deserted. Stumbling along a stony path, he looked around, trying to decide where the best place would be to bury the evidence of his crime. He scrambled down a small, grassy embankment to a row of dense, overgrown bushes near to the start of the lake. After sizing up the area he decided it would do, as the dense foliage growing along the path would shield what he was about to undertake. After reassuring himself that it was safe, he ran back to the car and dragged Molly's lifeless body down the embankment, carelessly dumping it on the ground.

Using the broken piece of tile, he began to scrape and dig at the dry, sandy soil. He swore out loud as he realised that a lot of the roots were near the surface and it was going to take longer than expected to dig a large enough hole. Frantically trying to pull them up and failing, he had to bend and twist the roots out of the way instead. He scraped and dug for what seemed an eternity until he had fashioned a big enough depression. Satisfied with his work, he rolled Molly's body out of the duvet and into the shallow grave, before quickly and unceremoniously covering her body with the loose soil. Checking yet again that there was no one around, he went in search of a leafy branch and finding one a little way away, began sweeping it backwards and forwards over the disturbed soil, carefully erasing any drag marks and foot prints. Standing back, he admired his handy work and allowed a self-satisfied grin to cross his face.

Riffling through Molly's handbag he found her purse and took the five-pound note which her mum had given to her, stuffing it into one of his pockets. By now it was beginning to get light and he realised he needed to hurry up. Scrambling around on the ground, he found a heavy stone which he placed inside the handbag before zipping it up. Then he went down to the edge of the lake and threw it as far as he could. After hearing a satisfying splash, he hurriedly gathered up the soiled bedding and ran back to the car.

After driving to the next town, he drove round the back streets, searching for a building skip. Eventually he found one part-full of building rubble, and purposefully parked the car in an adjacent street. With the duvet and pillow tucked under his arm he ran back to the skip, and after checking that there was no one about, threw the broken piece of tile into it and buried the duvet and blood-soaked pillow under the rubble. With adrenaline still coursing through his veins, he drove back to the row of garages, parked the car in its original position, and satisfied himself that he had left no evidence behind by carefully and meticulously wiping over anywhere he might have touched. 'No finger prints, no way back to me,' he reasoned.

Running back to his bedsit, Gareth felt edgy but excited. With each stride he could hear his heartbeat thudding in his ears, and the pungent smell of Molly's perfume in his flaring nostrils made him feel exhilarated and invincible. His mind raced manically as he planned what he needed to do to get rid of any evidence left in his room. He hoped that Tony was still unconscious, otherwise he might have to kill him too. Letting himself back into the house, he held his breath as he stood in the hallway. He listened for a while at the bedsit door for any movement from inside his room but everything was deathly quiet on the other side of the door. Fumbling for his key, his nerves began to get the better of him as he let himself back into the scene of his crime. He tiptoed around the bed before giving a sigh of relief — Tony was in the same position as when he had left. He checked that he was still breathing and then left him to sleep off the effects of the drink and drugs for a while longer while he set about cleaning up the room. Gareth wiped the bedside lamp, making sure that there were no traces of blood left on it, and placed it back on the table. He would strip the bed completely once Tony had gone and put everything through the washing machine at the local laundrette as soon as it opened. Next, he ran hot, soapy water into the sink and carefully washed the three used glasses, removing any trace of Molly's lipstick and Tony's fingerprints before placing them back in the cupboard. Finally, he flushed the used condoms down the toilet.

Checking that everything in the room now looked okay, he suddenly noticed a mobile phone under the bed. Crouching down, he reached for it and examined it and immediately realised it was Molly's. He turned it over and over in his hands, realising that it must have fallen out of her handbag when he'd knocked it of the table. All he could think about was that he had to get rid of it, as it was incriminating evidence. Gareth slipped the phone into one of Tony's jeans pockets before shaking him awake and telling him the party was over and it was time to go. Tony groaned at being disturbed, groggily looked at his watch, and then reluctantly stumbled out of Gareth's bedsit and into the early morning air, barely able to walk in a straight line.

Gareth opened another can of lager and revelled in the knowledge that he had got away with murder. Tossing the empty can at an already overflowing bin, he stood in the middle of the dank, dingy bedsit and falling to his knees, began to laugh hysterically. He laughed so hard that his sides hurt and his eyes stung with salty tears. Gareth was tired, so very tired. Getting up off the floor, he stumbled across the room and falling onto the bed, lapsed into a dreamless, troubled sleep.

He awoke with a jolt; he could hear angry, raised voices coming from the corridor outside his door — two of the other tenants were arguing over who was to use the shared bathroom first. He lay motionless, listening to the fracas which was unfolding less than eight feet away. Agitated, he wanted to shout for them to 'shut the fuck up and sod off,' but thought better of it. Focusing through bleary, bloodshot eyes, he noticed a thin trickle of sunlight forcing its way through the threadbare curtains. Gathering his thoughts, he remembered what had happened just a few hours earlier. He leapt out of bed and pressing his ear against the cold, wooden door, strained to hear what all the commotion was about. Instinctively he began to shallow breathe as he stood motionless, hardly daring to move a muscle. It was some minutes before the argument eventually subsided and the voices became muffled and distant. It had now become quiet in the corridor again and feeling himself relax a little, Gareth made himself a cup of very strong, black coffee and smoked a spliff before going back to bed.

Chapter Five: All That's Missing

<***>

Annie Roberts started her day early as there was housework to be done and then she needed to pop down to the shops and the outdoor market. She opened the kitchen curtains, letting the early morning sunshine flood the room, which instantly made everything seem bright and cheerful. The cat purred around her legs, and weaving its furry slender body in and out of her ankles, demanded attention. Retrieving an open tin of cat food from the fridge, she fed the impatient feline and bending down, stroked its sleek form. Straightening up, she stretched and yawned before setting the table ready for breakfast. A glance at the kitchen clock told her it was 7.15 am and she suddenly realised that there was no sign or sound of movement upstairs.

Annie bustled through to the hallway and shouted up the stairs, "Molly! Molly! Are you getting up for work? You'll be late again and you know what that means."

Annie was a stickler for punctuality and couldn't understand how she'd come to have a daughter who had no sense of urgency and whose time-keeping was virtually non-existent. Going back through to the kitchen, she turned the radio on and absentmindedly hummed along to the tune which was being played. At 7.30 am the news came on and she realised that Molly still wasn't in the bathroom. She stomped up the stairs, muttering and berating Molly for being so lazy and chastised her for going out clubbing on a week night. "Molly, get your lazy bones out of that bed. If you can't get up on a weekday, you shouldn't be going out on a weekday night," she remonstrated.

Entering Molly's bedroom, Annie expected to find a dishevelled heap in the middle of the bed. She stopped in her tracks, as a glance around the room showed her that the bed was empty and that things were exactly as they had been the previous night, when she had put a pile of ironing on top of the chest of drawers. Going over to the window, she swished open the curtains, allowing a bright burst of sunlight to fill the lavender-coloured room. She peered out of the window, craning her neck to look down the road and half expecting to see Molly coming around the corner, but there was no sign of her. With a disdainful tut, Annie crossed the bedroom floor and closed the door behind her. Going downstairs again, she went into the kitchen. The kettle was boiling, so she made a pot of tea, and got on with preparing breakfast. Nan wandered in, and sitting at the kitchen table, reached for her packet of cigarettes. Taking one out, she lit the end with a flick of the lighter; it was her seventh cigarette of the morning. Glancing sideways with a disapproving look, Annie asked her if she had slept all right.

"No, not really. I had an 'orrible dream and couldn't get back to sleep. And me rheumatics are playing up sommat chronic, so there's no point in just lying there, suffering," she sniffed.

Annie turned to look at her. "You all right? You're not ailing for sommat, are you? And them bloody things will see you off!" she said, pursing her lips to show contempt.

Nan just inhaled all the more. "Aye that's as may be," she retorted, blowing out a plume of smoke which also came down her nose, "but I could drop dead right now, should our good Lord choose to take me. Besides, they're the only pleasure I have left in life anymore — these and chocolate."

Annie raised her eyes to the ceiling with a flick of her head and tutted to herself.

Nan inhaled again on the cigarette. "Our Molly not come home again?"

"No. Anyways, what do you mean, again — you make it sound like she does it all the time. She's probably stayed over at Debbie's, is all," said Annie, in Molly's defence.

"Huh, and I suppose a phone call wouldn't have entered her head? Selfish mare! I don't know, only thinks about herself, that one. She's got one of them flashy, all-singing, all-dancing, bloody la-de-da mobility phones. I don't know why she bothers having one — obviously doesn't know how to work the thing. You know what will happen, don't you? Give it five years and you'll not be able to find a phone box on a street corner for love nor money — you see if I'm not right. I'm telling you, GPO will wonder what the hell's hit 'em."

Annie kept her back turned towards Nan, so that Nan couldn't see her pulling faces.

"I'll have some honey on me porridge for a change, seeing as how you're making a bowl for yourself."

Annie raised her eyes to the ceiling and tutted again before letting out a deep sigh. "Well, you'd best fetch in the milk off the door step then. There won't be enough here for the two of us."

After breakfast Annie cleared the dishes into the sink and waited for the hot water to come steaming through the tap. She stared out of the kitchen window in a daydream, as she rinsed the soap suds off the bowls and cups. Suddenly she remembered that she needed to get something out for tea, but nothing in the fridge or freezer appealed to her. She decided that she would get a nice bit of fresh steak and kidney for tea from the butchers instead when she went out shopping. Sitting at the kitchen table, she made out a shopping list, folded it in half and put it in her shopping basket. Putting on her coat, she fastened the buttons before going into the hall to put her shoes on.

"Right Nan, I'm off to the shops. Do you want owt fetching back?" she shouted.

"Only me fags. Oh, and a quarter of liquorice allsorts — the proper one's mind, not the cheap, pretend ones they have on the market. Oh, and get me a packet of decimated coconut — I fancy baking a cake this afternoon."

Shaking her head at Nan's lack of diction, Annie decided that it wasn't worth the argument. "I've got my phone with me, if Molly calls, get her to ring me."

Nan heard the front door slam and slowly climbed the stairs, needing to pause to catch her breath on the landing. Wheezing and coughing, she went into her bedroom to get on with the business of getting dressed. She opened the curtains a chink and sitting down on the soft, padded stool at the dressing table, began to remove the curlers from her hair. Combing her hair carefully so as to keep the curls, she sprayed near half a can of lacquer to hold them in place. She looked at the face which stared back at her in the mirror. The eyes were the purest blue and still shone clear and bright. Leaning forward to check that no more wrinkles had appeared overnight, she dabbed a little powder onto her nose and cheeks, before adjusting the gold chain and crucifix which she wore around her neck. It had been one of the few gifts that Ged, her late husband, had given her and one which had never been pawned. She remembered it had been the very first Christmas present from him, and she had never taken it off since the day he had given it to her.

Gerard Elliot had spent most of his married life within the confines of her Majesty's hostelries. Unfortunately, he had died many years previously, while serving a two-year sentence for handling stolen goods. The stroke which he had suffered had been fatal. Nan had been glad that he had gone quickly and not suffered; seeing him as a useless invalid would have been too hard to bear. She had caught herself dissecting the word 'invalid'. 'In-valid' — that about summed it up, she'd thought at the time.

Nancy Atkins first met Ged when she was in her early twenties. She'd been working as a receptionist at the local doctor's surgery and had just finished work. She was waiting at the bus stop as Ged, who had just done a bit of business in the pub opposite, ambled over to chat her up. He had fancied her from the moment he first saw her. Pretending that he was waiting for the same bus, he had even paid her fare. They had chatted for the entire journey and then he'd walked her to her door. The fact that it was completely in the opposite direction to where he lived hadn't mattered, nor that he hadn't any more money on him. Ged hadn't minded in the least that he'd had to walk the fourteen miles back home to his house. The following day he had waited again at the bus stop for her, and plucking up courage, asked if he could take her out to the pictures at the weekend, and if she would like to go for a drink afterwards. She had jumped at his offer, and they agreed to meet at the local cinema.

Ged, who had got there slightly early and had already bought two tickets, waited in the foyer for her to arrive. They sat together on the back row which had double seats, and kissed and cuddled. That particular picture house became their regular meeting place irrespective of which film was being shown. They would also frequent the local dance hall after which Ged would treat them both to a bag of chips on the way home at the end of the night.

After a brief courtship, Nancy had discovered that she was pregnant, much to the dismay and shame of her parents. Walter and Violet Atkins were strait-laced, plain-talking Catholics, born and raised. Being regular church goers, the news that their daughter was going to have a child out of wedlock came as a huge shock, and Nancy's mother, Violet, made light work of whisking her into the confessional at the local church to confess her sins before God, certain that she herself would die of shame if any of the neighbours found out. Walter Atkins was a man of few words, and decided it was probably best to leave it to the women folk to sort out.

Ged's parents weren't particularly perturbed. They thought that Nancy seemed a nice enough girl and as long as Ged did right by her, that was all that mattered. The decision that they should get married as quickly as possible was orchestrated at Mrs Atkins' insistence. It was decided that the next available date which they could get for a wedding would have to do, so Nancy and Ged could tie the knot before Nancy was showing.

Being a woman of principles, Nancy's mother made a very unforgiving mother-in-law, and Ged absolutely refused to live under the same roof as her. Ged and Nancy had to find a place of their own and although it was a struggle, they managed to scrape together enough money for a deposit on a rented two-up, two-down, end-of-terrace house. Nancy hadn't really minded that it was damp and somewhat dilapidated — to her it was their own little love nest. Unfortunately for Nancy, life with Ged had been a constant struggle, as he could never manage to hold down a job long enough to bring home a dependable wage. Her entire married life was lived in uncertainty — everything on tick and the never-never, getting by on goodwill and dodgy deals. Never one to miss an opportunity, Ged could always be found in the local pub doing a deal and flogging things which had 'fallen off the back of a lorry'. That was how her life had been — living hand to mouth and dodging the rent man on a Friday night.

Nancy had got used to having to visit Ged in various prisons up and down the country. Like a fool, she had stuck by him whatever happened. He was a good man, after all said and done but unfortunately for Nancy, a hapless one. Nancy always told friends and neighbours that Ged was working away on the oil rigs, to avoid having to explain his long absences — not that anyone believed her. Although absent for most of his married life, Ged nonetheless managed to father three children — all daughters — and Annie had been the youngest. She had idolised her father and missed him terribly when he was away. Annie had always looked forward to the times when he would be home from the 'oil rigs'.

Chapter Six: In-Consideration

<***>

A nnie hurried to the shops still worrying about Molly. She'd just bought some steak and kidney and a pound of sausages from the butchers and was putting her purse away, when looking across the road, she noticed Beth Travis, Debbie's mum, waiting at the bus stop. She rushed over to thank her for letting Molly stay the night.

Beth looked confused. "I'm sorry Annie, but your Molly didn't stay with our Debs last night. Debs came home alone and went straight up to bed."

Annie was taken aback. "You sure? Only Molly didn't come home last night, so I presumed she was at your place."

"No, like I said, Debbie came home on her own. Do you want me to ask Debbie for sure? Maybe Molly stayed at someone else's. I'll give you a ring when I get home. Gotta go love, the bus is here. Speak to you later."

A frown crossed Annie's face as Beth got on the bus. She had a nervous, jittery feeling deep in her gut and distracted, she almost got herself run over as she crossed the busy main road. When Annie got home, Nan was in the living room reading her Woman's Weekly magazine.

"You took your time! Did you get me fags?"

Annie went straight through to the kitchen and taking her coat off, hung it over the back of a chair and started to unpack the shopping. "Aye I've got your fags. They've gone up tuppence, like just about everything else," she grumbled.

Annie busied herself with the chore of putting tins away in the cupboard, and the fresh food into the fridge, before putting the kettle on to boil for a much-needed cup of tea. "I'm making a brew - do you want one?" she asked Nan as she came through to the kitchen.

"Well seeing as how there's one on the go. Did you get them biscuits I like? I'll have a couple of them with it as well."

Carrying the tea tray through to the living room, Annie set it down on the coffee table. "I've got us all a lovely bit of stewing steak and some kidney for our tea. Do you want a pie crust with it?"

Nan returned to her recliner chair and moving the magazine that she had been reading, plonked down awkwardly onto the soft cushion. Studying her daughter's face, she asked, "What's up? You look proper mithered."

"Oh, it's probably nothing. I saw Beth, Debbie's mum, at the bus stop, and she reckons that our Molly didn't stop over at theirs last night."

"Well that's her all over! Thoughtless, feckless and useless! I don't know what these kids are thinking half the time."

Annie glared at Nan. "Oh, don't start, I don't want to hear it. I'm getting really worried, and you're not helping any," she retorted, as she rummaged in her handbag. "Where's my phone? I'll just check to see if she's sent a text." She eyed Nan with a look that said, 'and if she has, you can stop your criticising.'

Nan saw the disappointed look on Annie's face. "You know what she's like love. She's probably on someone's floor, or worse still, in some idiot lad's bed."

Annie ignored Nan's comment and called Molly's number. It rang the usual four rings before going straight to her voicemail. Annie listened impatiently, 'Sorry can't talk right now. Leave us a message.' Waiting for the beep, she asked Molly to call her as soon as she could. Placing the phone down on the coffee table she kicked off her shoes.

"Told you," said Nan smugly.

"For God's sake! Honestly, you make her sound like a right floozy."

Nan smoothed down her apron. "Do I? Yes, well if the cap fits… Shall I be mother? I think a crust will do nicely with that steak and kidney, seeing as how you asked. I quite fancy a bit of flaky."

Annie finished her cup of tea, took the tray through to the kitchen and rinsed out the cups, before wringing out the dishcloth and wiping over the Formica worktops. She wandered back into the living room, picked up her phone and once again tried to contact Molly but it went straight through to her voicemail again. Nan clicked her tongue as she always did when she disapproved of something.

For all Nan's nastiness towards Molly, Annie was sure that she loved Molly in her own way — she just had a funny way of showing it. When Daniel left them, Molly had been no more than six years old, yet although Annie had suspicions that he was messing around and seeing other women, she had reasoned that life was better with him than without him. How stupid she had been as he had left anyway. Daniel had cleared out the joint bank account and left her penniless, homeless and clueless as to his whereabouts. She had never had him down as being that selfish. Sometime afterwards she heard through the grapevine that he had gone off to Cornwall for a new start… or rather, a new tart, the tart in question being a blonde bitch from Sutton Coalfield who was ten years older than him.

After Daniel had gone, the easiest and most sensible option had been for Annie to move in with Nan and try and get her and Molly's lives back to some sort of normality. Valerie, Annie's eldest sister, had offered to take them in, but there had been more than enough room at Nan's house. Those first few years had been a struggle in more ways than one. Just to make ends meet Annie held down two jobs, and Nan had a part-time cleaning job at the Town Hall. The quarrels and full-blown arguments they had could be heard half way down the street, but Annie knew not to say too much in the early days for fear of being turned out of the house. As the years passed and Annie grew braver, she would stand up to Nan and give her as good as she got.

Annie had hoped and prayed that one day Mr Right would make an appearance and sweep her and Molly off to a better life. Unfortunately, she was a long time waiting, and her knight in shining armour never did materialise. Then one day out of the blue there came a hollow, thumping rap on the front door, and a prime example of callous officialdom had come to inform Nan that Ged was dead. Annie and Nan came to rely on each other even more, as both of them grappled with their own grief and sense of loss. Annie had watched her mother wrestle with the realisation that she was now a widow, and in the early days it was all Nan could do to get out of bed. Some days she didn't even do that.

Molly had always been a handful, and by the time she was in her early teens was rebellious, gobby and in Nan's words, 'a right stroppy, selfish madam'. Annie often asked herself where she had gone wrong with Molly's upbringing.

Molly, being stubborn and defiant, hung on to dreams of a better future with aspirations of becoming a model with one of the top modelling agencies, or to even being on TV. When Molly was a little girl, Annie would sneak upstairs and peep through the crack of the bedroom door and watch as she cavorted up and down the room, stopping in front of her dressing table mirror before giving a twirl and a pout as she practiced various poses and struts across the floor, walking the way models do. Now that she was older, Molly constantly moaned about her boring job and her dull life and couldn't wait to escape the hum-drum, boring existence which she was leading. Many a time Annie had reminded her that she was lucky to have a roof over her head and a job to go to, and berated her for being so ungrateful. Similarly, Nan would remind her that she would never realise her daft dream of becoming a model, as to do so she would actually had to get off her arse and go and get her name on the books of a modelling agency and show them a 'portfolius, or whatever it was called'. Molly just raised her eyes to the ceiling and tutted under her breath.

Sinking back into the comfortable armchair, Annie felt the sunshine which was streaming through the window fall across her face. She closed her eyes and basked in its warmth as she gently fell into a welcome nap. Suddenly she jumped with a start — she was sure she'd heard Molly shouting out to her. But then she realised that she had nodded off and it wasn't Molly calling, but rather Nan shouting to let her know that Sheila was standing on the doorstep as it was time to go to Bingo.

Annie had first met Sheila at one of the Women's Institute meetings which were held monthly in the Community Centre. They had been asked to run the book stall at the local church's Bring and Buy sale and had immediately hit it off. They had swapped and shared recipes and discovered that they liked similar things and had similar interests. The following month they both entered the baking competition which was being held at the county flower show and they had come joint first. It was only when they began packing away at the end of the competition that Annie had come clean and admitted her deception to Sheila — she had entered a shop-bought cake. Sheila thought it hilarious and roared with laughter, promising to keep Annie's secret. They had been firm friends ever since.

Sheila lived on the other side of town and drove a very tired Morris Minor. She was very proud of her classic banger and would pick Annie up and drive them both to the Bingo Hall. Being a divorcée, she had been on her own for the past three years, not that she minded in the least. Her marriage to Peter had lasted all of twenty-six years, which was when she had discovered that darling Peter, the successful lawyer, entrepreneur and senior partner in a very successful law firm, was in fact a fully-fledged, lying bastard who preferred to have sex with other men instead of his wife.

Being the kind of woman who, when wronged, went all out for vengeance, she had successfully wreaked havoc on his career and had brought mayhem to his social contacts, including his associates at the private and exclusive golf club of which he was a member. It was amazing how telling a little white, if somewhat embellished lie, to one of the wives who moved in their circle could bring a man to his knees. Then of course, there was the matter of his bank accounts, which included some off-shore accounts in Switzerland. She was delighted to learn that his assets had later been frozen while they were investigated by the Inland Revenue. Although nothing irregular was found, Sheila had relished the fact that it would have been a major inconvenience and pain in the arse for darling Peter. She quite liked that analogy, given his sexual proclivities.

Throughout the whole ordeal, Annie had been there for her friend and had supported and advised her as best she could. It was the least she could do, and Annie knew that had the shoe been on the other foot, Sheila would have done the same.

Annie and Sheila were sitting at their favourite table in the Bingo Hall. They had clear sight of the numbered balls as they were drawn from the machine, and were also able to see the numbers flash up on the big illuminated board which was placed behind the caller.

"Well I'm feeling lucky today — think I might have a win," mused Sheila.

Annie smiled but knew her mind was elsewhere and that she felt distracted. She really wasn't paying the amount of attention that a bingo session required these days.

Sheila noticed that Annie's heart wasn't in it. "What's up, Annie, You're quiet today. You look like you've the woes of the world on your shoulders."

Annie shrugged her shoulders and started to tell Sheila about how upset she was at Molly's thoughtlessness. "I've rung and rung her, but not so much as a by-your-bloody-leave. I'm really beginning to worry about her, Sheila. She's been out all night and according to Beth she didn't stay overnight with them either. Honestly Sheila, I swear to God I could kill her at times!"

Sheila was trying to pay attention to the numbers which were being called out. "Well you know what kids are like. She's probably not given it a second thought, or her phone's off, or the battery's flat. Have you tried ringing her at work?"

Annie shook her head. "No, she'd go mad if I did that. I've just been ringing her mobile."

Sheila put her marker pen down, before lightly resting her hand on Annie's arm. "Look Annie, I'm not being funny love, but seeing as you're this worried, call her at work — to hell with what Madam will say, at least it will put your mind at rest. Have you got her work's number?"

Annie frowned and mulled over Sheila's suggestion. "I suppose you're right. It won't do any harm will it?"

She scrolled through the address book listings in her phone. "Yes, I've got it here. You know what, I'm going to ring her and give her a piece of my bloody mind, if nothing else."

Sheila carried on marking the bingo cards as the numbers were called out. "No joy?" she asked distractedly, as Annie finished her call and put the phone down on the table.

Annie shook her head as a worried frown furrowed her brow. "Molly never showed up for work today. Christ, Sheila, what the hell is she playing at?"

"Well that's kids for you. I'm sure she'll be home for her tea. They usually are… 'BINGO!! Bloody hell, I've won a full house."

Waving goodbye to Sheila, Annie let herself into the house. "Nan, I'm home," she shouted from the hallway. Wandering through to the kitchen, she saw Nan was in the back garden, bringing in the washing off the line. Annie stood on the door step watching her.

"Oh, hello love, I didn't hear you come in. How's Sheila? Did you win?" Nan asked, as she folded each item of clothing, before putting it into the wicker laundry basket.

"What? No, Sheila did. Has our Molly showed up yet?" Annie asked expectantly.

"No love, not a dickey bird, I haven't seen sign nor sight of her. Oh, the gas man came to read the meter while you were out. That's all that's happened, really," she said as she hung the peg bag onto the washing line, before raising it up with the prop.

Annie glared at Nan, irritated at her apparent lack of concern. "For God's sake, can't you see I'm really worried? She wasn't in work today either, and all you can say is that the bloody gas man called. Jesus Christ! I'll try her phone again and if there's no answer this time I'm gonna ring the police and report her as missing."

Chapter Seven: The Morning After The Life Before

<***>

Molly opened her eyes and blinked several times. She felt really strange — heavy yet light, cold yet hot, and absolutely ravenous. Struggling to sit up, she looked around expectantly, presuming that she was in her bedroom, surrounded by her familiar belongings and snuggled under her duvet. She blinked again and rubbed her eyes. She looked around but all she could see was an expanse of whiteness and shades of light and dark grey. Rubbing the side of her head, she groaned and then chastised herself, thinking she must have the hangover from hell. 'That will teach me. Never again! Huh... I probably said that the last time.'

Continuing to look around, Molly felt confused and disorientated. "Where the hell am I?" she asked out loud to no one in particular. Squinting with one eye, she suddenly realised that she couldn't see anything familiar, no furniture, no messy pile of clothes left on the floor, just a vast expanse of white and greyness, stretching way into the distance. Suddenly feeling panicky, she tried to remember what had happened the previous night, but nothing came to mind or made any sense — she couldn't remember anything. She struggled to get to her feet but felt woozy and clumsily sat down again. Continuing to rub the side of her head, she stared into the distance and realised that someone was walking towards her. Through bleary eyes she watched as the figure approached. A deep-seated memory suddenly began to surface, and she realised it was her grandfather, her grandfather Ged. Molly sat rooted to the spot as he knelt down in front of her.

"Hello Molly, are you okay? You look a little... shell shocked."

"That's cos I am. You're my grandpa, aren't you! You're Grandpa Ged, right? I don't understand — where the hell am I?"

Studying her closely he said, "Don't you know Titch?"

"No, I really don't know," she answered in a mocking voice, while still rubbing the side of her head.

"Oh, well this will come as a bit of a shock then, and there's no easy way to tell you. The thing is, for you to be here means that you're dead," replied her Grandpa simply.

"Shit!! Dead? Dead? What the hell do you mean, dead?" she gasped. "How can I be dead, for God's sake. …Did you just call me Titch?"

Ged eyed her carefully. "Yes, I've always called you Titch, right from when you were a youngster, and I also used to sing, 'Good Golly Miss Molly' to you as well."

"Oh," she replied, somewhat perplexed, "I don't remember and I don't know what the hell's going on either. You've just told me I'm dead, so how the hell did that happen?"

Ged had always loved his granddaughter's forthright personality — she reminded him of how he had once been. Molly had been eleven years old when he left the mortal realm, and he had watched over her ever since. He had tried to point her in the right direction, keep her on the straight and narrow and help her make the right choices, and in the scheme of things, he thought he hadn't done too bad a job, all things considered. Now, with the realisation that they were together again, he couldn't help but feel immensely happy.

Earlier that day he'd been instructed by the Elders to collect and escort her to where she needed to be. He was glad he was the one to meet her, but knew he had a hard task ahead of him to get her to accept what had happened.

"So, come on then. Why am I dead? Is this some kind of joke?" she asked in a sarcastic tone.

"Well see, that's the million-dollar question and one that I don't know the answer to, but believe me, it's no joke," replied Ged.

"Well, that's just great," she glowered.

She felt herself becoming frustrated and irritated, and suddenly began ranting about the injustice and unfairness of it all. Ged looked at her somewhat bemused, waiting for her to finish her outburst.

"Blimey, Molly! Have you done having your strop? You can carry on like that all you like, it won't change owt. And before you start creating again, I have to take you somewhere else. You can't stay here. You … we… need to leave this place."

Molly studied her Grandpa. "What do you mean leave? Jesus, I've only just flaming well got here, wherever here is."

Ged reached for Molly's hand. "I think that whatever's happened to you has changed something. You need help to complete your crossing, which is why I have been sent to meet you. This place is what we call the astral plane. We can visit here — although why anybody in their right mind would want to is a mystery to me — but we can't stay. Like I said, we need to leave."

Molly frowned. "Yeah, well seeing as I know nothing about any of this, feel free to do whatever," she retorted derisively.

Ged scowled at her and anxiously looked around as if expecting something to happen.

"Still a gobby mare, aren't you? Look, if we're not careful we can get stuck here, and stuck here isn't the best place to be. It's an interim stop, like waiting at an airport gate. It's a means of making sure that you get the right flight to the right destination, as it were."

Molly looked all the more puzzled.

"Okay, I need you to do exactly as I say. I've never done this before… I just hope it works. Right, take both of my hands, close your eyes and step towards me."

Molly hesitated. "Yeah, right. Why should I? You just said yourself that you've never done this before — whatever it is you're going to do."

Ged glared at her. "Because you should, Miss Know-it-all knows-nowt! Just do as you're damn well told for once and have a little faith, else you can stay here for all I care," he fumed, in an attempt to call her bluff.

Molly was taken aback at her grandpa's curt outburst and decided that she'd better do as she was told. Tentatively she held her hands out. Gently taking hold of them, Ged encouraged her to move towards him. She took a cautious step forward and immediately felt herself falling at great speed. A second later she was being lifted higher and higher, as though she was being sucked up in a powerful uprush of air. Her head felt like it was spinning and she could hear a roar like a gale force wind in her ears. Then just as suddenly as it had started, it stopped. Molly kept very still, too afraid to move.

"You okay?" asked Ged.

"Uhm, I don't know… I think so. Jeez Grandpa, what the hell did you do?"

"Not too sure actually, but it worked. You can open your eyes now, or at least feel with your senses."

Apprehensively daring to open one eye, Molly looked around and gasped. She couldn't believe how beautiful it all was. There was an intensity of colour and brilliance everywhere, and the space around her felt pure and fresh. With an over-powering sense of joy, she felt free and exhilarated as she realised that she was floating. Smiling to herself, she became aware of a low, throbbing beat which was soothing and comforting and reminded her of a heartbeat. Reaching upwards, Ged gently pulled Molly down level with him and held her at arm's length.

"You okay, Titch? You're home now; this is where you should be."

Molly continued to look around in a bit of a daze. "Whoa, that was amazing! This is nothing like I imagined it would be. It's beautiful… the gardens… the buildings… oh my God, it's lovely! But I'm still dead, right? So, this must be Heaven, yeah?"

"Err, we'll talk about that 'being dead' thing later, but yes, you could call it Heaven. Actually, it's whatever you want it to be… it's whatever your reality was. Some call this Heaven; some call it Shangri-La."

Molly frowned. "Shangri what?"

"…La. Oh, no matter, wherever it is though, it's a damn sight better than where you were. I just hope that was the first and last time I ever have to do that. It was quite daunting and very draining on the old energy supply."

Molly looked concerned. "Are you okay, Grandpa?"

"Yes, I'll be fine, don't worry about me. What's more important is, how you are. I know you've got lots of questions which you're dying to ask, and I will do my absolute best to answer them, but you have to realise that there are some questions which will never yield an answer. Once you accept that, things suddenly get a whole lot easier to understand. You need to accept that sometimes it just is."

"Ha-ha, very funny Grandpa… 'dying to ask'. Yeah, I'm dead, I get it but what did you mean by it being a reality or something?"

"Well, when we come back here, to the spiritual realm — Heaven, Shangri-La or whatever you want to call it — we bring the memory of what we identified with on earth back with us. Initially it helps us to make sense of here. We actually re-create our own reality, a kind of mental blueprint, depending on what the reality of being there, on earth, was. Of course, it's only temporary, until we get our bearings, as it were. Oh dear, are you following any of this?"

"Yeah, I think so. You mean like how I can see buildings and gardens and what not?"

Ged nodded encouragingly.

"Well, that makes sense I suppose, cos there's no way that any of those things could really be here, right? So, supposing I'd lived in say Egypt, I'd see pyramids or if I'd lived in China or Japan, I'd see temples and the like. Is that what you're saying?"

"That's exactly what I'm saying. Quick, aren't you, though you needn't look so smug. Just understand that there are many tiers, levels and layers to this one particular dimension alone. The hard part is recognising what your reality was and what really exists here. That's the tricky bit."

Molly shrugged and grinned confidently, "Piece of cake!"

Ged raised a questioning eyebrow. "You think? You look jiggered, by the way. Do you see that tree over there? Let's go and sit for a while. It will give you the chance to recuperate. You look like you could do with a rest and even if you don't, then I could certainly do with one."

Molly followed her grandpa over to where the tall, elegant tree stood, and together they sat beneath its canopy of translucent pink- tinged leaves. Resting her back against the tree's trunk, Molly looked up above her and watched as the leaves rustled and swayed in a breeze she couldn't feel. As she watched, she realised that she could hear the leaves whispering. She strained to hear what they were saying.

"Whoa… that's weird, Grandpa. Are the leaves really whispering?"

Ged smiled. "Ah now, this is what I'm talking about! Is the tree really whispering or not? Is this your reality or not? Actually, I'm teasing you. You're not imagining it; they really do whisper. This tree is the Tree of Loving Intent. Its canopy holds more leaves than anyone could ever count, and the leaves capture every loving thought that's ever made — every loving thought that's sent out as a prayer, or deed or intention. All that loving energy is captured by the leaves and then they tell one another. They share the love, as it were, and once shared, the energy of love is released and recycled back into the universe."

"Aww… how cute is that? But how will I know? How will I know what's real and what's not, I mean?"

"Well, it's quite easy when you think about it. Much like this tree, if it's never been part of your reality on earth, you just have to ask yourself 'Could I ever have imagined or visualised such a thing?' or 'Could I ever have seen or heard such a thing?' If you couldn't, then there's your answer. Another way, of course, is just to accept what you see and hear as being your reality now."

Molly felt even more confused at her grandpa's explanation. Continuing to look around, she unexpectedly became aware of a small light coming towards them. It seemed to be bounding and jumping up and down.

"What the bloody hell's that? No, don't tell me — I'm imagining it!"

Suddenly she realised it was a dog and it was licking and greeting her excitedly, wanting to play. "Whoa, okay, okay! Hello boy! Well I never thought I'd see you again. Grandpa look, its Harry! It's our old dog, Harry!"

Ged smiled and leant forwards to pat the dog. "Hello boy, I was wondering when you were going to show up. You're never far away, are you lad?"

Together they patted and stroked the dog as it revelled in the attention.

"Wow, this is just like the old times. Do you remember, Grandpa?"

Ged nodded and a broad smile crossed his face, as memories of his last time on earth came flooding back.

Molly looked away into the distance. "So how do we get here, Gramps? When we die, what happens?"

Ged smiled at her, surprised that she had called him Gramps. "Gramps, eh? Well, quite easily really. When we reside in a physical body, we are only aware of what is purported to be three dimensional. As human beings we have no concept or awareness of the many other parallel dimensions which exist around us — here being one of them. When we 'die' as you put it, we are, in fact, merely released from the physical body which we've inhabited. As Spirit, we simply shift or cross over into this dimension. It's really that easy and that simple."

Molly looked confused. "Oh! I always thought that when we died, we'd go to Heaven or Hell, I'd always imagined Heaven was someplace up above, like in the sky or outer space or somewhere, and Hell was…. yeah, now you mention it, where exactly is Hell?"

Ged laughed. "Yes, well, we think that Heaven and Hell exist because it's what we've been led to believe. As humans we don't question things or work it out for ourselves. Strange when you think about it — I mean how could any of that be true? Imagine the reality… it would be ridiculous! Yet we don't think about it logically, we simply accept it because that's what we've been told to believe."

Molly frowned. "Yeah, s'pose so. So, what you're saying is that there is no Heaven or Hell."

"Yep, exactly that. It's bizarre really but that's just us, as human beings, trying to make sense of something that makes no sense. Much like the concept of Man being made in God's image, with the assumption that God has a human form. I mean… seriously? We are Spirit energy, so as we are in his image, then it stands to reason that he is Spirit energy too. I'll tell you Molly, you'll find things are totally different here. When we're on this side, living as Spirit again, it makes you sad that when we go back to the earth realm, we forget all of this." Ged waved him arm to indicate the vastness which lay before them.

Molly yawned. "Yeah, well, I'm kinda struggling to remember anything about being a human being, let alone being back here. I'm really tired, Gramps… would it be okay if I had a nap, I can hardly stay awake."

Not waiting for Ged's reply, she lay down on the greenest, sweetest grass she had ever laid on, and fell into a deep, languid sleep.

"Molly... Molly... wake up! There's someone here to see you. Someone you need to meet."

Looking around groggily, Molly was momentarily confused before she realised where she was. Jumping up quickly, she felt herself wobble and holding on to her grandpa, steadied herself.

"Whoa... shit! I don't feel so good. My head still hurts, I'm hollow and empty and feel like death warmed up," she moaned.

"Well, it's hardly surprising that you should feel those things. You've been dead to the world for the last couple of hours — excuse the pun! Like I said, there's someone here to see you."

Molly glared at her grandfather. "Dead to the world... funny...not! And now you want me to meet someone? Who's there to bloody meet?" she groaned.

Suddenly she became aware of an energy standing behind her as Ged shifted to the side a little. "If you will allow me to introduce you, this is Orick, your spirit guide."

"I know," replied Molly, surprised. "I don't know how I know, I just do." She pursed her lips almost afraid to ask what she was about to. "You're telling me that Orick here is my guide, so I guess that's it then. It's final and there's no going back, is there."

Ged sighed. "No Titch, there's no going back — not to your physical existence anyway. It's been too long."

Molly felt a wave of sadness wash over her as the implications quickly dawned on her. Orick gently placed his hand on her shoulder, and was taken aback when she shrugged, as if to dislodge it.

"Don't do that! Don't touch me. Where the hell were you? It's your job to protect me, isn't it? Or do whatever it is that guides are supposed to do."

Ged glared at his granddaughter. "Molly, don't be so rude, how dare you speak to Orick that way."

Orick smiled uneasily. "It's okay, really, she's just upset."

"No, it's not okay, I'm not having her speak to you that way," scowled Ged.

Molly was fuming. "I don't bloody believe this. I thought spirit guides were supposed to protect us… save us… look out for us," she ranted.

Orick glanced at Ged. "Look Molly, I appreciate that you're upset, but that's because you haven't been fully reintegrated with the spiritual realm, which is why I'm here. I have to escort you to the Halls of Wisdom where you are to have, shall we say, a reconnection with the Council of Wise Ones. They need to discuss with you how and why you are here with the utmost urgency before you can have your life review and evaluation," Orick said stoically.

Molly moved nearer to her grandpa. "Re-connection… life review… evaluation… Well that's a bloody joke, when I haven't even had any life. Twenty I was! Twenty for God's sake!" she replied sarcastically. "Do I have to go Grandpa? I don't want to leave you — I've only just found you again," she whined.

"I'm afraid you do have to come with me. There are many factors that need to be addressed, and sooner rather than later. Obviously, your being here under these circumstances is, shall we say, a little unconventional compared with the normal way in which things are done," urged Orick.

"Oh my God. Unconventional… unconventional?" she repeated, "Really… well you should try being me"

Sensing Molly's distress, Ged stepped between them. "Now, now, what's the rush? Another few minutes won't hurt, surely?"

Orick shifted uneasily. "Very well, I shall wait yonder," he said, as he nodded in the direction of a glistening, white marble staircase which glinted in the distance. Looking in that direction, Molly suddenly realised that she could see him standing on the lowest step, surrounded by other spirit guides. They occasionally looked over in the direction of Ged and herself, and Molly was aware of them nodding to one another in quiet discussion.

Staring into the shimmering distance, lost in thought, she tried to make sense of what was happening to her.

"Oh Grandpa, I'm so confused. Why do I feel like I don't belong here? Well not yet, anyway. Please, you've gotta help me. I need to know why I'm here and what happened to me. I have no memory of anything. And how the hell did he just do that?"

"Do what?"

"That… he… him… Orick! Disappear, then reappear over there!"

"Oh, you mean, here one minute and gone the next?" he chuckled. "Well he is a spirit guide after all. Besides which, you'll be able to do that too, when you get the hang of it."

"Really!" she replied dismissively. "Yeah, well like I was saying, I want to go back. I want to know what happened to me."

"That might be a problem, Molly. You can't just go and do what you like, you know. You can't go against the divine order of things — it's just not done. And you can't take it upon yourself to meddle or defy or change things just cos it suits you."

Molly frowned. "Why the hell not? What's the worst that can happen?"

"Damned if I know, and I'm not willing to find out. Look, all I know is that everything which happens to us when we are in the physical dimension is for a reason — everything is in divine order. How we live and end our mortal days is pre-ordained. That's just the way it is, but right now you evidently have a big dose of amnesia, and I'm not sure why. We get amnesia when we are born, not when we come back to the spiritual realm," he explained.

Molly suddenly began to snivel and cry, as she became overwhelmed with sadness and frustration. Ged was taken aback and tried to console and calm her as she howled and whimpered.

"Oh well, that's just great. I can't remember anything, and you don't know anything, and just exactly when do I get my memory back?" she moaned, in between racking sobs.

Ged hugged her and with a measured voice said, "I haven't the faintest idea, but look on the bright side — at least you're in the right place now."

Molly stopped crying and pulling away from him and glowered incredulously. "Right place? Right place? No Grandpa, I'm not in the right place. There's absolutely no bloody way on earth that I'm in the right place. There must be some mistake. I don't want to be here, I don't belong here and I sure as hell don't want to stay here," she fumed.

Ged was shocked at Molly's outburst and show of ingratitude and chastising her said, "Watch the attitude, girl. You aren't at home now, giving cheek to your mother. Show some respect, you're in the Divine's domain now."

Molly shifted uncomfortably, realising that she had probably just overstepped the mark. "I'm sorry, Gramps but this is just a pile of poo. And yes, you could say that I'm feeling a little bit miffed. And that's an understatement, by the way."

Ged scowled at his granddaughter, and moving opposite to where Orick was standing, indicated to Molly that she should follow him. Taking a deep breath, he sighed. "Okay, as far as I can tell, something went very wrong when you crossed over. Obviously, we need to find out what that something is. You seem to have forgotten everything a spirit knows or should know; it's like your memory has been wiped clean. You should know all this stuff — that's what's strange, you don't know or remember any of it."

Molly stared somewhat bemused at Ged, unsure of what to do or say.

"It's like you didn't have time to make the transition and your soul hadn't prepared itself to leave. It's like you didn't know what was coming — well your soul didn't anyway. Tell you what, I'll help you to find out what happened, and I'll try and put Orick off for a while but we'll have to be quick mind, because you can bet your bottom dollar we'll be missed."

Ged looked around nervously. He knew that what he was proposing to do was going to be hard and virtually unheard of, and if anyone found out it would more than likely take decades to correct. There'd be endless Council meetings to attend and appearances to make in front of the Elders and whoever. Ged knew that if his plan went pear-shaped then he'd have a lot of explaining to do.

"So, what's the plan? What are we going to do? Do you even have a plan, Grandpa?"

"I don't know for sure. All I'm saying is that there are a lot of 'ifs', 'ands' and 'buts'. Oh, blow it, what the heck! What's the point in having life-ever-after if you can't get to enjoy it or at the very least stir things up a bit?" Muttering nervously to himself, he looked over to the stairway and quickly turned away again to avoid Orick's gaze, hoping that he hadn't read his thoughts.

Molly was becoming impatient, and staring defiantly at her grandfather, pouted. "Well, what are we waiting for? You said yourself that we have to be quick; come on Grandpa, pretty please, pleeease," she begged, "I need your help; I need to find out what happened to me."

Ged sighed deeply. "Shush a minute, I need to think. I need to plan a way of doing this. I need a plan of action and right now you're not helping, what with all your questions and whingeing and carrying on. Jeez, I'd forgotten how much of a pain in the rear you can be."

Molly pouted again but thought it best to stay quiet.

Chapter Eight: Lost Cause

<***>

Growing up on the local council estate, Tony Collins had lived in the same council house with his mother, Sally, for as long as he could remember. He had lost his father and his sister in a fire when he was nine years old, and his mum had remarried a few years later.

Tony wasn't one to readily conform to the ways of the world. Having sauntered aimlessly through life so far, he had unwittingly managed to avoid the responsibilities of adulthood. He had never held down a job for more than a couple of weeks at a time, which meant that his drug addiction was largely funded by means of dole money and petty crime. Now, and not for the first time, he was on probation for possession of cannabis, for which he was required to report to his probation officer every week.

Often having rows with Jack Monroe, his stepfather, Tony knew he could quite easily lose control and end up hitting the silly old buggar, even though he was twice Tony's height and build. Tony knew that if he lashed out, he would be out on his ear as his mum always sided with Jack. Knowing full well which side his bread was buttered on, he figured that in the scheme of things, keeping his fists to himself was a small price to pay for free board and lodgings. His mum, Sally, worked part-time at the local pub as a barmaid. Jack was unemployed and unemployable due to a 'back condition'. Tony knew that there was nothing wrong with the lazy sod, as his bad back didn't prevent him from going to the local bookies or doing odd jobs, for which he got paid cash in hand.

On this particular Thursday morning Tony struggled to open his eyes as he felt the worse for wear. He had a raging thirst with a hangover and headache to match.

"Tony, get up!" shouted his mum from his bedroom door. "Just look at the time. You're supposed to be there for 11 o'clock. You know what they're like if you give 'em cause."

Tony fumbled for the bedside clock. "Yeah, yeah," he mumbled, pulling the sheet over his head, and tried to shut out the unwelcome intrusion as Sally continued her disapproving tirade. Stumbling into the bathroom and slamming the door shut, he stood at the sink staring at his reflection in the mirror. His eyes were bloodshot and his tongue felt like it was glued to the roof of his mouth. After brushing his teeth and showering, he hurriedly got dressed in clean jeans, T-shirt and his favourite grey sweatshirt. Bounding down the stairs two at a time, he slammed the front door behind him.

"Bye," Sally shouted sarcastically, as she shook her head with disdain.

The dole office was a thirty-minute bus ride into the centre of town and the probation office was just around the corner. Tony was sick of having to see his probation officer, but knew that he would only have to do it for another couple of weeks and then he would have the tag removed. It had been ten months since he had been stopped by two local coppers when he and Gareth had been walking through the shopping precinct, on their way to the Swan pub for a quick pint. They had frisk-searched him and found the drugs, and he had been done for possession. Gareth was clean — he had made sure that he wasn't carrying anything incriminating, as he always did. Gareth was free to go but Tony was in it up to his neck, with a lot of explaining to do. Tony reckoned that Gaz was a mate; Gareth just thought that Tony was an idiot.

The bus was running late, but Tony managed to get to his appointment in time. His probation officer was nice enough, and Tony answered all of his questions and said all the right things. Afterwards, he had collected his dole money and laughed all the way to one of the local dealers. After buying his usual, he ambled over to the local park and sitting on a park bench which was recessed into a wall, he took the plastic bag out of his pocket along with a packet of paper Rizlas, and expertly rolled up a joint. Pulling deeply on it, he inhaled the smoky drug which snaked its way down into his lungs before hitting his brain. In a haze of jumbled thoughts, he began trying to piece together what had happened the previous night. He couldn't put his finger on it, but deep down he knew something wasn't right — he didn't feel right. Closing his eyes, he began to relax. He remembered that he had been to the pub with Gaz and had chatted up two girls. He remembered watching them sing karaoke on the stage and... what else? There was something else.

'Molly and Debbie, that's it! Those were their names. This is weird. Why can't I remember stuff? Must be the weed. Christ this must be good shit,' he thought, smirking to himself.

Suddenly he had a flashback. He had really got on well with the girl called Molly, even though he realised that Gaz also fancied her. He vaguely remembered really liking her and fancying his chances, but after that everything else was sketchy.

Staring out over the green of the playing field which stretched out in front of him, he watched one of the council workers drive up and down the field, cutting the grass on a mechanised lawnmower. He looked over to where the kid's playground was, and watched as two teenage girls pushed their latest additions in battered buggies with a couple more snotty-nosed brats in tow. Tony smirked to himself; they were the easy lays — girls with a reputation for sleeping around. He watched one of the girls in particular, as he recognised her from his old school. She had a cigarette hanging out of her mouth and was screaming and shouting at two of her grubby brood. With a passing thought he fantasised that one day he could see himself having a couple of sprogs.

Tony remembered coming to the park for a kick around when he was a kid, and recalled how he and his mates would ride their bikes across the bowling green lawn and get chased and shouted at by the park keeper. He thought about how they used to build dens in the bushes and hide in them when they played truant from school. Abruptly his mind wandered back to the previous night's events, as Molly's face began to swim in front of his eyes. 'Oh, sod her.' he thought. She was just another slapper who probably hadn't given him a second thought since last night. The problem was though, he had given her several second thoughts; he knew that he fancied her something rotten and couldn't get her out of his head. He resigned himself to the fact that he would just have to wait until next Wednesday before he could see her again.

He had just finished smoking his joint when his phone rang, and the photo that it displayed showed it was Gaz who was calling.

"Hi mate, I'm going for a pint in the precinct. Fancy a swift one with us?" asked Gareth.

"Yeah, be there in a bit. See ya in there."

Tony made his way to 'The Swan' pub where he found Gareth standing at the bar, downing the last inch of his pint.

"Get 'em in, will you? I'm just going for a slash," Gareth said casually.

Tony got two pints of lager and sat down in one of the alcoves next to the pool table. He looked out of the window as faceless people scurried past, trying to get out of the sudden downpour.

Gareth strode over and sat down opposite him. "Cheers mate. You been into town yet?" he asked, taking a swig of lager.

"Yeah, saw me probation officer. Bastard gave us a right lecture about reforming me character and all that bullshit. Blah, blah, bleedin' blah!"

Gareth saw this as his chance to manipulate and plant seeds of doubt in Tony's mind. "So, what do you remember about last night?" he asked eagerly. "Christ man, you were well oiled!".

Tony thought for a minute. "Yeah, not bleedin' much, now you mention it."

Gareth smirked. "Well, let's just say you had your fun before you crashed out."

"Yeah well, I don't remember having fun. I don't remember jack shit as it happens, so come on, spill. What happened, did you get your end away or what?"

Gareth suddenly lost his nerve and felt tense and uncertain. He needed to get his story straight and watertight; he had to make sure that he was convincing, otherwise Tony wouldn't buy any of it. Reaching for his phone, he pretended that he had just received a text message. "Huh, what the 'ell does he want?" he feigned, "Gotta go — just got a bit of business to see too. Catch ya later, big boy. Fill ya in then."

Tony nodded like he understood, as Gareth swiftly downed the rest of his pint and winked at Tony cheekily. Watching as he hurriedly grabbed his jacket and disappeared through the double doors into the rain, Tony always felt like he was kept at arm's length. The reality was that he didn't know Gareth, not really. He was a bit weird at times, but to Tony's way of thinking, a mate was a mate and besides which, he felt sorry for him in a way. Tony finished his pint and decided to go home as he knew that the house would be empty. Knowing that he could please himself as to whether he played on his computer or watch television made it all the more appealing. He even toyed with the idea of going back to bed. Pulling his hood up he ran to the nearest bus stop as the rain continued to bounce off the pavement.

Letting himself in through the back door, he found the house in silence; all the same he checked the downstairs, making doubly sure that no one was home. Sprinting up the stairs three at a time, he stood on the landing listening; he thought he'd heard something, but wasn't sure. Flopping down onto his bed, he plumped up a pillow to lean on and finding the television remote, began flicking through the channels. Finding a programme which he liked, he began to relax and was soon drifting into a deep, empty sleep.

It was sometime later when Tony stirred. He could hear that strange noise again, the same as he'd heard when standing on the landing. He swung his legs off the bed, and sat on the edge, trying to organise his thoughts. Switching the television off he crossed the room to the heap of clothes left on the floor from the previous night. He fumbled through the jeans pockets and found a mobile phone. Tony was puzzled and tried to think how he had come to have somebody else's phone. Turning it on, he saw it had eleven missed calls. He thought about dialling the last number which was displayed but decided against it. Shrugging his shoulders, he threw it dismissively onto the bed; he'd ask Gaz about it later.

The house was still and quiet save for the kitchen clock which ticked relentlessly. Glancing at the time he knew that his mother would be home soon. He looked through the cupboards for something to eat — weed always gave him the munchies — and decided on a bowl of cereal. Helping himself to two bowlfuls, he slouched into the lounge and flicked the television on. Tony tried to concentrate on the programme but his mind was elsewhere. Suddenly he remembered the mobile phone and raced back upstairs to examine it again. He looked at the screen but this time it was blank; the battery was flat. He got out his phone charger and tried plugging it into the phone but it was a different type of connection socket. Putting the phone into the top drawer of his bedside cabinet, he flopped onto the bed and fell back to sleep.

A short time later something roused him and he woke with a start. His head was pounding as he heard his mother shout up the stairs, "Tony, are you in?"

Rolling over onto his back he stared at the ceiling. "Yeah, be down in a minute," he shouted back. He fumbled to see what time it was on the bedside clock — 6.15 pm. Stretching and yawning, he stuck a mint in his mouth and ambled downstairs into the kitchen, where his mother was peeling potatoes for the evening meal.

"I see you didn't read my note. I asked you to peel the spuds ready for tea. You know I'm pushed for time and have to be back at the pub for seven o'clock.

Tony slumped down onto a kitchen chair. "Yeah, sorry, I didn't see it," he lied.

"Have you seen Jack at all?" asked Sally, flustered.

"Hmmm… no," he said, as he bit into a thick round of buttered bread.

Sally busied herself as she put some chicken drum sticks into the oven. "Chicken and chips for tea. What have you been up to all day, or shouldn't I ask?"

"Nowt much. Saw me bleedin' probation officer, got me dole money, then just been up to the precinct and met Gaz for a pint."

"Well, I hope you're keeping yourself out of trouble. Keep your nose clean — do you hear me? I've just about had enough of your shenanigans, and I don't trust that Gareth as far as I could throw him. You'd do right to do the same. I keep telling you he's bad news, that one," Sally scolded.

Plating up Jack's meal as usual, she left it in the microwave before setting him a place at the table. She never knew when he would be home these days. Sitting in the kitchen with Tony, they ate in silence. Sally knew damn well that Tony was still smoking dope, in spite of all his promises that he had given it up. She could smell it in his hair and on his clothes, but she didn't have the fight in her for another row. After clearing away the plates, she left to go back to work.

Tony was lying on the settee when he got a text from Gareth inviting him round to hang out for a while. Since he had nothing better to do and also as a means of avoiding Jack, he decided to walk round to Gareth's. On the way he called in at the off license and picked up a couple of cans of lager and some Rizlas, but all the while his head was filled with thoughts of Molly.

Gareth had thought long and hard about what had happened the previous night, and kept replaying the events and scenarios over and over in his head. He had practiced getting his story straight all afternoon, and now he was eager to gloat at his conquest — a conquest fabricated with fantasy and lies. Of course, he wouldn't admit to murdering the silly bitch. No, the important thing was to convince Tony that he was implicated in the sex, and to blackmail him into keeping quiet about last night.

Tony took a swig of the cold lager and looking round Gareth's room, noticed that the bed wasn't made. He still couldn't remember much of what had happened, so was happy to listen to Gareth filling in the gaps. He vaguely remembered leaving the pub and going back to Gareth's place, and he remembered downing a couple of vodkas, but after that his memory was non-existent. Gareth nonchalantly began rolling a spliff and was enjoying being in control. He was bragging about the great shag he'd had, how Tony had really enjoyed having a threesome, and how the slag had been up for anything.

"Christ man, you were fuckin' amazing! I thought I was up for anything, but you were an animal. I'm telling you man, it was fuckin' amazing. She was squealing like a good 'un — couldn't get enough of it. Fit as fuck! I thought she was gonna wake the whole fuckin' street at one point. Then when we got it on, well, you were sommat else."

Tony took the offered spliff and sitting back in the chair, took a long, deep toke. "What do you mean, 'we got it on'? What ya talking about? Cos I'm telling you now, there's no bleedin' way I would ever be shaggin' a bloke, not even you. No bleedin' way!"

Gareth pretended to be hurt by Tony's remark. "Awe mate, sorry to disillusion you and shatter your macho image and all that, but you were well up for it. Said you loved me and all sorts."

"Nah. Don't believe you. Piss off! Us, shaggin? Nah, you're a lying bastard!"

Gareth grinned. "Yeah, well not from where I'm sitting, darlin'. But don't worry, your dirty little secret's safe with me."

Tony suddenly felt sick in the pit of his stomach and standing up, began to pace the floor. He was shocked and confused at what Gareth had just told him, though he still didn't believe it. He couldn't even begin to let himself think that he would do such a thing — he wasn't gay or even bi! No, Gareth was a lying bastard, he had to be.

Tony sat down hard on the chair again and put his head into his hands, shaking it in disbelief. Gareth knew that he had Tony on the back foot and continued to elaborate the lies, knowing that he had Tony exactly where he needed him. He was pretty convincing and managed to leave Tony with just the right amount of doubt. God, he was so easy to manipulate, and blackmailing him into silence was easier than Gareth had imagined it would be.

"So, where's Molly now?" Tony asked, genuinely concerned.

"How the fuck do I know? What do you care, anyway? She left while you, my sleeping beauty, was snoring your pissed, fuckin' head off."

Tony continued to shake his head, hardly daring to believe what Gareth was saying. He certainly hadn't had Gareth down as batting for both sides, yet what if he had done those things? Just because he didn't remember doing them didn't mean that he hadn't done them, did it? Suddenly he began to feel uncomfortable at being alone with Gareth.

Swigging from another can of lager he noticed that Gareth kept rubbing his leg. Wanting to change the subject but keep Gareth on side he asked, "What's up? You been bitten or sommat?" He looked around the dingy, dank bedsit and continued contemptuously, "Jesus Christ, how the hell do you live in this flea pit, man? It's bleedin' rancid."

Gareth rolled up his trouser leg to have a look. "Ah, it's nothing. Like you said, it's a fuckin' flea pit."

Tony suddenly remembered having found the mobile phone. "Anyways, how come I've got a bleedin' mobile that's not mine? I found the bleedin' thing in me denims."

Gareth took a long swig from the can of lager he was holding. "Phone, what phone?" he asked, pretending to know nothing about it.

"I've just said, haven't I. The bleedin' phone I found in me denims."

"Oh, that. I found it on the floor and thought it was yours. Why, where is it?" he asked, keeping his voice steady.

"Left it in me bedroom. It's no good any road — bleedin' thing's flat."

"Shame, must be hers then. So, what ya doin' tomorrow?" Gareth asked, trying to change the subject.

"Nowt much. Suppose I'll have to wait and give it back to her next time I see her then," replied Tony. Yet all the while he was aware that a multitude of questions he didn't dare ask, hung unanswered in the air.

Feeling nervous and somewhat uncomfortable, Tony quickly finished his can of lager, made an excuse and hurriedly left Gareth's bed-sit. He toyed with the idea of catching the bus home but decided to walk instead; it would give him thinking time. He ambled home, not in any hurry. Lost in thought, he mulled over what Gareth had told him. His head was all over the place, particularly with what had supposedly gone on between them, and he still couldn't get Molly out of his head either. Gaz had made her out to be a right slag, but he just didn't buy it. Yes, she had been well and truly pissed — he remembered that much, and also that she could barely walk, but she certainly hadn't come across as being a slag. No, something wasn't right — it just didn't fit. If she were that drunk, she would have been incapable of doing half the things that Gaz had said they'd done. And as for him and Gareth — no way! He was a bleedin' liar, he had to be. Rounding the corner near his house, he checked that there were no nosy neighbours about before he went down to the tool shed at the bottom of the garden and sitting alone in the gloom, began to quietly sob.

Gareth was pacing his bed-sit floor. He knew that the phone was evidence, so had he done the right thing by slipping it into Tony's pocket? He began to question himself, doubting his rash decision, going around in circles with the same worry — would they be able to trace it to him through having his finger prints are all over it? He was trying hard to suppress a feeling of rising panic, then relaxed a bit as he realised that because Tony had the phone and had handled it so much, it wasn't likely that they would now be able to trace it back to Gareth.

Gareth replayed the fantasy he had created over and over in his mind until he knew it verbatim. He couldn't stop smirking. After all, knowing that Tony didn't remember much was a master stroke because Gareth could say whatever he liked and Tony would have to believe it. Tony only had his word and version of events, a version which he would obviously want to be kept secret. Snatching the tab off another can of lager and taking large swigs of the cold liquid, he continued to pace the room. His whole body was awash with excitement as he recollected the events of the previous night and once again revelled in the exhilaration, the lust, the sheer power. He remembered how soft her skin had been, how her hair had smelt of shampoo and how her perfume had lingered. Closing his eyes, he visualised her perfect form of curves and womanliness and began to taste and feel her again. As his desire mounted, he felt a familiar stirring as he became all too aware of his hardness. God, how he had loved loving her!

Chapter Nine: Unimaginable

<***>

Beth loved her home — it was a little palace in her eyes. She and Frank, her husband of twenty-two years, had lived on the same council estate ever since they first got married. They had bought the house from the local council while she was working full-time as a bank clerk and Frank had joined the fire brigade. It was a neat, three-bedroomed semi-detached with a pristine lawn in the front garden, a landscaped rear garden, and a conservatory built onto the back of the lounge. Yes, Beth was very proud of her little palace. She knew that they had been the first in their road to have a conservatory built, and she had loved showing it off to anyone who happened to express an interest. However, the conservatory had soon become a bone of contention; Frank would moan about it being too hot in the summer and too cold in the winter, and grumbled at the cost of the heating bills, not that Beth really cared. The weekends were mostly spent entertaining friends from the golf and tennis clubs, of which they were both members. Beth especially looked forward to hosting dinner parties on Friday or Saturday nights. She loved cooking and baking and would effortlessly throw a three-course meal together with coffee and mints to follow.

Today, Beth had been out to the local market to buy some fresh meat and vegetables for the evening meal. The bus was always full on market days, but Beth had managed to get one of the front seats on the lower deck of the double decker; she was relieved, as the thought of having to struggle up the stairs to the upper deck with a load of shopping filled her with dread. She sat down next to a heavily pregnant young girl who she thought could not be older than fifteen and stared out of the window as the bus pulled away. Beth soon became engrossed in thought as she started thinking about what Annie had said about Molly not coming home and silently prayed that everything was all right.

Getting off the bus at her stop, she walked the few hundred yards to her front gate and expertly flicked the catch up. She kicked it shut with her right foot, and it slammed noisily behind her. Precariously she balanced the shopping bags on the front doorstep, fumbled in her pocket for the door key, and let herself into the house. Going through to the kitchen, she set the bags down on the counter top.

"I'm home — anybody in?" she shouted to no one in particular, as she went back into the hall to close the front door. The house was quiet; Frank must still be working his shift or doing a bit of overtime, she thought. "Anybody in?" she shouted again, as she took her coat and shoes off. She made herself a cup of coffee and standing at the open back door, lit a cigarette and inhaled deeply, enjoying the taste and smell of the tobacco.

"Caught you!"

Beth rounded to find Debbie standing in the kitchen doorway. "Jesus Christ!" Beth shouted out in fright. "You nearly gave me a blooming heart attack! I thought everyone was out. Why the hell didn't you answer me when I shouted?"

Debbie smirked to herself. "I was on the computer with my head phones on."

Beth shifted awkwardly. "Well, don't you be telling your Dad I'm smoking again. You know what he's like with his bloody holier-than-thou attitude. I won't hear the bloody end of it, him being a fireman and all."

Debbie smiled sweetly and replied that she wouldn't breathe a word. Instead, she just stored it in her memory as blackmail currency for getting what she wanted at a later date.

Finishing her cigarette, Beth started to unpack the shopping. "I saw Molly's mum while I was out. She was under the impression that Molly stayed over last night. I put her straight like, and told her that you had come home by yourself."

Debbie flopped down on to one of the kitchen chairs. "Actually Mum, I've fell out with her."

Beth turned around. "What do you mean fell out? You ain't never fell out, you and Molly, never."

Debbie looked sullen and started to recount what had happened the previous night. She told Beth how she and Molly had sung on stage, how Molly had won a bottle of wine, and how they had been chatted up by a couple of lads.

"They were a right laugh. Molly really fancied one of them — Tony I think his name was — but the other was just way too creepy. Gareth or Gaz, I think he was called — not my type at all. Anyways, they were buying, so we were drinking. We must have downed quite a few between us."

"Oh, you did, did you? So how many did you have?"

"Like I said, quite a few. Molly was really knocking them back."

"Well I hope you had more sense. That kind of thing is bound to cause no end of tears. You youngsters think you can do what you like, when you like, how you like."

"For God's sake Mum, stop going on! Are you listening or not?" Debbie scowled.

"I'm listening," Beth said as she closed the cupboard door, giving Debbie her full attention.

"Anyway, afterwards at chucking out time, Molly decided that she was gonna head off into town with them to a party or something. The last I saw of her was her backside getting into a taxi. Honestly Mum, she never gave me a second thought. She was really drunk though but when I tried to talk her out of it, she told me to buggar off and get a life. Can you believe that? Me… get a life! Cheeky cow!"

"Oh, did she now? Well you know she can be a bit of a stroppy madam."

"Stroppy? You didn't see her, Mum. Off she went without a second thought. It was like I wasn't there. She just wouldn't listen to me, and we ended up having a blazing row, so I walked home on my own."

Beth could see how upset her daughter was and put her arm around her shoulders. "Ah, don't worry love, I expect it will all blow over. She'll be sorry and you'll be sorry, and you'll both make it up again. You two not being best friends is unimaginable." But a flash of concern had already crossed Beth's face as she picked up the phone and dialled Annie's number.

Chapter Ten: Gone Home

<***>

Molly sat quietly while Ged pondered on what to do next. "Right, you need to think long and hard about last night. You really need to try hard and remember exactly what happened."

"Really, well it's not like I'm not trying is it?" she replied insolently. "All I remember is going to the pub with Debbie. Jeez — give us a chance!"

Ged scratched his head. "Well then, maybe that's the place to start. We should go back to the pub to see if that helps. It might jog your memory."

"Back to the pub? Well that's great. And just how do we do that, seeing as how we're dead and all?"

Ged eyed his granddaughter. "Well, have you got a better idea? You're a right cocky mare, aren't you — I don't know how your mother put up with you. And as I've told you before, we aren't dead; existence as Spirit is eternal and this, the spiritual realm, is the place where we always return to — our real home, if you like."

Molly shrugged her shoulders. "Home? You keep saying that, but I don't know what you're talking about. How can this be home, for God's sake?

Ged sat down and gestured for Molly to join him. "You'd try the patience of a saint, so you would! Look, as Spirit this is who and what we are. This is where we are. We incarnate back to being mortal and reside in the physical — mostly to the earth realm but sometimes even to other planets and alternative dimensions. We do that to learn, to experience difficult situations and emotions. We are Spirit and we are multi-dimensional, immortal energy beings."

Molly felt belligerent and was beginning to think that her grandfather had lost his marbles. She decided that it was probably best not to say anything more, well at least for the time being.

"We exist as Spirit in a body, not as a body with a spirit. We learn from each and every incarnation we undertake. We return to the earth realm to have a physical experience in a physical body. With each lesson learned we progress, until eventually we move up through the ranks, as it were, and we don't have need to come back any more. That's called 'ascension' — think of it as getting a promotion if you like. When we ascend, we draw closer to the Great Spirit... closer to Source."

"'Sauce'? What do you mean, 'sauce'? Like in tomato ketchup or brown?"

"What? Not 'sauce' you idiot — 'Source' as in God, the entity who oversees this vastness. You have no idea, no appreciation of just how wonderful and unlimited this whole thing is," exclaimed Ged, exasperated.

"All right, keep your hair on. How was I to know?" she said impudently. "So how does it all work then?"

"Truly, I don't know where to begin. That would take an eternity in itself to explain, and I don't think you're ready yet to even have the basics explained, judging by what you've just said. 'Sauce' indeed!"

Molly shrugged her shoulders again and feeling slightly embarrassed, changed the subject. "Are we going to the pub or what? Cos if we are, how do we get back?"

Ged smiled to himself. "Ah, that's the easy part, once you've done it a couple of times that is. We call it energy shifting or transformational transference."

"Transformational transference?" Molly repeated, rolling her eyes.

"Yes, actually it's just a fancy name for altering our energy. First you imagine that you're taking a deep breath, like you did when diving underwater. Do you remember when you used to go swimming? Well that's the equivalent of gathering your Spirit essence and condensing your energy field. It helps to lower your vibration, making it easier to slip across into the earth realm dimension. Oh, and as you're doing all that, you just think yourself where you want to be. That's how we visit whoever or wherever we want, whenever we want. Don't forget, you're not in a physical body anymore."

Molly stared blankly, trying to comprehend what Ged was saying. She eyed Ged with a look which said, 'Okay… whatever.'

"Don't look at me like that, Molly girl," he said sternly, "Actually though, I'm thinking that you just might struggle a bit, seeing as how you haven't connected to your essence and whatnot yet."

"What do you mean?" she asked, frowning.

"Well as far as I can tell, you haven't got all your energy and vibration together, so it might be that you're too weak to do transference anyway, or you might manage to get there but not be able to get back again."

"Oh, is that gonna be a problem?" she asked, puzzled.

"Don't know till we try. We'll just see how we get on and if it's a problem I'll have to ask Orick to help us out."

"Will we be in trouble if that happens? If you have to get Orick to help, I mean"

"Why heck, sure we'll be in trouble — a big shed load of trouble — but I'm guessing they can't exactly do much about it. Maybe give us a stern talking to."

"A stern talking to…" Molly repeated.

"For goodness sake, Molly, how would I know? I've never done this sort of thing before, but working on the principle that love is all there is in the universe, then the higher echelons are hardly going to punish us or harm us in any way, are they?"

"Well I don't know, do I? All this is new to me and there's no need to get all shirty!" she said, indignantly.

Ged felt bad and instinctively gave Molly a hug. "I'm sorry Titch, it's just so frustrating that you don't remember things, and it's hard for me to stop taking things for granted. Look, I'll tell you what, maybe what we need to do is be a bit more tolerant of each other. What do you say?"

Tutting under her breath, she rolled her eyes. "S'pose so… I will if you will."

"Good, that's settled then. Right, what was I saying? Oh yes, Orick stepping in if needs be. I'm hoping we won't need to involve him but you never know."

Molly looked all the more perplexed. "So, what you're saying is that if this all goes pear-shaped, we still have a lifeline, as it were, and I'm not gonna die again?"

Ged spluttered at Molly's remark. "What? Die again? Why of course not! No one and nothing can kill a spirit. It's only the physical body which perishes."

Molly flinched. "Really…tell me about it!" she said sarcastically.

"Another thing which might be useful for you to know is that there are people in the physical realm who are sensitive to our vibration. So just bear that in mind if ever you find yourself needing to communicate with them."

Molly rolled her eyes again. "What do you mean, communicate with them?"

"Well, there are people who can sense when we are around, because they are sensitive to our vibration. They can tune in, as it were. They're usually called psychics or mediums. Remember I mentioned my Auntie Vera being one"

Molly retorted, "Oh yeah, you mean those nutters or weirdos who are supposedly able to talk to the dead?"

Ged raised his eyebrows in surprise. "But they're not nutters or weirdos, Molly. They're the folk we depend on when we need to get a message through. I remember arranging it a couple of times for your Nan when I needed to tell her something. Absolute Godsend they are, too."

Molly didn't fully understand why her grandfather was getting so animated. "So, this is important because….?"

Ged looked at her incredulously. "It's important because it means we can talk to our loved ones through them — it means we can communicate. It's a way of proving to them that we're not dead and that life is eternal and everlasting."

"Okay, keep your hair on…" said Molly, defensively, "I only asked."

Ged frowned and taking her hand, said, "Have you ever heard the expression, 'seeing is believing'?"

Molly nodded, "Of course I have, Nan said it all the time."

"Right then, well hearing is God's own truth — remember that, if nothing else."

Lapsing into a long silence, Molly thought about what her grandpa had just told her and looking around her, surveyed the enormity of what lay before them. Becoming a little impatient, she started to fidget. "So, what now? What're we doing?"

Ged stood up, and looked at Molly with concern. "Are you all right? You look a little out of it."

Molly rubbed her eyes. "Yeah, I'm all right — stop fussing for God's sake. Can we go now? Can we go to the pub?" She was eager to try this thing which Ged had called transformational transference. "You said that we can go wherever we want, whenever we want."

"Yes, that's the size of it, but you have such a lot to remember. I think you have transitional amnesia because you haven't fully reconnected to the spiritual realm yet. Hopefully, once you've been to see the Elders, everything will be okay. You have a lot to learn and a lot to do, so if we are going to go back to the pub, we need to get cracking. I just hope that nothing goes wrong in the meantime."

"Oh yeah, 'the Elders'…" she said mockingly, doing the inverted comma gesture in mid-air, "mustn't forget them now, must we." Molly stood defiantly with her arms folded. She really didn't give a damn if anything did go wrong. All that mattered to her was that she found out why she was here when she shouldn't be.

"It's not funny, Molly. This is serious stuff. You will be summoned and I'll have to go with you. I was the one to meet you, and I've been given the responsibility of being your custodian. Don't you get it? What we are planning on doing is sacrilege and potentially very dangerous. Why its tantamount to… to… whatever its tantamount to. I can't believe I'm now even considering doing it, let alone agreeing to do it. I was wrong to make light of it. This just isn't done, and you'd do well to remember that," he snapped.

Molly was taken aback at her grandpa's outburst and tried to smooth things over. "I'm sorry Grandpa, it's just that I need to know the truth. I need to know why."

Ged relaxed and softened his voice. "I know Molly, I'm sorry too. Guess I'm a bit stressed with all this. Look, just remember what I've told you to do, and go and practice over there for a bit."

Molly nodded and wandered a couple of feet away. She imagined herself taking a deep breath, like she used to do just before doing a duck dive. It wasn't as easy as she thought it would be, as it took a great deal of concentration and felt a bit weird as well. It was like feeling light and weightless, while at the same time having the sensation of a heavy pressure pushing against her. Molly practiced for a while and soon started to get the hang of it.

"How's it going — you ready?"

"Sure am! Oh, this is so exciting."

"Right then, follow me."

Following her grandfather's vibration and light, she found herself at his side in the Lounge bar of the Horse and Jockey public house.

Although Orick had been some distance away, he had heard what Ged and Molly were planning. He wasn't in the least surprised that Molly would disobey cosmic laws. As her life guide, he knew that she had always been headstrong and stubborn, and they were the very reasons that Molly had got herself into bad situations and endless amounts of trouble throughout her many lifetimes. He was, however, very surprised that Ged was about to instigate an ill-thought-out plan. A plan which Ged surely knew could end really badly, and yet was still going to go along with.

Orick thought back to all the occasions when he had had to intervene and come to Molly's rescue. Maybe that was part of the problem; perhaps he should stop intervening and let her sort her own messes out. Yet although he knew that the 'Guides Guild Code of Conduct' was there for a reason, he had admittedly been a bit lax in adhering to it of late — well the last couple of centuries, actually. He thought back to his inaugural ceremony and silently recited it, congratulating himself on remembering it. Tutting he then chastised himself. 'More's the pity I didn't put it into practice as often as I should have,' he thought, whilst continuing to mutter under his breath.

Truth be told, he wasn't entirely happy with the way things were panning out; he had growing concerns and was beginning to feel quite tetchy. He muttered even more to himself as he remembered the many lifetimes he had shared with Molly and how she had often got it woefully wrong when it came to making the right choices in important life events. But somehow things had always come right in the end, for which Orick took full credit. The problem now was that Molly was back home in the spiritual realm, and that was a whole new ball game, especially as she was an incomplete spirit, at least as far as energy and memory were concerned. He decided that for the moment he would do nothing but observe; he would stand back and let her and Ged do whatever it was they were planning to do. But at the first sign of trouble he would have to intervene and, if necessary, consult the Elders. Orick really hoped that it wouldn't come to that.

Chapter Eleven: Reportedly Missing

<***>

Annie listened to the dialling tone and then changed her mind and replaced the phone's handset into its cradle. No, it would be better if she went to the police station in person, she decided.

Arriving outside the foreboding building, she paced up and down the pavement a few times. The imposing wood and brass swing door seemed to mock her, daring her to enter. Letting nerves get the better of her, Annie got cold feet and decided not to go in. She felt sick, her insides churned, her legs were like jelly, and she felt like she would collapse in a heap from adrenalin and nerves at any moment. She wished she felt braver. After walking round the block a few times trying to clear her head, she took in some deep breaths until she finally summoned up the courage. She pushed the heavy oak door open, crossed the old Victorian tiled floor of the reception area, and went over to the closed glass window, next to which was a sign giving instructions to press the buzzer fixed to the wall. Annie pushed it twice and chewing her lower lip, waited impatiently for the glass window to slide open. Glancing around at the multitude of posters which were haphazardly Sellotaped to the walls, she realised that they were mostly about fraud and burglary and how to report criminal acts anonymously; there was nothing about reporting a missing person.

She glanced nervously at the other people who were sitting in the waiting area and decided that they all looked of dubious character. Keeping her eyes cast down, she did her best to avoid making eye contact and seeing an empty seat, made her way over to it. She shifted uncomfortably on the hard-plastic chair and clutched her handbag tightly, silently wishing the ground would open up and swallow her whole in one huge gulp.

Annie never thought that she'd ever have the need to venture into one of these places. She remembered the many derogatory remarks which Nan she used to make about Police Stations due to Ged's career in crime. Nan had called them 'The Sties', because that's where pigs lived and as Annie started to recall some of her childhood memories, she understood why she had developed such a dislike and mistrust of the police. She remembered that they were the ones who knocked on the door and took her father away, usually for questioning or to help them with their enquiries; strangely this often seemed to happen soon after he was home from the oil rigs.

"Hello, can I help you? Excuse me... can I help you there?"

Annie was lost in thought when she suddenly realised that a Police Officer had appeared at the window and that the question was being addressed to her. Standing up quickly, she approached the open glass window and the smiling face on the other side.

"Hello there, how can I help you?" the smiling face repeated.

"Erm... yes. I'm... erm... Mrs Roberts... Annie Roberts and I want to report that my daughter is missing."

"Oh, righto, sorry to hear that. Just have a seat again and I'll get someone to come and speak to you. Shan't be a minute."

The smiling face disappeared as the glass window slid shut. Annie felt a dozen eyes turn on her as she returned to her seat. She went over in her mind the conversation that she'd had with Beth and decided she was being foolish in involving the police so soon. She had just made up her mind to leave when a door opened and a young constable appeared within its frame. "Mrs Roberts?" he enquired, looking over in her direction. He was tall and of slim build, and it crossed Annie's mind that he looked like he was just out of school.

Getting to her feet, she hesitated. "Yes, that's me."

"Hello, Mrs Roberts. Would you like to come with me — we'll go somewhere a bit more private."

Annie followed him down a brightly lit corridor into a room which smelled of furniture polish. He deftly changed the sign on the door to 'Engaged' and pulled out a chair for Annie to sit on.

She was acutely aware of the desk which was between them — a barrier between him and her.

"I'm Constable Morris. I understand that you want to report a missing person?"

Annie reached into her pocket and fumbling for a tissue, said, "Yes, that's right; I want to report my daughter, Molly, as missing — Molly Roberts."

Constable Morris opened a black box file and taking out the necessary forms, hovered over them with a biro pen. "So, if I can take some preliminary details… When did you last see your daughter, Molly?"

Annie blew her nose. "It was last night… I've not seen her since last night. She always goes out on a Wednesday to the local pub, the Horse and Jockey — you know, the one on the estate? She loves to sing and they do a Karaoke night there on a Wednesday."

"Did she go with anyone else?"

Annie reached for the glass of water which had been thoughtfully placed in front of her and took a sip, as her mouth was dry. "Yes, Molly went with Debbie — Debbie Travis, her best friend." Annie opened her handbag and rummaged inside. "Here, this is a photograph of her." She passed it to him, and he studied the smiling girl who looked back at him. Annie recounted everything she could remember — what clothes Molly had been wearing, what time she had left the house. She mentioned all the unanswered phone calls and texts that she had made to Molly's mobile phone that day and how Molly hadn't been into work either. She added that no one had seen her since the previous night and that she had spoken to Debbie's mother who told her that Debbie had come home on her own, a little after 11.30 pm.

Constable Morris took a detailed statement and said he would file a missing person's report and take things from there. He told Annie she was not to worry as lots of young girls did this sort of thing all the time, only to turn up a couple of hours later.

And if she did turn up, would Annie please let them know immediately.

Annie sniffed indignantly and glared at the officer. "Not my Molly. No, not my Molly. You're wrong, I know my daughter and she would never just stay away like this without letting me know where she was. I'm telling you; something isn't right."

Pushing the heavy door open as she left the station, Annie gulped in the fresh air. She felt very uneasy and prayed to God that Molly was all right and that her visit to the Police Station had been just a waste of an evening. On the bus home she sat, lost in thought, hoping that Molly was now curled up on the settee watching television, swigging from a can of Coke and eating a packet of crisps. If she was, then she would throttle Nan for not ringing her to let her know.

As Annie entered the hallway, Nan took one look at her daughter's face and wished she had gone with her. She took Annie firmly by the shoulders, steered her into the kitchen, and sat her down at the table. Rummaging in a kitchen cupboard, she got out two crystal cut tumblers, retrieved a bottle of 12-year-old malt whisky from the back of the drinks cabinet, and poured two stiff drinks.

"Well, what did they have to say?" she asked nervously, sliding her crucifix back and forth along its gold chain.

Annie stared into space trying to make sense of what was happening. "She's not here then? Well, I made a statement and told them as much as I could remember, and I gave them a photograph as well. You know, the one we have on the mantelpiece." She looked at Nan and felt hot tears roll down her face, the salt stinging her dry lips.

"You know what? I don't think they are going to take it seriously. I think they will brush it off as just another silly girl that's run away or whatever the hell it is that they think these young kids do." She took a sip of the whiskey and felt it warm the inside of her mouth and throat. "He kept asking me if we'd had an argument, or did I feel that she was making a point? I put him straight: Molly would never go off like this, never! I kept on telling him that." Taking another sip of her whisky, she started to weep.

"Now then, don't take on so," Nan said, trying to reassure her daughter. "She'll more than likely come flouncing through that door anytime soon, you'll see."

Annie wished that she could feel the same optimism.

Chapter Twelve: Happy Days

<***>

Don and Maggie Holden sat in their newly fitted kitchen enjoying a leisurely breakfast of cereal and wholemeal toast. Don was finishing off his coffee and helping himself to the last round of buttered wholemeal as Maggie cleared the table. Loading the dishwasher, she flinched as she straightened up.

"Are you all right?" he asked, concerned, as Maggie rubbed her lower back.

"Yeah, I'm fine. Just a twinge. Nothing a good walk won't cure."

They were both newly retired and were beginning to enjoy their new-found freedom. Having previously lived in Newcastle for most of their married life, they were excited to have moved out of a busy city to a more rural setting.

Don had worked as a welder for one of the big shipyards on the Tyne. It had been hard work, but it had been his one and only job since leaving school; having started off as an apprentice and worked his way up. Back then it had been a job for life. He did miss the old routine and some of his workmates but he would never admit that to Maggie.

Maggie had trained to be a midwife. She had loved every minute of it, and the thrill of delivering a new-born baby safely into the world had never lost its shine. She was always amazed at how nature 'did its thing'. Some thought it strange that Maggie had been a midwife all her working life, yet had not been able to have any children herself. The irony hadn't been lost on her and although they had looked into adopting, it was an option which neither of them had whole heartedly pursued. Still, she enjoyed babysitting her nieces and nephews when the need arose.

It had always been Maggie's dream to retire to a lovely little cottage in the country, and a year ago she had realised that dream. The cottage was chocolate-box picture-perfect, with rambling pink and white roses around the porch, wooden beams in the ceilings, and its own cottage garden. It was near enough to the village shops but far enough from the busy town for them to enjoy the peace and quiet. Every so often Maggie almost had to pinch herself just to make sure that she wasn't dreaming.

It had become their morning routine to take the two dogs out for a romp to the local country park. It was a large estate with its own Manor House and manicured gardens, along with a lake and a deer park. On the way back they would usually call in at the village pub for a coffee and to read the morning papers, before returning home for lunch, although on a Sunday they would often stay for the home-cooked roast. They had made lots of new friends, including the pub's landlord and they both loved the quiet village way of life.

Maggie bustled through to the hallway. "Don, you ready then? I've got the leads," she shouted up the stairs.

"I'm in the bedroom. Won't be a minute love, just putting my shoes on. Have you seen my glasses anywhere?"

Maggie had already climbed the stairs and popping her head round the door, replied somewhat disparagingly, "They're on top of your head, you daft beggar."

It was a bright, sunny morning and a gentle, warm breeze was blowing down the valley — perfect for a morning stroll. Don locked the back door and together with the two dogs they set off across the village green. Once out of the village they continued down the lane, heading towards the country park. Keeping to the path which skirted the edge of the estate, they picked up the bridle trail which meandered down towards the lake. Don and Maggie strolled at a leisurely pace, stopping and chatting to a couple of people they knew from the village as they went. They had just rounded a bend when they met Mrs Richmond from the village Post Office. Don groaned inwardly as she dismounted from her bike and braced himself for an onslaught of useless information and questions, the answers to which would never be heard.

"Good morning folks, and how are we all today? Beautiful day for a walk, isn't it? My, my, your dogs are growing — they're a bit bigger every time I see them, and so well behaved! So how are you both settling in? Now let me tell you, did you know that Mrs Hughes from the bakery has been taken into hospital? Dickey ticker, I believe. Apparently, her son found her on the floor, poor dear. And let me tell you, Doctor Green will be retiring at Christmas, so expect a locum if we're lucky. Oh yes, what else… did I mention the scout's jumble sale next Saturday? You are both coming, aren't you? It's at the Church Hall, kick off 11 o'clock — I'll expect I'll see you both there then. Anyway, must dash, jam to make and scones to bake and all that. Bye for now, see you on Saturday."

With a cheery wave and a bit of a wobble, Mrs Richmond peddled off as Maggie assured Mrs Richmond's somewhat broad back that they would both be there and wouldn't miss it for the world. Don elbowed her in the ribs knowing that it had taken all of Maggie's self-control not to giggle.

"I pity her poor bloody husband, I thought she was never coming up for air!" muttered Don under his breath.

"He probably can't get a word in edgeways anyway," laughed Maggie.

Continuing to stroll along the lake's edge, Don threw a rubber ring for the two spaniels to chase after and retrieve.

"So, what shall we do this weekend?" Don asked as he bent down to pick up the ring which one of the dogs had dropped at his feet. He fancied going to the seaside for a little break but knew that Maggie wouldn't be keen. "I thought we could pop over to the coast and see my Aunt Connie."

Maggie visibly bristled as obviously irritated by Dons request, purposefully picked a loose thread off one of her sleeves. "I don't see what pleasure there is in sitting in miles of traffic, inhaling all those nasty fumes, and then sharing a beach with the world and his wife," she argued. "Tell you what, why don't we just potter at home and enjoy the garden and the nice weather that we are having at the moment? Besides, we can always go to the coast mid-week when it's a bit quieter."

Don looked deflated and knowing this was an argument he couldn't win, thrust his hands into his pockets, resigned to having lost the battle. Maybe he could get a round of golf in later that afternoon, he thought.

Maggie loved this time of year. Filling her lungs with fresh air, she raised a hand to shade her eyes and looking out over the lush green fields, tried to guess which of the crops would be harvested first in little under a month's time.

"God, I love it here, don't you? Have you thought any more about my suggestion?" she asked.

"What suggestion's that, then?"

Maggie scowled. "The one about getting an allotment, of course."

"Oh, that. Well, I've thought about it good and hard but I think I need to do a bit more thinking yet."

Maggie laughed out loud. "You do that. I know you too well, Don Holden — you're not keen then?" she retorted with a knowing smile, as she brushed some wispy stray hairs off her face and put her sunglasses on. She watched and fussed over the dogs as they bounded along at a ridiculous speed before jumping into the water, scattering the ducks and geese in a flurry of feathers and squawks. Don had repeatedly tried to stop them, but the dogs hadn't taken a blind bit of notice and had carried on regardless.

Don tutted and scowled. "Haven't got the bloody sense they were born with," he complained.

Maggie shook her head. "They're dogs, Don — they don't have any. It's a good job I washed and dried their towels ready for when we get back. Just look at the state of them!"

Ben, the larger of the two Spaniels, suddenly took off into the bushes and began scratching and digging. Nosing around he began to bark excitedly as he ran backwards and forwards between the bushes and Maggie.

"Oh, what's he doing now? Must have picked up a scent. Ben… Ben… come here! Here boy! What the devil have you got now?" shouted Maggie. "You got one of them damn rabbits?"

Re-emerging from the undergrowth Ben came lolloping up to her and dropping a shoe at her feet, sat wagging his tail, looking very pleased with himself.

"What have you got there, boy?" she asked, as she bent down to pick it up. Turning it over in her hand she showed the black, stiletto-heeled shoe to Don. Ben ran off again back towards the bushes, and continued to bark excitedly before disappearing through a gap.

"Damn dog. Oh, for goodness sake, shut up Ben! Don, put him on the lead, he's going frantic," Maggie ordered.

Crouching down and managing to grab Ben by the scruff of his neck, Maggie struggled to control the excited dog. She snatched the lead from Don's hand and deftly attached it to the dog's collar, snapping the clip home. She yanked at the lead, trying to bring the excited dog to heel. Ben refused to obey her commands and barked and whined all the more. Passing the lead to Don, she lifted her sunglasses and set them on top of her head as she peered into the undergrowth.

"What the hell's got into him? and what on earth is that?" she asked out loud. Edging closer on her hands and knees, she pushed some of the branches out of the way so that she could crawl forward for a better look.

Don was trying his best to restrain the dog as it barked and pulled against the restraints of the lead. "What is it? What have you found, love?"

"I'm not sure Don, it's difficult to see, just a minute!"

Maggie edged further into the bushes, allowing her eyes to gradually adjust to the gloom. Reaching her hand out she grabbed what looked like an oddly-shaped, pale tuber. Tugging it, she realised with horror that what she was holding was somebody's big toe and attached to the big toe was a slender foot and ankle, which were now protruding from the mound of loose earth.

Scrambling backwards she screamed, "Don! Oh, dear Lord! Oh, good God!

Chapter Thirteen: Transition

<***>

The pub was in complete darkness and had a heavy atmosphere about it. Obviously closed, the place was silent apart from the humming of the refrigerator unit behind the bar. The green Exit sign above the door gave the place an eerie glow, and Molly instantly recognised the familiar smell of stale beer and musty carpets.

"Whoa, that was pretty amazing, Gramps. Who'd have thought it's that easy," she said excitedly.

Ged smiled affectionately. "Yep, easy when you know how. It certainly doesn't involve crossing any veil as they seem to think we need to do."

"What do you mean, 'crossing any veil' — what veil?"

"Exactly – what veil!! When I was a young boy, I used to hear my Auntie Vera talk about Spirit having to 'cross the veil' to communicate with her. Remember me telling you about her? She was a psychic, and used to read tea leaves as well for the neighbours and such like. But as you can tell, actually there is no veil or any such barrier — it's just a matter of shifting our energy from there to here or wherever, and back again. I think it's just one of those common misunderstanding or a misguided notion, making it seem like it's some great super-natural feat. Turns out to be a load of mumbo-jumbo."

Molly shrugged her shoulders, indifferent to what her grandpa had just said. Looking around the empty pub, she floated across the room and hovered near the table where she and Debbie had been sitting. Falling quiet, she gasped as she tried to claw at a memory which was just out of reach. She suddenly felt scared and unsure, not liking what she was feeling.

"You okay?" asked her grandfather in a concerned voice.

Molly nodded. "Yeah, I'm fine. It just took me by surprise, being back here — in this place, I mean."

She floated over to the small, raised stage when something suddenly jogged her memory. Excitedly, she began to tell her grandfather that she remembered how she had won the karaoke competition and that Debbie had been there with her. Molly casually floated over to the bar area, and just as she drew level with the beer pumps began to feel strange and dizzy, like she was about to faint. Quickly she turned away and joined her grandfather, who was examining the jukebox.

"Remember anything else?" he asked.

"No, not really. It's like it's there but I can't quite reach it, like the memories are buried in a deep black hole. I keep trying to remember the names of the two lads who chatted us up but..."

"Well, there you go, you've just remembered that there were two lads. See, something's happening but maybe you're trying too hard. What a load of rubbish there is on here, I don't recognise any of these songs."

Molly frowned, and going back over to the table again, waited for Ged to join her. "I'm sorry Gramps, it's all a blank. This has been a complete waste of time and energy."

"Well, not to worry, it was worth a try; at least you remembered winning the karaoke and that there were two lads."

Molly gave a wry smile. "S'pose. Anyways, what do we do now?"

Ged thought for a moment. "Well, we could go back home or visit Nan and your mam, or Debbie, even."

"Yeah, let's visit Mam and Nan — I want to give Mam a hug. Hang on... what's that?"

Glancing at a framed photograph which was hanging on the wall behind the bar area, Molly noticed that it appeared to be glowing. Cautiously she floated over to it, making sure that she didn't feel woozy again. Feeling okay, she studied the photograph, which was of a family posing together and laughing and smiling at the camera. Just below the frame was a brass plaque on which the names of the family were engraved. Molly noticed that two of the names were followed by 'In Memoriam'. She continued to stare at the photograph.

"What's up? What are you staring at?" asked Ged, puzzled, as he floated next to her.

"Hmm, I'm not sure. The face of the boy standing on the end seems familiar, but I don't know why."

Ged peered at the photograph and then at the plaque. "Says here that the girl and father died in a fire."

Molly couldn't take her eyes off the boy's face, until suddenly she knew who he was. Giving a visible shudder, she felt her energy levels plummet and she staggered backwards. Whirling around, off balance, she knocked an empty wine glass off the bar and watched as it smashed on the floor.

"That's him…that's Tony! He's one of the lads who chatted us up, Grandpa. It's him! He's the one who… who…" Molly fell silent.

"Who what? Come on Molly, you're so close. What did he do? Come on love! Remember… remember…"

Molly sat down at the table, trying to visualise and recall some shred of memory. "I know one was tall and dark-haired, and the other was blonde and a bit shorter."

Ged nodded in encouragement. "Well, that's something to be going on with."

Molly was disappointed and despondent. "Oh, it's useless, Grandpa."

Hovering over the stage, she tried to feel something — anything — when with a sudden jolt she remembered leaving the pub and getting into a taxi. She was just about to say as much when she heard something.

"Hello," said a voice from behind them. They both spun round to see where the voice had come from. Standing in the corner was a young girl who Molly instantly recognised.

"Whoa! You're the girl in the photograph," said Molly in a surprised voice.

"Yes, that's right. I'm Jenny — Jenny Collins. Pleased to meet you," she said, offering her hand.

"Well hello, Jenny Collins. This is Molly and I'm Ged, her grandpa."

"Yes, I know," said Jenny, turning to face Molly. "I know who you are. I've seen you before — you're the girl who likes to sing. You come in here quite a lot, don't you?"

Molly was somewhat taken aback. "What, you mean you've seen me before?"

"Oh, I know all the regulars. You come here with your friend... Debbie, isn't it?"

Molly glanced at her grandfather. "Hang on a minute! You saw me? When did you see me?"

"The other night, like I said. You were singing karaoke and you won."

Molly realised that Jenny might be able to piece together the events of Wednesday night. "Jenny, I need your help. Can you tell me exactly what you saw? Can you do that? Something happened to me, but I don't remember what. Maybe you could fill in some of the gaps. Could you do that for me?" she coaxed.

Jenny was quiet for a moment while she organised her thoughts. "Well now, let me think. After you won — only just mind — you and Debbie got chatted up by Gareth and Tony. I don't much like that Gareth. He's the one who does bad things. He's the one who thought it was clever to put nasty drugs into your drinks."

"Whoa! What do you mean, 'put nasty drugs in my drinks'?"

"Like I said, I saw him putting something into your drinks — little white tablets they were."

Molly reeled in horror. "What? Why the scheming, two-faced bastard! He spiked my drinks. Did you hear that Gramps? What an absolute bas..."

"Molly, watch your language," interrupted Ged, somewhat shocked at Molly's choice of expletive.

"Sorry," she apologised. "Jenny, you've been a big help. At least I know some of what happened to me now. Thank you."

Jenny looked pleased with herself and a beaming smile crossed her face.

"Right, so one was called Gareth. Who did you say the other one was?"

"Oh, that's Tony, my lovely Tony, my brother. Tony often comes for a drink here and my mum works as a barmaid. She and my dad used to own the pub before the fire."

"Ah, I get it. That's Tony in the photograph, isn't it? I knew I recognised him."

Jenny smiled and began to dance on the stage. "It's lovely to have someone to talk to — I do get so lonely sometimes. You coming here has been quite the loveliest surprise." She stopped dancing before sighing deeply. "I'm really sorry, Molly. I'm sorry that I couldn't stop Gareth doing what he did. I've tried to stop him doing it but I can't seem to."

"You mean he's done it before?"

Jenny nodded. "Yes, lots of times. He's a bad person. He's not nice at all."

Molly gave a weak smile. "Thanks Jenny, you've been a big help, hasn't she Grandpa?"

Ged nodded before suggesting that she should perhaps have a rest whilst he and Jenny had a chat. Molly made her way over again to the table where she and Debbie had been sitting. She was feeling frustrated and confused. Suddenly, without warning, she started having vivid flashbacks, as chunks of memory seemed to drop back into her mind. To her surprise, she found she could now remember most of that Wednesday evening and realised that Debbie would have had no idea what had happened to her — how could she have?

Leaving Molly to her own devices, Ged had steered Jenny to the opposite side of the room. Looking intently at her, he noticed that her energy field was lacklustre and appeared to be full of holes and small tears.

"Anyway Jenny, you'd started to tell us about what happened to you. You mentioned something about a fire."

Ged listened as Jenny went on to explain about the accidental fire which had happened a year after her mother and father had taken over the pub. An electrical fault had caused the main fuse box to short out, and the pub had gone up in flames. Jenny and her father had both perished that terrible night.

"You poor thing. You mean to say that you've been stuck here all this time, unable to go anywhere?"

Jenny nodded. "Well, I suppose I haven't noticed if it's been a long time or not. I've just been waiting for my dad to come back and get me, and I suppose I wasn't so bothered because I still got to see Tony and my mum."

Molly re-joined them and glancing over at her grandfather, let a huge smile cross her face.

"What's up with you? You look like a Cheshire cat who's had the cream."

"I know, that's because I've just remembered a whole load of stuff," she said, grinning.

Ged smiled fondly. "Terrific, you can tell me later but for now we have to help Jenny here get home."

Ged could sense Jenny's anguish and knew that she needed help to be with her loved ones again. She needed to be nourished and nurtured and helped to heal, so that eventually she'd be able to incarnate into another life. Ged realised that if she didn't, she would become stuck, which meant she would continue to haunt the pub and forever exist in frustrated turmoil and torment. He certainly didn't want that for her and knew that he had to help.

Turning his attention back to Jenny he said, "Look Jenny, you've done a good thing — a fantastic thing in fact. You've been a tremendous help to Molly, but you need to leave here. You have to get away from this place. You need to go home and we can help you do that. Of course, you'll be able to come back to the earth realm and visit anytime you like once you've rested, but at the moment it's not healthy for you to stay here in this atmosphere."

Molly nodded in agreement. "He's right, although I haven't the foggiest idea as to how we'll get you home. What about you Gramps, any ideas?"

Jenny was hesitant. "But what if my dad comes? I've been waiting for him to come back for me."

Ged embraced Jenny. "Look sweetheart, while you stay locked in this dimension, nothing can change. It's like being in treacle — you're stuck. Your dad's gone — gone to the light — but for some reason he hasn't been able to reach you. The thing is though, once you return to the spiritual realm, you'll be able to find him. Now, I'm sure that if we can call in your guides and the angels, they can take you to where your dad is, or to where you need to be. Would you like that?"

Jenny clapped her hands excitedly. "Really? You can do that?"

"Yes, well I think we can. Shall we give it a go? We've nothing to lose by trying," said Ged, scratching his head. "Jenny, could you stand over there in the middle of the room, please," he instructed.

Molly came to Ged's side and together they prayed for Jenny to be taken home to the light of the spiritual realm. They remained silent, waiting for something to happen, hardly daring to move. Suddenly a shimmering haze of luminescent silver and purple mist appeared. It spiralled down, enveloping Jenny. They watched as the mist expanded and swirled around her, almost filling the room. Through the haze, Molly and Ged could see an angelic form holding out its hands towards her, and as she placed her hands into those of the angel, she was lifted and carried higher and higher up into the shaft of silver and purple mist. Instantly a flurry of golden wings and translucent hands blurred their view as Jenny was carried higher and higher. They heard her squeal with childish delight, and then with a gentle sigh, she was gone.

"Whoa, that was amazing! They don't hang about do they?" exclaimed Molly. "She will be all right, won't she?"

Ged smiled. "Of course, she'll be all right. She's home now, isn't she!"

Floating over to the bar, Ged perched on a stool and became lost in thought as he began to recall why some spirits failed to return to the spiritual realm. He knew about spirits getting stuck within the upper dimensions of the astral plane. There were any number of reasons why that happened though mostly it was because spirits who had experienced a sudden or violent death sometimes became confused and disorientated, much like Molly had. They hadn't fully realised that they had left their physical body, so didn't get to go through the usual transition phase. They stayed trapped, continually re-enacting the final part of their life, searching for answers, unable to move on into the light.

Ged continued to sit quietly and ponder. He thought about how some spirits actually chose to stay in the building or place in which they had lived, particularly if they thought they had unfinished business or had committed some awful crime or deed. The thought of going into the light to face their Karma was just too awful to contemplate. They would rather haunt and stay in a familiar place, locked in fear, not realising that just one small step would release them.

Ged sighed as he thought about Jenny, and suddenly felt mixed emotions sweep over him. On the one hand he felt sad that she had been trapped, and he knew that had she not been rescued she would have eventually become a ghost, a shadow of her former self, as it were. But now that she was released, he felt a great sense of joy in knowing that he and Molly had helped her return home safely.

He thought back to when he had ventured into the astral plane in search of Molly, and felt his energy quiver at the memory. The thought of actually meeting or coming face-to-face with the Shadowers — the Lessers who were held there — made him shudder. Their dense negative energies were so impure, it was necessary that they be contained. For the most part they were held within the deeper dimensions of the astral plane, but some of them were able to find distorted energy portals and use them to cross back into the earth realm dimension, where they caused no end of mischief and mayhem. Ged thought himself fortunate to have never had any encounters with the likes of them.

Thankfully he knew that the majority of Spirit were just like him. They had traversed back into Spirit light without any problems and, when necessary, had been nurtured and healed by Elder Hamneth and his team of Adjusters or by their soul group family or by healing guides and angels. He remembered how uneventful his own crossing over had been and thought himself lucky. Even now he still felt the exhilaration of having fully completed his transition and of being free to use transference and return to visit whenever he liked. Being able to visit the earth realm meant that he could keep an eye on Nan and Annie and, of course, Molly.

"Penny for them," said Molly, as she sat down next to him.

Ged sighed. "I was just reminding myself why some of us end up like Jenny."

Molly smiled and snuggled up to him. "Well whatever the reason, I'm so grateful to her. I'm sure that it was Jenny who helped me to remember a lot of stuff, and she answered a lot of my questions too."

Ged kissed her forehead. "Well, that's great. So, what have you remembered?"

"Huh, that can wait, but I know that without her I'd still be fuddled."

"Fuddled, eh? What makes you think that you still aren't?"

"Why, you cheeky thing!" Molly said, laughing as she playfully poked him.

"Right then, come on bossy boots. Our work here is done, let's go home," he said, smiling as he gave her a little hug.

Chapter Fourteen: A Policeman's Lot

<***>

Detective Sergeant James Millington had been a policeman for the past twenty-two years. He had carved out a career for himself which he and his parents were very proud of, and this coming September he was to receive his long service medal and a series of commendations to add to his already illustrious collection. James was six foot two tall, with an athletic build, chiselled features and thinning hair. He was careful about what he ate, due largely to a mistrust of corporate food chains, although he did enjoy a good curry and a couple of beers at the weekend. He kept himself fit by going to the gym regularly and also played squash twice a week at the local sports centre. After all, you never knew when you might have to chase a scumbag, and James Millington always got his man, or women as the case might be.

From being a kid, it had always been his ambition to join the police force and become a bobby, just like his uncle Ken. Uncle Ken had given thirty years of service to the Metropolitan Police Force and had always encouraged James to join as soon as he could. James had left school with the required exam grades and after successfully passing the entrance exam, was accepted as a police cadet when he was sixteen years old. He had studied and worked hard, passing each of the courses and examinations with flying colours, and had gradually worked his way up the career ladder. He loved every minute of his work and even now, after all this time, he never got bored of the buzz rush of adrenaline which each new 'job' brought. He had certainly put the hours in, sadly at the cost of his relationship and marriage.

He and the lovely Emily had first met in the car park at the local gym when Emily accidentally reversed into his car. Although the incident caused nothing more than a scuffed bumper, they had nonetheless swapped insurance details and phone numbers. Ringing her the following week on the pretence of asking how she was, he had steered the conversation round to asking her out on a date. The rest, as they say, was history. After a three-year courtship they were married in the little rural village where Emily had grown up. Both the village and its church were quaint and Emily and her mother had been in their element. Nothing had been left to chance — the whole modus operandi had been planned and executed with military precision. It had been an 'all bells and whistles' sort of a wedding, which had cost an absolute fortune. Not wanting to appear ungrateful to his future in-laws, James had gone along with it — after all, if Emily was happy, so was he. As she had walked down the aisle to be by his side, he couldn't take his eyes off her. He couldn't believe how beautiful and radiant she looked and how happy he felt.

Emily had been a high flyer — ambitious, focused and incredibly headstrong. She too had worked her way up the career ladder and had achieved the enviable position of Marketing Manager for a world-leading advertising company. James had mistakenly taken it for granted that they would be the perfect average couple, spawning the perfect two point four children, having the perfect life and bagging the perfect whole caboodle. However, Emily wasn't the kind of woman who was prepared to be put in second place to her husband's job and career, and not being one to suffer fools gladly, had made it known in no uncertain terms that she hadn't worked that hard 'just to be a housewife'.

Regrettably, over the latter years that they were together, the dream of the perfect couple wasn't to be. They couldn't seem to agree on anything and had countless arguments and bitter rows, which usually ended with Emily packing an overnight bag and leaving to go back home to 'Mummy and Daddy'. James would wait for the storm to blow over and would welcome Emily back with open arms, promising to forgive and forget. The pattern became a habit, but each argument became more bitter and hurtful, with each accusing the other of being selfish and self-centred and each thinking they were in the right and the other was being unreasonable.

James had never questioned the sanctity of marriage, as he was of the opinion that once you were in it, you stayed in it. Unfortunately, he was proved wrong and they finally got divorced after four tumultuous years. James had been glad that the divorce had gone through as quickly as it had; he hated having to deal with life's dramas. Unfortunately, the divorce proceedings had led to further bitter rows and raw accusations, and the divorce had been anything but amicable, at least for James. Emily — 'poor Emily' — had got the house and half his pension and he had got saddled with the dog. Since the divorce, he had heard through the grapevine that Emily had moved to the East coast to somewhere near Whitby. He also later heard that she had remarried. The gossip was that she had landed herself the CEO of an international pharmaceuticals company, who was on a six-figure salary. He had also heard that they now had two children as well — twins, he believed.

He'd been working with the Missing Persons Unit for the past eight years when Molly's file landed in his in-tray. Making himself a strong cup of black coffee before sitting down at his desk, he read through the missing person's report and a relative's statement. Recognising the familiar sinking feeling in the pit of his stomach, he knew that this one wasn't going to end well — call it copper's intuition, call it what you liked. Taking a gulp of black coffee, he let out a heavy sigh, just as his desk phone rang.

Ged and Molly were planning where their next visitation was going to be and eventually decided that they would go and see Annie and Nan. It was late in the afternoon and Annie was sitting in the lounge, staring into space. She was wishing and praying that Molly would walk through the door, or at least ring her. Constantly checking her phone just in case she had a missed call, Annie was agitated and although the television was on, she wasn't paying any attention to it. Suddenly the doorbell rang.

Jumping up, she went over to the window and peered through the net curtains. Standing on the door step was a woman police constable and a tall, smartly dressed man in a suit. Annie rushed to open the door.

"Mrs Roberts? I'm Detective Sergeant Millington and this is Police Constable Webber. Can we come in?" he asked, as he showed Annie his warrant card.

Annie stepped aside. "Yes, yes, please come in. I'm all at sixes and sevens, forgetting my manners," she said, as she showed them through to the living room before introducing them to Nan. "This is my Mother, Nancy. Please have a seat, won't you?" Annie nervously glanced at Nan. She could feel her throat beginning to tighten and her stomach knot, as the anticipation that they were about to receive bad news began to seep into her consciousness.

"Mrs Roberts, please will you sit down too," Millington said, clearing his throat. "On Thursday you reported your daughter as missing. I'm sorry to have to break the news to you, but I believe we have found her body." He let the words hang momentarily in the air, waiting for their impact to hit home.

Annie threw her hand to her mouth to muffle an audible gasp, as the shock of what she had just been told slammed into her brain. "Where? When? I don't understand. You're mistaken, you must be — Molly can't be dead."

Millington shuffled awkwardly. "I'm sorry Mrs Roberts, but we have every reason to believe that the body of a young women that has been discovered on the Trigshaw Country Estate, is Molly."

Molly and Ged materialised just as D.S. Millington was breaking the news to Annie and Nan. Realising what was happening, Ged steered Molly into the far corner of the room.

"Molly, you need to listen to me carefully. I need to remind you that what you're about to witness will bear no resemblance to anything you've experienced before. How you're existing now as Spirit is different to how you existed as a human, a person — you understand that don't you?"

Molly nodded. "Of course, I do, I'm not completely stupid."

"I never said you were but you're something else at times — you know that! Okay, because we are energy, we are able to discern different frequencies — we're aware of the various vibrations of other energy fields. You no longer have any need for the five embodied senses. Essentially, you'll sense vibrations instead, because all vibrations are energy."

Molly nodded again. "Yeah, I get that."

Unaware of their presence in the room, Millington continued to break the terrible news to Annie and Nan.

"The body was discovered in a shallow grave, so obviously… well there's no easy way to say this, but if this is Molly — and we have no reason to believe otherwise — then she was almost certainly murdered."

Molly suddenly shouted out, startling Ged. "Murdered … murdered? Oh my God, I was murdered! Why the little bastard, I knew it, I knew he was up to no good."

Recovering from Molly's outburst, Ged too was visibly shocked. "Oh Molly," he said in a whisper, "That explains a heck of a lot."

"You think," she said abruptly, before floating over to her mother's side to give her a hug.

Ged observed the impact that the news had caused. Molly too began to notice how dull her mother's aura was becoming. It was like a light or spark had gone out, almost like a shadow had fallen across the window and pervaded the room. She could also sense that Nan's aura was taking on a dull, muddy hue as well.

"What's happening, Grandpa?" asked Molly, alarmed.

Ged put his arm around her to steady and support her. "Well, it's like this. You know how we are made of energy? Well, so too is the physical body. Actually, every living thing emits an energy field, although as humans we don't readily see it. It's called the aura and it surrounds the physical body and is made up of several different layers. With me so far?"

Molly nodded.

"Good. Now then, the etheric layer of the aura is the one closest to the physical body, then there's the emotional layer, then the mental layer, then the astral layer and so on — can you sense them?"

Molly nodded as she became aware of the different vibrations.

"There are layers of aura beyond that lot as well, and a healthy aura can expand anywhere up to several feet from the body. Still with me?"

Molly once again nodded.

"Marvellous! Now, we also have energy centres, or chakras as they're called. They're like energy vortices. The seven main ones that run down the centre of the body, but there are lots of other sub-chakras dotted about, like in the hands and feet. The chakras and the aura are connected to each other to form a huge energy field, I'll tell you a lot more about them later."

Molly nodded her understanding again, as she observed her Mam's and Nan's energies shift.

"The chakras and the aura all vibrate in harmony and in synchronisation… or at least they do until something happens which causes the vibration to become distorted, such as disease or illness, or if something happens to make them have a wobble, like just now. Look, the thing is, when news of a death is given suddenly, it shocks the chakras' energy vibrations. Have you ever heard the expression 'a shock to the system'? Well, that's literally what happens. That's why your mam's aura has dimmed — it's like a part of her energy field has just been… well… extinguished."

"Oh, Grandpa! Will she be all right? Will Nan be okay too?" Molly cried.

Ged looked sombre as he replied, "Yes, they'll be fine. It just takes a while, is all. Not to get over it mind — as humans, we never do that. The thing is, they already carry a vibrational distortion from when I died. That's what grief does. Effectively, it leaves a scar in the heart chakra and distorts some of the others too, and it's true when they say that someone is broken-hearted, because, in effect, they are. The human perception of death is distressing, we perceive it as the finality of life, but in reality, it's all part of a cycle — the cycle of physical birth and spiritual rebirth."

Turning their attention back to the events unfolding in the room, Molly and Ged heard Millington continue, "Obviously we need to make sure, so if you feel able, we would like you to come and make a formal identification, if that's okay."

Ged and Molly watched as the two women put their coats on. Through habit, Nan applied her lipstick while Annie rummaged in her handbag for a packet of tissues, as unsuppressed sobs escaped from her slight, heaving frame.

After escorting the two women down a well-lit, linoleum-floored corridor, D.S. Millington showed them into one of the family rooms, knowing that on the other side of the corridor lay the body of the young girl who had been found in suspicious circumstances. The room was tidy and neatly arranged, with comfortable armchairs and a coffee table. Nan noticed the vase of artificial flowers placed in the middle of the window sill. The walls were painted in standard issue white emulsion and had cheap pictures of seascapes and countryside scenes hung on them. Nan noticed the distinctive smell of formaldehyde permeating the room's very fabric.

Motioning to the chairs, Millington invited the two women to take a seat, while he went to see if the mortuary technician was ready for them. He was soon back and asked them to follow him into an adjoining room which housed rows of refrigerators used to store bodies until they could be identified by relatives or friends, or until a post mortem was performed and a cause of death found. The bodies would then be released to the undertakers so that funeral arrangements could be made.

On the opposite side off the refrigeration storage area was the autopsy room and laboratory. Positioned in the centre of the room was a state-of-the-art, stainless steel autopsy table, which was as shiny and pristine as the day it was first bought. On the walls were cupboards, each labelled with a list of its contents, and a stainless-steel workbench ran the length of one side of the room. On top of the bench were microscopes and various pieces of equipment used for examining and collecting specimens. Three fluorescent lights stretched from one end of the laboratory ceiling to the other, giving a cold, bluish tinge to the room. Molly noticed that the middle strip light was flickering. Off to the right of the laboratory was a much smaller room which was used as an office, one wall of which housed floor-to-ceiling shelving units onto which were crammed box files, folders and reference books. Two large filing cabinets were pushed against the opposite wall.

Molly shivered as she followed Annie and Nan into the refrigeration area. "Blimey, you wouldn't want to hang around here too long would you, Gramps? It's not exactly warm and cosy is it?"

Molly and Ged hovered at the far end, as the technician respectfully nodded his head towards Annie and Nan. Positioning himself next to the technician, Ged waited for him to open the fridge door and glanced along the row of stainless-steel doors with their shiny handles and dull, chrome hinges.

"Looks like you're not on your own. I reckon these fridges are mostly full."

Molly went to her mother's side and hugging her, looked around the room. She noticed an iridescent, purple shimmer radiating from one of the fridge doors.

"Grandpa, why is that fridge door a different colour to the rest?"

Ged went over to where Molly was pointing and peering at the door, frowned. "Ah, I've heard about this but never actually seen it. The person who's in there committed suicide. They're called Strugglers. A Struggler is someone who couldn't deal with the life events and experiences that they found themselves having to cope with, so they opted out, as it were."

Molly felt a touch of sadness sweep over her. "So why is the door glowing purple then?"

"Because when they did whatever they did to end their physical life, their soul vibration became so distressed it got stuck in their physical body and their spirit guide had to help release it. As you can tell it makes a bit of a mess so a special healing balm has to be used, but the balm is so powerful that it permeates throughout the entire body and leaves this purple residue."

Molly nodded like she understood, and Ged thought it best not to say much more. He could see how morose she had become and decided to keep his thoughts to himself for now. He knew that for a spirit to have made such a decision meant that they must have been deeply distraught. He also knew that they would have a lot of work to do on their return to the spiritual realm, although they would receive unconditional healing, guidance and love from specialist guides and teachers. They would have to re-do the lessons that they hadn't learned in that particular lifetime, and incarnate again. Ged smiled to himself, thinking that at least they would be better able to cope next time round.

Annie suddenly realised how chilly it was in the room and giving a visible shiver, stood motionless, desperately trying to swallow the saliva which was rising up into her mouth. Clutching her coat tightly around herself, she dug her fingernails into her clenched palms and repeated silently to herself, 'Please don't be Molly. Dear God, please don't let it be Molly.' Holding herself proud and erect, she dabbed the well-used tissue to her eyes, mopping away the tears which rolled freely down her cheeks.

Nan stood at her daughter's side, fingering her crucifix and chain, as the fridge door was opened and the technician pulled out a sliding tray. Slowly and carefully he unzipped the black body bag and turned it down sufficiently for the corpse's face to be seen. Nan managed to stifle a cry as she looked at the child who would no longer be giving her cheek and backchat. Recoiling in shock, she felt like she had been punched in the guts. Instinctively she put a supportive arm around Annie's shoulders, as she felt her daughter slump at the realisation that against all her hopes and prayers that she was there under false pretences, her nightmare had come true. Annie trembled as the silence was shattered by the sound of her voice saying, "Yes, oh God, it's Molly."

Millington knew he would never get used to having to deal with the relatives of murder victims. Most of the time he was able to predict or pre-empt how people would react on hearing such devastating news. With his years of experience, he had just about seen and heard everything there was to see and hear from the bereaved. Some relatives became quiet and seemed to go into a state of catatonic shock, some were verbally abusive and shouted accusingly, as if it were the police officer's fault that their loved one was dead and he was having to bring such devastating news, while others just crumpled in a heap. Annie did none of these.

Molly stared down on herself. Her face was pale with a dull, sallow, waxy complexion and her eyes were closed and sunken. She frowned at how her hair was pulled back off her face and secured with a red rubber band, and saw that small flecks of soil clung defiantly to her lips and ears. Noticing the deep gash and bruising to her temple, she made Ged jump as she shouted out, "Wow, look at that, I look a right mess! Now I know why my head hurt so bloody much and why I can't remember anything. Blimey, it's no flaming wonder!"

Ged came to her side. "Crikey, I see what you mean! You still look beautiful though — well you do to me," he said, smiling as he gave her a hug.

Molly looked on. "Poor Mam. Poor Nan. They both look so sad."

"Aye, to them it's the finality of it all. They think we're not around anymore. Obviously, we are, but usually people either don't know that or have forgotten it, so a big part of their grief comes from the missing. Yet the missing bit is kind of one-sided."

Molly suddenly felt her sadness deepening. "It's funny really, I never thought that I would be this important." She fell quiet as she contemplated what was to come. "I never thought that I would ever end up like this," she whispered.

Ged looked lovingly at his granddaughter. "Oh Molly, of course you're important! You're very important, especially to your mam and Nan and to me and the coppers and to so many others who care about you. I know you've had a short life, and the way you got here has been traumatic, not only for you but for everyone. There will be a lot of people who will struggle to come to terms with what's happened. You do know that, don't you sweetheart?"

A sorrowful frown crossed her face, as Ged reached out and gave her a gentle squeeze.

"Now see, there's so much you need to be reminded of and to relearn, so the sooner you have your reunion with the Elders, the better. But right now, I'm gonna help you find the answers as to what happened to you, just as I promised. Come on, moping around here isn't going to change owt."

Molly smiled at her grandfather. She had many questions to ask, yet she also knew that all would be revealed to her when it was the right time; after all, time was one thing she had plenty of.

After being escorted back to the family room, Annie and Nan sat in silence, both locked in their own inner turmoil. Annie absentmindedly lifted the teacup which had been placed in front of her to her lips. Her hands were visibly shaking and the warm insipid liquid did nothing to sooth or calm her. In a state of shock, she and Nan sat listening to what the detective was saying, not fully hearing the words. All Annie knew at this moment was that her Molly was gone — murdered and God knows what else.

Replacing the cup back onto the saucer, she sat with her hands in her lap and tried to block out the horrendous images and scenarios which played over and over in her mind. It was just too hard to imagine the horrors that Molly might have endured — possibly she had been raped, beaten, even tortured. Annie was trying really hard to concentrate and take in what the detective was saying to her, but the reality was that she had retreated somewhere safe and deep within herself, somewhere dark and protective, where she harboured an internal suit of armour and where arrows of pain couldn't penetrate to wound her any further. Millington was saying something about further investigations and examinations, forensic autopsies, toxicology screening and statements, words which were swimming round her head but she wasn't able to make sense of. Reaching for Nan's hand, she held it tightly in her own and wept silently into another tissue.

Nan too was stunned as she tried to make sense of something which made no sense. The blackness of dark memories once again began to surface, as she remembered how she had felt all those years ago when she received the news that her Ged had died. The shock and disbelief had been unimaginable and now, once again, she felt the familiar pervading numbness coursing through her as she remembered that awful June afternoon. The knock on the front door had been loud and intrusive and had reverberated throughout the entire house. Nan had cautiously opened the door to find two prison officers standing on the door step. They had introduced themselves with an air of awkwardness and unease, and standing in the middle of the living room, had been curt and to-the-point in informing Nan that Ged was dead. He had died from a stroke two days previously in the infirmary, and there had been nothing anybody could have done to save him. Yet even after all this time, Nan could never reconcile the fact that she hadn't been there at his bedside. They had not called her to let her know that he'd been taken to the infirmary, and the bitter contempt and resentment which she harboured for the authorities was still as raw now as it had been then.

It was just before midnight when Annie and Nan got home. They had been driven back by PC Webber, who had been assigned as their Family Liaison Officer. Taking Annie's keys from her trembling hand, he opened the front door, gently ushered the two women into the house and watched sadly as Annie and Nan stood in the hallway holding one another tightly. "Why Nan, why?" Annie sobbed. Nan didn't answer, because there wasn't any answer to give.

Molly and Ged stayed with Annie and Nan for the rest of the night, trying to console them but unable to penetrate the blackness which surrounded the two grief-stricken women. PC Webber made endless cups of tea, yet each was left untouched and allowed to go cold. Neither of the women went to bed — instead they morosely shuffled from the living room to the kitchen and back again, alone with their own muddled thoughts. Every so often one of them would allow a sob or cry to pervade the chasm of silence.

The sun had yet to breach the horizon, when Ged made the decision that he and Molly should return to the spiritual realm.

"Come on, we're not doing anything useful here so I think we should get back. I have a feeling that Orick is beginning to get a little fraught and tetchy, and you still need to speak with the Elders."

Molly began to protest that she wanted to stay with her mother and Nan but Ged had made up his mind. Condensing their energies, they simultaneously arrived back in the Halls of Wisdom. Molly immediately noticed a light coming towards them rapidly.

"Hello, nice of you both to come back," Orick said curtly.

"Yes, sorry. We had something to do earth-side but as you can see, we're back now," Ged replied crisply. Molly shuffled nervously towards her grandfather.

Orick glowered at Ged before turning his attention to Molly. "As you were away for quite some time, I became increasingly concerned for you both, so it was with much reluctance that I felt the need to seek advice from the Elders. On their instructions you are to accompany me urgently to have an audience with them, as amongst other things they wish to discuss the matter of your loss of memory of all things spiritual."

Ged looked relieved. "Oh good, the sooner the better I say."

Orick frowned. "Yes well, had you been here… Come Molly, you can catch up with your grandfather later."

Looking sheepish, Molly followed Orick's light as he led her to a vestibule outside one of the chambers. Glancing around her, the first thing she noticed were the high ceilings and absence of windows.

Orick nodded in her direction. "Are you all right?"

She gave a shiver, suddenly aware of a tingling feeling which seemed to ripple through her. The sensation was strange and reminded her of when she had gone to see the dentist and he had used those funny, vibrating instruments on her teeth. Molly nodded, "Yeah, I think so. What's going to happen now?"

Orick stared straight ahead before answering her, "I don't know for certain but hopefully all will be well."

They were approached by a small man whose beard was nearly as long as he was tall and whose white robe appeared to pool around his feet. Beckoning for them to follow him, he showed them into a large, empty chamber. He motioned for them to wait in the centre of the pure white marble floor. Molly couldn't help but notice how it glinted and sparkled; it reminded her of a winter day when the first snowfall was hit by the rays of early morning sunshine. Looking around, she gawped and squinted at the brightness of the room, despite the fact there were no windows or other means of lighting.

Orick nudged her and nodded towards the seated gathering who were assembled before them. Molly did a quick head count as the thirteen Elders who constituted the Council of Elders looked back at her. She hadn't been aware until that moment that they were seated in front of her and were the source of the illumination which filled the chamber. She watched with trepidation as the most senior Elder rose from his seat. He was tall and willowy, with kind green eyes and a serious frown, which seemed to be permanently fixed to his features. Elder Pettruf approached them, connected with Molly's energy and led her to the far side of the chamber. The others turned in unison to face them, and with all eyes upon her, Molly felt a shiver of anticipation run through her core as the Elder addressed the gathering.

"Blessings. It is with a heavy heart that I have called this Congress. As you are all aware, yet another disturbing incident has occurred. The Beloved who is before you returned to the spiritual realm with very few memories of her last life-lived on the earth realm. Her memories of her own spiritual existence and identity are also impaired. As you are all aware, it is necessary in such events to orchestrate the Beloved's recovery, not only in the restoration of the lost experiences of human memories, but also in the spiritual memory loss. The instigation of healing to repair the damage inflicted on our Beloved's soul, energy and vibration is paramount."

A muted murmur swept through the chamber as the Elders muttered amongst themselves. Raising his hands, Elder Pettruf commanded silence before continuing, "I believe that Guide Orick and also our Beloved One's custodian have taken matters into their own hands and foolishly tried to remedy this regrettable situation themselves." He looked over in Orick's direction while continuing to speak. "A matter which they clearly know nothing about, I hasten to add."

Realising that he was being reprimanded, Orick tried to protest his innocence but the Elder had already turned his attention back to Molly.

"This entire debacle will be dealt with by this Council and the Council of Wise Ones. There is to be no further meddling, no more interfering, and definitely no additional transference back to the earth realm. Do I make myself clear?" Pettruf's eyes bored into Orick's vibration and then into Molly's as he held their attention. "I will liaise with Guide Orick when it has been decided how best to restore your memories. I think it would be prudent if, in the meantime, Guide Orick were to commence reteaching you the knowledge which you have sadly lost."

Molly and Orick flashed a look at one another.

"Until then, Beloved, you are free to explore the spiritual realm, and only the spiritual realm. I would also suggest that you continue to be guided and coached by your custodian." Giving Molly a kindly smile, he turned to leave the chamber as the other twelve Elders rose and followed him.

Orick winked at Molly. "Phew! That wasn't so bad really, I thought we were going to get a right ticking off. So, come on then, I'm all ears — just what did you get up to?"

Molly smiled, relieved that at least that particular meeting was over. Looking around her, she whispered, "Quite a lot really. We went to see my mam and my Nan and I also saw myself dead in the morgue — that part was a bit yucky though. And we think we know what happened to me. Obviously, there's much more that we have to find out, but it's been very exciting."

Orick shook his head. "You heard what Pettruf said. You aren't to go gallivanting where and when you like anymore. I'm telling you; you'd be an idiot to defy him."

Molly shrugged. "Yeah, well, like he's going to know. Especially if you don't say anything."

Orick glared at her. "Don't be so stupid! I won't have to tell him. He…they will know anyway. You forget that nothing, and I mean nothing, gets past that lot, trust me."

"Well, we'll see about that," she said as she nonchalantly turned and strolled out of the chamber. She had other things on her mind.

Chapter Fifteen: Evidence Mounts

<***>

It was Saturday morning and Annie, still in her dressing gown, was sitting alone in the kitchen and staring into a cup of cold coffee, lost in thought. Suddenly the shrill ring of the telephone made her jump as it startled her back to reality. Nervously lifting the receiver, it was all she could do to speak.

"Mrs Roberts? It's D.S. Millington. I'm ringing to let you know we've found what we believe to be some of Molly's possessions. We're pretty sure we've found her handbag. Do you think you could come to the station?"

"What? Why yes, of course I can. Do you want me to come now?"

"Yes, if that's okay with you. PC Webber will pick you up and drive you over. She's on her way."

Millington met Annie and Nan at the Police Station and after showing them into a small, airless room, asked them to take a seat. On the other side of the room a row of wooden trestle tables was pushed against the far wall. "Thank you for helping us, Mrs Roberts. I realise that this will be quite traumatic for you but it will be invaluable to us." Taking Annie by the elbow he gently steered her towards the tables. "Please just take your time but don't open any of the plastic bags. You just need to look at the items and confirm if they belonged to Molly. Like I said, take as long as you need."

Annie cast her eyes over the display of polythene evidence bags and felt herself being drawn to one that was much larger than the others and had the words "FORENSIC EVIDENCE" marked clearly on the front in bold, red lettering Inside it she could see a handbag which she recognised immediately. She felt her knees go weak as bile began to rise up into her mouth and hot tears begin to prick her eyes. She took a few seconds to compose herself, refusing to let the tears fall, fearing that if she did, they would never stop.

The handbag was obviously damp, as droplets of moisture had formed on the inside of the bag and the colour had faded slightly. Annie knew there was no mistaking it; it was definitely Molly's. The contents of the handbag had been removed and each item had been individually sealed in clear plastic evidence bags. Annie stared at each of the items in turn, before carefully examining them. Turning them over and over in her hands, she could hear and feel the crackle of the plastic barrier. She examined the compact mirror; it was the one that she had given Molly for her eighteenth birthday. And the perfume which Molly always wore was also there, intact in its glass bottle. Annie walked the length of the tables on which Molly's belongings were displayed, wanting desperately to touch and hold them, even smell them, as each item triggered a memory.

Millington cleared his throat. "I'm sorry Mrs Roberts, but I have to ask you — is this Molly's handbag and do these items also belong to her?"

Annie nodded and looking the detective in the eye, sat down heavily on one of the chairs. "Yes, they are," she replied in a small dry voice.

Nan also stood gazing at the array of items. Tears began to well up in her eyes as she recognised the brand of lipstick Molly used and the keyring shaped in a big initial 'M' which was studded with diamante crystals; it was the one she had given Molly a couple of months ago. She remembered buying it from the local market, along with the address book which had a picture of a cartoon rabbit on the front; the rabbit was now blurred and sodden.

Nan rushed to Annie's side and kneeling on the floor, threw her arms around Annie's neck and incoherently sobbed, "I'm so sorry Annie, truly I am."

Somewhat dazed, bewildered, and numb, Annie continued to stare unseeing at the collection of plastic bags. Abruptly Nan released her hold as she felt a shiver run down her spine, and she had a sudden compulsion to search through the objects again.

Unaware that Molly had just whispered into her ear, she began to frantically rummage through the items on the table. As if on automatic pilot, she went from item to item and repeatedly checked each plastic bag to make sure that she hadn't missed or overlooked anything.

"Oh, Sweet Jesus — her phone! Where's her phone? It's not here. Why isn't her phone here?"

Millington shifted from one foot to the other, hurriedly reading through the inventory which was fixed to the metal clipboard clenched in his hand. "We didn't find a phone — there's no mention of a phone. Everything here was found in the lake by the Underwater Search Team. There was definitely no phone found where she was buried either."

Annie rushed back to the table and also began frantically searching for Molly's phone. "Nan, you're right, it's not here. Jesus! I have rung and rung that bloody phone of hers so many times. She's never without the damn thing. Maybe it's still in the lake."

Millington reached for his biro and began busily writing a note alongside the inventory of Molly's belongings. The fluorescent light overhead was becoming quite distracting and annoying as it flickered and buzzed loudly. Clearing his throat, he asked, "Can you give me the number and details of Molly's phone, please?"

Molly and Ged followed Millington back to the police incident room. Going over to his desk, Millington sat down heavily on the black leather chair, holding his head in his hands as he tried to organise his thoughts. After a few seconds he walked over to the white evidence boards and stared at the information which had been gathered so far. Finding a red marker pen, he wrote in bold letters across the top of one of the boards, "FIND MOLLY'S MOBILE PHONE!!!" Standing back a little, he scratched his head in frustration; it was like trying to fit a jigsaw puzzle together when half the pieces were missing.

Floating behind him, Molly also studied the information which was amassed on the boards. She too followed the black felt-tipped lines which criss-crossed over other black lines. There were lists of the names and contact details of everyone the police had interviewed, along with statements cross-referenced and verified, as well as someone's attempt at a time line. Abruptly her attention was drawn to a display of photographs and going over to them, she studied each one in turn. They showed her dead body lying half-in and half-out of the ground, her life force extinguished. Staring at them, she realised that each one had been taken from a different angle, each one giving a different view, a different perspective.

Annoyed, she suddenly shouted out, "Well, they're hardly flattering, are they? Look at the state of my hair, and — oh my God — look at my dress. I loved that dress as well; it's absolutely ruined now."

Ged was startled at Molly's sudden outburst. "Will you stop doing that! You nearly gave me a flippin' heart attack, shouting out like that. It's a good job this lot can't hear you, and let's face it, you won't be needing that dress again any time soon, anyway."

Molly pouted, continuing to study the information boards. She followed a black marker pen line down to the names of the people who had discovered her body. "Sorry! Anyway, look Gramps, these are the people who found me, Don and Maggie Holden. Maybe we can pay them a visit sometime to see how they're doing. We might even get a bit more information if we have a nosey." Continuing to look at the boards she saw Debbie's name. "Aww, poor Debs, she'll be in a right state. I'll pop in on her sometime to see how she's doing, as well."

Studying the other boards, she realised that the two key witnesses to her murder weren't there. Why hadn't Gareth Shaw been arrested? Molly sighed heavily. "Well, Gramps, looking at this lot is a waste of bloody time. Most of what Jenny told us isn't even here. We'll have to make the coppers aware of just who it is that they should be looking for."

Ged thought for a moment. "I think you're right. We need to play detectives ourselves. Maybe we can give this lot a bit of a helping hand; looks like they ruddy well need it."

Millington suddenly turned his back to the boards and called for everyone's attention. "Right chaps, as you are all aware, we have a lead. We know that Molly Roberts had a mobile phone which at the moment is unaccounted for. The next of kin have been very helpful by giving us the number, make, and model — I've written it all on the board. Is everyone clear on what they're meant to be doing? Bradley — anything else to add before we split up?"

DC Bradley nodded in confirmation and standing up, addressed the team, "Err… yes, as it happens, I was just about to tell you actually. I've got hold of some video footage taken from the pub's CCTV. The player's all set up in the vid room."

"Very salubrious," said Millington, rubbing his hands together. "Great, let's have a shufty then. The rest of you know what you're doing. We'll regroup here in two hours."

The two officers watched the monitor screen intently. The video footage taken from the Horse and Jockey showed Molly and Debbie entering the pub and sitting near to the stage. It also showed two lads sitting together at the bar.

Bradley leaned in for a closer look. "I know him on the right — that's Anthony Collins. He was nicked a few months ago for possession. I'm sure that's him."

"Really? So, who's the other lad then?" asked Millington, as they continued to watch the flickering images.

Bradley studied the screen. "Don't know yet, but I'll bet a pound to a penny on him being one of the local scroats. I'll make some enquiries. Have you noticed how it's always him that goes to the bar to get the drinks in?"

Millington thoughtfully stroked his chin as he continued to study the footage. "There! Just rewind a couple of frames will you. Watch… there! See how he fumbles in his pocket, then hunches over the tray of drinks. Strange that, don't you think?" he said, cracking his knuckles.

"Yeah, you're right," said Bradley as he freeze-framed the footage. "I'll get a couple of images of him as he's coming out of the toilets as well. I'll use them as mug shots and get them circulated."

Next, they turned their attention to the footage which had been captured from the CCTV outside the pub. Although it was in black and white and quite grainy, it showed Molly and Debbie arguing in the car park and Gareth intervening. He was holding Molly's arm as he roughly steered her towards the waiting taxi. It looked like she could barely stand, let alone walk, as he wrenched the rear door of the taxi open and forcibly pushed her into the back of it. Tony got into the front passenger seat, and the taxi drove off towards the town centre. The two detectives continued to watch as Debbie walked off alone in the opposite direction. Bradley reached for a pen and briskly wrote down the taxi's details.

"Right, chop, chop. I think we need to find this lad for a serious word," Millington said, heading back to the incident room. After diverting to the coffee machine on the way, he entered the noisy incident room which was filled with excitement and apprehension.

"Okay everyone, can I have your attention? Just to bring you all up to speed, we've looked at the CCTV footage, and Bradley is chasing up a lead on the taxi which picked up Molly Roberts from the Horse and Jockey, along with two males."

Millington proceeded to distribute the grainy black and white photographs. "Everyone, have a gander at these. Does anyone recognise this lad?" he asked, holding up the photograph of Gareth. "Bradley already knows the other one — Anthony Collins, or Tony as he's known. Bradley had him up for possession recently, and we've also managed to trace the missing phone to his address. D.S. Johnson and a couple of his team are already feeding back surveillance."

Everyone in the room fell silent as they studied the photographs.

"Whittaker — will you and Turner go and see Debbie Travis and show her the mug shots. See if they jog her memory and get an additional statement if they do. Rodgers — you go to the Horse and Jockey and see what else you can find out from the bar staff."

Molly excitedly punched the air and whooped loudly. "Yeah, at last! Now we're getting somewhere."

Bradley drove to the taxi company's premises. It was a well-known local firm whose office was on the High Street in the town centre. Questioning the manager, he obtained the details of the taxi driver and the address at which the fare had been dropped. Bradley then interviewed the taxi driver and got a full written statement. On his way back to the station he was feeling confident that they were going to solve this murder case in record time. He hated it when murder investigations dragged on, particularly the ones which went on for years and years or even became cold cases. Bradley got a buzz from the challenge of bringing all the evidence together, nailing the suspect and then getting a conviction. He was hoping to smash his personal best for solving a case, which currently stood at nine days.

Some five hours later, the police team were descending on the local council estate in three police cars and two vans. Parking just around the corner from the suspect's house, they waited as Millington calmly and deliberately dialled the listed land-line phone number for the address; it was answered by a male on the sixth ring. Tony was caught by surprise when the front and back doors of the house were simultaneously battered down. He was in the kitchen making a brew at the time and only realised what was happening when several police officers appeared in the kitchen doorway, batons drawn, shouting and commanding him to lie on the floor face down.

By chance, Gareth was on his way to Tony's house. He had decided to call round as he wanted to keep the pressure on Tony and control exactly what he remembered — if anything. Just as he rounded the corner of the road where Tony lived, Gareth realised that a full-scale police raid was taking place and that the whole area was crawling with coppers. Dodging back out of sight, he watched the whole event unfold from a safe distance and looked on as they frog-marched Tony out of the house in handcuffs, before bundling him into the back of one of the police vans. Gareth was momentarily confused and stood rooted to the spot, as more and more people from the estate gathered to see what was going on. Willing his feet to move, he knew that he had to get away before someone recognised him, and it would only be a matter of time before the cops found his connection to Tony. He knew it wouldn't take them long to find out who he was and where he lived; Tony was sure to shoot his mouth off.

After running back to his bed-sit, he nervously ducked behind one of the neighbouring walls and hid in the undergrowth, checking that everything was as it should be before he made a move. He let himself into the building and stood in the hallway, out of breath and panting, aware that the pulse in his temple was throbbing and his heart was thumping so hard it felt like it was trying to escape through his chest. He struggled to steady his breathing as he fumbled for his door key, dropping the key twice before finally managing to push it home into the lock.

Gareth was scared — very scared. 'Shit… shit… shit! Calm down, it will be all right, it will be all right,' he repeated to himself. He had to get a grip and think calmly and rationally. What the fuck was happening? How did the cops know where Tony lived? He knew that stupid Tony would sing like a canary once he got any semblance of memory back, and what had that gob shite told the cops already? What did he know, anyway — Jack shit by all accounts. And anything he did know was just what he'd been told, and he was hardly going to admit to any of that was he, the stupid bastard?

Following the successful raid, the police cordoned off the area surrounding Sally Monroe's house, and the Forensics team started to go through it with a fine tooth-comb, searching for, and gathering any evidence which would implicate Tony in the murder of Molly Roberts. They carefully and systematically picked over Tony's bedroom and soon found Molly's phone in one of the bedroom drawers. One of the officers picked up the pair of jeans from the bedroom floor and searching through the pockets, came across two small, clear plastic bags. Holding them up to the light, he studied the contents and concluded that one bag probably contained marijuana but he wasn't so sure about the contents of the other, which appeared to hold traces of a white powder. Carefully bagging and labelling the two bags, he moved on to examining the other items of clothing which he'd found.

While the search took place, Molly and Ged were sticking like glue to the police officers. Molly couldn't contain her excitement. "Wow, this is brilliant, I'm starting to remember things! Who would have thought that my phone would lead the cops here? They must have pinged it."

Ged raised an eyebrow in surprise.

"I wonder where Gareth hangs out though. He's the one they need to get," Molly continued, "He's the bastard who murdered me."

Ged raised the other eyebrow.

"Sorry, Grandpa," she said, as Ged looked at her with a surprised expression.

"They 'pinged' your phone? 'Pinged' — where on earth do you get it from?"

"Why? That's what they call it. They're always doing it on the telly. You really need to get with the times, Gramps!"

Meanwhile, Tony was being detained in one of the interview rooms. He was shocked and confused and didn't seem to know what was happening. Millington and Bradley had started the interview and were showing him photographs, and questioning him about the two girls he had been with at the Horse and Jockey pub. Tony was trying to answer the questions, while also trying to remember and make sense of what had happened on that Wednesday night. Bradley was putting the pressure on, and Tony felt himself spiralling deeper and deeper into confusion and despair. He was becoming sick of hearing the same questions, and being asked, over and over again, how he knew Molly Roberts, why he had her phone, and what the drugs were that they'd found in his jeans pocket.

Tony raised his voice in frustration, "I don't know what you's is goin' on about. I found the phone in me bleedin' denims and I know nothin' about no bleedin' drugs"

Molly and Ged hovered behind the two officers, listening to what was being said. "Oh my God! He's trying to frame him. Gareth...he's trying to frame Tony. What an out-and-out shit-head!"

"Molly, that will do," Ged said sternly.

"What? Blimey, excuse me for breathing! I'm just saying... it was Gareth who murdered me, but poor Tony here is gonna get the blame."

Ged nodded. "Yeah, you could be right."

Positioning himself in front of Tony's face, Ged studied his features closely. "I always prided myself on being able to suss out a liar but his eyes are blank. There's nothing — not a spark of guilt or anything."

"Yeah, well, what's that got to do with it?" Molly asked, irritated.

"Well, they say that the eyes are the windows to the soul and there's nothing in his eyes to suggest that he knows anything about your murder. I'd say that he doesn't have a clue — he's as much in the dark as this dozy lot are."

"Oh, so now you're a self-confessed lie detector?" she mocked, as she raised her eyes, tutted and flicked her head, not fully comprehending what her grandfather was talking about.

"I think you mean 'self-professed'! You know what, you look just like your mam when you do that," Ged said, smiling.

"I don't know if that's a good thing or not," Molly replied, as she continued to shake her head.

"Course it's a good thing. Anyway, come on. We need to find this Gareth Shaw fella, then maybe we can give these two the heads up. They obviously need all the help they can get."

Molly averted her eyes and looked down awkwardly. "Actually, I was going to ask if you wouldn't mind doing that yourself. I want to go to my post mortem if that's okay. It's today, and I'd like to go and watch."

"Well yes, if you're sure. Do you want me to come with you, love?"

"No, honest, I'll be fine. I'll see you in a bit."

Ged smiled tenderly as Molly left. He couldn't help but think how much he loved her and how he would do his absolute best to help her. He would do everything within his power to help her regain her memory and start to enjoy being home once again. But he knew that without her memories she would struggle to be her true self. He smiled as he thought about her quirky human mannerisms and just how un-spiritual, she was.

Ged's attention was suddenly diverted as Millington and Bradley abruptly left the room, leaving Tony to stew.

Chapter Sixteen: The Truth Shall Out

<***>

Nathan Bennett was one of the two on-call Forensic Pathologists who were covering the rota that particular weekend. At fifty-eight, Nathan was what people termed 'a confirmed bachelor', which was just the way he liked it. He had been a Forensic Pathologist for almost thirty-two years and now held down one of the most prestigious positions in the entire country. Nathan was extremely proud of how he had developed a team of experts and a department to be envied.

Nathan was a man who didn't suffer fools gladly and saw no point in engaging in conversation if it didn't serve a purpose. He was thorough and meticulous; every detail, measurement and all observations were systematically logged and analysed, following procedure and protocol to the letter, so as not to miss any shred of evidence that a deceased body might reveal. In fact, it had been Nathan who had written all the protocols and procedures in the first place, with the intention of developing and maintaining a gold-standard service. He never tired of telling his understudies that they should never forget that every post-mortem was as individual and unique as the subject's finger prints.

Although he considered himself to be a workaholic, the impromptu invitation to a round of golf had been gratefully received, and as he was the most senior of the on-call pathologists, he hadn't expected to be called in to work that day. Unexpectedly his pager had gone off just as he was about to drive his ball up the eighth fairway. Looking down at the number which was illuminated on the display, Nathan knew that the only reason for him to be paged was in the event of a serious case.

"Well, that's put paid to that! Sorry fella's, got to go. Thanks for the game all the same, have a couple for me at the nineteenth."

After parking the Aston Martin which was his only indulgence in the named space in the car park, he walked briskly to his office. Entering the laboratory, Nathan picked up the clipboard which the technician had left on the bench and studied the details which were attached. Dating and entering the time, he signed the form and mentally noted the case number. He could see he was about to examine a twenty-year old, white Caucasian female.

Molly positioned herself above the wall cupboards, watching as Nathan booted and gowned himself and waited for Bob, the technician, to position the body in readiness for being examined. "Bob," he grunted, by way of a greeting.

Nathan carefully studied the corpse of the young girl which lay before him on the cold, stainless steel table, while Molly just gawped at what had been her physical shell. Nathan's eyes purposefully and methodically scanned the body, looking for obvious marks or tell-tale signs to suggest any indication of a struggle having taken place, or restraints having been used. His gloved fingers expertly prodded and probed the pale, waxy flesh, and he noted that she had an almost serene look on her face. He thought that rather surreal, seeing as how she had met with such a violent death, judging by the skull indentation and black eye which she was sporting. Positioning the microphone over the table, he started to record his observations and findings into the Dictaphone. Proceeding to carefully remove her clothing, he handed each item in turn to Bob for him to bag and label.

Studying her face, he could see dried soil and twigs stuck in her hair. He noted that the left eye was blown and that there was dried blood crusted inside the left ear. There was bruising over the throat area and around the left breast. The right breast had more extensive contusions, with deep, pronounced bite marks around the areola. Picking up the camera, he photographed the bruising and soft tissue trauma, and recorded all other visible injuries on the post-mortem anatomy chart. Molly hovered around Bob, and with curious interest, continued to stare at what had once been her flesh and bones. After taking blood and urine samples, Nathan carefully examined the fingernails, looking for any debris which may have been lodged underneath them. It didn't look very promising but he took scrapings all the same, in the hope that she may have scratched her assailant. He documented that there were no broken finger nails or defence wounds, which strongly indicated that she hadn't put up much of a fight, if any.

Positioning a body block under the torso to arch the body, Nathan expertly made a 'Y' incision from the shoulders to the pubic bone, and after separating the sternum and ribs with a rib cutter, removed the chest plate. Next, he began to remove the internal organs. He was careful when lifting the stomach out, as he needed to examine its contents. Bob expertly and efficiently passed instruments and various sized bowls to Nathan to receive the organs so that they could be examined later. Carefully re-positioning the body block to raise Molly's head off the table, Nathan noted that there were extensive haematomas and soft tissue swellings, suggestive of multiple facial fractures. Examining the obvious depression to the left temporal lobe, he carefully measured the depth, width and breadth of the indentation.

"Make sure you get a couple of X-rays and pictures. Pass me the scalpel and bone saw, will you."

Bob expertly did as Nathan requested, before handing over the shiny, stainless-steel instruments. "That bone fragment looks pretty deep — whoever bashed her skull in must have given her one almighty thwack," he commented.

Nathan skilfully resected the area and carefully lifting the bone clear of the rest of the skull, placed the bone fragment into a stainless-steel kidney dish. Grunting and taking a sharp scalpel, he made a careful incision behind Molly's right ear. After cutting across to the opposite ear along the top of the head, he eased the front half of the scalp forwards and the other half of the scalp backwards, exposing the top of the white cranium. Picking up the bone saw, he manoeuvred and angled it into the best position and expertly began to saw through the top of the cranium. Selecting a skull chisel to carefully prise off the top of the skull, he exposed the brain beneath. Immediately he could see that there was a substantial blood clot at the site of the traumatic impact.

"That's it. The resulting bleed would have been enough to have caused her death — not necessarily immediately, but eventually."

Bob inhaled sharply. "Christ almighty, poor kid — that's one hell of a haematoma"

"Bloody hell!" winced Molly.

Carefully removing the brain from its cranial vault, Nathan placed it on the scales and weighed it. Next, he inspected the haematoma before examining the dura mater and found more evidence of a substantial haemorrhage within the delicate tissue. Proceeding to carefully dissect the brain. Slicing through it with a knife, he separated the two hemispheres, examining each one in turn. After studying the cortex of each half, he frowned.

"That's strange! Hand me a magnifying glass, will you."

Bob rummaged around in one of the drawers and finding one, passed it over to Nathan.

"Well I'll be dammed — look at that! The impact must have been so violent it's actually sheared the pineal gland clean from its stalk."

Bob also looked through the magnifying glass and studied the area where the pineal gland should have been.

"I can't see it either. You're right, it isn't there, unless its buried in the tissue somewhere else."

Nathan retrieved the magnifying glass and once again studied the two sliced hemispheres. "Hmm, how bizarre. Must be somewhere, though. I've seen this sort of thing once before. It's a case of getting the angle of the blow to hit the skull in such a way that it sends shock waves through the brain. The resulting force is sufficient to do that kind of damage."

"Must be like having a volcano go off in your head"

"Yeah, pretty much. I'll have a good look later when I fully dissect the brain"

Nathan grunted to himself again, and returning his attention to the corpse, continued to work quietly and methodically. It was evident that she had recently had sexual intercourse, as there were small skin tears to the entrance of the vagina and anus, suggesting rough penetration, probably rape. But there were no visible traces of semen in the vagina, rectum or mouth. Nathan took the intimate swabs regardless, while Molly looked on somewhat perturbed, before pulling an indignant facial expression and averting her stare.

The remainder of the post-mortem revealed no other pathology, and Nathan busied himself with completing the relevant paperwork, while Bob did the necessary cleaning and tidying away, ready for the next one. Nathan suddenly felt a tingle run up and down his spine. Just as Bob was about to push the body back into the refrigeration unit, he crossed the floor and stood in quiet reverence at the foot of the trolley on which the body lay.

"Hold on a minute," he said. Bowing his head, he recited a silent prayer, and as he opened his eyes, he felt drawn to look at the corpse's feet. Turning the sheet back, he noticed the pink toenail polish and had a sudden compulsion to examine the right foot. He immediately noticed that the big toenail was torn and jagged on the outer edge and it had a vertical split running down its length.

"What have we got here? Pass me the camera and a pair of sharp tweezers, will you."

Bob watched as Nathan angled the examination light to see better.

"Well, well… what have we got here, indeedy?"

Molly smiled to herself and moving to a better position, looked over the pathologist's shoulder. After taking several photographs, Nathan proceeded to grip the foot. Holding the tweezers firmly, he carefully removed a tiny sliver of pale tissue which was lodged underneath the broken toe nail.

"Hmm… pass me a specimen bottle, will you."

Unscrewing the lid, Bob passed him a small bottle which was half-filled with Formalin. Nathan gently tapped the tweezers on the inside of the bottle, dislodging the tissue sample, which slowly sank to the bottom. Screwing the lid back on tightly, he carefully placed it onto the trolley with the other specimens.

"Make sure you send that off with all the other tissue and blood samples, will you."

Bob held the sample up to the light for a better look.

"On second thoughts, label it separately as high priority and be sure to write on the form the site it came from; that's from under the toenail of the first hallux, of the right foot."

"Yes, Bob, make sure you label that properly," repeated Molly, disparagingly.

"Oh, and will you get an electrician to fix that bloody ceiling light — the constant flickering is getting on my nerves."

Removing his gloves and apron, Nathan continued to mumble under his breath as he went into the office to finish off writing his report.

"Damn cheek! You should think yourself lucky mate — if it hadn't been for me, you wouldn't have found that scraggy bit of skin," Molly shouted after him, somewhat affronted.

"Sure thing," replied Bob, as he repositioned the sheet and pushed the body back into the refrigeration unit.

"And I'll put a soddin' brush up my arse while I'm at it," he muttered under his breath.

Chapter Seventeen: The Pressure's On

<***>

Picking up two coffees, Millington went back to the interview room where Tony was being detained. He was eager to get the interview underway again.

"Coffee?"

"Ta," said Tony, "So, what's goin' on? Why's I 'ere? I ain't done nothin'," he said nervously.

Acknowledging the officer standing quietly in the corner of the room, Millington pulled out the chair from beneath the table and sat down opposite Tony.

"Let's just say that we're having a little chat and that you're helping us with our enquiries, shall we?"

Tony drained the coffee from the polystyrene cup and began to drum his fingers against the table top. Millington leaned forward to further intimidate his scared prey.

"Who's the lad who was in the pub with you, Tony? I've just been looking at some very interesting video footage, and you and 'what's his name' are looking very pally together, very pally indeed."

"Oh, you mean Gazzer. Gareth Shaw, I think his name is."

"So how do you know… Gazzer?"

"We met down at the probation office. He's just a mate."

"Just a mate, eh? Well, you look like bezzie mates on the tape. Come on Tony, cut the crap! We watched you and him arrive together and then leave the pub with two girls, one of whom got into the taxi with the both of you."

Tony continued to stare at the bottom of the empty polystyrene cup.

"What's up, Tony? Not figured on a camera? Well, let me tell you just exactly what's on that tape, shall I? It's there, Tony, it's all there. You and Gazzer together with Molly Roberts, one of the girls you and matey boy picked up, all cosy like, getting into a taxi. Where'd you go Tony? Into town? Back to your place? Or back to matey boy's place?"

Tony shifted in his seat and squashed the empty cup. "Honest mate, I don't knows what ya on about. All I knows is getting in a taxi and going back to 'is place. We downed a couple of vodkas but after that, it's all a blur. I knows I was pretty wasted, cos Gazzer told me I was, but I don't knows nothin' else, so's I'm not saying another bleedin' word till I've got a legal."

Tony clammed up and stated to pick and bite his nails, which he always did when he was nervous or stressed, and right now he was both. Millington stood up abruptly, causing his chair to fall backwards. It hit the floor with a loud clatter, making Tony jump. Towering over him, Millington thumped the table with his clenched fist as he glared down on him.

"You honestly think that this Gazzer fella is a mate? Don't make me laugh. Do you honestly think that Gareth Shaw, that little toe rag, would give a damn about you? Well, do you?"

Tony continued to bite and chew his nails and avoided making eye contact with the detective. Millington maintained his stance.

"I suggest you find your memory pretty smartish my friend, as all the evidence that you murdered Molly Roberts is flashing over your head like some huge feckin' blue neon sign. You're going to need more than a feckin' solicitor, pal. Capisce?".

Tony recoiled in shock. "Murdered? What do ya mean, murdered? What the hell you talking about? I don't knows nowt about her being bleedin' murdered. Christ almighty! Murdered?"

"Yes, murdered. So why don't you start to tell me exactly what you do know."

"Yeah, well I'm telling you, I knows nothing and like I said, I'm sayin' nowt else till I've got me brief," he stammered.

Frustrated, Millington terminated the interview and stormed out of the interview room. Bradley and Millington met back in the incident room, which was noisy with banter and ringing phones. Together, they studied the information written on the ever-expanding boards, scrutinising the new leads and evidence threads.

Running his hands through his hair, Millington took a step back, turned and addressed the team. "Okay, right, listen up people; this is what we have so far — feel free to interject at any point."

"Yeah, you lot, shut up and listen," shouted Molly.

The room fell silent as all eyes turned to the boards.

"From the pub's CCTV footage, we got a positive ID of the taxi firm, and Bradley got a detailed statement from the taxi driver who took the fare. We know that all three of them went back on the Wednesday night to a bed-sit where Gareth Shaw lives. When we raided Collins' home address, we found drugs and Molly's mobile phone in his bedroom. And we also know how Molly died; for those that don't, it was a single impact blow to the temple, but as yet we haven't found the murder weapon. She also had high blood levels of alcohol and traces of Rohypnol, and she had been raped as well."

The room's atmosphere changed as Millington divulged the disturbing information.

"What we don't know at the moment is the whereabouts of this Gareth Shaw, aka Gazzer. We need to work on that, although he's probably done a runner by now. You should all be familiar with his picture. We've now got details and know that he has an existing record of criminality with numerous charges of violent assault, drug offences and aggravated burglary. He's one of the nicer ones — a real gent by all accounts," he added sarcastically. "As soon as we're done here, I want Bradley, Church and Donnelly ready to come with me. Oh, and some builder has just brought in a blood-stained pillow and duvet — Crawley, will you see to that?"

Bradley stood up and looked round the room at the expectant faces of the team.

"He's our man — I'm sure of it — but DNA and some forensics are still being processed, so we won't know for certain for another twenty-four hours or so." Millington pointed to one of the boards. "Tony Collins claims to have no memory of what happened after he and Molly went back to Shaw's bed-sit. I get the feeling that he knows more than he's letting on but he's clammed up. I intend to interview him again, later. Truth be told though, I've a hunch that Collins was drugged the same way Molly was. As I said, Molly's tox screen results showed a lot of alcohol and traces of Rohypnol. It would certainly fit with his story — no memory and the like. We need to move fast on this one. His twenty-four hours are nearly up and we haven't got enough to charge him, so he'll probably walk, but for now he's still a suspect."

Millington absentmindedly scratched his head and then continued, "Right, when he's released, I want Jenkins and Fowler to keep an eye on him. I want him under twenty-four-hour surveillance. I want to know who he meets and where he goes. Oh, and put a tap on his phone before you give it him back — I want to know if these two are in cahoots. I'm going over to Shaw's place now. Bradley, are you ready? Forensics are meeting us there. I want this Shaw bugger caught as soon as."

Molly and Ged were also listening to what Millington was saying. Molly was still having a hard time trying to understand the events which had happened that Wednesday night.

"Why me, Grandpa? I can't believe that this was how my life was meant to end. I can't believe that there was a point to any of it. It's like my life didn't have a purpose."

Ged said nothing but carried on looking at the boards. Shaking his head, he turned to Molly who was looking out of the window, watching the hustle and bustle in the street below.

"Molly I know that's how you see it at the moment, but once we get you back with Orick, everything will fall into place and make more sense," Ged said as he continued to look at the white boards. "Come on, we need to get to Gareth Shaw's place before that lot do, so we can see what's there and look for clues ourselves."

Fixing onto her grandfather's energy vibration again, she followed him. They found themselves in the pokey, dank bed-sit where Gareth lived. Looking around the room, Molly started to pick up on the negative vibration of violence which filled the atmosphere.

"This is it," she gasped, "This is where I was murdered." Hovering over the bed, she felt a distortion in her energy as she began to remember what had happened that awful night.

"Oh my God! It was here — here on the bed. Jenny was right. I vaguely remember now. He drugged me and brought me back here. I must have passed out and then he... he... oh God, I started to come round and struggle, so he hit me. He hit me on the side of my head with that table lamp."

Molly's voice faltered and trailed off as she pointed to a lamp next to the bed. She began to feel sick as the negative energy which now pervaded the room became cloying and oppressive. She started to shiver uncontrollably and began to feel cold and empty. Dismissing the strange feeling, she carried on searching, trying to find anything that would prompt her memory.

"Bloody hell! I wasn't the first to be drugged and raped here either, but I was the first to die."

Ged went over to the lamp and studied it. "Well if you're sure that's what he used to hit you with, the police need to find it — they'll need it as evidence. I think we should wait until the coppers show up. They'll more than likely turn this place over big time."

Molly nodded. "I bloody well hope they do. There's no telling what else they might find."

"Well, in the meantime I think we could be a while waiting, so it might be a good idea to conserve our energies and condense our vibration."

Molly looked bewildered. "What do you mean?"

Ged smiled, "Well you know how to use transference to get around, don't you?" Molly nodded. "Well, we can conserve more energy by lowering our vibration level even further."

Molly was intrigued. "Really? Oh wow, I've gotta see this."

Ged gave her a knowing smile. "Okay, now then, what we need to do is to find some water. We can use water to create a type of energy conductor and form an outer shell around ourselves. Ah, over here, there's some water droplets in the sink."

Molly went over and peered into the stainless-steel sink. "Okay, what do we do now?" she asked, puzzled.

"Watch — just do what I do."

Molly watched as her grandfather focused his attention and stared intently at the water droplets. She could see a faint mist starting to rise from the droplets, and in an instant, he had changed his whole shape and transformed himself into a round ball of energy which hovered at her side.

Molly did a double take. "Blimey, Grandpa, how did you do that?"

"Ha, easy when you know how. You should give it a try," he said encouragingly.

Molly stared into the sink and focussed on a water droplet. She began to see a faint mist beginning to form above it, and using all of her concentration, felt herself absorbing the water vapour. In an instant, she too shifted her energy into a ball.

"Whoa, amazing! Grandpa, look at me… whee!" she squealed in delight. Molly felt energised and charged as she realised she could whizz around at speed, or float leisurely to wherever in the room she wanted to go.

Ged smiled and then floated and drifted effortlessly across the room to join her. "Full of surprises, aren't I? You'd never have thought that we can change our form at will, and contain our energy in a ball — or orb as they're called these days."

Molly didn't care what they were called. She was ecstatically happy in her new-found form. "Grandpa, this is so cool. You have a kind of a yellowy-green colour around you."

"Do I? Well you're kind of see-through, and your aura is a very pale grey."

Continuing to float around the room, Ged and Molly were enjoying their shape-shifting, when suddenly they were taken by surprise as Gareth barged into his bedsit and slammed the door shut behind him. He leaned against it, gasping for breath. He could feel his heart pounding in his chest, and it felt like it was about to explode as he gulped in air and struggled to calm himself. Frantically he began opening cupboards and tossing everything he thought he'd need onto the bed. Reaching up on top of the wardrobe, he retrieved an old, battered holdall and hurriedly shoved everything which was on the bed into it. Next, he rummaged in a drawer, and retrieving a bundle of papers and documents, proceeded to squash them down the sides of the holdall. 'I'm not gonna make it easy for them bastard coppers,' he thought. Molly and Ged couldn't believe what they were seeing, and floating high up near to the ceiling, they watched as Gareth orchestrated his escape, unaware of their presence.

Suddenly remembering the stash of drugs which was hidden in an old biscuit tin under a loose floorboard just in front of the fridge, Gareth pulled back the stained rug covering it and expertly pressed down on the end of the floorboard to flip it up. Retrieving the tin, he quickly emptied its contents onto the bed, and pushed the small plastic bags of drugs down one of his socks. Next, he rummaged through his coat pockets and fumbled for his wallet, as he remembered the wad of cash which was stuffed inside. 'Lucky I got my dole yesterday,' he thought to himself, as a smirk crossed his lips. He was about to leave the room when he noticed the lamp at the side of the bed. Picking it up, he forced it into the holdall but as he did so, he broke the shade. Angrily snatching at it, he completely sheared it free from the lamp, threw it onto the floor and stamped on it in temper. Picking the lamp up again and thrusting it back into the already overstuffed holdall, Molly could hear his thoughts as he planned to dump the lamp somewhere later.

Molly was so incensed that it caused her to shape-shift back into spirit form, and in a fit of rage she started to shout and hurl abuse at him. "You pig!" she shouted, "You shit! How could you? How could you do what you did to me, you murdering bastard? Don't think you're going to get away with it. Jesus! Where are the police when you bloody need them?"

Ged was caught unawares at Molly's sudden outburst and quickly shifted his shape back into spirit form, too. It took all of his strength and determination to stop Molly throwing things around the room. Gareth was largely oblivious of the torrent of anger and rage being rained down on him but feeling a sudden chill run down his spine, he stopped and gave a quick glance around the room. Satisfied that he had left nothing incriminating, he checked that the coast was clear before quietly crossing the hallway, entering the bathroom, and locking the door behind him.

Molly was so angry and distraught, that she didn't realise just how drained she was feeling. She tried to follow Gareth but rapidly found that she didn't have the energy.

"I'm sorry, Grandpa, but I feel weird. I feel like I'm… fading away."

"Molly, you can't be doing outbursts like that — you haven't gathered your essence yet. We have to go back immediately or you'll be so weak you won't be able to get back."

Molly felt light-headed and dizzy, and before Ged realised what was happening, she collapsed into his energy field. Feeling a sudden shift and down-turn in his own vibration as Molly sapped his energy levels, Ged struggled to gather every ounce of his remaining strength. With some difficulty he managed to get them both safely back to the spiritual realm.

Chapter Eighteen: A Fatal Mistake

<***>

Gareth leant against the bathroom door and listened; the last thing he wanted was to be seen leaving his bedsit by the front door. He was grateful that the bathroom was opposite his bedsit. Opening the bathroom window as wide as it would go, he clambered out onto the window sill and dropped the holdall to the ground, before jumping down. Quickly looking around and checking that no-one had seen him, he hauled the holdall over his shoulder and set off running, heading off through the back alleyways and away from the life he knew. Gareth Shaw was on the run.

Gareth was scared — so scared that he couldn't stop himself from shaking. Making his way out of town, he ran himself nearly to the point of exhaustion. His breathing became laboured, and the stitch in his ribs hurt like hell. Part running, part stumbling along a small stream, he kept checking behind him, making sure that no one was following him and hoping his trail would be masked should the police be using dogs to pursue him. Eventually he stumbled, exhausted, into a small copse, where he decided to have a short rest. Crouching down in the thicket to catch his breath, he tried to estimate the distance he had covered, and thought it must be ten miles or more. Knowing that the sun would be setting soon, he decided to stay where he was for the night and then continue to head to the coast at first light. After concealing himself as best he could, he tried to settle down to sleep, but the towering trees around him threw dark, menacing shadows which had his senses in overdrive, and he imagined that every creak and crack was made by pursuers. Eventually though, he fell into a restless sleep.

At first light he awoke and smoked a spliff, before setting off at a steady run. After he had covered a few more miles, the woods ended abruptly and the land suddenly fell away into a steep drop. Distracted by his thoughts, he nearly missed his footing but managed to regain his balance and stop himself plunging down into the ravine. Collapsing on the ground to catch his breath, he realised how lucky he had been not to have fallen over the edge. He lay on his back for a few seconds, looking up at the sky through the canopy of branches, trying to work out where he was. He estimated that he must have covered a fair distance by now. As his breathing became regular again, he was suddenly aware of sporadic traffic noise and realised that there was a lane on the other side of an unruly Hawthorne hedgerow.

Heading in the direction from which the sound was coming, he came upon the lane. Breaking his cover, he walked along the road for a mile or so until he heard a truck approaching from behind him. Pulling his hood up over his head in an attempt to hide his face, he flagged down the delivery van, and asked the driver for a lift into the next town. Never in his life had Gareth felt such relief and gratitude when the driver agreed to take him there. The driver made small talk as he drove, but Gareth was careful not to say anything which was likely to give any clues to where he had come from, or where he was heading. At Gareth's request, the van driver dropped him off at a lay-by on the outskirts of the next village, and with a cheery wave drove off without giving their chance encounter a second thought.

Walking through the narrow streets, Gareth mingled unnoticed with the crowds of shoppers and tourists. He bought himself a couple of sandwiches and cans of lager from a small convenience store, as he was beginning to feel thirsty and weak with hunger. He knew he had to find somewhere to sleep and hole up for a while. Deciding that he wasn't going to chance a Bed and Breakfast, he headed out of the small village, hoping to get lucky and find a shed or garage to hide in for the night. Scampering over stiles, dry walls and fences, he skirted the edges of fields and kept to the quiet country lanes and hoped that he hadn't stirred anyone's curiosity.

Just as it was starting to get dark, he came across a detached farm house which had a 'For Sale' board planted in the garden. Surrounded by countryside and farmland, Gareth reasoned that it would make the perfect hide-out. He rang the doorbell, then rapped loudly on the porch window before hiding behind a large rhododendron bush which gave him direct sight of the front door. He waited apprehensively for someone to answer, but no-one came. Skirting around the outside of the house, he looked through each window until he was absolutely sure that it was deserted. He couldn't see any signs of life but to be safe, he waited until it was completely dark before he made his move. Smashing a small glass window pane in the back-porch door, Gareth carefully turned the key which had been left in the mortice lock, taking care not to cut himself. Cautiously opening the door, he stepped into the porch, crunching the broken glass underfoot. He quietly closed the door and stood listening, straining to hear any sounds of movement over the pounding heartbeat which was thumping in his ears. The inner door was old and flimsy, and didn't stand up to his shoulder charges for long; after a couple of attempts, the rusted lock and bolts sheared away from the splintered door frame.

He entered the room and allowed his eyes to gradually adjust to the gloom of the kitchen. Holding his breath, he crept over to the opposite door and opened it slowly, trying to avoid making any noise. Then he stepped into the hallway and listened again; silence and the smell of damp had his senses reeling. Going from room to room, it soon became obvious that the house had been empty for a while, as all the furniture and trappings of a home had long since been removed. Checking the water taps and light switches, Gareth was disappointed to find that there was no running water or electricity; it never occurred to him to look for the stop-cock or electricity meter. Still, he reasoned, at least he could shelter and stay low for a while, until he had sorted his head out and had decided what he was going to do.

He returned to the kitchen, and wedged the door back into place. Pleased with his good luck, he sat down on the quarry-tiled floor with his back leaning against the wall, and drank thirstily from a can of lager. The room was now illuminated by the light of a full moon which shone hazily through the dirty kitchen windows. Rolling himself a spliff, he idly watched the smoke drift upwards to the once white ceiling, before disappearing into nothingness. For the first time in his wretched life, Gareth Shaw cried. He sobbed uncontrollably, and as each sob shook and racked his body, he felt that he would never stop. Shivering as the cold and damp began penetrating into his very core, he curled up into the foetal position and through sheer exhaustion, drifted off into a troubled sleep.

The next morning, Gareth awoke with a jolt as the faint light of dawn began to fill the empty room. Images of Molly, which had up until then been suppressed deep in the recesses of his mind, began to surface and he remembered the dreams and terrors he had wrestled with during the night. He struggled to stand up, as every inch of his body ached and protested when his stiff joints and muscles were forced to move. He limped to the kitchen window and peered out, his eyes darting over the misty fields as he searched for movement. There was nothing unusual to see; the landscape was undisturbed, as nature went about its seasonal business. He glimpsed a fox, and watched as it wended its way along the hedgerow of the harvested field, obviously in search of breakfast. The startling 'caw, caw' squawks of a murder of crows, which had congregated in a nearby sycamore tree, were strangely reassuring.

Gareth knew he had to plan what to do next. It made sense to stay put, but he would have to go back into the village and get some more supplies. He needed food, water, and a blanket at least, and laughed to himself as he realised that he was making a mental shopping list. Deciding to explore the upstairs rooms first, he climbed the stairs. There were four big bedrooms and a bathroom, all needing a good clean and decorating. Finding an old bucket and some candles in one of the bedrooms, he decided that they would come in very handy. Placing them on the kitchen worktop, he added matches to his mental shopping list. Leaving by the back porch, he hoped that when he got back, the house would be exactly as he had left it.

Returning a few hours later with everything he thought he would need to keep him going for at least a couple of weeks, he hid out of sight for a while, making doubly sure that the place was still deserted. Entering by the back-porch door again, he quietly closed it behind him and carefully lifted the inner door out of its frame, listening for a long time before going into the kitchen and setting the items down on the counter top. He looked over the selection of tinned beans, soups, biscuits, crisps and chocolate bars laid out in front of him and immediately wished that he had got more. He was disappointed at the limited amount of water and lagers which he had managed to steal due to their weight and bulk. But he laughed to himself as he remembered the rush of adrenalin he had felt when he had managed to steal a radio right from under the shop assistant's nose. And even better, he had managed to steal a sleeping bag which had been hanging on a washing line.

Opening one of the cans of lager and taking a large swig, he wandered through to the dining room end of the through-lounge and started to set up his make-shift camp. He had quickly decided that this was the best part of the house to be in, as he could see through to both the front and the rear gardens; if anyone called at the house, he would see them first and would be able to hide or escape. Although the room was cold and stark, with bare floorboards and old draughty sash windows, it did have an open hearth, so at least he could make a fire. Glancing around the room, he saw that the only furniture left in it was an old wooden card table and a footstool, whose tapestry design was now threadbare; he would make firewood out of them later, he decided.

He waited until it was completely dark before making a small fire in the grate, figuring that people would be less likely to notice smoke coming out of the chimney at night. Blowing dust and a dead spider out of a saucepan which he found at the back of one of the kitchen cupboards, he carefully balanced the saucepan on the edge of the fire grate. He tipped half a tin of beans into the pan and huddled around the small fire to keep warm, eagerly stirring the beans so that they wouldn't catch and burn. Although his meal was meagre, he felt sated. Opening another can of lager, he saluted the air with it and then suddenly remembered the radio. He retrieved it from the kitchen, and tuned the dial into a national radio station so that he could listen to the hourly news bulletins and updates.

Over the next few days he watched and waited, living on his wits and nerves with every creak and sound driving his anxiety higher. The days eventually began to blur together, and although the radio news bulletins reported Molly's murder and that the police were looking for him, no new developments were broadcast. Gareth stayed in hiding, occupying himself by smashing up the kitchen cabinets, as his need to keep the cold at bay meant that he had to keep the fire going. He was also careful to eke out his ever-dwindling supply of food and bottled water.

By the middle of the second week, Gareth had begun to feel quite ill. He had a constant headache and was shaking and shivering all the time, unable to get warm no matter how many layers of clothing he put on or how much wood he burned. He thought he must be coming down with the flu, and convinced himself that he would begin to feel better in a couple of days. But as each new day dawned, the relentless pain and aches which racked his body began to wear him down, and the cannabis did little to relieve his discomfort. He began to dread falling asleep, as his dreams morphed into awful nightmares, and the night terrors which followed were like demons, come to terrorise and haunt him.

Then one morning, while listening to the news broadcast on the radio, he heard that the police had received new information: the van driver had come forward and had given them a statement, describing how he had picked up a hitch-hiker matching Gareth's description. Gareth was surprisingly calm as he figured that he would be all right, since by his reckoning the driver had dropped him off miles away from where he was now. Still, it would do no harm to be extra vigilant from now on, he thought, as he positioned himself in the middle of the room to best keep a look-out.

It was during the beginning of the third week that Gareth, now totally exhausted, realised he was getting weaker and beginning to lose his grip on reality. The hallucinations were becoming ever more grotesque in his confused brain and all the more terrifying, and he just couldn't seem to stay awake for very long. His left leg was red, painful and swollen, with green pus oozing out of the big, open sore on his shin and the smell coming from it was indescribable. It was only now that the seriousness of his predicament began to seep into his fuddled brain, and a feeling of helplessness and foreboding began to envelop him. Curling up in the sleeping bag, in front of a fire which had long since burned itself out, he waited. The sepsis which was coursing through his body made light work of destroying his major organs, and one by one they began to fail. Within a few short hours he lapsed into a coma. The dining room, in which he had spent his last few miserable weeks, was now as cold and as empty as his life had been. It was during the dark, early hours that his heart shuddered and gave its final quivering beat, as death came to claim its trophy.

Chapter Nineteen: Chamber of Transcendence

<***>

Molly woke with a start, and looking up at a translucent, green-domed ceiling above her, cried out, "Oh God, where the hell am I now?"

Ged was sitting by her side. "It's all right sweetheart, I'm here. Just rest — you're going to be fine. You're in the Chamber of Transcendence. I got you here just in time, by all accounts."

Molly thought it best not to ask anything more, as she sensed that whatever had happened to her must have been serious. She felt different, although she didn't know why. Relaxing a little, she felt a great sense of peace and love sweep over her. It felt like she was snuggled in a blanket which was so soft it caressed every part of her fragility. She became aware of a prickling sensation which seemed to ripple and surge through the whole of her being. It was a peculiar feeling, as if she was completely immersed in a warm, silky liquid. Looking down towards her feet, she realised that she was indeed immersed in liquid — a liquid which was the most beautiful, emerald-green colour that she had ever seen. She watched it flow around and through her, and thought it strange that it felt solid and dense, yet fluid-like, simultaneously.

She caught sight of a movement and instinctively knew she was in the presence of an archangel. The angel was sombre in his healing ministrations and totally absorbed in what he was doing, yet he frequently gazed at her, checking her flow of energy and auric layers. Turning her head to get a better look at the archangel, she saw that he towered above her and appeared to emit a shimmering, translucent, green energy which sparked and crackled. His face was serene, yet troubled, and Molly sensed an unfathomable depth of ancient knowledge and wisdom. He moved effortlessly around her, as he laid his healing hands gently over each of her chakras before gently tapping them with what looked like a small stick. The Caduceus wand he held calmed the torrid, swirling energies which coursed through each of her energy vortices. Molly lay perfectly still, revelling in the healing vibrations, and began to feel her vitality returning. With love and inexplicable compassion, the Archangel looked tenderly upon her and although no words were exchanged, she knew that he too was deeply wounded, just as she was. Then she once again lapsed into a deep, rejuvenating sleep.

"Will our Beloved recover and be healed from her sufferance?" asked Kyah, the keeper of the Akasha, as she tenderly stroked Molly's hand.

Archangel Raphael shook his head slowly, releasing a deep troubled sigh. "Kyah, it is with a great heaviness of heart that I must tell you I have undertaken what the Great Spirit has asked of me, but our Beloved has sustained a virtual depletion of energy and vibration, and it has taken a lot of love, healing and nurture to stabilise her. I have managed to merge and reconnect what was left of her shattered soul, but sadly I haven't been able to fully restore her. I will have to apply further restorative healing to her memory re-emergence later, when she is a little stronger perhaps. But even then…."

Kyah detected the depth of sorrow in his voice. Nodding, she rose from Molly's side and whispered, "I understand, and it saddens me immensely to learn of this. Obviously, the ramifications are going to be very challenging, especially as you have now confirmed what I had feared."

Archangel Raphael nodded sombrely. "Indeed Kyah, but I am hopeful that she will be strong enough to support and uphold her astral chakras, or at the very least keep them aligned."

Kyah glanced once more at the recumbent form and after bowing respectfully, left the Chamber of Transcendence with a heavy heart.

<><><>

Several days passed before Molly stirred and woke again. Stretching and yawning, she looked around the chamber and marvelled at the vast, open space, which was a hive of activity. Molly could sense all manner of Ethereals and elementals bustling around, as she was now able to discern the varying vibration of the many healing sprites and faeries. She noticed two imposing archangels on the far side of the chamber, and watched as they effortlessly tended their charges with an air of unspoken authority. They appeared to be supervising the benevolent therapies which were being given to returnee spirits who needed succour and restorative healing. Molly instantly recognised one of them to be Raphael, and watched as he worked his way around the chamber. Studying some of the altars which were adjacent to hers, she could see what looked like spider's webs hanging down over each of them. In the centre of each of the webs was something resembling a large, golden sphere, which seemed to pulse and vibrate and emit various colours. Each web had a network of silver, thread-like energy lines which criss-crossed backwards and forwards, cocooning the recovering spirit who was laid beneath it. Suddenly understanding the purpose of the altars, she realised that most of the returnees were tired and frail. Many were suffering from malaise and fatigue, having used up most of their energy during the physical life they had just left.

She noticed that many of the threads were silvery-white and appeared to glisten, and suddenly she was aware of a memory that dropped unexpectedly into her consciousness. The threads reminded her of the time when she had been in hospital with a burst appendix and had been given antibiotics through an intravenous drip. She remembered that the doctors had told her that she had nearly died. 'Oh, the irony,' she thought. Continuing to look around, she could see that high above the webs were clusters of what resembled huge balls of tangled string. They too were in various colours and Molly watched as they periodically lit up and sparked like fork lightening.

Sometime later, she sensed that Orick was at the foot of the healing altar on which she was laying. She could hear his voice in her head as he spoke to her. "Welcome back, I thought I'd lost you this time. You don't know how lucky you are — if it hadn't been for your grandpa…. well, who knows what might have happened? Zadkiel and Raphael have been tending to you for what seems like an eternity," he said, placing his hands on her feet.

Molly remained motionless, hardly daring to move.

"Have you anything to say for yourself?" he asked, more sternly than he had intended.

Molly looked away.

"You didn't tell your grandpa what Elder Pettruf said to you, did you? Honestly Molly! After all he told you… told us… you still went ahead and defied him."

Molly realised that Orick was telling her off. She didn't really care and going on the offensive, nimbly jumped off the healing altar. She stood cockily with her hands on her hips.

"No Orick, I didn't tell my grandpa because I knew that he would still help me regardless, unlike some others I could mention."

Orick glared at her. "What's that supposed to mean? What you did was pure defiance, and was pig-headed and stupid, and it could have put Ged in difficulty too."

Molly glowered back at Orick. "Yeah, well, at least I know that whatever happens, my grandpa will always protect me. He will always be there for me, and you know what, he will always love me regardless. Because without stating the obvious, he was there for me, unlike you! So no, Orick, I didn't tell him."

Orick was astonished at Molly's outburst, but noticing Archangel Zadkiel looking over in their direction, lowered his voice. "Right, lets sort this out here and now. Why do you speak to me like that? Why all the contempt and anger towards me?"

Molly glared at Orick, suddenly feeling defiant. "Because… because… you didn't save me! You weren't there," she replied angrily, stamping her foot in temper.

Orick suddenly realised why Molly was so antagonistic towards him. "Oh Molly, that's not true. There is so much that you don't understand, please be patient. Until your recovery has been fully completed, you are more fragile than you think. Archangel Raphael and his angels of healing have performed nothing short of a miracle to get you to where you are now."

Molly scowled. "A miracle? You'll be telling me next that God had a hand in all this, too."

"Actually, yes. The Great Spirit — who you refer to as God — has done everything possible to orchestrate your recovery."

"Oh, whatever! Yeah, well you would say that. Anyway, I'm fine now. I'm feeling much better, so if you don't mind, I'd like to go. I have things to do, and places to be, and anyway, where's my grandpa? I really need to see him."

Orick stared at her. "Oh, you do, do you? Well, you know what? Why don't you try finding him yourself, seeing as you're fine? And when you do find him, maybe a bit of honesty on your part wouldn't go amiss, either."

Molly pouted as Orick's sarcasm was lost on her. Haughtily, she condensed her energy and headed back towards the Gardens.

Chapter Twenty: In Memory Of

<***>

It was a beautiful day for a funeral and the church was filled with beams of sunlight which streamed in through the stained-glass windows. Molly and Ged hovered above the altar, as a church bell sombrely began to strike its timed note. Watching the grieving mourners — journalists, police officers and the down-right nosey — begin to reverently file in, Molly was a little perplexed. Soon, every pew was filled and it became apparent that there would be standing room only. Organ music suddenly cut through the sad atmosphere as the organist began to play the notes on the sheet music in front of him. As he concentrated on the chords, not wanting to hit a wrong note or pull an incorrect stop, a sad lament began to fill the church.

Molly and Ged watched the procession of six smartly-dressed pallbearers carry her coffin down the nave of the church, before carefully lowering it onto the trestles which were placed in front of the altar. Molly admired the mahogany coffin which her mother had chosen for her. She approved of the wood, which was shiny and polished and she loved the gold-plated handles, which glinted in the sunlight. Molly gave an involuntary shudder at the realisation that her physical remains were inside the wooden box. Looking down on the coffin, she admired the arrangements of wreaths and posies which had been carefully placed on its lid; her mother knew they were her favourites — pink roses and baby's breath. Annie had requested that the floral display which spelled out Molly's name be positioned in front of the coffin, while an enlarged, portrait-sized photograph of her was placed on an easel next to the altar. Molly remembered the photograph being taken two years ago on her eighteenth birthday, when her mother and Nan had surprised her with a party at the local social club. Looking around, Molly noticed that there were floral tributes all around the church.

"Blimey, it looks like a flower shop in here — Interflora must have had a field day," she quipped to her grandfather.

Catching sight of Debbie who was sitting with her mother and father, Molly went over and sat next to her. Debbie held herself erect and adjusted the veil of the black pillbox hat she was wearing. She couldn't stop looking at the coffin which now held the body of her dead, beautiful, best friend.

"Don't blame yourself Debs, it wasn't your fault," Molly whispered, as she heard Debbie's thoughts. Debbie shifted position on the hard-wooden pew.

"You okay love?" Beth whispered, concerned. She reached over to give Debbie's hand a gentle squeeze.

"Yeah, I'm okay Mum. I just can't believe that she's gone."

Taking a small compact mirror out of her handbag, she checked that her eye makeup wasn't smudged. But in that instant her eyes brimmed with tears as she recalled the last time she had used that same mirror.

Molly wrapped her energy around her best friend and giving her a hug, whispered, "Don't fret, Debs. I'm fine and we can still do Karaoke if you want to."

Debbie suddenly became very hot and casually unfastened the buttons on her jacket before fanning herself with the order of service booklet.

Molly thought back to when she and Debbie were kids growing up together; how she wished that they could have grown old together as well. She remembered when they used to play truant — it had usually been during the religious study period, which to her mind had been 'dead boring', so they had never given it much thought. After all, religion and going to church hadn't been cool. She tried to remember the last time she had even been to church. Like a bolt out of the blue, she suddenly remembered that it was when her grandfather had died. She knew she had attended his funeral, but as hard as she tried, the memory of the event eluded her. Returning to her grandfather's side, she looked out across the congregation. She was pleased that so many people had come to her funeral to say their last goodbyes. Molly floated around the church and eavesdropped on conversations and quiet whispers. She felt momentarily sad as she looked at all the people dabbing at their eyes in a sea of white tissues and handkerchiefs.

"Look Gramps. Just look at how many people are here. Even the local newspaper and national television are here, and that nice policeman who looked after Mam and Nan is here too. Does this mean I'm famous?"

"Well that's one way off looking at it," he replied with a frown. Ged floated down into the congregation and hovering behind Nan, gently placed his hand on her shoulders, giving her a gentle squeeze.

"Jesus, I swear somebody just walked over me grave," she said, and gave an involuntary shiver. Taking another tissue from the small packet which was clenched in her fist, she continued to wipe her tears away. She was glad that she had waterproof mascara on. Molly nestled next to her mother, who kept her head bowed while quietly sobbing into the open hymn book.

Continuing to glance around the church, Molly could see spirit guides and guardian angels standing next to the people they were assigned to. "Getting busy in here, isn't it?"

Ged gave a nod as he looked around the full church. "Aye, a good funeral is always a crowd puller."

Molly noticed the sudden change in atmosphere within the church, which had begun to feel charged and energised. Looking round, she realised that lots of other Spirit orbs were joining the gathering, and she watched as they began to settle into prime positions within the rafters and joists, almost as though they had a ring-side seat.

"Grandpa, who are all these other Spirit people? And why is that old lady waving at me?"

Ged looked round and smiling, waved back. "Oh, I'm sorry Titch, I forgot. They are all your relatives. You will get to meet and catch up with them all later. I can't wait for you to meet your Auntie Alice and your Great Grandma Hilda. She's a scream. She's the one who's waving."

Molly returned a wave, before turning her attention back to the altar as the sad dirge of the organ faded and her farewell service began. Looking over Nan's shoulder, she read the 'Order of Service' and enjoyed singing along to the hymns that her mother had chosen. She even joined in with the Lord's Prayer, before getting bored and transforming into an orb. She floated effortlessly around the organist and the priest, and laughing to herself, played tricks on people in the congregation. Floating above their heads, she stroked their hair or gently blew onto their faces. She laughed as they would suddenly scratch their heads or brush aside an invisible cobweb. Molly was delighted with her mischief, and giggling, went back to join Ged who had found a nice little niche, up in the church rafters.

"So how long does this go on for?"

"Why, are you bored?" asked Ged.

"Yeah you can say that again — bored to death," Molly replied, grinning and laughing at her own joke.

"Really Molly — talk about inappropriate!"

They both looked on as the priest asked the congregation to stand in prayer. With heads bowed and eyes closed, the quietness only served to amplify the blowing of sniffles and the wiping away of tears. Suddenly, just above the middle of the nave, a dot of light appeared and seemed to hang in mid-air over the congregation. Molly and Ged watched, fascinated, as the dot of light began to expand, before turning into an enormous funnel of the brightest white light that Molly had ever seen. It grew larger and larger until it filled the entire church, and expanded across and above the congregation.

"Whoa, what's happening?" exclaimed Molly, as a broad smile crossed Ged's face.

"Ah, see now, it's the angels of mourning — they've come to give upliftment to everyone here. The Great Spirit knows that this can be a very difficult time for some folk, especially for the ones who have forgotten that life is everlasting, so he sends the mourning angels to help them carry their burden of grief and sadness."

The brilliant light began to permeate into every space and recess within the fabric of the church, and through the light Molly could see a multitude of angels descending. They floated serenely among the congregation, going about their work, gently and delicately touching the heads of everyone there and blessing each person in turn. The air was filled with angelic singing and chanting voices, and golden specks of healing energy fluttered and wafted downwards off the angels' resplendent wings, coating the congregation in a fine layer of healing dust. A movement suddenly caught Molly's attention as she noticed four different angels standing close to her mother and Nan. They were tall and elegant, yet serene in their approach, and each of them glowed and radiated a different colour. One of the angels was dressed in robes of the most beautiful hue of violet, another was in cerise pink, the third had cascading robes the colour of green chartreuse, and the fourth was illuminated in russet and umber browns.

Each of the angels wore a sapphire blue braid around their waist, and as Molly watched, the braids began to loosen and unfurl. Through unseen forces they began to twist and entwine, taking on a life of their own as they blindly but purposefully searched for one another, each end finding its counterpart as they joined to form a blue healing mesh around the two grieving women, who were standing in silent prayer. The four angels unfolded their wings and moved closer, surrounding Nan and Annie. Each angel bowed forwards and manoeuvred themselves so that the tips of their wings touched, becoming intertwined to form an umbrella-like structure over the two women. Molly watched, fascinated, as pearlescent beads of pink, silver and gold began to explode around them, raining miniscule droplets of healing energy; they were being enveloped in love, peace and serenity. Mesmerised, Molly looked on as the four angels started to sway backwards and forwards, and began gently rocking her mother and Nan in a slow, rhythmic movement which was hypnotic and soothing to watch. The angels then appeared to meld into a single mass of white, shimmering energy, which began to swirl around the women, starting at their feet, and gradually rising until it was level with their hearts. Molly noticed the energy begin to change colour from white to pink, then green and blue and finally to yellow, after which they separated into prisms of colour which curved over the women in an arc of intense, shimmering light. Then, just as suddenly as they had appeared, the angels were gone and the funnel of light shrunk back to the size of a rain drop, and evaporated in a shard of sunlight which glistened through a stained-glass window.

Molly sat speechless, amazed at what she had just witnessed. "Wow! Did you see that, Grandpa? That was so cool! Do they do that at everyone's funeral?"

"Absolutely — each and every one," he replied. "Spectacular, wasn't it? And those four angels, the ones who were gathered around Nan and your mother, well, they're called the pillars — the pillars of strength — and they come to give support and sustenance to those who are bereft. They work with Archangel Azrael."

Molly was in awe. "Yes, they were amazing, and the colours were beautiful, Grandpa — so bright and vivid."

Ged pondered on what Molly had just said and then replied, "Yes, they do appear to be intense when seen from our side, just like when you're in the Garden or Library or wherever. But you do realise that as Spirit we don't have need of any of the human senses?"

"Huh, I was beginning to, but wasn't completely sure," she replied, a little perplexed.

"Well, obviously we don't need to taste anything, we hear and speak by telepathy, and we don't need to touch. We just need to be able to sense our surroundings. It's the same for colours. We sense them by the vibrations that they emit, or we can recall them as a memory."

Molly looked even more puzzled as Ged continued, "In reality Molly, there is no such thing as colour. As you know, there is a whole spectrum of light, and when we are in a physical body part of the spectrum is visible because our eyes and brain respond differently to each frequency and wavelength. We perceive the intensity, shading and depth of visible colours through our physical eyes."

Molly scratched her head, deliberating. "Yeah well... whatever. All I know is that the angels' colours were beautiful and I get the feeling that the colours are symbolic of something. The problem is I can't remember which colour is for what — don't suppose you know do you?"

Ged considered the question himself. "Hmm, let me think. Oh... got it. The pink is for unconditional love, the green is for healing, both of body and mind, the brown is for earthly connection, and violet, well that's for the unbreakable bond that we have to the spiritual realm," he said, pleased with himself for remembering them all.

"And the blue braids are for conscious connection!" interrupted Molly excitedly. "Wow! How did I know that?"

Ged smiled to himself. "You've always known it — you just needed reminding of it."

Molly inched nearer to her grandfather, slipped her hand into his and gave it a gentle squeeze, while they continued to watch her funeral. As the church service finally ended, the pall bearers reverentially carried the coffin out of the church, and placed it gently and carefully into the back of the black hearse, before neatly arranging the floral tributes around it again. Molly felt very special as the procession of mourners respectfully followed her to what would be her proper, final resting place.

The sadness was palpable, as tearfully locked in their own capsules of grief, the mourners watched as the shiny, wooden coffin was gently lowered into the body of the earth. Inching forwards towards the gaping hole, each of the mourners gathered round to throw handfuls of dry earth, flowers, and personal mementos, including one teddy bear, into the grave. Molly looked on, contemplating what purpose the gifts served. It was bizarre really, she thought to herself. After all, what the hell was she meant to do with them, given that she was dead! Positioning herself between the two most important women she had ever known, she gave each of them a huge Spirit hug and watched as most of the mourners began to drift away and return to their everyday lives.

Molly and Ged accompanied Annie and Nan back to the house, where the small family wake was to be held. Relatives who had faded from memory suddenly re-appeared and indulged in the free food and drink which was on offer. Tears flowed as easily as the sherry, but Annie knew that she would probably never see half of these people ever again — for which she was actually quite relieved. Eventually the guests left, and the house quietened and became their own once again. Molly was ecstatically happy in the knowledge that there was so much love for her. She sat with Nan, and snuggling up to her, began to tell her all about the family and friends she had met up with from the spiritual realm. Not that Nan heard though.

Annie was in the kitchen making a pot of tea. Carrying a tray laden with the best china and a packet of biscuits through to the living room, she set it down on the coffee table.

"Good turnout for our Molly, and the priest said some lovely kind words. I thought the service went very well. And all those people taking the time and trouble... I didn't know half of them, mind. Reckon some folk will do ought for a free butty," Annie said, a little peeved.

Molly smiled to herself and went over to her mother and gave her a hug.

Coughing into a crumpled linen handkerchief, Nan cleared her throat. "Aye, I know. It's bloody amazing who comes out of the woodwork. Bloody vultures, the lot of 'em! it was the same when your Dad died — haven't seen one of the greedy sods since, not a one."

"Honestly, Nan, you're such a cynic. Folk mean well, I suppose, it's just that they feel awkward. They probably don't know what to say for the best."

"Well that's as maybe, but where were they when we needed 'em, eh? Answer me that. Load of bloody freeloaders!"

Annie raised her eyes up to the ceiling and tutted under her breath. "Anyways, I was thinking about her headstone. Will you come to the stonemasons with me tomorrow? We need to choose one and get it engraved. I don't know which to go for, black or white marble, or even granite — what do you think? Mind, I suppose it all depends on the price."

Annie poured the hot, steaming tea into the nearest teacup, not seeming to care that some was splashing into the saucer. Nan helped herself to milk and sugar, and then proceeded to dunk a biscuit, managing to get it into her mouth before it had a chance to fall back into the cup.

Looking thoughtful, Nan said, "Suppose a white one would be fitting. There's no rush any road, the ground will have to settle first. I wonder what she's doing now. Probably out clubbing in the big disco in the sky, knowing our Molly, or singing in one of them daft karyacky things," she said, with a mouthful of digestive.

Annie suddenly burst out crying, as wracking sobs forced their way out of her slender frame. Nan was taken aback at the suddenness of it, but felt relieved that Annie had finally let at least a little of the burden of grief go. Nan knew how strong Annie had been, and how she had fought to keep her composure during the funeral. Passing her the box of tissues which was on the sideboard, she gently rested her hand on Annie's shoulder. Taking one of the tissues, Annie forced a weak smile and took her cardigan off, neatly folding it before laying it over the back of the armchair. Sitting down again, she nestled into the chair and sighed deeply.

Nan frowned. "You all right? God, I'm roasting. Is it hot in here, or is it me?"

Ged smiled to himself, knowing full well that Annie and Nan were being showered with loving energy which he and Molly were sending to them.

As nightfall began to steal what was left of the day, Molly and Ged reluctantly returned to the spiritual realm.

"Oh Grandpa, that was amazing. It was lovely meeting up with everyone again. You were right about Great Grandma Hilda — she is hilarious. And as for Uncle Bob, he was so kind. Did you know he had a soft spot for Nan? I had a really great time and I enjoyed my funeral. I had forgotten how much fun there is in a 'fun'eral."

Ged laughed at her drollness and play on words. "Get you! Quite the wit, aren't you? I'm really glad you had a great time. After all, funerals are the biggest welcome home parties imaginable, and you'll get to meet up with them again anytime you like. They will always be there for you Molly, because as you can see, we're one big family after all."

Chapter Twenty-one: Discovery

<***>

Mr Arthur Ambrose, the owner of a 'Double-Fronted, Four-Bedroomed, Detached Family Home, Set In A Beautiful Rural Location', was driving over to the said property to check that everything was as it should be. The Estate Agent had rung him earlier in the week to tell him that a couple had been into their office and having seen the property details, would like to view the property this coming weekend.

Mr Ambrose was feeling optimistic about selling the house. Yes, it needed some work doing to it, but it was a fair asking price, and the house was, after all, in a lovely part of the countryside and also came with several outbuildings. Being recently widowed, he had reasoned that there was no point in continuing to live in such a large, rambling family home on his own. After Jean, his wife of fifty-eight years, had passed away, Arthur had moved in with his daughter, Hillary, and her family. Both Hillary and Jason, his son-in-law, had busy professional careers and although Mr Ambrose had offered them the house, they had declined, preferring instead to stay in the city. They had built an extension to the downstairs of their house and turned it into a granny flat, a turn of phrase which the three grandchildren had found hilarious.

Moving in with his daughter had been one of the best decisions he had ever made, and although initially he had had some doubts about selling the house, he knew it was the right thing to do; the prospect of moving into a retirement home just wasn't for him. He had every intention of giving the money from the sale of the house to his daughter anyway — God knows she deserved it.

Having made an early start to avoid most of the traffic, Arthur pulled into the driveway just as dawn was breaking. Looking across the rolling farmland, he felt a tinge of nostalgia, as memories of the happy life he and his family had shared in the house surfaced unexpectantly. Breathing in the fresh, cool air of the autumnal morning, he made a mental note that the front lawn could do with a mow — it would probably be the last one of the year — and the flower beds needed a tidy up too. He also had to get around to repairing the side gate, as it was half hanging off its hinges, and the guttering over the front bedroom window needed attention. Still he thought, if this couple were serious, then perhaps he wouldn't need to do any of the repairs.

Fishing out the bunch of keys from his jacket pocket, he selected the mortice key which opened the front porch door, and pushing it home, wiggled it in the lock, which turned stiffly, protesting at being disturbed. Stepping into the porch, he noticed the black mildew on the paintwork around the window frames, and let out a heavy sigh. He opened the front door, walked into the hallway and immediately gagged as the smell of damp and death snaked its way up into his nostrils — he'd know that stench anywhere. Arthur had served in the British army as a medical officer in the Medical Corps during the Second World War and had been stationed at a military hospital in Bologna in Italy. During the war he had attended to many soldiers who had been badly injured and maimed. Once that smell became impregnated in your nostrils, you never forgot it; the stench of death and gangrene had become permanently etched in the memory.

Continuing to gag and wretch involuntarily, he found a freshly ironed handkerchief in his jacket pocket and covering his mouth and nose with it, mentally thanked his daughter for her thoughtfulness. Surmising that a field mouse or some other such rodent had got into the house and met with a grisly end, he pressed the handkerchief even tighter against his face. Venturing further down the hallway and tentatively opening the door into the living room, he waited for his eyes to adjust to the gloom and began to recognise a make-shift camp. Nervously walking into the middle of the room, he called out to see if anyone was there and nervously listened for a reply; none came, for which he was very relieved. Arthur looked despairingly around at the mess which was strewn everywhere. Empty cans, food wrappers and half-eaten scraps of food were scattered all over the floor, making the stench even more unbearable. He ran over to a window and hurriedly released the catch, opening it as wide as it would go. Gulping down lungfuls of cool fresh air, he fought to regain his composure. Stealing several deeper breaths, he braced himself, and pressed the handkerchief even more firmly to his face, before leaving the comfort of the open window. It was all he could do to suppress his gag reflex and curtail the rising bile.

He wafted his hand ineffectively at the buzzing flies which had annoyingly begun to circle around his head, and peered into the gloom. His attention was drawn to the far end of the through room, where he could just make out a shape in front of the Adams fireplace. With trepidation he slowly approached the unmoving, blue mound, and giving it a gentle poke with his foot, suddenly realised that it was a body curled up in the foetal position. With its knees drawn up to its chest, the decomposing remains of the body lay half in and half out of a sleeping bag.

It took Arthur a few seconds to fully comprehend what he was looking at. Then he staggered backwards as the full realisation hit him. Retching violently, his stomach parted company with the full English breakfast he'd eaten earlier, narrowly missing his newly polished, leather shoes.

D.S Millington placed the phone handset back in its cradle, and a wide grin crossed his face. "Bradley, you're not gonna believe this! They've found a body, and would you believe, it's only bloody Gareth Shaw. The local lads are there now. I've told them to hang fire and wait till we get there. Don't want any cock-ups now, do we?"

Since her funeral, Molly had been very proactive. She regularly checked on what was going on in the incident room, and happened to be there when all hell was let loose. As the two police officers ran to one of the waiting police cars, she followed closely, and settling herself on the back seat, clapped her hands with anticipation. Millington switched on the blue lights and sirens, and felt the adrenalin surge through his veins as he pulled out of the station compound.

It was the frantic phone call which Mr Ambrose had made to the local police station that had caused P.C Brendan, one of the local bobbies, to go over to the farm house. He was as shocked as Mr Ambrose at the terrible discovery, and had identified the remains from the ID card which he'd found in the kitchen. If it hadn't had been for the fact that Gareth's name was being circulated on the national list of most wanted criminals, P.C. Brendan would have thought that the incident was no more than a case of a squatter who had taken up residence in the empty property having met with a grisly end.

Molly, Millington and Bradley arrived a couple of hours later. Entering the house, they went through to the room where most of the activity was taking place. Introducing themselves to the other officers already there, Millington and Bradley navigated their way through the living to get to the dead. Molly excitedly followed the two policemen but abruptly stopped in her tracks as she stared at what lay before her. She stood transfixed as she studied Gareth Shaw's face; not that there was much of a face left to study — the maggots had seen to that.

Standing over the decaying corpse, Millington lifted the lapel of his jacket and pressed it firmly over his mouth and nose in an effort to stop the reek of death permeating into his olfactory bulb. Looking around Mr Ambrose's dining room, he gave a self-satisfied grin. He had started to think that Molly's murder investigation was going nowhere, with the real possibility that it could even become a cold case. His greatest fear had been that they would never find Gareth Shaw, or bring the scumbag to justice, as it appeared that he'd gone to ground and had totally dropped off the radar. Millington felt elated that at last he had found Molly's murderer. A dead murderer, true, but nevertheless, he had finally got his man, and what would subsequently come to light was anybody's guess. The chaotic mess in the room was already telling a story of someone who had been in total desperation.

Millington stepped to one side as the Forensics team arrived, and the room suddenly became a hive of activity. Molly was bewildered at the number of people dressed top-to-toe in white overalls, their faces hidden behind masks as though they were masquerading at a fancy-dress ball. Cameras flashed sporadically, and the rustle of plastic tape and evidence bags being unfurled filled the air. Millington knew it would be a long process, and half the afternoon was already gone. Standing over by the open window, he let them get on with their job. One of the Forensic officers was bagging and labelling any items which were in his assigned gridded area and was immediately suspicious when he came across a bedside lamp secreted in an old battered holdall. "Guv, over here!" he said, looking in Millington's direction. "I'm not sure, but I think I might have found something," he exclaimed as he pulled off his face mask and repositioned it on his forehead. Millington craned his neck to get a better look at the item that was clenched in the officer's latex-gloved hand. Molly went over and looked too.

Millington scratched his forehead. "Hmm, very salubrious. When we searched his bed-sit, there was nothing there which we could identify as being a likely murder weapon, but I remember seeing a broken lamp shade. Looks like this may be the lamp it belonged to and given that the sneaky bastard took it away with him, I'd put money on this being the missing murder weapon. I think you'd better take special care of that," Millington said gravely.

"Yeah, you'd better take special care of it," repeated Molly, wagging her finger in the forensic officer's face.

Millington stood next to Bradley and thrust his hands into his trouser pockets, jingling the loose change. They watched in tentative silence as Gareth Shaw's remains were placed inside a black body bag. Glancing surreptitiously at each other, they couldn't help but give one another a knowing smirk as they heard the sound of the closing zip. Looking around the room, Millington was satisfied that there would be more than enough evidence to nail the bastard, even though he was dead. He was counting on it for Molly and her family — after all, seeing justice done was what being a copper was all about. Turning on his heel, he strode out of the room, and felt a tingle run up and down his spine as he left the house to its memories.

The following morning Millington was back on duty, and sifting through the ever-increasing mound of papers and files, felt more than a little pleased with himself. He waited until it was after nine am before he dialled the number for the Coroner's Office. After waiting impatiently for his call to be answered, he asked the receptionist what time the post mortem was going to be performed. He could hear the familiar tapping of the computer keyboard and felt strangely reassured.

"It's scheduled for ten thirty tomorrow morning. I'll make sure that you get the Pathologist's report as soon as possible."

Molly had been waiting for Millington to show up and had listened to the conversation. She immediately decided that she would be attending Gareth-bloody-Shaw's post mortem.

Lifting the handset again, Millington dialled Annie Robert's number. In an instant Molly was standing behind Nan as the phone rang. Annie got up wearily from the kitchen table to answer it, and absent-mindedly fumbled with the coiled wire of the handset as she listened intently to the caller's voice.

"Mrs Roberts? It's D.S Millington. Is it okay if I come round? There's been a major development in our investigation."

Annie's hands were shaking as she put the phone down.

"Who was that?" Nan asked, puzzled.

"It was D.S. Millington — he's calling round. He said there's been a major development."

"Major development. About bloody time an' all. Major development, my eye! What the hell does that mean?" Nan chided, shaking her head.

Molly knew exactly what it meant. Although it felt strange being able to eavesdrop on conversations, knowing that she was invisible made it all the more thrilling. She went over to her mother and gave her a big cuddle before settling down beside her on the couch.

"Is it hot in here, or is it me?" Annie asked, taking off her cardigan.

Nan clicked her tongue. "Bloody hell, Annie, you and your hot flushes! You should go and see the doctor or sommat, I bet you're starting with that menaclause thing. I remember when I went through it — okay one minute, then sweating buckets the next. I think it started just after your dad died, as if I didn't have enough on my plate! Right, I'm going to put the kettle on for a cuppa. Do you want one?"

Annie shook her head as she fanned herself with a half-folded magazine. "No ta, I'll wait till he comes, if it's all the same."

Chapter Twenty-two: Further Evidence

<***>

Nathan Bennett mentally prepared himself for the autopsy of the case which had come through the doors of the morgue the previous day. The entire building appeared to be busier and noisier than usual, and he couldn't wait for the circus of people to leave so that he could get on with his job. Stealing himself for the long haul, he hurriedly made himself a cup of strong coffee, anticipating that it would be a while before he would have time to have another one.

He entered the ante-room, and gowned up in the standard green coverall before donning the required splash-proof boots. He tied a full-length, protective apron around his middle and grabbed a pair of large-sized latex gloves which were in a box fixed to the wall. Going through to the autopsy room, he waited for the technician to position the remains of the corpse on the gleaming, stainless steel autopsy table. The odour of decomposition exuding from the remains reminded him that it had been a while since he had performed a post mortem on a body with this amount of putrefaction.

Nathan was aware that 'Gareth Shaw (Deceased)', was the main suspect in a police investigation into the murder of a young woman — the same young woman that had been lying on this same table only a couple of months before. He knew the case very well, as he was still waiting for the courts to decide on an inquest date.

Casting a glance over the equipment which had been set up by the technician, he checked to reassure himself that everything which he was likely to need was to hand. He hated it when it was a new 'techie', especially one who didn't know his routine and wasn't used to his ways of working. Nathan became easily irritated if he had to wait while they scuttled off to find something which was missing, when through sheer incompetence they had forgotten to put it on the trolley. He glanced at the wall clock, making a mental note of the time, and turned the extractor fan onto its maximum setting. Going over to one of the wall cupboards, he retrieved a small bottle of aftershave and dabbed some of the fragrant liquid onto his top lip, in an attempt to disguise the smell of putrid flesh. Then he set to work, mainly in silence which the young assistant was grateful for; she didn't mind not having to exchange pleasantries with Nathan, and she had been forewarned that he was a man of few words. He carefully scrutinised every inch of what remained of Gareth's corpse, and after satisfying himself that he had gathered as much material evidence as he could, selected a sharp scalpel from the prepared trolley. Hesitating slightly, he delivered the first incision into the decayed flesh.

Molly positioned herself so that she could look over his shoulder for a better view. Completely engrossed in the unfolding event, she failed to notice the uncharacteristic chill which pervaded the atmosphere of the mortuary, as Gareth's spirit materialised high up in the corner of the room — a vantage point he'd chosen to give him a bird's-eye view of what the pathologist was doing. Becoming totally absorbed, Gareth watched, fascinated, as the pathologist cut open and dissected the decayed body which had once been his physical vessel. He couldn't help thinking what a waste of time this all was, and laughed to himself at the thought that the living always needed to find a cause of death. It was as if they needed to find an explanation why someone had died as their way of keeping the books straight, as it were. Yet, if truth be told, what did it matter? After all, by then the vessel had already served its purpose. Suddenly Gareth noticed another spirit light just behind Nathan's shoulder and instantly recognised it. Momentarily perturbed, he kept still so as not to be noticed and watched Molly, watching his post-mortem.

Performing the examination with his usual level of care and attention to detail, it took Nathan just under five hours to complete all the procedures. He made sure that every sample and specimen was bagged, labelled and logged; he knew that the evidence which he collected had to be the very best it could be. Nathan was fully aware of how the legal system worked, and knew that having to stand in the witness box and give evidence on his findings at the inquest could be just about as tough as it got, especially with a murder investigation. He wasn't about to give some jumped-up, wet-behind-the-ears, smarmy lawyer any reason to discredit the evidence — his evidence. Nathan Bennett wasn't going to let that happen, because Nathan already knew that Gareth Shaw was guilty as charged, and even though it would be a couple of days or so before all the forensic tests were processed, the evidence confirming his guilt was as plain as the nose on Nathan's face.

Removing his examination gloves, he dropped them into the clinical waste bin and looked over to where the assistant technician stood. Taking a deep breath, he bristled. "I thought that light had been fixed. It's really getting on my bloody nerves, flickering and buzzing like that. See to it, will you?" Nathan hurriedly removed the rest of his garb, and leaving the assistant to finish off cleaning and clearing the room and the equipment he had used, he went into the office and made himself a much deserved, fresh cup of coffee. Molly followed him, and positioning herself so that she could see what he was doing, waited impatiently for him to start writing his report.

Nathan already knew what the cause of death was, because of the amount of tissue necrosis which was evident, particularly to the left shin. Damage like that, together with the resulting major organ failure, could only mean one thing and that was an untreated infection. The resulting infection would probably been as a result of some sort of injury, even something quite minor like a toe nail being scratched down the shin. After becoming infected, such an injury could easily have caused blood poisoning, if left untreated.

Molly read the computer screen over Nathan's shoulder as he typed up his notes. At the bottom of the template form there was a box labelled 'CAUSE OF DEATH'. Nathan typed in the blank space, *'Multiple organ failure due to bacterial sepsis.'* After reading the words, Molly punched the air ecstatically, allowing a broad grin to cross her face. She couldn't begin to describe the jubilation she felt. 'At last,' she told herself. At last she felt retribution, at last she could gloat and relish his demise.

Nathan's attention was suddenly drawn to the flickering ceiling light, and looking up, he tutted to himself in irritation, before drawing in a deep, exasperated breath.

Wandering back to the room where Gareth's remains had been stored, Molly went over to the refrigeration cabinet, and pressed her energy against its door, allowing herself to seep through the metal and into the space which lay behind. Looking down at the putrid mass, she revelled in the knowledge that he too was now dead and couldn't help breaking into hysterical laughter. Then she suddenly became livid with anger and rage and found herself screaming at what remained of the soulless shell, "Damn you, Gareth Shaw, you piggin' bastard, you absolute piece of shite! I hate and despise you so much that I hope you rot in hell."

Gareth Shaw didn't witness any of Molly's rantings; he had already left the mortuary and returned to the spiritual realm.

Chapter Twenty-three: The Keepers of Akasha

<***>

Orick was waiting for Molly to return as he had been instructed to escort her to the Halls of Wisdom. As soon as she entered the spiritual realm, he got a fix on her light.

"Where have you been?" he enquired.

"Nowhere, why?" she lied.

Orick stared at her intently. "I'm to take you to the Halls of Wisdom, where you're to be given access to the inner sanctum. You're to meet with the Keepers of the Akasha and they've requested for you to be brought before them as soon as possible."

Molly looked down, somewhat sheepishly. She realised that he knew damn well where she'd been, yet she didn't really care. Following him down one of the corridors, she entered the room which Orick indicated. Bracing herself in anticipation, Molly stood before the Keepers. They were the guardians of knowledge, the seers and sages of what had been and what was to come, and they held the collective wisdom of cosmic law and divinity. Glancing around, she vaguely remembered having been in the sanctum on previous occasions, or at least she thought she had.

Molly felt nervous, and fidgeted while daring to furtively glance at the light-beings that made up the revered Council. She couldn't actually see them, but somehow sensed that they were seated in a semi-circle before her, and she could feel them scrutinising her. Orick had positioned himself to her left and suddenly she became aware of an energy-being standing to her right. Glancing to her side, she saw an enormous, glowing ball of intense white and gold light. In a moment of recognition, she realised it was Thumus, her guardian angel. Molly gave an audible gasp of surprise as she suddenly remembered him.

"Thumus!" she cried out, forgetting herself as she affectionately flung her arms around him. At that moment she felt her own light energy reconnect with his, as a spark of energy leapt between them. Molly couldn't stop herself from grinning. Feeling her heart swell with love, she knew that having Thumus with her would make everything all right; he gave her a sense of great reassurance and comfort.

Molly swallowed hard as one of the Keepers glided over to a huge marble lectern which held centre stage. He was carrying a large but very slim file, which he placed carefully on the lectern. Looking affectionately over to where Molly was, he bowed his head respectfully before returning to his seat. Molly tried to avert her gaze, but her attention was drawn to the file which looked like it was made of layer upon layer of compressed, white feathers. Transfixed, she watched as the file opened by itself and the words written within rose above the gleaming, white, translucent pages. The edges of the pages began changing colour from gold to purple, then to silver before changing back to gold again. She stared as the pages began to turn themselves over, one by one.

Molly noticed a strange flickering behind the seated gathering, and realised that the file had somehow become a projector, and pictures were being projected onto the wall of the sanctum. It reminded her of being in a cinema watching a film, but a film which had depth and detail, and an almost tangible texture to it. Molly was suddenly aware that she was actually watching the events and memories of her last life, her last incarnation. She gawped in awe as she observed her spirit light entering what was to become her new mortal body. Molly smiled as a glowing, yellow, pulsating light illuminated the womb in which it was nestled. Mesmerised, she watched as the life-force energy of Prana began to surge and pulsate, circulating throughout what was to become her physical vessel, as she and the unborn baby became completely connected and co-dependent. She felt pure joy as she witnessed her transition into physical consciousness, and watched as she developed into a human baby. Molly couldn't begin to describe the mounting elation and excitement she felt as she witnessed herself being born, and she found herself thinking about the symmetry of being born into light and then ultimately returning to light.

Without warning, the leader of the Keepers crossed the floor, and Molly was abruptly distracted as the movement broke her concentration. She dared to sneak a sideways glance at the great being, and was dazzled by her beauty and elegance. The Keeper radiated a shimmering pink and yellow aura and had deep-set, blue eyes and high cheek bones. Molly quickly cast her glance down as she realised that she was staring. Standing in front of the lectern, the Keeper studied the file as the pages continued to turn. With eyes full of loving expression, she periodically looked directly at Molly before returning her attention back to the file. Finally, the Elder finished reading, and stepped away from the lectern. Molly sensed a movement, and realised that one by one, the Keepers were raising themselves to their full stature and looking over in her direction. Then each one turned respectfully, nodded and returned to their seated positions. Molly struggled to control herself and barely managed to stifle a giggle, as the scene reminded her of a Mexican wave. Orick and Thumus both glanced at her and scowled.

Turning to face Molly, the Leader of the Keepers waved her hand across the file.

"Beloved One, welcome. We are the Keepers of the Akasha and I am Kyah, leader of the Keepers. It is our collective duty to oversee all Akashic viewings, but only I will converse with you this day."

Molly was transfixed and suddenly realised that the great light-being was speaking to her telepathically.

"Do you know what this is?" Kyah asked, indicating the white-feathered file. Hardly daring to move, Molly shook her head.

"This is the Akashic testimony of your previous life-lived, and this element will eventually blend with, and into your entire

Akashic record thus far. Your Akashic record holds the essence and verification of your pure energy vibration; it is the cosmic validation of who you are. It records and holds what you've learned and authenticates all of your deeds and experiences, both good and bad, within the earth realm, within the cosmos — including all dimensions of time and space — and within the spiritual realm. It holds the transcript of what is your soul's karmic journey, and ultimately your soul's evolvement."

Molly listened intently but decided to say nothing as it was evident that she didn't need to — the Elder would know what she was thinking anyway.

"Your Akasha holds, amongst other things, the cosmic imprint of your soul's spark, which is the Great Spirit's ultimate plan for what will be your definitive destiny, a destiny which is never replicated, much like a fingerprint. Your pre-determined soul's journey, its destiny, and its chosen name are all unique, but because you have severe memory loss we are allowing you to re-integrate with your full Akashic narrative, in the hope that witnessing your past lives again will help you to regain most, if not all, of your lost memories. As for those memories which you cannot reconnect to or recollect, well you will have to trust that they are in existence."

Molly shuffled nervously, conscious that all eyes were upon her as she began to fidget.

"It saddens us all deeply, as it does the Great Spirit, that you need to have this done, and similarly it saddens us that you have forgotten your soul name. Beloved, here you are known as Brenth, for that is your chosen name, a name which is as divine as you are."

Molly frowned and momentarily forgetting herself exclaimed indignantly, "Unique? You're telling me that I'm one of a kind and that I chose that name? Really? Brenth... what a daft name! Why on earth would I choose that? Can't I just be called Molly – I like that name, and it's way better than a rubbish name like Brenth." Molly continued to moan and complain, seemingly indifferent to whom she was addressing.

Orick moved forwards to remonstrate with her, but Kyah raised her hand to prevent him.

"Very well. For now, you may continue to use your earth name, but eventually you will come to be known once again as Brenth. It is, after all, the name you chose for your own divine self. As for everything else, all that is will be, and all that is to come, will manifest."

Molly felt herself relax, and was just about to give a sigh of relief when Kyah addressed her again.

"There is, however, another facet to all of this, one which you are obviously unaware of because of your memory loss. Brenth, I have need to remind you that you have reached your conscious ascension."

"What do you mean?" she asked in a surprised voice.

Smiling, Kyah answered, "It means that you have learned all of your earthly lessons. It means that having completed your physical life experiences, you have fulfilled your soul's contract, and you are now on the cusp of accessing a higher level of consciousness. Your ascension to a higher dimension was imminent; you were about to exist in a higher realm of continuation and way of being."

Molly didn't know what to say and glanced over to where Thumus was standing. Thumus could see the expression of confusion and bewilderment cross her face just as Kyah did. "You look somewhat disconcerted," she remarked.

Molly nodded slowly. "I'm just trying to take it all in. Ascension! Blimey, I had no idea. Jeez, there's more to this dying lark than I thought. I mean that's good isn't it, the ascension bit?"

"Yes, of course! Ascension is what every spirit and its soul ultimately strive to achieve. Ascension is the culmination and fulfilment of your soul's purpose — it is after all a soul's destiny to ascend. And just to remind you, there is no death, only eternal existence. However, Beloved, it has come to light that you have one final incarnation to complete which would have finalised your accomplished development, as it were. Alas, the other Keepers and I are not entirely certain that you currently have the ability to function again within a physical vessel, or that the implementation, or indeed, completion of another contract would be achievable, or even prudent for that matter. The decision as to whether you should experience that final incarnation, and what it would mean to you and to us if you didn't, has yet to be made."

Stooping down in front of the lectern, Kyah picked something up, and gliding over to Molly, held it out for her to take. "In light of what I have just told you, take this sacred scroll and be dutiful in your fulfilment."

Molly accepted the scroll and was about to unfurl it but thought better of it. "What is it?" she whispered,

"The content of this scroll is exclusively yours. It holds a strategy for your quest to recall your lost memories. It is also the foundation for your future preparation, should the decision be that you are not to incarnate. Study it well, Beloved One — study it well. Thumus and Orick will assist you in your required understanding."

Frowning, Molly was just about to ask further questions when she sensed that the other Keepers were leaving the room. She thought it best to say nothing further, and assuming that she had been dismissed, headed eagerly for the door.

Ged was waiting outside for her and breathed a sigh of relief as she appeared. "Well, how did it go?" he asked, nervously,

"Oh, it could have been worse, I s'pose. Orick and Thumus were with me, so I wasn't completely on my own, thank God. Honestly Grandpa, I've never felt so nervous or so… I don't know… lost! It's really a lot to take in, although Kyah was very kind. Just give us a minute while I read this."

"What is it?" he asked, as Molly unfurled the scroll.

She glanced over the words and let out a groan. "It's a… well, I suppose it's like a to-do list of things to help me regain my memory. I think Kyah said it's to prepare me for not going back to the earth realm again. Oh my God! No way… look at this…

"Firstly, I have to spend time with my soul group. Guess I'll be in the gardens a lot more then…

"Secondly, I'm to work with Orick to relearn my lessons and study cosmic law…

"Thirdly, I've to go to the library for tuition from Archangel Metatron, whoever he is… Let's see, what else? …

"And lastly, I've got to have lots of healing from Archangel Raphael and meet regularly with the Keepers and the Elders. Huh, they don't define 'regularly'."

Ged was reading the list over her shoulder. "Well that lot will keep you out of mischief for a while. And that's just for starters, I would think. They really are trying to help you to get your memory back," he said, scratching his head. "Anything else?"

Molly shook her head before suddenly remembering something. "Oh yeah, something about ascension. I couldn't really make sense of what she was saying. Anyway, I think I've got enough here to keep me going for a while, although there was… what was it? Oh yes, there is one other thing — apparently my name's not Molly, it's Brenth."

Ged smiled. "Ascension, eh? I must admit I did hear a rumour, and I was wondering when they would get around to telling you your actual name. Brenth is your divine name, after all. But if it's all the same, I'd like to keep calling you Molly. I don't think it matters really, not for the time being any road."

Molly bit her bottom lip. "Actually, I was a bit cheeky and told Kyah I'd much prefer to be called by my earth name. I can't believe that I told her that I thought Brenth was a rubbish name."

Ged frowned. "Really? You said that to Kyah? Well you might have lost your memory, but you sure as heck haven't lost your metal."

Molly frowned. "What do you mean, lost my metal?"

"You know — your confidence, your self-assurance, although I'd call it cockiness. Truth be told, I've always admired you for that. Anyway, getting back to the scroll — talk about jammy! You got off lightly considering what we got up to. You do realise that, don't you?"

Molly shrugged her shoulders. "Actually Gramps, I've a confession to make. The thing is, when I went with Orick to see the Elders... oh what's his name... you know, the leader one?"

"Pettruf."

"Yeah, that's it — Pettruf. Well, he said that I wasn't to leave the spiritual realm again."

Ged's face turned solemn. "He told you that? Then why did you?"

"Come on, Grandpa, you know full well why. Because I needed to find out what had happened to me. I needed to know. I'm sorry I didn't say anything and was a bit economical with the truth, but ..."

Ged shook his head. "But nothing. Honestly Molly, I don't know what to say. It never entered my head that you were, in effect, grounded. They must have been really concerned about you. But to not tell me — well that was downright dangerous and stupid. It never even occurred to me that you would do such a thing. How could you have been so silly?"

"I'm sorry, Grandpa. I know I should have told you, but if I had then, well, let's face it, you wouldn't have helped me, and I wouldn't have remembered anything, and just think of all the adventures we would have missed out on," she said cheerfully.

"Adventures!" Ged repeated, shaking his head at the absurdity of the whole mess. He sat down and put his head in his hands.

Molly sat down next to him and slipped her hand into his. "It's all my fault, I know and I'm really sorry that I didn't tell you, and I love you all the more for doing what you did for me, but there's no harm done, is there? Everything will be all right in the end."

"No harm done?" he retorted incredulously as he turned to stare at her. "No harm done?" he repeated.

Molly brightened. "Yeah, like I said, it will be all right. Anyway, what's the deal with you and Orick? What happened when you went to see the Elders — did you get into trouble too? And you haven't told me what your soul name is either yet"

Ged shook his head, realising that he couldn't stay annoyed at her for long. "Oh yeah, Orick and I got a rap on the knuckles, as it were — no thanks to you. We thought that we'd be in a right load of trouble, but I've not done too badly, all things considered. I'm expecting that there's more to come though, especially if we get hauled up before the Council of Wise Ones."

Molly pursed her lips guiltily, knowing full well that she had been the cause of her grandpa's admonishment.

"They've told me to work on a couple of lessons, such as honesty and truth. Same could be said for someone else not too far away — can't think who though," he said, winking. "And seeing as you've asked, my soul name is Cloiff, if you must know."

Molly couldn't contain herself, as a fit of giggles came over her. "Cloiff? What sort of a name is that? Cloiff?" she repeated. "Really, Grandpa, what were you thinking when you picked that one? Anyways, as far as I'm concerned, you will always be my grandpa, my grandpa Ged.

Chapter Twenty-four: Re-union

<***>

Molly left her grandfather in the Halls of Wisdom as she wanted to go back to the Gardens. As she entered, she realised why they were called the Gardens of Tranquillity. The atmosphere was calm and serene, and the air was both soporific and stimulating, with a sweet heady perfume. They were filled with the most amazing, vibrant, coloured flowers and trees that she had ever seen. Looking around, she noticed that the Gardens were actually larger than she remembered, as they seemed to disappear beyond the horizon, and completely surround the Halls of Wisdom. She was surprised that she hadn't previously noticed how they seemed to bring perfect balance and harmony to the imposing building which she had just left.

Molly was looking forward to meeting the members of her soul group again, and full of excitement, she quickly climbed up a small hillock to gain a better view. Looking into the distance, she searched for their familiar spirit lights and recognised two of them instantly. She rushed over to where Braugh and Vimprn were sitting together, and they embraced and hugged her as she arrived. Molly was overcome with emotion as she basked in their light energies.

"Wow, it's great seeing you both again. I'm so excited to tell you about what's been happening to me. Oh, I'd forgotten just how beautiful and tranquil it is here. Mind you, that's the problem — not remembering, I mean," she said ruefully.

Braugh and Vimprn had been instructed by the Elders to help Molly recall her past life memories. They were part of quite a large soul group, of which the three of them were the most advanced. They had reincarnated over many lifetimes, sometimes together, sometimes separately, depending on which lessons they were to learn and what life experiences they were to learn from. Braugh had assumed guidance of the group as he was the most experienced, with an energy print so powerful that his vibration rippled far from his core, and his light was so bright that he could be seen from a great distance, shining like a beacon.

Molly was eager to share with them what had happened to her and she recounted how she had been murdered, and how it had all gone horribly wrong. Braugh listened intently, periodically smiling and hugging her when she became over-awed or seemed distressed. Encouraged by Braugh, she began to relax and surrender to a feeling of euphoria.

Braugh suggested that she try to remember some of the past lives which they had shared together. Prompting her, he asked, "Do you remember the incarnation when we were both doctors and worked together in a leper colony? That was the lifetime in which we learned compassion and about being in service. That time we were man and wife."

Molly didn't remember and shook her head as a frown furrowed her brow.

"Or the lifetime when we learned tolerance? We were sisters for that one."

Again, Molly shook her head. "Honestly, Braugh, I don't know what I remember anymore. Hopefully my memories will come back eventually; I just wish they'd bloody well hurry up, that's all."

Braugh gave a weak smile. "I hope so too, Brenth, I really do hope so," he said, sighing deeply.

Molly suddenly reeled backwards in surprise, and a beaming smile crossed her face. "You called me Brenth — you called me by my soul name. I remember now. Oh Braugh, this is fantastic — I think you've triggered something! I've just had a rush of memories come flooding back. It must have been because you used my name."

Braugh looked pleased. "Wow that's great, but we'd assumed that you were fully merged — that you were once again melded."

Molly looked confused. "What do you mean? Merged? Melded? I don't know what you're on about."

"We thought you'd reconnected — you know, that your spirit and your soul had been re-united. We thought that you'd done that. Vimprn and I were under the impression that you were complete. but obviously, you're not."

"What do you mean, complete?"

Braugh looked perplexed. "That's when your soul, your higher self, is in alignment with your spirit, which is your connection to the Great Spirit and is part of your energy and vibration — your essence if you like."

Molly sat down; she was more confused than ever. "Oh, for God's sake, Braugh, I don't know what the hell's going on. You're saying that I need to reconnect with my soul? Well that's just great, seeing as I have no idea where my soul is right now. All I know is that I've had lots of healing, and everyone's trying to fix me, and everyone's talking about me, and… and…whatever!" She sighed, despondently.

Braugh fell quiet and thought for a while, while Molly became restless and began to pace backwards and forwards. Suddenly he had a flash of inspiration and shouted out excitedly, "Got it! It's obvious — all we need to do is to locate your soul, of course."

Molly looked incredulously at him. "Right, Sherlock, and just how do we do that?"

"Erm… I'm working on it. Don't rush me."

"Great, you do that. But do you think you could hurry up?"

Now it was Braugh's turn to pace up and down as he muttered and mumbled to himself. Vimprn and Molly exchanged glances as Braugh let out a deep sigh and abruptly sat down next to Vimprn.

"You got any ideas?' he asked, hopefully.

Vimprn shook her head.

"Okay, as I see it, the first problem is that we don't even know how to locate a specific soul. Second problem is, when and if we do locate your soul, how do we get it to you, or you to it?

And the third thing is doing the melding bit. This isn't going to be easy at all."

Molly tutted, flicked her head and rolled her eyes, exasperated with the whole thing. "Okay… whatever!" she said disappointedly. "Jeez, is he always like this?"

"Yeah, pretty much."

"Bloody hell, nightmare then. See, I'd even forgotten that."

Molly was becoming increasingly impatient as she and Vimprn watched him resume his pacing.

"Well, anything?" she asked briskly.

"Erm… no… not yet. Bit of a challenging dilemma this one. The thing is, if you haven't remerged with your soul then I'm pretty certain that you can't reincarnate. You can't go back to the earth realm ever again."

Molly looked pensive, and suddenly understanding the implications of what he had just said, scowled at him as if it were his fault.

"I'm sorry, Brenth, but I don't see how I can help you. This is way out of my league," he said apologetically.

"Well that's just great. All this has done is make me even more confused."

Braugh sat down but seemed agitated and unsettled. "Thing is Brenth, you've probably forgotten that I have only one further incarnation to do, after which I will be able to complete my ascension."

Molly caught her breath. "Ascension? No! Oh God, yes, you're right, I had forgotten, although what's-her-name… Kyah, told me I was close to ascension too. Well, like that's gonna happen now."

Abruptly she felt a sudden jolt, as she comprehended the implication: her final incarnation should have been at the same time as Braugh's. Molly reeled as the realisation hit her like a physical blow. Trying to disguise her disappointment, she managed a weak smile.

"Oh Braugh, you're nearly there — the final stage of your development. I'm really pleased and happy for you."

Holding his gaze but feeling utterly wretched, she hugged him, realising just what a momentous occasion it would be for him. Once Braugh had completed his final physical existence, he would never have to return to the earth dimension again. He would never have to subsist in a physical vessel again. Instead he would elevate to the next level of existence. She was happy for him, but began to feel a gnawing emptiness inside, as she knew that she would miss him terribly. Braugh tried to hide his disappointment, as he too realised just what it meant.

Molly reached for his hand. "It's okay Braugh. I understand, and you must know that I only have the purest love for you. This is too important for you. Please, you must go, you must fulfil — you have to evolve."

Suddenly another surge of memories came flooding back as she remembered that they had indeed shared many lives together. They had been husband and wife and sister and brother many times. They were true twin flames, and she knew deep down that she would never love anyone the way she loved him. She revelled in the depth of her feelings towards him.

Reading her thoughts, he unexpectedly enveloped her with his energy and together they inter-mingled into one another's essence. She felt weightless yet heavy, fragile yet strong, and as they merged and intertwined their cosmic blueprints, they became one, as their knowing of all things imploded within and beyond them. They embraced for what seemed an eternity, and as Braugh gently released her, dazed and overwhelmed in a stupor of elation, she floated downwards, re-joining Vimprn.

"Whoa, that was incredible! Absolutely bloody amazing! I'd forgotten how fantastic it is to be on a one-to-one connection."

Vimprn had been listening to their conversation before they had merged their energies and she had witnessed their union. She had felt a little discomfited at witnessing the act of true universal love which had completely caught her unawares. yet a knowing smile had crossed her lips. Teasingly she said, "Well, if you two have quite finished your little tête-à-tête, can we get back to doing what we're supposed to be doing.?"

Having been swept up in the moment, Molly gasped as she suddenly realised that Vimprn had witnessed her surrender. "Oh Vimprn, I'm sorry," she said somewhat awkwardly.

Vimprn shrugged her shoulders and patted Molly's hand reassuringly. "No really, don't mind me. Please don't give it a second thought, although I'm glad I've got your attention again! Now then, where were we?"

Vimprn began to recount some of her own past life experiences. She told them how her lesson of learning temperance and forgiveness in her last life had been very hard. She had been a prostitute and an alcoholic, and had died before she'd had the chance to learn those particular lessons. Now she was having to prepare to contract her return again, in an effort to complete those teachings. As Molly sat listening, she began to remember many of her own lifetimes spent with Vimprn — times when they had been father and son in ancient Greece and Egypt, and a time when they had been brothers during a particularly bloody civil war. Molly smiled as she recollected times when she and Vimprn had been together as life-long friends as Nuns in a convent, and when they had been mother and daughter, sisters and even twins.

"Oh my God! Do you remember that time when we were sisters, and we were tried as witches? We were accused of using black magic and devil worship... remember? We were both burnt at the stake; what an awful life that turned out to be, although I can't remember which particular lesson that was for."

"Vimprn looked thoughtful. "Erm... persecution, I think."

"Oh, and what about the time we were brothers, and you were convicted of treason? I remember you were jailed and tortured, then beheaded, just for good measure. God, if I've remembered that one, then you must too," said Molly confidently.

Vimprn was taken aback as she too recalled the memory. "Oh yes, of course I do remember that one. You're doing really well, you know. Do you remember living as peasants when that awful winter saw you off with starvation, and I got sick with some horrible disease?"

Nodding, Molly suddenly became aware of a torrent of memories which came flooding into her thoughts. A multitude of past lives seemed to flash through her consciousness, yet at the same time she felt an all-consuming sadness and emptiness inside her. It was like nothing she had ever felt before, and she suddenly knew that a major part of her being — a major part of her essence — was missing, and nothing and no-one would ever be able to fill the abyss where her soul essence should have been.

Chapter Twenty-five: Unwanted Visitor

<***>

Molly was enjoying herself in the company of Braugh and Vimprn as they watched a particularly beautiful sunset. Suddenly she started to feel restless; she had an uneasiness which she couldn't explain. Hurriedly she went over to the nearest tree and hiding behind it, stared into the distance.

He was coming — coming towards her. She recognised the approaching light and energy print and, in an instant, she knew that she had to make sure he didn't see her. Remaining completely motionless, she pressed herself against the tree, confused and shaken. This wasn't supposed to happen — what the hell was going on? Pushing herself further into the tree and wishing she could completely melt into its warm, loving energy and camouflage herself in its aura, she waited until the energy had passed her by. Had he seen her? She wasn't sure. But even if he hadn't seen her, had he sensed her, as she had him?

Braugh came over to her. "What's the matter? Why did you hide?"

"Oh Braugh, I'm so confused. I don't know what's happening. I need to see Orick — don't suppose you happen to know where he is?"

Braugh fell silent and scanned the spiritual realm before homing in on Orick's location. "He is with Adzullon over in the Towers. He is assisting with the process of harmonising spirits, ready for their return to the earth realm. You'll have to wait until they have completed their task — you'd best not interrupt when such a delicate and important process is taking place." His voice softened. "Maybe I can help you, though — what is it that troubles you so?"

Molly crumpled to the ground, aware of how confused and helpless she felt. Braugh sat down beside her. "Who was that anyway? I didn't recognise the energy print."

"That's because he shouldn't be here. He's a lower spirit — I've fathomed that much at least. He's the one who murdered me in my last life. He went by the name of Gareth Shaw, and I don't understand why he is on our level. I really need to speak with Orick."

Braugh sighed deeply. "Indeed, you do Brenth, indeed you do. He shouldn't be too long."

Molly wiped away a tear as Braugh tried to comfort her. "Anyway, who is Adzullon, and what did you say he and Orick are doing?"

Braugh frowned. "What? You mean you don't even remember that? Adzullon is the Overseer of Dates. He helps an incarnating spirit connect to its chosen parents. I can't believe that you'd forgotten that. Goodness, that's basic stuff."

Molly shook her head sadly. "No, I'd forgotten. I think I need to take things more slowly, at least until I've regained the bulk of my memories. But it's weird, because sometimes I think I do remember, then it's like the memories lessen or become dulled. It's really hard to explain."

Braugh patted her hand reassuringly. "Well, I suppose it's down to the damage done to your circuits, as it were. And don't forget, you haven't had all the healing you need or even had your soul merged, so don't stress about it. Maybe it's good to keep being reminded of things. I suppose that eventually you will remember and retain most, if not all, of the knowledge and ways of this realm and its cosmic laws. Do you want me to continue to teach you?"

Molly nodded. "Yeah, s'pose you might as well, but don't be surprised if I need reminding again. My mam always used to say that I had a memory like a sieve — I know what she meant now."

Braugh gave a weak smile. "So, you remember that there are soul groups, don't you?"

Molly nodded indignantly. "Why yes, silly, I know that! Obviously, you and Vimprn are part of my soul group, otherwise why would I be here?"

Braugh frowned, surprised by her response. "Okay, so a spirit and a soul are joined together by a thread of vibrational energy, but here they can choose to exist independently if they wish. Obviously in my and Vimprn's case we are complete — we have chosen to be fully merged. Now, when a spirit wishes to incarnate again, that particular spirit's soul makes a contract with the Great Spirit, or God as you call it, for one or more lessons or life experiences which it wants to have. That's when the spirit and soul converge again, which is why the memory of here — the memory of knowing — has to be erased as we leave this realm It is Adzullon who, amongst other things, oversees and implements the natal amnesia, as it is called."

Disparagingly, Molly retorted, "Pah! So how come my rubbish, supposed life guide is doing what seems like such a responsible job?"

"Whoa, you need to tone it down! Yes, it is a responsible position. Orick has been procured by the Elders and given the task because you were about to undergo ascension, which meant that he too was coming to the end of his service as your life guide. All spirit guides whose charges have evolved get to evolve themselves — guides get promotion too, as it were."

Molly shook her head in disbelief. "Really? Unbelievable! And here's me wondering how I got lumbered with such an idiot? I mean, he didn't do me any favours, did he?"

Braugh looked at Molly incredulously. "What? Is that what you think? Well, you'd best keep that one to yourself."

Braugh's response was totally lost on her, and for the rest of the evening Molly stayed close to Braugh and Vimprn, keeping a wary look out and fearing for herself, even though Braugh tried to reassure her that everything would be okay.

The following day, Molly met up with Orick again, and still feeling angry and upset, was curt and disgruntled as she informed him that Gareth had been in the Gardens, and that she was almost certain that he was there for one reason, and one reason only — he was trying to find her. And she didn't know why.

"So, what the hell's going on?" she demanded to know. "Why is that utter loser strutting round here like he owns the bloody place? For God's sake, Orick, have you any idea how I feel? Have you any idea how upset I am? No, you probably haven't. Do you even care? No, I don't suppose you do. Well, do you know what? I'm bloody sick of you — not only do you let me get murdered, but now you're letting the bastard who murdered me do as he likes. Jesus! What is it with you guides? Waste of bloody space the lot of you, if you ask me. And another thing, what's going to happen to me?"

Orick was completely taken aback at her outburst, and didn't quite know what to say or do to calm her down. "I'm sorry that's how you see it, Molly. There's nothing I can say or do at this time which will change how you perceive this. Just trust that all will be well, and know that there are aspects of your questions which I cannot answer."

"Can't or won't?" she fumed.

"Look, everything is being overseen by the Keepers and the Elders; it is they who are instrumental to your recovery. I've even heard that they feel it is time for you to meet with the Archangel Metatron."

Molly stared defiantly at Orick, determined to have an argument with him. "Archangel Metatron? Yeah, well like he's going to be any bloody use, either."

Orick glared and then inhaled deeply and counted to three, trying to remain calm. Exasperated, it was all he could do to keep a level voice as he retorted, "You go too far, Molly. For your information, Archangel Metatron is the ultimate Keeper and Protector of the Akashic archives. He is therefore the quintessential ethereal being in the whole of existence, and you are very blessed to have him tutor you. So, when you do eventually receive that great privilege and have an audience with him, ask all the questions you like, because, just for the record, right now you're coming across as a spoilt brat, and you're beginning to really try my patience."

Molly stared defiantly. "Try your patience? Well that's rich. Come on then, just when do I get to meet the great Metatron or whatever his name is?" she asked cockily, doing the inverted comma gesture in mid-air.

Orick was struggling to remain composed. Molly was intentionally pushing his buttons, and her indifference and downright rudeness and arrogance had begun to grate on his nerves. "I don't know for certain — soon I would think," he said, mustering all the patience he could, "But when you do get to meet him, you'd better have lost the attitude, and I'm also going to suggest that you show some gratitude and respect — both of which, it has to be said, appear to be very sadly lacking."

Molly glared at Orick, and finally lost for words, pulled a face before sticking her tongue out at him. Then, in defiance and without so much as a backwards glance, she flounced off.

Chapter Twenty-six: An Understanding

<***>

The following dawn, Molly was instructed by Kyah to attend the Temple of Deeds, which was a large, imposing building constructed out of pink marble and quartz crystal, and situated opposite the Halls of Wisdom. As she approached, Molly was impressed at the sheer size of the building. She noticed how it appeared to hover in mid-air and glint and sparkle in the sunlight, yet for all its enormity, it cast no shadows. Orick was also there and they sat in an awkward silence, waiting for the great Archangel Metatron to appear.

It was Molly who spoke first. "So, what's this place again?" she asked tentatively, "It's huge."

Orick smiled, pleased with her interest. "This is the Temple of Deeds. It is here that the Akashic records are held in their very own library, although it also holds the archives of Judgement, Prudence, Knowledge, Discretion, Counsel, Understanding and Power — otherwise known as the seven pillars of wisdom."

"Oh blimey, sorry I asked," she said huffily, as she sat nervously wringing her hands.

Orick felt uncomfortable with the silence which hung between them and wishing to break the stand-off, began to explain that Metatron was one of the most powerful archangels in existence, and was reputed to know everything about anything. It was said that if Metatron didn't know about it, then it wasn't worth knowing about. Molly looked disinterested and haughtily folded her arms, making it obvious that she was still annoyed and irritated with Orick. As far as she was concerned, he had let her down, big time. After all, where the hell had he been when she'd needed him? Weren't spirit guides supposed to help and protect you? To her mind he was supposed to have been there for her, but he had been less than useless, and so this was all his fault. Still, she couldn't help but be in awe of his knowledge, not that she'd admit that to him, and she was certainly impressed at the enormity of the building,

Suddenly there was a swirling rush of cool air as Archangel Metatron swept into the vast vestibule, accompanied by a loud whooshing sound which reverberated around the chamber. He was extremely tall and graceful, with a purple aura so magnificent that Molly had to avert her gaze until she became accustomed to his radiance. She gawped in total astonishment as she studied the angel standing before her. She noticed that his robes bore the most beautiful hues of orange and persimmon, and gracefully rippled and shimmered as they returned to their natural cascade. Glancing over in their direction, the archangel silently folded all thirty-six of his wings in one seamless action. Molly stared at them, mesmerised. They glinted and shimmered as bright as the morning star, and within each wing Molly could see thousands of what looked like iridescent bicycle spokes. Each spoke held a multitude of all-seeing eyes running down its length.

Transfixed and in awe, Molly watched as the great archangel glided over to where she and Orick were waiting, and silently raising his hand, held out what, at first glance, looked like a chunk of rock. Smiling, he encouraged her to take it and reaching out, she accepted his gift and stared at it, somewhat bemused. As she studied it, she could see that it was actually a piece of crystal fashioned into a cube. Her attention was captivated by the colours within it, which formed dazzling light prisms in all manner of shapes and patterns. Intuitively she knew that the patterns were made up of multiple geometric shapes, and she smiled to herself as she remembered that sacred geometry, healing and esoteric wisdom were what Metatron was renowned for.

Telepathically he instructed her to follow him, while she awkwardly fumbled with the cube which he had given to her, not sure what to do with it. Taking it from her, he smiled and slipped it into a pocket secreted within his robe. Leaving Orick in the vestibule, Molly did as the archangel had instructed and meekly followed him down a long, wide corridor which had marble flooring, quartz crystal pillars and numerous gushing water fountains. Droplets of water splashed out of the enormous fountains, and glinted with colours found only in the prisms of perfectly cut diamonds. Molly noticed how they formed a curtain of rainbows with no beginning and no end. The corridor stretched far into the distance and Molly realised that the walls on either side were shimmering and that the lower parts of the walls were vermillion red in colour, while the top parts were deep, amethyst purple. The two sections were separated by a wide, gold-coloured border which glinted and sparkled. At intervals along the upper walls there were recesses which were illuminated with brilliant, silver light. They held screens which displayed moving pictures of animals and insects, birds and reptiles and all manner of other living creatures. Molly realised that she was seeing all of creation, and gasped as that realisation dawned on her.

Looking upwards, she realised that there was no ceiling above them as she could see the most beautiful, clear, azure blue sky, yet there were strange, white flakes falling all around her. At first, she thought that they were snowflakes but they didn't appear to be settling. Looking more closely, Molly saw that the flakes appeared to wriggle and dart, and go in any direction they pleased. She suddenly recalled that what she was seeing was a sort of energy, of a kind which gave harmony, balance and healing to the universe. She suddenly remembered that it was called Chi.

As she continued to look around, something else caught her attention as she noticed a variety of glistening spheres of differing sizes and colours which flitted and fluttered all around her, before swiftly darting into one of the many fountains which adorned the corridor. She suddenly remembered that the spheres were the light energies of elementals — animal spirits and sprites, faeries, undines and sylphs — and that they were using the fountains as portals. The fountains were a means of dropping back to earth, disguised as rain drops. This clever illusion allowed them to blend into nature and emerge camouflaged and unseen by humans. She watched mesmerised, as a pair of unicorns pranced and gambolled towards the fountain nearest to her.

They were spectacular and majestic, and Molly couldn't help but notice their single horns of pure, white light energy. She wanted to reach out and touch their translucent manes, which flowed and glistened as they moved, and she noticed how their bodies seemed to emit a soft, white glow which shimmered as they were caught in a myriad of rainbow colours. Watching in astonishment, her gaze followed them as they both simultaneously reared up onto their hind legs and leapt forwards, before disappearing into the heart of the fountain.

Realising that she was lagging behind, she quickened her pace along the corridor to catch up with the archangel. She could see his energy vortex in the distance, and became aware of a heady aroma which lingered in the air. It reminded her of spices and vanilla, chocolate and baking. Or was it a childhood memory of fresh sea air and candy floss? She wasn't sure — to be honest she wasn't sure of anything anymore. She noticed there were numerous doors fronting the long, straight corridor, most of which were made from different varieties of wood; some were made from cedar, some from oak or banyan and others were made of acacia or ficus. Molly also noticed that a few of the doors were made of stone or marble and others of gold or silver. The doors were of varying heights and widths, but each had ancient Sanskrit writings and sacred geometrical symbols carved into or above them. They were all closed, and each seemed to glow and pulsate with a different colour. She found herself running her fingers playfully over the surfaces, before becoming aware of a low humming sound which felt strangely comforting and reassuring. It suddenly dawned on her that all her senses were now in overdrive and she recalled that what she was sensing was the resonating, thrumming vibration of the universe, the rhythmic heartbeat of the cosmos.

Metatron stopped abruptly in front of a particularly large and imposing door, which appeared to be made of opaque crystal emanating a very subtle green hue. Molly studied the ancient symbols which were embellished above the door, but couldn't recognise or understand what they meant. The archangel stepped forward and disappeared through the door, leaving her in the corridor. She hesitated, uncertain as to what she should do — should she follow him or wait to be invited in? Suddenly a hand appeared through the door, pulling her into the room. At first, Molly was surprised and a little shocked at being dragged through a closed door, before realising that the door wasn't solid and was actually a veil of shimmering, crystal energy. Metatron stood in the middle of the room and motioned her over with an almost indiscernible nod of his head. Approaching him, she hovered to the side of the formidable and powerful angelic being.

Looking nervously around her, Molly realised that the walls were shimmering with a palette of radiant and vibrant hues of light. Some were subtle and pastel-like, while others were vivid and bright. She was somewhat taken aback as she realised, she didn't recognise any of the colours and certainly couldn't have named them. The room was vast, and housed row upon row of shelving, some made from quartz crystal and some from a strange-looking green and pink crystal. Each section towered above her, and the whole structure appeared to be floating. Each shelf looked to be filled to capacity with varying sizes and shapes of folders, files and books, some thick and bulky and others thin and flaccid.

Molly's attention was suddenly drawn to the centre of the room where a colossal heptahedral-shaped crystal was emitting a green-coloured mist. This appeared to be the source of the throbbing, pulsating beat which resonated throughout the building. The axis of the crystal was tilted away from the vertical by an angle which Molly somehow knew to be 36 degrees, and it looked like it might fall over at any moment. Metatron motioned for Molly to approach it, and retrieving the cube from his robe, handed it back to her. Molly could feel the weight of it, and was just about to ask what she should do with it when Metatron instructed her to position it into a small recess halfway up the crystal's side. Nervously she did as he had instructed, and as she let go of the cube, a flash of white light jumped across and entered her. It startled her and she yelped in surprise, while simultaneously jumping back and falling over. Metatron gave a loud, booming chuckle as he headed towards the other side of the crystal.

"What just happened?" asked Molly in a daze, as she followed him.

The archangel continued to chuckle, before placing his hands on the pulsating crystal. "Most Beloved, the geometric cube which you have just returned to the Goddess Crystal is imprinted with your cosmic DNA. It is all that remains of your cosmic blueprint, and it is all that I could salvage. It was agreed that for your sustenance you need to reconnect to the whole and you need to be reconnected to Love. The energy within this crystal is the resonating beat of universal love. Its pulsing energy sends love in its purest form out to the cosmos."

Molly smiled. "Wow, no wonder it knocked me over."

Metatron gazed into the crystal and replied, "Indeed, the energy of love is very powerful, and yet the understanding of love in its purest form has sadly eluded the human race. Humanity think they only hold love within their hearts, when truly they don't; love isn't held anywhere, love just is."

Molly didn't know what to say, so decided to say nothing, not wanting to distract the great archangel from his task.

"Pah, no matter, let us continue."

Molly followed Metatron as he swept majestically to the far end of the room. Mesmerised by the archangel's swishing robe, she nearly bumped into him as he suddenly stopped in his tracks. She edged around his frame of energy, and noticed that at the far end of the room there was a vast screen which filled the entire height and breadth of the walled area. Molly vaguely thought she'd seen it before, but she wasn't entirely sure. She approached the screen and floating in front of it, realised that images had begun to appear, just as had happened when she had been in front of the Keepers. Staring at the screen, Molly realised that the images being replayed were of her previous lives; the whole collection of her past lives was being played as three-dimensional images similar to a hologram.

Molly was excited but nervous as she settled at the side of Metatron and silently watched herself on the screen. She observed each of her births and deaths, and gazed in amazement as she realised that she was actually viewing all of her lives in reverse order. After the first few hundred, she began to notice that the pictures were starting to merge into a jumbled blur.

Metatron gently placed his hand on her shoulder. "Are you all right, Beloved?"

Molly stared in amazement, and turning to face the archangel, asked him why she couldn't remember much of what she had just seen.

Metatron remained sombre. "You will remember in time. Maybe not everything, but you will recall many of your past lives-lived. The more times you watch, the more you will remember, and as you remember, each of your viewed lives will become separate from the others, so they too will become a recollected memory."

She began to feel calm and serene, and basking in the archangel's healing light, also felt safe and protected. Continuing to watch the screen, she realised that Metatron was right — the more she watched, the more she remembered. Eagerly she began recounting each memory as it was triggered, and chattered non-stop as she shared each event with Metatron. He was pleased that her amnesia was beginning to fade, but knew that there were some memories which even he could never recover. Taking a deep breath, Molly found the courage to ask the great archangel why her last reincarnation had been so short and seemingly uneventful.

Metatron considered his reply carefully. "It was what you contracted for. It was pre-ordained that you were destined to have your last life curtailed at the hands of another, because you didn't wish to stay away from the spiritual realm for longer than was necessary. You wanted an easy, uncomplicated life experience. Unfortunately, the toxic concoction of drugs, alcohol and the trauma inflicted to your vessel at the time of your crossing over has damaged your energy print and vibration. Some of your memories are lost, never to be remembered or recovered, and I have to tell you that sadly, despite our interventions and my best efforts, that part of your soul which had accompanied you has been irreparably damaged."

Molly gasped as a wave of sadness and realisation crashed over her. "Irreparably damaged..." she repeated.

"It is recorded within your Akashic record that your previous twenty-three incarnations were to learn the lessons of love and forgiveness."

Molly was trying to make sense of what Metatron was saying. "Forgiveness... damaged... twenty-three... I don't remember. I don't remember any of that," she whispered. Molly realised that she had more questions than answers, as a wave of confusion consumed her.

Metatron softened his gaze and gliding over to a large, shimmering swing, motioned for Molly to join him. The seat appeared to be suspended in mid-air, and swung gently backwards and forwards in time to the pulsing vibration which was all around them.

"Beloved, there are some life lessons which are not learned so easily — most Spirit struggle with the harder ones. It doesn't matter how long it takes, because we know that eventually the lessons will all be learned. Spirit are proud of their achievements, just as we are proud of Spirit. Spirit revel in knowing that every lesson learned will bring them closer to the Divine, so if a lesson is hard earned, then all the better."

Molly smiled and pondering to herself, suddenly thought that on the whole she must have done something right.

"I'm also told that you want to know the name of the one who, shall we say, abruptly instigated the fulfilment of your contract. You know him by his earth name, Gareth Shaw. but his soul name is Dolf. As you have already surmised, he is troubled, a lost soul if you will, and he is in much need of love and understanding. And as his actions have demonstrated, he has an almost unprecedented need for guidance."

Molly sat motionless, hanging on to the great archangel's every word, yet feeling abject turmoil inside.

"Although Dolf was instrumental in ending your physical life as was agreed, it was the way in which your physical life was ended which is unjustifiable. To commit such a nefarious crime and knowingly act in such a way as to intentionally destroy the vibration of another's soul, especially when that soul has been rendered totally defenceless, is abhorrent to the laws of nature and cosmic law. Dolf pre-meditated his actions — on some level he knew full well that the combination of toxic poisons and an orchestrated blow to a physical vessel would render it totally powerless. He abused the trust which was placed in him — your trust. His deed also sought to undermine universal law and that is what makes this situation all the more abhorrent. He fully understands that the penance will be his, and his alone. Dolf knows, as do all Spirit, that their Karma, be it good or bad, is their own; he is his own judge and jury, and he alone must reconcile his actions and take responsibility. His Karma, his betrayal to you, will cost him an immeasurable amount."

Metatron sat reverently in quiet contemplation before he spoke again, choosing his words thoughtfully. "Dolf is attempting to acquire your forgiveness, because the forgiveness which would have been granted automatically upon his return to the spiritual realm has evaded him. Because of your circumstances, shall we say, dharma has not been fulfilled, don't you see? Dharma is the natural way of things; it is the natural cosmic law and way of the Divine."

Slowly processing what Metatron had just said, Molly felt her vibration quiver and she recoiled in horror as the magnitude of what was being asked of her gradually began to dawn on her.

Chapter Twenty-seven: Choice Decisions

<***>

After her meeting with Metatron, Molly had thought long and hard about what had been asked of her. She was wrestling with having to make a decision and decided to ask her grandfather to meet up with her to see if he could advise her.

"Blimey Molly, you're in a right old quandary. So, what are you going to do?" asked Ged.

"I'm still undecided — there's so much to think about. Metatron told me that my soul essence is damaged beyond repair and I now have a permanent scar within my energy vibration, which means I will carry it with me forever. I finally get what Kyah was telling me now. I can't believe I was so close to ascension and now he's gone and ruined it for me."

Ged sighed and thought for a while. "Then would it be so hard to forgive Dolf for what he did? After all, like Metatron said, he's the one who has to deal with the fallout of his actions. Karma like that will be retribution enough, believe me."

Molly pursed her lips and slumped down under a big, old cedar tree. She angrily pulled and poked at the grass as Ged sat down next to her.

"Sweetheart, finding it within yourself to forgive someone is a huge deal. We all know that — it's one of the major lessons we contract for and learn from. The thing is though, here there are no differences between us. As Spirit, we are equal. We are all energy beings, connected to each other and to the Great Spirit. Yes, there are various stages of development, and Gareth — or Dolf if you like — obviously isn't as evolved as you are, but essentially that doesn't matter; we are all connected by, and through, unconditional love."

There was a long silence between them as Molly mulled over what Ged had just told her.

"When we come back to the spiritual realm, we retain many of our human character traits — you know, mannerisms, gestures and such like — but what you need to do is get past the emotions that come from being human. Anger, hate, resentment, jealousy, bitterness, in fact any of the negative emotions which are prevalent and portrayed on earth, do not serve humanity, yet they chose to give them power and let them influence their everyday lives and everyday decisions. If humanity realised that, then their world would be a much better place to be in. Which is why as Spirit, we know and recognise that there is no place for negative emotions and actions. There is no worth to them — no substance — yet we have to experience them to realise this."

Molly didn't say anything as she was still too upset to trust herself. Still seething with anger and resentment, she couldn't believe what had been asked of her and feared that she would completely lose control. How could she not have retribution? How could she not have revenge?

"Look sweetheart, eventually the mortal vessel, and the spirit and soul within it, get it right. It might take a while, granted, with many life-times having to be lived, but eventually we learn all the lessons and ditch the repeated bad character traits and old patterns of being. Heck, eventually we even let go of the ego. Don't you see, at some point in one of our incarnations the vessel — the person we are — begins a spiritual path of enlightenment, and it is at that pivotal point that we begin to evolve as a human being, which in turn allows us to also evolve as spirit."

Molly suddenly began to sob. "Oh Grandpa, what am I going to do? I hate him so much. What if I can't forgive him? What if I can't get past this?"

Ged reached out to console her and embraced her. "My poor girl, I fear that all this is getting too much for you. I was afraid that this might happen. Nevertheless, I'm going to tell you something — something fundamental which every spirit knows.

Obviously, you have forgotten, and it's possible that you will forget again, but try and remember this, if nothing else."

Molly shifted position and sitting up, gave her grandfather her full attention.

"What we experience physically is stored in our Akashic record, be they good or bad experiences. The main thing Molly, is that we learn from them. After we have completed a life lived, we return to the spiritual realm where we have to reconnect to the energy veil which we left behind, because we can't take all of our energy with us when we reincarnate. The majority of the energy we leave behind is our soul energy — our higher self. It's the soul which formulates and authenticates our contracts with the Divine, the Great Spirit. Our soul energy knows everything we need to achieve in a particular lifetime to fulfil that particular contracted lesson. Our soul is the essence of who we are as Spirit, yet our soul also has many facets."

Molly remained quiet as she desperately tried to remember what was already held deep within the recesses of her memory.

"Right then, let's see if you can get your head around this little nugget. When a spirit is ready to reincarnate it chooses a physical vessel that's about to conceive — its parent-to-be, if you like. Now at about seven weeks gestation, give or take, the spirit enters through the posterior fontanelle of the embryo and into physical consciousness. This fontanelle will later become the crown chakra. Now at the same time, a fragment of the soul's essence is also guided into consciousness, into a part of the brain called the pineal gland. We also know it as the third eye or brow chakra."

Molly smiled as she realised that what her grandfather had just told her was what she had previously watched on the big screen. "Go on," she said eagerly.

"You sure? I don't want to tire you out with all this."

"No, no, honest, it's fine. Carry on, I'm fine, really."

"Okay, do you remember me telling you about the aura and the chakras?"

Molly nodded. "Oh yeah, I do remember you telling me when we were with Mam and Nan, when they found out about me being dead."

"That's right, and you already know that our physical body has a crown and brow chakra. Well there are also chakras at the throat, heart, solar plexus, sacrum and base of the spine, also known as the root. Each chakra resonates at a specific vibrational note and has its own unique colour. These are the main seven chakras, but actually there's a whole load more which surround, and are part of, our energy field. They form a kind of grid."

Molly frowned. "Well how come I never saw any of them — well not that I remember?"

"Because chakras are energy vortices. They aren't made of flesh and bone; they're made of cosmic energy. They act like power stations, receiving energy in, and transmitting energy out. They go through the physical body front to back, and work in tandem with the aura and each other to keep our physical vessel healthy. They are also connected to tiny little channels called meridians which help to circulate our essence — which some people call the life force energy, or chi. You've probably never heard of it."

Molly closed her eyes, trying to concentrate on what her grandfather was explaining to her.

"You okay?"

"Yeah, I'm fine, carry on. Actually, I have heard of chi. Mam's friend, Sheila, used to go to yoga and she used to talk about it"

"Oh good. Right, where was I…? Oh yes, now just above the crown chakra, which if you remember is the one on top of the head, there is the soul star chakra. Then above that there's the stellar gateway. These chakras are collectively known as the astral chakras. All the chakras are aligned and they're all kept in line by the hara line."

"The hara line… never heard of it! Sounds like it should be part of the London underground, like the Circle line or Jubilee."

Ged smiled to himself before carrying on, "As I was saying, smarty-pants, the hara line starts at the soul star chakra and passes vertically through the other chakras downwards into the earth. It transports or channels white light energy — healing energy — through the physical vessel. The thing is, you've still got yours attached to you and it's a bit wonky and looking the worst for wear. If you look up you might just be able to see it."

Molly looked up, trying to see her hara. "Oh yeah, I can see it. But it's very faint and looks a bit lop-sided"

Ged nodded. "Like I said, yours is... well look, don't worry — I'm sure whoever's sorting things out for you will be on to it."

"Okay, so what's those astral and stellar thingies again?"

Ged took a deep breath. "Right, concentrate will you. There are three astral chakras, the first one is the crown, then the soul star, and then the stellar gateway. Collectively the three astral chakras enable the soul essence to assimilate and accumulate all the learning and all the experiences we undergo over our entire history of incarnations."

Molly smiled. "Oh, I get it, that's what Metatron was showing me and what Braugh and Vimprn were talking about. Actually, I've just realised something. The chakra which you said is on top of our heads is the crown, right? So actually, we all wear a crown!" She grinned, feeling proud of her little witticism.

Ged smiled to himself, amused at Molly's analogy.

"Well yeah... kinda. Actually, it's through the crown chakra that we receive divine healing, and it's also a means of staying connected to the Great Spirit and higher realms. Now, the soul star is our connection to the cosmos and our higher self, and the stellar gateway is the portal between the physical dimension and the ethereal. The stellar gateway is the access portal into the greater universal consciousness, and that's where the fun starts. It's only accessible when we've achieved our spiritual conscious enlightenment — our ascension."

"Wow, so when I ascend, I'll be able to... what exactly?"

"Erm… not have to go back to the earth dimension."

"Right …"

"No, really! When we ascend, I believe it's incredible. We come to realise our full potential, and get to exist and explore other dimensions. We can explore the cosmos and travel with other light-beings, and begin to encompass what the true meaning of unconditional love and life eternal is."

"Oh, great… can't wait"

"Well you could at least be more enthusiastic and show a little bit of excitement."

Molly scowled and shook her head. "Excitement… oh yeah, remind me what that is, will you?"

"Oh, don't be such a grump. Once you've lost the human attitude, you'll be fine."

"Whatever!"

Molly didn't feel like she wanted to be fine. What she really wanted was to punch 'whatever-his-face-was' senseless, and beat him to a pulp, just like when she had seen his mortal remains in the morgue.

"Do you want to carry on?" Ged asked, frowning.

"Yeah, you may as well. I'm not promising that I'll remember any of it though."

Ged reached out to give her a hug. "I understand, Molly, really I do, and if I can help to make this easier for you then that's what I want to do. If I can teach you things and explain stuff to you, at least it might help you to understand a bit more. It might even jog your memory."

Molly felt herself relaxing again as she leant back against the cedar tree. "I know, Grandpa, it's just that I feel isolated and detached from everything, I feel wound up and on edge all the time and angry and frustrated. I'm trying to understand and remember stuff, it's just hard being like this. Actually, it's horrible."

Ged patted her hand and edged closer to her. "It will be all right you know. You'll be all right."

"I wish I could share your certainty, Grandpa. Anyway, you were telling me about conscious ascension and the stellar gateway."

"Well get you — you remembered! Okay, when we are in a physical body, we not only have physical obstacles to overcome, but also emotional and mental ones to contend with as well. We have a lot to surmount but because of the amnesia we are all given, we forget about our connections, not only to the Great Spirit, but also to each other and nature — oh, and not forgetting the animal kingdom. But if we get back on our spiritual pathway, and if we advance enough to realise that we're all connected to everything as a whole, and if we strengthen that connection for example by praying or meditating, we develop a raised awareness, an enlightened consciousness. This enables our soul essence to raise up from the third eye chakra, which is known as the gateway for the soul, and move into the soul star chakra, which funnily enough, is actually known as the seat of the soul. Once that happens it allows us access to a greater realisation, a higher perception, which enables us to astral travel or enjoy lucid dreaming — that sort of thing. That conscious shift means we can have any number of spiritual experiences while we are in a physical vessel."

Molly rubbed the sides of her head. "Blimey, Gramps, there's so much to take in. I'm never gonna remember even half of this."

Ged looked concerned. "Maybe you should get some rest."

Molly straightened up. "I'm okay, I've just got a throbbing pain in my head — here, at the side. I'll be all right in a bit."

Ged looked closely to where she was pointing, and realised it was the exact place where she had suffered the fatal blow. They sat together for a time, neither of them speaking.

It was Molly who broke the silence first. "Grandpa, can I tell you something?"

Ged changed his position so that he was sitting opposite her. "Of course you can."

"I'm scared, Grandpa, really scared. I want to know what's going to happen to me — I mean what happens if I don't get my memories back? What happens then? Or what if Gareth — Dolf — tries to harm me again?"

Ged let out a long sigh. "Honestly sweetheart, I have no idea, but what I do know is that you will be looked after. There is nothing here to hurt or harm you and there is certainly nothing to fear, please never doubt that. As for Dolf, he cannot impair you any further."

Molly threw her arms around Ged's neck and hugged him tightly. "I love you so much, Grandpa, I really do," she whispered into his ear, before kissing him on his cheek.

Ged tucked her hair behind her ear and whispered back, "I love you too, Molly — always have, always will."

Molly smiled and snuggled into him. "Gramps," she said quietly, "When I was a little girl, did you come to see me? Cos I always felt that there was someone with me, someone watching me, and I remember seeing glimpses of things, like shadows or flickers of light. And I'd have dreams about you — was that you?"

Ged smiled and pulled away to look at her. "Yes, Molly, it was me. I was never far away, though as you got older your ability to see or sense me got a little bit dulled."

"Hmm... I thought so. I remember thinking about you sometimes and feeling like you were with me."

Ged smiled again. "That's the beauty of being Spirit. I could hear your thoughts, and if you needed me, I'd be with you in a flash, as it were. You see, thoughts are a vibration of energy — in effect they are a living thing — but they aren't tangible in the sense of a physical object because they are energy. What you give out as a thought observes the laws of attraction. Negative thoughts attract negative vibrations and positive thoughts attract positive vibrations. They're like little magnets. That's why they say to be careful what you wish for."

"Little magnets, eh, I wished I'd have known that, I would have wished harder," she said, giving a little sigh.

After embracing a while longer, Ged pulled away again. "Right, you soppy happeth, where were we? Do you want to carry on a while longer?"

Molly furrowed her brow. "Sure, why not?"

"Okay, that's my girl. Now just to make things interesting, we also have what are called the three cords, or to be more exact, the three cords of attachment. The first cord connects and nourishes us while we are in the womb. That's the umbilical cord. Then our soul, or higher self, is connected to the Great Spirit — the Divine, Source, God or whatever you want to call it — by an unbreakable gold cord."

Molly although a little perplexed nodded again.

"And finally, we have a silver cord. That's the one which connects and anchors us into the physical body. One end is attached to our energy vibration and the other end feeds into the brow chakra, same as the gold cord does"

Molly pursed her lips. "It's okay, I get it; I just need to remember it is all."

Ged smiled. "We're not quite done yet, there's also the earth star chakra."

"The what?" she asked, sleepily as she gave a big stretch and yawned.

Ged chuckled. "The earth star chakra. It's the same distance below our feet as the soul star chakra is above our crown. It keeps us grounded, connected to the Earth, to Mother Nature. We also have a chakra in the sole of each foot. These connect energetically to the earth star and are called earth chakras. Our aura extends beneath us too, so effectively we are cocooned in a bubble of energy, if you like to think of it that way.

Unfortunately, like I said earlier, most people are so wrapped up in themselves that they never reconnect with their knowing."

Molly realised that although she had a lot to relearn and remember, she was happy and content at that moment. Sitting together beneath the gnarled branches of the old cedar tree, Molly was oblivious to the fact that she was in fact sitting beneath the Tree of Wisdom. A comfortable silence hung between them, as together they watched the silvery light of the cosmos glisten in the heavily scented air before they both succumbed to sleep.

Some time passed before Ged stirred. He yawned and stretched, before rousing Molly. Sitting up, she too stretched and yawned. "I nodded off — I must have needed those forty winks. Huh, listen to me, I sound like Nan."

Ged smiled. "Ha, yes you do. You even have similar mannerisms as well. You remind me so much of her. Right, I'm off. I've got a few things to do, so I'll see you later."

Giving her a hug, he left her alone to contemplate what she had learned so far and what would possibly happen next. Distracted, she ambled her way around the Gardens, captivated by the beautiful colours and scents, and oblivious to the fact that an orb had followed her to the Gardens, and had been keeping out of sight, waiting by the temple steps until she was alone. Being so distracted with her thoughts, she didn't see him approach.

"Molly! Please, I really need to talk to you."

Momentarily caught off guard as he appeared at her side, she stared in disbelief as the orb changed into Spirit form.

"You need to talk to me? Well, I don't want to talk to you. Go to hell, Gareth… Dolf… whatever your bloody name is! Drop dead! Oh no, you can't, you're already dead, and so am I, you murdering monster. I have nothing to say to you, and I sure as hell don't want anything to do with you, so just go away and leave me alone."

As she turned to leave, she unexpectedly bumped into Orick. "And what the hell do you want?" she shouted angrily.

Orick was taken aback at Molly's outburst. "Well I saw you two together, so I came to see if you were all right. Obviously, you're not. Can I help?"

"Help!? Help!?", she repeated, incensed. "And where the hell were you when I needed your bloody help? Where were you when he staved my head in? Oh, leave me alone, the pair of you. Just leave me alone."

Molly turned her back on both of them, and hurriedly returned to where she had been sitting with her grandfather moments earlier and then slumped down onto the grassy mound. She was furious; in fact, she was so incensed that the level of anger she was feeling even scared her.

"How dare he!" she seethed. "How bloody dare he! Forgiveness? Forgiveness? I'll show him bloody forgiveness."

She hated him for what he'd done to her, and she hated him even more for the way he made her feel. She was having a hard time trying to come to terms with what had happened and felt confused and out of control. Molly knew that she had to get away for a while. Taking a deep breath, she decided to go and visit Nan and her mother.

Chapter Twenty-eight: Karma - Amrak

<***>

Dolf had just about resigned himself to the fact that Molly wanted nothing more to do with him. He didn't blame her really — he'd want nothing to do with himself either, given the amount of trouble he'd caused. He remembered that when he had crossed over and returned to the spiritual realm he had been consumed, in his own way, with remorse and guilt, not that anyone had noticed. When he met up with Prenge, his spirit guide, for a one-to-one life review, he had been severely reprimanded. Prenge had told him in no uncertain terms that what he had done earth-side had been wholly unacceptable, and that there would be consequences which only he himself could address.

During his life review Dolf had been reminded that although he had incarnated a total of eighty-seven times, he was still inexperienced in the workings and protocols of both the spiritual and the earth realms. Prenge had also pointed out that he had made very little progress, not only in the last life lived, but also in many of his past incarnations. He had frequently made wrong choices and failed to learn from lessons and experiences. It had also been duly noted that even though he had contracted on several occasions to live full and rewarding lives, he had never actually managed to reach 'a ripe old age' in any of them. As each life had ended, Dolf had met Prenge to re-evaluate and assess his life lessons, and although Prenge was a patient and understanding guide, he was nonetheless becoming exasperated by him.

Prenge was beginning to realise that he had made a huge mistake in trusting Dolf. His error of judgement had snow-balled out of control, especially as it had been him who had agreed and instigated the last contract which had been made between Dolf and Brenth. Prenge knew that he would have to reconcile that mistake with Shelmuthe and the Council of Justice, amongst others.

Having spent a lot of time together in the library replaying Dolf's Akashic record, Prenge had come to realise that Dolf clearly had an insatiable compulsion trait. Every incarnation he'd experienced had been lived with violence, and in most of his lives he'd succumbed to every type of addiction you'd care to name; essentially every physical body that he had ever been blessed with had been abused, neglected and harmed. Prenge was concerned by Dolf's apparent inability to cope with the earth realm and its ways, and had begun to surmise that in all probability Dolf would have to return either to the dimension from which he'd originated from or relocate to an alternative realm, as it was becoming increasingly obvious that his behaviour needed to be re-appraised and his energy reconditioned, possibly even re-coded. Prenge had escalated his concerns to the Elders, and having admitted his mistake had been given clear instructions on how to redress the situation. Reticently, he broached the subject while they were sitting together on the steps of the library.

"Dolf, we need to have a serious talk. The thing is that when I agreed to become your life guide, it was intended that I was to help develop and influence you for your highest good and greatest joy. In the scheme of things, we have known one another but for the briefest of moments, yet although I was aware that you had originally transferred from one of the lesser evolutionary constellations, it was felt that with nurture and guidance there was hope for you. Realistically, I think that's not the case anymore. It has become glaringly obvious that you are not capable of undertaking earthly existence. I have to tell you therefore that I see this as a failing on my part, and I apologise unreservedly to you for that. I have consulted with the Elders for their advice and guidance. They recommend that you spend time with the healing angels and also your soul group, in the hope that you will be influenced by their love, nurture and healing."

Dolf stared into the distance to avoid Prenge's questioning stare.

"You don't seem to be in the least bit perturbed."

Dolf shook his head. "That's cos I'm not… not really. You're right, all I've done is make a huge mess of things."

Prenge sighed. "Yes, well that's as maybe. Let's see how it goes and hope that something is salvageable. As yet, nothing has been finalised or fully decided, but all the same, I think you should prepare for change, as it were. There's every chance that you won't be incarnating again anytime soon — well, certainly not back to the earth realm. You've become too much of a liability — you do realise that, don't you? I must say that you're taking all of this rather well, though."

Dolf frowned. "Change, eh? Is that what you call it? Well, it's probably been a long time in coming. You gave it… me… your best shot, as they say. So, what happens now?"

"Like I said, I don't know for sure. I need to finalise my conclusion chronicle and report back to the Elders, but know this, once your cosmic destiny has been decided there will be no reversing the decision. You do understand that, don't you? You have amassed one of the most enormous karmic debts I have ever had the misfortune to deal with, one which is proving to be irreconcilable. I will see you later."

Sitting alone, Dolf thought back to the day when he and Molly had agreed their contract. It had been different to the normal way of doing things. Usually when two spirits and their souls make an agreement, they know each other already, as they are normally from the same soul group. Molly. however, was advanced and didn't want to endure a long, hard life as she had done in her many previous lives lived. The contract had been mainly drafted to her specifications, as she wanted to return home relatively quickly. Previously, Orick and Prenge had individually planned and overseen Molly and Dolf's incarnations respectively. This was to be the first contract that they all had agreed to plan together. Dolf remembered that he had only agreed to it because it was a way of earning brownie points as it were and because Molly was near to gaining ascension, he would do it as a favour. Between them they had added several additional clauses, before ironing out the finer points. Having so many variations and agreements to consider, they had sifted through the different formats and had even included a final lesson of forgiveness for Molly and for good measure, the lessons of temperance and compassion had been incorporated for Dolf's benefit.

Dolf knew that the main lessons of emotions, such as forgiveness, unconditional love, compassion, temperance, patience, non-judgement, empathy and acceptance were the toughest ones; they were the lessons which accumulated karma, whether good or bad. Prenge and Orick had scrutinised the details of both contracts meticulously, and had decided that in order for Molly to return home swiftly, she would have Dolf end her physical life. After much discussion it was agreed that the obvious way to fulfil the contract was for them to meet as passing strangers. Unfortunately, the fact that Dolf was somewhat unreliable and inexperienced had somehow been overlooked, and the cost of that error had been catastrophic. What they hadn't foreseen were the actions of an over-zealous taker and the consequential return of a spirit who was so energetically broken that a part of her soul essence was damaged beyond repair. The whole sorry escapade had turned into a right mess.

Dolf had only recently come to realise that what he had actually done had been above and beyond what Molly had contracted for. It was just that he felt compelled to commit violence and exert his will and control when residing in a mortal body; he just couldn't seem to help himself. He was trying to find answers to justify what he had done, but thinking about it only made him more confused. Maybe this was what was meant when they talked about someone being a tormented soul. He knew that Spirit have to experience life's hardships as a matter of course, and that all Spirit have to experience the act of taking a physical life at some point or other, just as all Spirit have to experience being murdered. He'd just fallen into a pattern and failed to learn from it.

Trying to rationalise it only made Dolf even more defensive, as he felt justified in having carried out what had been contracted for. Yet he knew in his heart that he was kidding himself, just as he knew that his karmic debt would take eons to heal. He also knew that his spirit energy was so impoverished it would never fully unite with his soul's vibration; it would never become a whole again. Hanging his head in his hands, he felt desolate and isolated. This wasn't how he had imagined things would turn out. Why the hell hadn't she contracted to go back as a dog or a horse or some such thing — at least it wouldn't have caused all this trouble. Yet he still clung on to what Lucifer had promised him. He was desperate to believe that what he had done wasn't that big a deal — after all, Lucifer had promised and assured him that it wouldn't be.

Chapter Twenty-nine: Insightful Perception

<***>

O
rick and Ged had been summoned to the Halls of Wisdom to stand before the Council of Wise Ones and the Council of Justice. Entering the vast hall, they waited for instructions and were directed to one of its many chambers. Nervously floating in the middle of the chamber, Ged glanced round at the assembled members of the Council. He noticed that their arms were hanging down at their sides with their hands facing outwards and that they were looking over in their direction with fixed gazes. Ged got the distinct feeling that things were about to get a whole lot more serious than when they had been up in front of the Elders, and that he and Orick were now in really big trouble.

In silence, the Council members respectfully parted to allow Riizlabll, their leader, to step forward. His stature reminded Ged of how he imagined the magician Merlin would have looked. He was exceedingly tall and had the brightest blue eyes Ged had ever seen. Pure white hair tumbled around his shoulders, and his white beard tapered down to his feet. He wore a robe of sapphire blue which had threads of silver running vertically through it and Ged noticed how it sparkled and glistened as though it were a bejewelled ocean. Around his waist he wore a wide, silver, braided belt upon which dangled three differently shaped gold keys. Ged struggled to take his eyes off them as they glinted hypnotically, seemingly by their own accord.

Managing to break his gaze, Ged whispered to Orick, "What are the three gold keys for that are hanging from his belt?"

Looking over nonchalantly, Orick smiled. "What? Oh, those keys. Well, one is the key which unlocks wisdom, one is for revelation and the other is… for his front door."

Ged was taken aback at Orick's answer. "His front door - really? Why does he carry a key for his front door?"

"Of course it's not for his front door! That was a joke — duh! The third key is actually for knowledge or knowing."

Ged glared at Orick and frowning, whispered, "You taking the mick? I'm asking you what the three keys are for and you're taking the mick?"

Orick laughed quietly to himself. "Yeah sorry, couldn't resist. Like I said, one's for wisdom, one's for revelation and the other one is for knowing or knowledge — thought you knew that. You can't have one without all the others.

"Erm… now you come to mention it, I do know, it just kind of slipped my mind. Blimey don't tell me I'm doing a Molly."

Orick chuckled. "Let's hope not - one's enough. The three keys represent the relationship which Spirit have with the Divine. They are metaphorical representations, to give humanity an understanding of their spiritual connection. Well, that's simplifying things of course. Anyway, shush, here goes — wish me luck!" murmured Orick under his breath.

Riizlabll turned his attention to Ged and Orick and addressing Orick in a commanding voice said, "So, Guide Orick, please explain yourself. Explain to all here present why you went against all that had been specified by Elder Pettruff — all that had been decided and agreed upon. Please share with everyone here why you colluded in our Beloved One's constant desire to keep returning to the earth realm."

Orick cleared his throat and clasping his hands behind his back, proceeded to pace backwards and forwards as though he were a defence lawyer delivering a statement of the facts to a jury.

"Thank you Riizlabll for giving me this opportunity to represent myself and explain my actions. Indeed, in my defence all I can say is that I acted out of love. I acted out of love, as I knew that Brenth, our Beloved, was finding it hard to come to terms with what had happened to her, and for the most part, blamed me for her circumstances. So yes, I failed to stop what was being done, and yes, I turned a blind eye, as it were, but I was never far away. I had hoped that Brenth would find satisfactory answers. I thought that she would come to terms with what had happened and recover more quickly if she were allowed to seek her truth. I knew that she would be safe, as she was with her custodian, Cloiff, for it was he who has guided and protected our Beloved since her return, and he has been nothing but a guiding light. He has sought to bring understanding and comprehension in the pursuit of the re-assimilation of her memory. So that is my defence; I did what I did out of love."

Turning to Ged, he winked as he swept his arm across his body in a flourish of exuberance, causing his cloak to swish around his shoulders. The chamber had taken on a sombre atmosphere and the Wise Ones, having listened to what Orick had declared, remained expressionless and impassive.

Orick continued, "Brenth has retained many of her character traits and human ways and is still very stubborn and unchanged in her mannerisms. We assumed that if we helped her to regain her memories, she would adopt a more spirit-like persona. Her error in all of this was that she failed to tell her custodian, Cloiff, what Pettruf had decreed. The reason for that failure, whether through deceit or due to her memory loss, is known only to herself. I must point out that at no time was she in any danger, and it was only because she suffered an energy inversion — and I admit that was an oversight on my part — that any of this would have come to light. But I was there with her every step of the way, although she didn't know it. I was there, along with Cloiff, protecting her, guiding her, doing my job."

"Doing your job? Well, I for one would argue that point. Had you been doing your job, as you put it, you would have realised just how fragile our Beloved was. You should have known that she hadn't merged or melded with her full energy and essence, but because you didn't, — well need I say more? Let this be a lesson to you, Guide Orick!"

A mumbled murmur began to reverberate around the hall before Riizlabll called the gathering to order. "Cloiff, we come to your part in all of this. I acknowledge that it was your desire to assist that made you foolishly pursue this debacle, and I have no doubt that through loving intent you sought to help this spirit, because in essence she was your granddaughter from your previous life lived. Is that correct?"

Ged nodded nervously.

Riizlabll continued, "Because of your, shall we say, misguided actions, certain problems were unnecessarily created, as I'm sure you are now fully aware. I do realise that your actions were made with the best of intentions, but regrettably they have caused complex ramifications."

Orick dared to look defiantly at Riizlabll, and was about to defend himself and Ged again when he noticed that Riizlabll was glaring at him, and his eyes flashed warnings of great infuriation. Orick knew to say nothing more. Riizlabll went over to a large wooden stand which was on the far side of the room. Positioned in the middle of the stand but hovering slightly above it, was an enormous, round, energy ball which appeared to emit a fluorescent, muddy brown-black colour around its outside. This was the all-seeing Orb of Peccancy. Within the orb's energy, shards of all malevolent deeds, thoughts and ill intentions of spirits who had incarnated to the earth realm were captured and safely contained. The malevolent energies were for now inert, and would eventually be totally destroyed once the spirits who owned each shard had fulfilled and made good their karma. The orb pulsed and made a crackling noise as it rocked backwards and forwards in an apparently haphazard way, although Ged knew that there would be nothing haphazard about it. Orick and Ged stared as Riizlabll positioned his hands just above the orb's energy field and gazed deeply into its depths. His eyes flashed backwards and forwards, as he became transfixed by its powerful force.

Ged was suddenly aware of movement coming from behind him as Shelmuthe, presider over the Council of Justice, crossed the room and joined Riizlabll. He too placed his hands just above the orb's energy and scrutinising it, also appeared to become spellbound. Moments passed as an atmosphere of trepidation hung in the still air and no one dared move.

Shaking his head solemnly, Shelmuthe turned, his eyes filled with sadness as he addressed Orick and Ged. "I am in full agreement with Riizlabll. Your meddling has indeed brought great consternation and disquiet. Your actions have delayed and all but jeopardised our Beloved One's recovery. Having heard what you so eloquently stated, I understand what you did and why you did it, however I'm afraid on this occasion your loving intent was misguided and misplaced. Where is the one known as Brenth?" he asked brusquely.

Ged cast a sideways glance at Orick. He was just about to speak when Orick interjected, "I believe Brenth, the Beloved One to whom you refer, has briefly returned to the earth realm."

"Oh, has she now. How ironic! I need not remind you that it was through that very action that this mess came about. This is a most unusual state of affairs that needs to be resolved as quickly as possible. I cannot allow this to continue any longer. I ask Council to locate her energy print and transfer her back here immediately," Shelmuthe commanded.

The Council members stood perfectly still and without any discernible movement, touched their palms together. A brilliant oscillating wave of white light silently rippled around the chamber and Orick and Ged were left in no doubt as to the serious dilemma that the spiritual realm was now facing.

Chapter Thirty: Decision Made

<***>

Molly was visiting her mother and Nan, and had arrived just in time to listen in on the conversation that D.S Millington was having with them.

"Mrs Roberts, I'm here to tell you that we've found the body of the man who we believe murdered Molly. We are still waiting on a couple of test results to come back from the laboratory, but we're pretty confident that Forensics will confirm that a tissue sample which was found under one of Molly's toe nails is a DNA match for this chap."

Annie and Nan looked at one another, then back at the Detective. "Dead? He's dead? Good. I'm glad he's dead, and I hope he rots in hell," spat Nan.

Annie slumped down onto a chair and in a shocked daze, tried to process her thoughts. "Sweet Jesus," she cried out, "It's not enough that I've lost my daughter, my child, but I've also lost any means of getting justice for her." An uncontrollable anger began to surface, as the realisation that there wouldn't be any punishment or retribution for what he'd done began to consume her. How was that fair? How was that justice?

Molly, however, couldn't contain herself and punched the air triumphantly. Just at that moment there was a flash of silver light, and without any warning, she was transported back to the spiritual realm. Orick and Ged were both taken aback as she suddenly appeared in front of them. Not realising what had just happened, Molly broke into an enormous grin.

"Grandpa, you'll never believe it! While I was with Mam and Nan just now, that nice policeman was visiting and told them that they've found Gareth Shaw's body. They know it was him who murdered me. Oh, I'm so happy — at last they…" She stopped mid-sentence. "What's going on? One minute I'm over there and the next I'm…"

Ged shifted awkwardly. "You might want to turn around."

Shelmuthe was looking at Molly with a surprised expression. "What is it that brings you so much excitement, Blessed One?"

Molly spun round in complete surprise and rooted to the spot, looked down, not wanting to meet Shelmuthe's stare.

"We are all well aware of the circumstance you mention, yet this brings you much pleasure because….?" he asked, somewhat austerely. Turning his attention back to Orick and Ged he continued, "I shall hand this fiasco over to Riizlabll. I want both of you to be left in no doubt as to the serious consequences that your actions have brought about."

Riizlabll nodded in agreement as Shelmuthe concluded, "I shall meet with Council again in conference in two dawns, to confer on this matter and mete out appropriate courses of action. Riizlabll, Council — I bid you farewell for now."

All those present respectfully bowed as Shelmuthe exited the chamber with an air of authority, leaving everyone in no doubt that he was most displeased. Crossing the floor to re-join the Council members in their debate, Riizlabll left the three of them to reflect on their actions, while the assembly occasionally looked over in their direction, nodding and whispering before returning to their huddle. Molly was beginning to get irritated and annoyed and was about to say as much when, without any warning, the gathering left the room.

When the last of them had gone, Riizlabll raised a hand, gesturing to Molly. "Approach, Blessed One."

Orick cast a glance at Ged, before bowing his head as he waited for the Wise One to speak.

Riizlabll rose to his full towering height and in an even voice addressed Molly. "I have been given knowledge from Archangel Metatron and Elder Kyah that this situation has caused you much turmoil, as indeed it has this entire realm. Nevertheless, I am sure that in time you will come to have faith, and trust in what is going to be."

Molly stood rooted to the spot, and looked over to her grandfather who gave her a reassuring smile and nod.

Riizlabll continued, "I believe that Kyah has given you direction already as to ways which should help in your recovery. I expect you therefore to fully avail yourself of her advice and guidance."

Molly glanced at Orick but he had broken eye contact with her. Riizlabll walked over to a solid, quartz crystal table which was set back into a recess and pondered a while before reaching out and selecting something off it. As he did so a silver spark flew to his hand. Approaching Molly, he gently took hold of her hands and carefully placed a crystal into each of them.

"I am hopeful that you realise that what happens next is largely down to you. The amount of memories you regain will be instrumental in your recovery, so I want you to take this amethyst crystal and absorb its energy and vibration. The Deva within will help you to heal. It will bring clarity and focus of mind and assist with memory recall and decision making. The rose quartz crystal is to heal your heart and instil unconditional love, not only for others, but also for yourself. Do not forget that you have choices, and the choices you make here are just as important as the choices you made while you were on the earth realm. Do you understand?"

Molly meekly nodded her head.

"I know that you will make the right choice and therefore come to the right decision," Riizlabll said kindly.

Molly didn't know what to say, so just nodded her head again.

Riizlabll turned to address Ged and Orick, his piercing blue eyes holding them both transfixed as he fingered the keys which hung from his waist. "Your actions necessitated me to seek additional guidance. I have, albeit reluctantly, consulted the ancient manuscripts, and you will appreciate that my having to take that course of action reflects the seriousness of what has come to pass. Your misguided deeds and participation in all of this has to be acknowledged as idiotic, to say the least, yet I know it was meant with the best of intention. That said, you will both be held accountable — how can you not be? You do understand that, don't you?"

Orick and Ged nodded in unison.

"I have to leave now, but as soon as I know what decision has been taken, you will be summoned. For now, I suggest that you all reflect on your misguided deeds and actions."

The three of them stood transfixed as Riizlabll left the room.

"What does he mean, be held accountable? What misguided deeds? Jeez, it's not like anything bad's happened."

Ged and Orick both looked at Molly exasperated. "No, I suppose not," replied Orick incredulously, "I suppose not."

Chapter Thirty-one: Intolerance

<***>

M olly met up with Vimprn the following day in the Gardens. She was delighted to see her again, and discuss what had happened with Riizlabll and the Council.

"So, how did it go?" asked Vimprn.

Molly shrugged. "Could have been worse, I s'pose. Thing is, I still don't know what to do. What would you do?"

"Me? Huh, don't ask me, I honestly don't know. But one thing's for sure, I hope that I never have a decision like that to make."

"No, I don't suppose anyone does. Anyway, enough about me, how's your new contract coming along? Didn't you say that you have a couple of specific lessons you need to do when you next incarnate — temperance and forgiveness, wasn't it?" enquired Molly.

"Yes, hopefully I'll get them right this time round. And well done for remembering — see, you are getting better. Oh-oh, don't look now but Dolf is watching. Actually, he's coming over," whispered Vimprn.

Molly was rooted to the spot. "Oh crap, what the hell does he want? Don't leave me alone with him, will you. Please stay with me," she pleaded.

"Of course, I'll stay with you," nodded Vimprn.

Dolf sauntered over towards them and somewhat awkwardly, sat down next to Molly.

"Please, Molly, I need to talk to you."

Staring at him in disbelief, she tried to contain her anger. "What do you want, Dolf? I don't have anything more to say to you. Not only did you mess up my energy and vibration, you also effectively shredded my soul in the process. Do you have any understanding of what that means? Well, do you?" Molly was furious and it was all she could do to control herself.

Dolf didn't move. "Please, hear me out. I know that what I did was wrong, and I know how bad things are for you, right now. Obviously, I've messed up big time, but I'm trying to make things right, not only for you, but also for me."

Molly couldn't contain herself any longer. "Make things right? Make things right? So just how do you intend to 'make things right'?" she said angrily, doing the inverted comma air sign. "Jesus, you have absolutely no idea, do you. It's all about you, isn't it? Get lost you stupid, stupid, selfish idiot! If I never see you again, it will be too soon," she shrieked.

"That's just it — don't you get it? I've got to leave, I'm leaving this realm, and I can't ever reincarnate back to earth."

"Good, then you'll be doing us all a massive favour. I'm glad, and I hope you damn well rot there. Do you know what, Gareth… or Dolf… or whatever your bloody name is? Not once have you actually said you're sorry. Not once have you actually apologised to me for what you've done."

"Me, apologise? That's rich! I'm back here having to deal with all of this crap. It's been just as hard for me as well, you know. When we made that contract — which if I remember rightly was done just so you could be Miss Hoity-toity-high-and - bloody-mighty — I didn't bargain on any of this happening."

"Hoity-toity? What's that supposed to mean? Hard for you! Well, my heart bleeds, cos do you know what? That's what I call justice… no, karma… yes, karma. Don't you dare expect me to feel sorry for you, you selfish gob shite. I can't believe that you've just moaned about being back here. Oh my God, I can't believe that you honestly think that you've been hard done by. You know what? Just get lost, Gareth… Dolf… whatever the hell you call yourself. I'm sick of the sight of you… you… God…, do you know what? I would cheerfully vomit my guts up if I thought it would help."

Vimprn moved between them to intervene. "I think it best if you left now, Dolf," she said, more forcefully than she had intended.

"But I need her to understand. She needs to understand. She needs to remember, because I sure as hell didn't contract to be back here this soon. That wasn't part of the deal."

"Part of the deal? Part of the deal? Me, remember? Christ almighty, what the hell do you think I've been trying to do all this time? And you're whinging just because you're here sooner than you think you should be! Well, like I said, ain't it a bitch when karma comes back to bite you on your arse. Just piss off will you, you pathetic excuse for a… a spirit."

Dolf looked defeated and cast a glance at Vimprn, still hoping to muster her support.

"Don't look at me, Dolf. You heard what she said — just go. She has other, more pressing things on her mind."

Vimprn and Molly watched as the retreating light disappeared into the distance.

"'Vomit your guts up.' I've heard it all now," laughed Vimprn.

Chapter Thirty-two: Retribution

<***>

Dolf was going over in his mind the conversation that he and Prenge had shared, and felt nervous and a little edgy. He had been instructed by the Elders to return to his soul group, and wasn't relishing the likely outcome. It was hoped that they might be able to understand what he had done, and although he was happy to reunite with most of them, he was feeling apprehensive all the same.

"Dolf... Dolf... over here."

Dolf gravitated over to where the shouted welcome had come from.

"Greetings my friend — long-time no see," said Hyptok as Dolf sat down next to her. Several of his soul group began to congregate, and form a circle.

"So, we hear that the Elders want us to help you to see the errors of your ways," said Hyptok lightly.

Dolf hung his head. "Yes, but I don't see how any of this is going to help," he replied curtly.

Hyptok was taken aback at his response. "I see. Well, maybe if you were to participate in a discussion with us, we might be able to help iron out a few problems for you — come up with a few suggestions even."

"Help me? Huh, it's too late for that. Didn't they tell you? Apparently, I'm a lost cause."

"Nonsense, there's no such thing," replied Hyptok brightly, as she rested her hand on his arm.

Abruptly one of the more senior members interrupted. "I beg to differ," said Edtus, "I believe that there are such things as lost causes. I will never understand why you did what you did, and I cannot for the life of me condone what you did, nor will I defend your actions. I wish to make it perfectly clear that I am of the opinion that you have only yourself to blame."

Hyptok scowled at Edtus. "Well, we know that you are never one to mince your words, but really…"

Suddenly everyone was talking at the same time and several heated discussions and arguments ensued. Dolf was beginning to form the distinct impression that none of them seemed able to reconcile his actions or suggest how to redress or reduce the damage he had caused. It was being made abundantly clear that he was the only one who could resolve this problem.

Rising above the rest of the group, Edtus raised his voice to make himself heard, as he scornfully addressed Dolf. "It is of course regretful that you find yourself in this predicament, yet I don't know how to counsel you. What I have observed is that you appear to be unable to take responsibility for any of your errant actions. Why should that be? Why do you persist in conducting yourself in this manner, when you know full well that what you have done in all of your incarnations is wholly unacceptable and completely goes against the love of the Great Spirit?"

Dolf remained silent as Hyptok nodded in agreement. "Edtus does have a point. It's as though once you inhabit a physical vessel, you have no conscience, no sense of obligation and dare I say it, no soul connection…" Her voice suddenly dropped to a whisper and looking him in the eye she added, "… and no self-love."

The others looked on, quietly contemplating what Hyptok had just said. Dolf stared into the distance as he realised that she was right — he didn't feel love or remorse or guilt. In fact, he didn't feel any of the things that he knew any self-respecting spirit should feel.

Edtus studied him, knowing that what he was about to ask would send ripples of alarm through the group. "Is it possible, that during your early formation as a star seed you were influenced by the… Lessers?"

Dolf visibly flinched as though a raw nerve had been exposed. "What do you mean, the Lessers?" he asked, almost a little too defensively.

Hyptok flashed an enquiring look at Edtus as he continued, "Come, come now Dolf, you must be aware of the existence of lesser energies. You must know that the Lessers prowl the lower astral planes of the spiritual realm. They purposefully seek out the new, the naïve, the star seeds, offering despicable yet irresistible rewards of untold power and influence in return for enactments of the lowest forms of depravity. Their influence over the wretches they target stretches far and wide. Were you ever approached, Dolf? Were you ever... recruited?"

Dolf shifted awkwardly as he fought to suppress a stirring of memories which started to float to the surface of his consciousness. Should he admit what he knew to be true? Alarmed at what was happening, Dolf suddenly felt waves of confusion, as inner turmoil and bewilderment washed over him. He sensed a jolt in his energy, and felt exposed and naked, as though he had just exposed his soul. But he felt relief too — it was as though the mask that he was wearing had slipped, exposing to all, what was really underneath. He suddenly felt Hyptok embrace him as his shuddering energy became calm once again, and in that instant Dolf knew that his inner light had been revealed.

"I don't know what to say to you, Dolf. You have just bared your true self. The Elders must be made aware of your involvement with the Lessers. I'm sure they will know what to do," said Hyptok reassuringly.

Surveying the expanse of the Cosmos, Dolf sat alone on the steps of the Halls of Wisdom. He looked out over the vastness of the spiritual plateau, observing the multiple dimensions which made up the immensity of it all. He was looking in the direction of the Towers when suddenly something caught his attention. He noticed a swirling funnel of glistening silver and golden light descending from one of the higher dimensions and realised that a group of angels was gathering at the bottom of the funnel. They were newly assigned guardian angels, about to take their first steps as qualified protectors. They shone with a dazzling, radiant light which pulsed and glowed, and each of them had an aura of pink and pale-blue translucency around them. Their silvery-white and yellow wings glinted in the morning sunlight as the new day began. Dolf was just thinking that they appeared to be somewhat sombre when suddenly they began to sing in harmony, lamenting in a final tribute to the heavenly realm. He watched as the funnel of heavenly light began to dissipate.

Dolf watched enthralled as the angels began to enter the Towers. Dolf knew that Adzullon would be assigning each of them to a baby about to be born on the earth plane. Dolf suddenly had an idea; what if he could meet with Thumus, Molly's guardian angel? Thumus knew about the agreement and contract between himself and Molly and Molly would believe Thumus. Yes, that was it, that was the answer; if he could convince Thumus to talk to her, then maybe she would agree to forgive him. Dolf immediately contacted Thumus telepathically, and the angel agreed to meet him later that day.

When they met up in the Gardens, Dolf quickly explained his idea and plan, and begged Thumus to speak to Molly on his behalf. "Please…" he urged, "Please… you have to try and get her to see reason, otherwise I'm well and truly scuppered."

"Look Dolf, I'm not promising anything — it's entirely up to her. You know full well that upon a spirit's return, all injustices are automatically forgiven. Nothing is harboured, no grudges are held, and there is no bitterness nor resentment, because Spirit know only love. The problem, my friend, is that you are failing to understand why Molly is thinking and behaving as she is. Don't forget that through your actions, Molly has had most of her memory erased. She is struggling to adjust and is still behaving like a human being, and so is unable to think or behave in any other way. Essentially, she's stuck. Her decisions will be made under the influence of human emotions and her retained human psyche."

Dolf nodded his understanding but looked somewhat deflated.

"You must realise that right across the realm, all are working hard to rectify what you have done. We are hopeful that the Elders will get to the bottom of this and be able to formulate a solution to rescue the situation. In any event, it will be a solution in which I would caution you not to meddle. I trust you understand that, at least."

Dolf sighed deeply. "Yeah, well it's worth a shot, isn't it?"

"I will see what I can do, but like I said, it's entirely up to our Beloved."

Watching pensively as Thumus disappeared into the ether, Dolf hoped against all hope, that Molly would agree.

Chapter Thirty-three: Guidance

<***>

The following dawn, Thumus telepathically summoned Prenge, Dolf and Molly, and instructed them to meet him in the Gardens of Tranquillity. Watching from a distance, Orick observed them as they walked together. Suddenly Molly stopped in her tracks. Raising her arms and flailing them in the air, she appeared to be arguing with Thumus and Dolf and Orick realised he could hear her angry shouts being carried on the breeze. He watched as she abruptly stomped off, and quickly set off after her. He managed to catch up with her at the same time as Thumus and they both tried unsuccessfully to calm her down. She was livid and Orick was stunned at the magnitude of her outburst, as she continued with her rant and tirade.

"Molly, you need to calm down; this isn't helping anyone, least of all you. What on earth has got you so riled? I was watching you all, and then you suddenly ran off. What's happened?"

"Happened? I'll tell you what's bloody happened. That murdering bastard, that piece of… of… whatever… got Thumus to try and persuade me to forgive him. That manipulating gobshite was all but demanding — yes, demanding — that I see my way to forgiving and forgetting. Can you believe that? Christ almighty! Bloody cheek, he's got some brass neck"

"Is that true, Thumus?"

Thumus nodded. "Yes, it's true; Dolf wanted me to try and persuade her to forgive him. Obviously, you saw how that went."

"Quite." said Orick somewhat subdued. "Although I have received guidance that there is another way of resolving this."

Molly glared defiantly. "Really! Then be my guest, cos I'm telling you now, there is no way that Dolf is getting anything off me, least of all my forgiveness."

Orick pondered about the best way of telling Molly his news. Bracing himself he said, "Molly, there's no easy way to say this, and I'm not sure how you're going to react to what I have to say."

Molly glared at him. "Tell me what? It can't be any worse than what that devious little... Well what are you waiting for? Oh, for God's sake Orick, spit it out. You're just as bloody infuriating as Dolf."

Orick looked hurt. "Well, the Elders have instructed me to inform you of their decision for your advancement and development."

"Really...their decision for... oh, for goodness sake Orick, get on with it."

"Now, promise that you're going to calm down — you're totally unreasonable when you're like this."

Glowering, Molly folded her arms and started to tap her foot impatiently. "Honestly, this whole thing is bloody ridiculous."

"They've told me that if you were to reincarnate, the damage which was done to your energy would leave you very vulnerable, and in all likelihood, there would be nothing to gain. However, you do still have choice and free will, which means you can choose to go back to the physical should you wish. But like I said, it would be with a very impaired energy print." He hesitated briefly, choosing his moment, then hurriedly let the words tumble into the space between them, "...Or you can train to be a spirit guide."

Molly was lost for words and stared at Orick as if he had completely lost his mind.

"Either way, I will teach and prepare you for whatever decision you make."

Molly couldn't believe what she had just heard. "Yeah right, train to be a guide? Are you stark raving bonkers? Me, train to be a guide? Don't be so bloody ridiculous. I've heard everything now!"

Orick was taken aback by Molly's reaction. "Why is it ridiculous? As far as I can see, it's a perfect solution to an impossible problem. Yes, it means that you will only be able to return to the earth plane when you have an incarnating spirit to take care of, but think about it — what have you got to lose? Besides which, I quite fancy the idea of being a teacher."

"Listen mate, I've heard some bloody stupid ideas but that just about takes the biscuit. You, be a teacher? That's just plain idiotic. When have you ever taught me anything, well anything that's ever been useful? Besides which, if I become a guide I can't go back and see Mam or Nan whenever I want to. No, I can't do that — I couldn't bear it."

Orick took her hand and gently placed it in his. "Molly, you have to understand that the Elders have explored all available options for you, and the reality is that there are none other than this one. When you think about it, really this will be the best outcome for all concerned. Look, your mother and Nan are going to be earth-side only for the foreseeable future, which means that in the dimension of their time, their return home will be relatively soon. So, in the scheme of things, becoming a guide makes perfect sense."

Molly sat quietly, thinking over what Orick had just said. "Okay, so what if I were to reincarnate with an impaired energy print? What would happen?"

"Well, I think that if you were to reincarnate, your energy print would probably be so weak that it wouldn't be able to properly function in a physical vessel anyway. And another thing — as you were so near to ascension, what's the point!"

Molly shifted uncomfortably, falling silent as she processed what Orick had just said. "Are you saying that having a weak or damaged energy print would only let me function in a disfigured or disabled body, or vessel as you call it?"

"Well yes, there is that. In all probability you…"

"So, what you're saying is that people who are born disabled or have some deformity or such like, are just like me?"

"What! No, that's not what I'm saying at all. As Spirit, they will have contracted for those conditions."

"Contracted? Why the bloody hell would any spirit contract to be in a vessel that's purposefully impaired to start with?"

Thumus smiled knowingly. "Because existing in a body that has… failings, shall we say, is seen as a huge act of love. Contracting to live in that type of vessel is a conscious decision to accomplish a selfless act. Humans with afflictions in whatever guise, have in effect made a sacrifice. As spirit when they contracted to reincarnate, they undertook that sacrifice in order to teach other human beings lessons such as tolerance, patience, non-judgment, acceptance or unconditional love. In some cases, it may even be as a means for that particular spirit to learn a difficult life lesson themselves. It's not a punishment or a penance, as some believe — that's just nonsense. And like Orick said, forget about Nan and your mother; they will be here soon enough anyway."

Thumus paused, waiting for Molly to comprehend what he had just told her before continuing. "It is my understanding that you have to make a decision, a choice. You must choose because you cannot stay as you are."

"Look, you are still thinking like a human being," Orick interrupted, exasperated by Molly's attitude. "You'll just have to trust us on this one. You have to let go of the human traits which are still imprinted on your energy. You are Spirit, and as such you need to start thinking, thinking and behaving like Spirit again. You must realise that events and past deeds and wrong doings which happened to you on the earth were all part of your learning and contract fulfilment."

Molly looked away and tutting under her breath, began to fidget.

"Molly, you have to understand that the one unwavering and resolute common denominator that binds Spirit together is love: it is a love of the purest form and highest vibration and is unconditional. The love from the Great Spirit is all powerful. Do you not see, do you not feel it, sense it? The Divine's love is everywhere. It's in us all and it's around us in everything. Love is

the Universe. Love is the glue that binds us, connects us."
enthused Thumus.

Molly shrugged, appearing almost indifferent. "Right, okay,
okay! Stop going on will you, I get it. And that's another thing —
just when do I get to meet the 'Divine'… 'God'… whatever?"
she asked cockily, doing the inverted commas air sign.

Orick pursed his lips. "What? You don't… The order of
cosmic law is that only very evolved Spirit — Ascended Masters,
Angels and higher beings and the like — can tolerate the
powerful, all-consuming expression of love that comes from the
Great Spirit. Like I said, you don't have to be in the Divine's
presence to know that love is in you and all around you."

Molly stayed silent as she realised that she had just been put
firmly in her place.

Orick raised his voice in frustration. "Look Molly, human
traits of negativity have no place here. They do not serve you, so
let them go. Forgive Dolf, send him love and then move on. Stop
being so… so… bloody human!"

Molly glared at Orick. "Oh, no pressure then! Stop rushing
me. And anyway, if I do decide to become a guide, what will
happen to me?"

Orick regained his composure. "Well, I'll teach you the
basics, which will give you enough knowledge to join the Guides
Guild, after which you will get to work with some of the more
experienced guides and senior Elders, before progressing to
learn from the Ascended Masters. Once they feel that you are
ready to advance further, you will be paired with a guardian angel,
after which you will be assigned to a spirit who is about to
reincarnate."

"Hang on, slow down! Ascended Masters? Who are they
when they're at home?"

Orick took a deep, exasperated breath. "You've never heard
of the Ascended Masters? What the heck do they teach you over
there? Ascended Masters are enlightened ones, like Jesus and
Buddha, to name just two. They were human beings once, but

have ascended because of their love and selfless service to humanity. They are pure energy and I mean, 'pure' in the true sense of the word."

"Buddha?" said Molly. "Jesus? You're joking right? You mean to tell me that they're the real deal? No way! And anyway, for your information, I do know who Jesus is. Nan was always banging on about him whenever she went to church. So yeah, I've heard of him, hasn't everyone? Anyway, just how long is all this going to take?"

Orick frowned, "Three, four, five years, give or take, does it matter? The reality is that it takes as long as it takes. I think you've earned concessions anyway, and as time has no relevance here, well, this is all there is. Time is an earthly constraint, an earth measure. If you agree to be a guide it means that you are in service and that's that. It is what it is. Quit complaining and think about it — it's a win/win solution. You still get to visit the earth realm but don't have to do any of the hardship stuff. It's a perfect solution, in my book."

Thumus nodded in agreement, trying to encourage Molly to see reason. "Orick knows his stuff. You know you couldn't get a better teacher. Give him a try, at least."

Molly shrugged her shoulders. "Well you're making it sound like I've nothing to lose. It's just that he makes me so mad — Dolf, I mean."

"It's okay, we understand, but Orick's right, what's there to think about? Look, in the normal scheme of things, Spirit have to incarnate as many times as it takes to learn all the lessons — the cosmic curriculum as it were. Now that usually takes about three thousand earth years, give or take a century or two. It's only then that Spirit get to ascend and be given the opportunity to become spirit guides," Thumus said reassuringly.

"Three thousand years? You've got to be kidding."

Orick snorted. "No, that's how long it takes the average spirit to learn and experience all the lessons. So yes, in case you're wondering, you really are that old."

Thumus continued, "Dolf's fate has yet to be fully decided, but if you forgive him it allows you to heal quicker because you let go of a very negative emotion. Normally that would have been an automatic 'done-deal', as it were, on your return. The problem's compounded because of your inability to let go of a common negative human trait — 'mountains into molehills' comes to mind. By your forgiving him, you activate the catalyst which gives you emotional freedom, then, hey presto, job's a good un and everybody's happy."

"Right, and if I don't forgive him, what happens to him?"

Thumus glanced over at Orick. "Look Molly, Dolf is obviously an immature spirit who bit off more than he could chew. He's going to have to leave this dimension and transfer to one of the lower astral planes, while he does the soul-searching bit and has the healing and teachings he needs. Having spoken to Prenge, we agree that one thing's for certain — Dolf isn't going to be allowed to reincarnate back to the earth realm any time soon, if ever again."

"Oh, I'm not sure about any of this. Okay, I need to be by myself for a while; I need to think and mull things over."

Rolling his eyes and shaking his head in exasperation, Orick looked over at Thumus. "Mull things over? She wants to mull things over! Heavenly realms, give me strength! What's to mull?" he exclaimed, sighing in frustration.

Chapter Thirty-four: To Err Is Human, To Forgive Divine

<***>

It took Molly the best part of three days and much soul searching to make her decision. Desperately needing to see her grandfather, she contacted him telepathically and arranged to meet in the Gardens. It had been a while since they had seen one another, and she was excited and overjoyed to see him. Molly knew that he had been visiting the earth realm a lot recently, so they would have lots of news to catch up on.

"Hi Gramps, oh it's lovely to see you again. What have you been up to? I haven't seen you in ages," she gushed as she recognised his light.

Ged smiled and hugging her, replied, "Well you've been busy and I've been busy — you know how these things go. What's up, what's so urgent?"

Molly could hardly contain her excitement. "I have something to tell you, and I wanted you to be the first to know," she said, beaming.

"Know what?"

"Well, it's been decided. I've made my decision — I'm going to train to be a guide." She let the words momentarily hang in the air before continuing, "Initially Orick is going to teach me and show me the ropes, as it were, but then I get to work with the Elders and Wise Ones and whoever else! Can you imagine? Oh Grandpa, I'm so happy now I've made my decision. I feel different — it's like a huge weight has been lifted off me."

Ged held her at arm's length. "Oh Molly, I'm so chuffed for you and so proud. Who'd have thought it, eh? It's like you've got your wings, well sort of. Well who'd have thought — you, a guide."

"I know, I can't believe it myself. Who'd have thought," she said happily. "But first I have to forgive that idiot Dolf, and to do that I have to undergo a 'Forgiveness Ceremony', whatever that is! That's why I wanted to see you — to ask you if you'll come. It's tomorrow — short notice I know."

Molly had felt a mixture of emotions since she had been asked to forgive Dolf, and even now she was still unsure and confused as to why this was necessary. She had to keep reminding herself that she wasn't constrained any more by human emotions and negative thought patterns, and as hard as it was, she knew that if she were to progress then she had to let go of all the hate and loathing that she felt towards him. Ged knew that Molly had struggled to come to terms with how things were going to have to be, and making the decision to forgive Dolf had been very hard for her. He felt so proud of her, and was delighted that tomorrow was going to be her special day.

"Of course, I'll come, just you try and stop me! I wouldn't miss it for the world. Oh, I'm so proud of you. So, what else have they got you doing?"

"Well, after the ceremony I'm going back to school. God, I sound like a kid! If I've remembered anything though, it's that I flipping hated school. Anyway, I'll have to study and I won't be able to visit Mam or Nan for quite a while, so will you keep an eye on them?"

"Ah, about that. You've probably gathered I've been away a lot lately because… well… I have something to tell you." Ged hesitated for a second. "The thing is… well it's Nan. She's not been so good, health-wise, and now… well, she's just been diagnosed with lung cancer."

"Oh… so how long till she gets back?"

"Don't know for sure. A year, maybe less."

"Oh Grandpa, how wonderful. I bet you're excited, aren't you?"

Ged gave her a beaming smile. "Yes, I am, it will be fantastic having her with me again."

The following dawn, Molly was to be prepared for her Forgiveness Ceremony by the Serenity Muses. She was escorted to an area which was set back a little from the Waters of Purity. It was a large, walled courtyard in which flowers, shrubs and small fruit trees were growing. The courtyard was laid out in a formal design which incorporated ancient, sacred geometry symbols and shapes. She recognised some of them and remembered that she had seen similar ones in the Akashic library. Molly noticed how the aroma from the flowers was heady and intoxicating and looking around her, she could see hundreds of elementals darting about. Fairies, sylphs, pixies and sprites were coming and going as they tended the flowers and trees.

Her attention was suddenly drawn to what appeared to be an enormous chunk of rock jutting out precariously from one of the walls. Floating over to it, she realised that it was a huge rose quartz crystal. Pulsating, pink energy emanated from it, and she sensed that the energy flowed around the entire courtyard. The crystal was fashioned in the shape of a tetrahedron and it appeared to be positioned at a strange angle, in a rather precarious position. Its facets were smooth and highly polished, and it reminded her of the huge green crystal which she had seen when she had been with Archangel Metatron. At the base of the pink crystal there was a semi-circular pool fashioned out of a huge piece of clear quartz crystal which glinted and sparkled in the brightening sky. Placing her hand on one of the crystal facets to steady herself, she sat side-saddle on the edge of the pool. As she peered into it, she noticed that it held the most crystal-clear water she had ever seen — water so clear that it was almost invisible, yet it glinted and glistened like ice. Gazing into the water, she studied her reflection, and she suddenly became aware that there were two reflections looking back at her and realised that someone was standing behind her. Spinning around, she was surprised to see it was her great grandma Hilda.

"Hello my darling," Hilda said as her bright smiling eyes fixed on Molly and the dimples in her cheeks expanded with her smile.

Molly flung her arms around her and embraced and hugged her. "Great Grandma Hilda! What are you doing here? What's going on?"

"Well my darling, isn't this wonderful? I have been asked by the Wise Ones to guide you and to show you what it truly means to forgive. Now, I'm going to have to be all business-like as this is a serious matter, so just do as I ask."

Molly stepped back a little with a confused look on her face. "Wow, the Wise Ones, eh? But why you, Great Grandma, why have they sent you? I didn't expect to see you again so soon."

"Please call me by my soul name — here I am known as Glyzha. The Wise Ones have decided that I would be the most appropriate one to assist you with this monumental moment of transformation because we belong to the same soul group, and because I too was murdered without compassion in one of my previous lives."

"What, no way! How so?"

"How, does not matter. What matters is that you get to do this and that you ultimately become a guide, because if you don't, you will remain locked within the human psyche and still behave and think like a human being. That cannot be allowed to happen — it would be too difficult for you to deal with. So you have to find it in your heart to forgive, and I am here to help you do just that. Now, I want you to fully trust and embrace what is about to happen. I need to get you ready and there is a lot of preparation to be made before the actual ceremony can take place."

Molly frowned and was about to ask a question but decided to stay quiet.

"In your quest to find forgiveness, you must first understand what it is to truly forgive. Forgiveness comes from the heart, as does unconditional love. The two are intricately entwined, inextricably linked. Their complexity is truly divine. This pool holds the energy of unconditional love and that beautiful, striking crystal before you embodies the pulsating heart-beat of the universe. The human heart is a replication of this crystal, and its design is that of a sacred geometry vortex. As you gaze into the waters, they will become turbulent, just as blood being pushed through a beating heart is turbulent. When your reflection truly holds the worth of unconditional love and compassion for yourself, then — and only then — will the waters become still once again. For it is only when you love yourself unconditionally that you can give unconditional love to another. Molly, you have to understand that a pure heart only knows forgiveness — how can it not?"

Molly looked forlorn. "But how do I find unconditional love, particularly for one who has so badly hurt and wounded me? How do I do that, Great Grandma — Glyzha I mean?"

"Through compassion. When you know compassion, then you will know unconditional love. When you feel compassion for yourself and you forgive your own wrong doings and shortcomings, then you will find it in your heart to forgive others their wrong doings and shortcomings. As humans, we are particularly hard on ourselves and therefore hard on others. Our expectations of others mirror our expectations of ourselves, and mirrored expectations are seldom met, so we feel let down or disappointed."

Glyzha motioned for Molly to kneel in front of the pool, and as she did so she saw the water within it begin to churn and swirl, distorting her reflection. Glyzha smiled as she knelt at Molly's side. Molly had to resist an urge to thrust her hands into the water, as she was suddenly overcome with rage and anger. Glyzha could see the torment that Molly was battling and embracing her, blended with her energy.

"It's okay, Molly, let it go. Release that which is holding you prisoner. Release what no longer serves."

Molly gave a heaving shudder as she sobbed and cried and thrusting herself forwards, wrenched herself free from Glyzha's embrace and plunged into the pool. Thrashing and flailing in the water, she released all her pent-up anger and rage, which spilled out of her like black ink, clouding and discolouring the water. Molly could feel herself sinking, almost drowning in the depths of despair, when suddenly she felt herself being pushed up to the surface again.

Glyzha reached out, and grabbing Molly, hauled her out of the pool. Holding Molly tightly, she whispered soothingly, "Oh my sweet, brave Beloved, your struggle is almost over. Calm yourself now and allow the energy of unconditional love to course through you. Release the burden which you carry. Shush now, shush."

Molly was spent; she was weak and emotionally drained. Looking into Glyzha's eyes, she suddenly understood, and feelings of elation and serenity swept over her.

"It's okay, I'm okay. I feel totally different, though. I feel lighter, like I'm complete, like I'm whole again."

Glyzha smiled tenderly, and speaking in a whisper said, "Your torment is at an end, for that is what you had sentenced yourself to. The negative emotions which we possess as humans only serve to disable and divide us, yet if we learnt to counter those dark elements, we would stop punishing ourselves and each other. You have released one of the very darkest, negative emotions that there is — the emotion of hatred."

Molly gathered her thoughts again, and sitting on the wall of the pool, continued to stare into the waters as they bubbled and frothed.

"Now focus on your reflection, Molly. See your light… feel your serenity… become aware of your beautiful energy. See how gentle it is, how calm it has become. Feel it embrace you…sense it… know it."

Molly stared at her reflection as if in a trance. Glyzha was making utterances in a language that Molly didn't recognise, but the words were calming and reassuring to her as she began to identify something which was cemented in the very core of her being. She recognised the emotion of compassion as it began to surface and envelop her, and with it came an all-consuming wave of love — love which was overwhelming, love which was all-consuming, love which was so beautifully crafted that she began to weep. And as her tears fell into the turbulent pool, the waters began to calm, until they became still and motionless as Molly shed her last tear.

Glyzha hugged her and stroking Molly's hair, said, "Now you can drink from the waters, for now you know what forgiveness is. You searched your heart and found what was buried deep within — once held in captivity, but now freed like a bird. You have let it go to soar on its own wings."

Molly bent forwards and cupping her hands into the crystal-clear water, drank thirstily from the pool. The water was refreshing and cooling, and as Molly savoured the fulfilling quench, she felt satiated and complete. Glyzha cradled Molly for a time, relishing the comfort and contact of a kindred spirit. She stroked Molly's hair one last time, before reluctantly releasing her embrace.

"Right then, shall we get you ready for this ceremony you're having?"

Molly smiled but still felt very apprehensive and a little nervous.

"The Serenity Muses are approaching. You need to go with them, my Beloved, to be made ready."

The Serenity Muses led Molly to an area on the other side of the courtyard and began to robe her in a beautiful ceremonial gown of vibrant, rose-pink energy which tumbled and pooled around her feet. The Muses were elegant and beautiful, with soft smiles which played across soft lips and dew-fresh skin, and Molly began to realise just why they were called Serenity Muses. A veil of delicate, pearlescent, green energy, which shimmered and glinted as though studded with peridot and emerald jewels, was placed gently over her head and was secured in place with a headband made of vibrant, pink rhodonite crystal. Around her throat was placed a blue chalcedony gemstone necklace, and her hand automatically explored the shape and feel of it. She stood entranced as a cloak of pure, white light was draped around her shoulders and secured in place with a crystal brooch made from angel tears. Molly immediately noticed how heavy the brooch was, and studying it closely, realised it was making a double rainbow which formed an arc above her. It created the most beautiful, intense colours which were so vivid that it was impossible to gaze at them for any length of time. Feeling happy and exhilarated, she wanted to dance and twirl and laugh with joy and elation.

Two of the Muses embraced her tenderly, and bringing her hands together, gently bound them with the Cords of Grace. Molly studied the purple- and gold-coloured cords and saw how they were woven and entwined together. She realised that she could feel an intense tingle as the cords' powerful energies pulsed and quivered with the purest expressions of love, empathy and compassion.

Molly felt radiant and incredibly happy, as the sunlight of a new dawn rose from behind the Towers and bathed her in its warmth. She was led down to the water's edge by the attending Serenity Muses, who scattered pink rose petals before her. Ged was overcome with emotion at how stunningly beautiful she looked, and feeling very proud of his granddaughter, brushed a tear away.

Orick motioned her to step forwards and instructed her to wade into the water until she was waist-deep in the crystal-clear fluid of purity. Looking along the edge of the lake, she could see the Elders, angels, and guides who had nurtured and healed her back to health, all waiting in excited anticipation. Scanning the large gathering, she saw two of the most important people who were now back in her life, her grandfather Ged and her great grandma Hilda. Molly was thrilled to see everyone gathered, although she was nervous and apprehensive — after all, they had all assembled to witness her releasing the burden of un-forgiveness. As the excited throng who had come to witness the ceremony looked on, she was suddenly aware of a very strange sensation which came from deep within her. It started to rise, almost bubbling out of her, and it was all she could do to contain the feeling of exhilaration and elation.

Dolf was standing at the water's edge next to Prenge. He was relieved that Molly had agreed to undertake the ceremony, as at last he would be able to clear his karma and face his remorse. He too had had to prepare himself for this moment. He had received healing and tutorage, and had been given time to reflect on his abhorrent actions. He knew that once he walked away, he wouldn't be coming back. Molly held out her tied hands towards Dolf and beckoned to him, inviting him to join her in the warm, glinting waters. Gesturing to him, she prompted him to untie the cords of grace from around her wrists, as the sun began to climb higher into the clear, azure-blue sky. Dolf pulled the end of the cord nearest to him and watched as it fell away easily, allowing Molly to open her arms to him.

They tentatively embraced and she whispered into his ear, "Dolf, I still don't fully understand what happened, nor is it likely that I ever shall. Maybe the fact that I will never completely regain or remember what your actions brought about will be my salvation. To be honest, I'm now past caring, but I want you to know that I do forgive you. My forgiveness for you is because I choose to release the burden of un-forgiveness, and I also relinquish the negative emotions of hatred and anger. I now realise how easily I could have crippled and damaged my already fragile vibration had I not done so."

Dolf remained still and looked down into the depths of the water to avoid making eye contact.

"I hope you find your inner peace and light and wherever you are destined to be, I have every faith that eventually you will blossom and thrive. But I also want you to know that I never want to see you again… ever. Do you understand?"

Molly glared. "Look at me," she commanded.

Dolf slowly lifted his head and looking into Molly's eyes, felt a sharp pain slice into his heart.

"Still can't bring yourself to say it, can you?"

"Say what?"

"Oh, you know, the 's' word… the 'sorry' word. Maybe that's something you need to work on, amongst other things," she said belligerently.

They stood side-by-side as each of the gathering approached them and in turn offered a blessing, before giving them both a loving embrace. When everyone had returned to the shoreline, Molly and Dolf faced one another again. Raising her arms and holding them outstretched in front of her, she encouraged Dolf to place his palms flat against hers. Standing erect and with her head held high, she once again fixed Dolf in her gaze and let her voice ring out for all to hear her proclamation.

"Dolf, you were instrumental in the premeditated obliteration of my soul. You also attempted to all but annihilate and damage my spirit. Your actions could have proved catastrophic for me. Were it not for the unquestioning love, teachings and healings which I have received, who knows where I would be right now? The realisation that all there is by decree is divine love, was the catalyst to my recovery. I will therefore grant you forgiveness, a forgiveness which is given to you through love and compassion, and which I give from the very core of my being, in the knowledge that you too need to be healed."

Dolf smiled gratefully, and advancing into Molly's energy field, merged and melded with her vibration, while a funnel of purifying water rose up around them and enveloped them both, washing away any remaining traces of negativity and hostility. Molly suddenly realised how buoyant and free her energy felt, now that the negative energies had been fully released and transmuted. After releasing their hold from one another, Molly watched as Dolf drifted away from her across the expanse of the

Waters of Purity. As he reached the opposite shore, he turned and shouted something. Molly couldn't quite hear him, but continued to watch as he slowly faded from view. Fleetingly she thought that she had heard him shout "Sorry" but she couldn't be sure.

Looking over to where her grandfather stood, she smiled to herself in the knowledge that she would never feel that burden ever again. She felt serene and at peace and realised that she had completed one of the major lessons to help her progress. And given how she was now feeling, she didn't really care that she had achieved it through unorthodox means.

Chapter Thirty-five: A Different Style of Learning

<***>

It had been arranged that the following dawn, Molly would meet once more with the two most senior Elders. Having watched and monitored her for further signs of improvement in her memory recall, they were pleased with the progress that she was making. Sitting with Riizlabll and Kyah, they talked at length.

"Beloved, you have been remarkable and all here are elated that you have made such progress. However, do not be under any illusion that what is to come will be easy for you. We need to make you aware that it may take some time for you to become a qualified guide, and you may be a trainee for quite a while, as you have much to understand, learn and process," explained Kyah.

Riizlabll smiled reassuringly, "Indeed Brenth, we have been advised by Archangel Metatron that you are not a spirit who readily follows instructions, and we know from your substantial Akasha that you have been and still can be quite challenging at times — I'm sure Orick will vouch for that. We are fully aware that your decision to do this has been a difficult one for you to make."

Molly frowned, not sure how to take what they had just said about her being 'challenging'. "Actually, I'd prefer to be called Molly, if it's all the same to you and as it turns out, I wanted to stay here anyway. I intend to give Orick a run for his money, as it happens," she said defiantly. Kyah and Riizlabll glanced at each other as Molly continued, "Anyway, what happens when I've done all the learning and stuff? What do I do then? I mean if I'm putting the effort in, you could at least tell me how I'm going to get to work as a guide."

Kyah nodded coyly and quietly replied, "When you have regained as much cosmic knowledge as you possibly can, and have completed the additional elements and filaments to your learning, then and only then, most Beloved, will a conclusive decision be made."

"Yeah, so you say — but what's gonna happen to me in the meantime, is what I want to know. And anyway, what are elements and filaments when they're at home?"

"Elements are the components — the nitty-gritty if you like — of what you have learned from the lessons which you contracted for. They will be added to, and eventually complete, your Akashic record. Filaments are the vibration or light threads which are the embodiments of your elements," replied Riizlabll, surprised at Molly's brashness. "You must be patient, Beloved. As I have just explained, when we feel that you are ready…"

Molly interrupted, "Yes, you say that now, but… oh, whatever… you know what, forget it! Blimey, you're as infuriating as Dolf. Why can I never get a straight answer to a straight question? And anyway, what did you mean when you said that I'm 'challenging'?"

Riizlabll let a wry smile cross his face. "We mean that your past lives have been… well… made somewhat more difficult than was necessary, shall we say."

"Indeed, which means that because you have agreed to accept what will be, you have changed a habit of many lifetimes," replied Kyah, chuckling at her own little joke. Molly looked blankly at each of them, having no idea what the hell they were talking about.

Meeting Orick in the Halls of Learning, Molly marvelled at the enormous sandstone building, which comprised within it many different areas. Looking around, Molly could see the Chambers of Power and Ignorance, the Halls of Prudence, the Halls of Wisdom and Counsel, as well as the Courts of Justice and Discretion. Molly felt a little nervous and disconcerted as she was still not fully sure it was the right decision when she had agreed to train to become a guide,

Orick greeted her, "You okay?"

"Sure, just a little overawed and nervous, I guess. I never thought I'd ever be doing this again — you know, the going back to school malarkey. But I have to say, this place is very impressive."

Orick smiled. "Yes. it is an amazing place. I love coming here, but like the Elders have told you, don't be under any illusions that this is going to be easy. It may take a while — possibly decades — for you to become a guide, and like they say, 'Patience is a Virtue'."

Molly thought she saw Orick wink at her.

"And just so you know, we will be visiting each of the halls and chambers in turn, and you will follow a timetable and curriculum as formulated by the Elders and myself. Now, are you ready to do some work?"

Molly nodded eagerly. They made their way over to a long, quartz crystal bench and sat down next to each other. Molly looked curiously around the immense space, and noticed that there were many other spirits and guides, all engrossed in what they were doing. She sat and waited expectantly.

"So, what happens now? Do I get books or something?"

Orick shook his head. "Be patient and watch. You are about to see a knowledge portal open — a vortex through which you will be able to access vast amounts of teachings and knowledge."

Waving his hand over the crystal bench directly in front of her, Molly watched as an indigo-coloured dot of light appeared.

"Okay, what's happening?"

"Shush, observe," commanded Orick.

Molly watched as the dot of light expanded, becoming larger and denser before dividing into two separate vertical light beams. They appeared to be suspended in mid-air as each started to rotate. Molly noticed that they were spinning in opposite

271

directions yet remained perfectly synchronised. Suddenly she felt a strange tingling sensation in the centre of her brow and then a gentle tug. She could feel her silver cord being pulled, as it began to advance towards the now entwined beams of light. Mesmerised, she kept perfectly still and waited for it to connect.

"Okay… this is weird… weird but awesome… actually, this is incredible," she breathed excitedly.

Becoming aware of a gentle, pulsing sensation, she looked closely at her cord and saw that it was only the thickness of a hair. The outside was covered in a translucent, silver filigree-like pattern which had a very intricate design etched into it. The design incorporated swirls and circles interweaved with lemniscate symbols — the symbols for infinity — which to Molly looked like lots of horizontal and vertical number '8's. She could also see that the cord had a gold core running through its centre and became aware of energy beginning to gently flow from the light beams and pulse down the cord into what had been her third eye.

Orick smiled as he too watched the knowledge download began to gather momentum. "You okay? Just stay still and relax while the helices download some of the more 'basic' information."

Molly did as she was told and soon realised that she was now able to recall vast quantities of knowledge again. Instinctively she knew that what had been lost was now once again firmly held within her universal DNA, her cosmic blueprint.

It was a little before sundown when Orick decided to call it a day, and waving his hand across the crystal bench, he disconnected Molly's cord from the light beam.

"That's enough for today. I feel it would be prudent not to overload you. We shall return tomorrow."

Molly sat as if in a daydream, and feeling completely stupefied by what had occurred, was slow to respond.

Orick became a little alarmed. "Are you ok?"

"Yeah, I'm fine. That was just… just… I can't find the words to describe it actually, other than it was just incredible."

Somewhat relieved, Orick smiled and nodded encouragingly. "Well, that's why you're here, after all. I'm pleased that you've handled the process so well and regained such a vast amount of knowledge and wisdom. Come now, it is time to leave. You will benefit from some rest."

Chapter Thirty-six: The Human Condition

<***>

M
olly had begun to lose track of time. Time had seemed so important when she had inhabited the earth realm — being on time for appointments, being on time for work, being early or late for other things — but just as her grandpa had told her, here it didn't matter; time had no importance in the spiritual realm. Was it days, weeks or even years since she had agreed to become a spirit guide? She didn't know and anyway, it didn't even seem relevant anymore. She liked that thought; it meant that there was no pressure, and she had got used to going with the flow, or going with 'the glow' as Orick called it.

Molly had proved to be a fast learner and had quickly absorbed and understood what Orick called her 'basic training', by which he meant the humdrum, ancient-times, happened-ages-ago training. She remembered how much she had hated being in school back on earth, how boring everything had been, and how suffocated she had felt by it all. This was far more interesting. It wasn't a case of swotting and reading and trying to remember and learn stuff —this was much more fun. Eons of information was being down-loaded and she didn't have to do a thing — it was just there, re-activated and ingrained again into her inherent spiritual database. It was like being given access to an instruction manual but not needing to read it. She was like a sponge, soaking it all up.

Then one day Orick decided that it was time to show her what happened over in the Towers. Molly was excited because she knew that being allowed to visit the Towers was like graduating to the next level. It meant that she was getting out of the Halls at last and was going to work in the field, as it were. Orick left her while he went to seek permission for their entry to the Towers, and after quickly finishing what she had been doing, she hurried over to meet him. Molly was excited, but also felt a little anxious, and was surprised to see that there was a lot of building work being carried out as additional towers were being erected.

"What's with all the building work?" she asked, somewhat puzzled.

"Ah, I'm not too sure myself. You'll have to ask Adzullon. He will be here any moment."

Molly looked at the new buildings which were half-finished. They had scaffolding around them and there were huge cranes lifting all manner of building materials from one place to another.

"Tell me about Adzullon. I've heard his name mentioned a few times. What is it he does again?" she enquired, as she continued to survey the extent of the building work.

Orick smiled. "Oh, he is someone I think you will find very interesting. He is a little eccentric and a bit impatient at times but I suppose that must go with the job. He's known as the Overseer of Dates. Ah, here he is now."

Adzullon hurriedly approached them. He was a small, hunched figure who carried a smooth and highly polished stick made of the finest sequoia wood. Within its handle Molly could see what resembled an array of coloured beads. They caught her attention because they twinkled like stars and appeared to be rotating by their own accord. Adzullon's persona was almost comical, and Molly tried to compose herself as he half hobbled, half hopped his way towards them. His hair was shoulder length and unruly, almost having an unkempt appearance. It was the colour of the blackest jet she had ever seen. His eyes were piercing but seemed to hold a great knowingness behind them and Molly thought that they could quite easily pass for pools of liquid chocolate. His complexion was un-lined and flawless and he wore what looked like a pair of white, silk pyjamas. Around his waist was a braided cord made from amethyst crystal. Molly noticed how intense the deep purple colour of the crystal was, as it glinted and sparkled. Stepping forward, Orick respectfully bowed his head and introduced Molly.

Adzullon peered at her as he studied her energy print. "Ah yes, it is our most Beloved. I have been looking forward to our meeting for a while now. I'm so pleased that Kyah and Hamneth orchestrated your safe return to the spiritual realm. Had it not been for them, and of course Cloiff, we would perhaps have lost you."

Molly glanced at Orick and was just about to say something about Cloiff being her grandpa when she thought better of it.

Adzullon tapped his stick on the ground and headed off in the opposite direction to which he'd come. "Follow me. Come, come, there's not a moment to be wasted. Busy, busy, no point in dawdling. Now, I want to show you something which I think you'll find very exciting."

Eagerly followed the Overseer of Dates, Molly thought that for a seemingly old man he was incredibly sprightly and agile, as they both had a job keeping up with him. He led them up a spiral staircase, across a hallway, down a flight of stairs, and then back up another spiral staircase and onto a vast, open- aired loggia. The floor was tiled in enormous slabs of sandstone which stretched as far as the eye could see. Molly thought that it resembled a library, as she could see row upon row of shelving which appeared to be laid out numerically. Each shelf was further divided into tetractys-shaped cubby holes which were stuffed to the gunnels with rolled-up paper scrolls. Molly noticed that each of the scrolls was securely tied around the middle with a silver braid.

Molly gazed around the terrace. "Blimey, what is this place?"

"A-ha. This, my Beloved, is where I store all my paperwork. These scrolls are my records which document the dates and times of every single incarnation that any of you spirits have ever made. 'One scroll, one soul', you might say." He gave a chuckle at his own joke. "All handwritten too. We leave nothing to chance here," he said, beaming proudly.

Molly shook her head in disbelief. "You're kidding, right? Why, that's amazing! Mad… but amazing."

Orick couldn't believe what he was seeing, either. "I knew about this place, but I didn't realise just exactly what was held here," he said, looking around flabbergasted.

Adzullon frowned to himself. "Yes, well all this needs to be stored somewhere and the new building work won't be completed for at least another lustrum — planner's error, shall we say. I did tell the architects in the very beginning that there wouldn't be nearly enough space, but did they listen? No! So now, well as you can see… It's the human population, you know — too many of them."

Molly continued to look around her, somewhat agog. "Guess you've never heard of a database then?"

Orick scowled at her before addressing the Elder, "Erm… sorry to interrupt, and with the greatest of respect, this is all very well, but do you think we could get a move on? I'm sure you will appreciate, we also have 'deadlines' to meet."

Molly struggled to suppress a giggle as she got Orick's little joke. Ignoring Orick's remark, Adzullon turned on his heel and led them both to the entrance of the main tower. Entering through its oak-panelled doors, Molly looked around and realised that all the other towers were connected to this main one by a series of corridors, moving stairs and walkways. She gawped at the enormity and beauty of the building, which almost took her breath away.

"Wow, this is amazing — it's huge! Oh, my goodness, I never expected anything like this," she exclaimed.

Adzullon gave a little shrug. "Oh, it's nothing, really."

Molly was eager to see more, and started to head down one of the long corridors at a rapid pace with Orick and Adzullon following her. At the end of the corridor, a cavernous room opened before them. Molly stared in astonishment, as she watched a variety of sprites, sylphs and other elementals darting around, busy with their tasks.

"What is this place?" she asked, in awe.

Adzullon looked very proud and pleased with himself. "This place, Beloved, is just one of many antechambers. It is here that the preparation and preservation work is undertaken." He ushered her towards a doorway and fidgeted excitedly in front of it. "Here, come and see." He waved his hand across a symbol which was to the left of the door frame and they watched as it slid silently open. Stepping over the threshold, Molly caught her breath as her eyes adjusted to the dimmed light. In front of them were countless shimmering veils which hung from the rafters of the huge chamber, some so long that they trailed onto the floor.

"What are those shimmering things? They're so beautiful," Molly exclaimed, mesmerised.

"Those, my dearest one, are just some of the many energy veils which are stored here. The towers are storage facilities for all of the energy veils of Spirit who have incarnated back to the earth realm."

Molly stared at the spectacle before her. The veils glistened and twinkled, appearing to shimmer and sway like sheer, gossamer curtains being caressed by a gentle, summer breeze. Having seen it all before, Orick stood over by the door and waited patiently.

"Impressive, isn't it. Each one of these energy veils is nurtured and lovingly tended until its owner returns," Adzullon said proudly.

Molly stared down to the far end of the chamber. "Wow, so each veil belongs to a spirit who is currently a person, a human being. Wow, there must be thousands… no, millions of veils, just in here alone," she gasped.

"Yes," Adzullon agreed, "But the veils don't just hold a spirit's energy — they also retain and house their memories of the Spirit world. And like I said, with an ever-increasing Earth population and people living longer, well, it's no wonder we're running out of space."

Orick was starting to get restless, aware that there was still a mountain of work to get through. Turning to Adzullon, he bowed his head respectfully again. "Well, thanks for the tour, Adzullon. We'd best be going now — I know how busy you are. Thanks for letting our Beloved see what goes on in here. Molly, I think we're finished — shall we go back to the Halls? We can talk and continue your studies and I can tell you more about all of this."

Molly hesitated. "Err… would it be okay if I stayed a while? Actually, I'd like to ask Adzullon a couple of things, if that's okay?" she said, giving Adzullon her best winning smile.

"Why yes… yes… of course. I'd be delighted. Go on Orick, off you go. You can run along now."

Molly caught Orick's eye and with a smirk, mouthed, "Go on then, run along." Realising that to all intents and purposes he had been dismissed, Orick glowered at Molly and mouthed back, "Oh shut up!" before he turned to leave.

Adzullon hobbled over to a marbled seating area and motioned for Molly to join him. "Now Beloved, what is it you wish to ask me?"

Molly sat down. "Well firstly, what did you mean about the increasing population? I always thought there was a balance — one in, one out, sort of thing."

Adzullon nodded. "Ah yes, you're quite right, that's how it was for quite a few millennia, but with the huge increase in the number and severity of conflicts which have happened on the earth realm in such a short space of time, and of course plague and famine and such like, the sheer volume of Spirit needing to incarnate has overwhelmed us somewhat. You see, when there is a major shift in the balance of life and death — like we see in wars and such like — Spirit often don't have time to learn the lessons they had contracted for, so a lot of them have to incarnate again sooner than they would have normally done."

Molly nodded, suddenly understanding. "Ah, so that's the reason for the new towers. Can I ask something else?" Molly shifted position, trying to think how best to ask her next question. Throwing caution to the wind, she blurted out, "Why do bad things happen? I don't mean to individual people — I get the contracting bit, and all that — I mean generally, you know, stuff like drought and famine and natural disasters and such like?"

Adzullon smiled, his eyes creasing at the edges. "Ah, from your question I take it that you are thinking that God is to blame? Well, let's see now. Disease, drought, famine and natural disasters, as you call them, are only to be expected when the great Mother Earth is trying to balance and harmonise herself against human interference and indifference. You see, humans need to understand that they are interconnected with the Earth; they are part of the Earth's biodiversity, not separate from it. Earth regulates and governs herself — or at least tries to — in an attempt to provide, maintain and sustain all life. In fairness, I cannot speak for God, as you call our Great Spirit, but my own personal opinion is that humanity is very much still in its infancy and therefore is still relatively primitive and it's behaving like a selfish, spoilt child. Maybe that's harsh and I should cut humanity a little slack and excuse it for its stupidity, but humans really are the most exasperating race that we have to deal with."

Molly began to wish she'd kept her mouth shut as she could see that he was becoming quite animated and somewhat austere.

Adzullon thought for a while before continuing, "As a species, humanity has proved to be greedy and egotistical. Humans are war-mongers and corrupt, and apparently hell-bent on destroying the very planet which sustains them. Like I said... stupid! Shall I continue? Oh yes, they are also doing a thorough job of annihilating just about every other living entity that has the misfortune to be sharing the planet with them. As I see it, your 'God' doesn't have anything to do with it. All the bad stuff, as you call it, is completely down to the human race. Mankind is master of its own destiny. If anyone is to blame, then it is mankind itself."

Molly didn't know how to respond, and thought it best to sit still and say nothing. Placing her hands in her lap, she settled back, as she could tell this was going to take quite a while.

"Humans are a species who have been blessed with free will and intelligence, as well as a host of other gifts which have been bestowed on them, yet they choose to abuse all of those gifts."

Molly was taken aback at Adzullon's belligerent and scathing honesty. "Blimey, I'm sorry I asked now! Guess you don't really like them much then, humans I mean."

Adzullon turned to look at her. "Oh no, it's not a case of liking or disliking humanity — we accept them for who and what they are. They just irritate the heck out of us. Don't get me wrong, there is more good than bad on Earth, or so I'm told. The thing is, humanity has a strong but unreasonable, inherent desire to possess all things, including things which are not theirs to possess. That flaw, amongst many others, is unfortunately a primordial trait — a trait interwoven and integrated so deeply, so powerfully, that we even had to give it a name. It is known as the 'human condition'." Adzullon gave a little chuckle to himself. "Unfortunately, such conditions will ultimately be humanity's undoing as they focus on and sustain negativity which does not serve any useful purpose. And as we know, negativity begets negativity, hatred begets hatred, and corruption begets, well… you get the picture?"

Molly nodded, not daring to do otherwise.

"You see, humanity as a whole has become so disconnected and detached from what has been gifted to it that it has lost its energetic connection. Many humans now only exist in the ego. For most, that is what being human is all about, and I have it on good authority that there have been some really vile ones — still currently are, in fact. Human beings have been tasked to evolve. It is their destiny and also that of their world. Sadly, what started as a ripple has now become a torrent, and a large proportion of humanity no longer has the ability to express empathy or love. This is something which concerns us all greatly, but as I am responsible for their natal amnesia, I am the one who is troubled the most, because it has proved to be a double-edged sword, you might say. Humanity seems to think that it can carry on doing what it's doing with little or no consequence for the harm it's causing, yet it is imperative that the human race, as a collective consciousness, sorts out its affairs; otherwise the sustained abuse of power, greed and ego will eventually bring about humanity's demise."

Molly didn't say anything but sat thinking about what Adzullon had just said, before sighing despondently.

Adzullon continued, "We are hopeful that with minimal intervention on our part, humanity will once again become enlightened and rediscover what has been lost. For some, the rediscovery of their soul's purpose has brought them a greater understanding of their 'knowing', shall we say. That in turn will begin to influence other humans — we call that the 'ripple effect'. We remain confident that eventually both humanity and the Earth will ascend to a higher frequency and vibration. The giving of unconditional love to one another and the nurturing of Earth and Nature must prevail. We must remain optimistic — who knows, maybe in a couple more millennia humanity will turn out okay after all."

"What if they don't? What if they don't turn out okay, I mean?"

"Then that depends. If human activity remains contained and doesn't exert any negative influence beyond the planet, or pose a threat to other cosmic affairs, then mankind will be allowed to continue, and guidance will remain. If not, then the cosmic guardians will have to make the decision as to whether they allow the continuation of humanity as a species. For the foreseeable future, they have been quarantined. But therein lies a potential problem, because Earth is one of the best worlds on which Spirit can develop and progress. The relationship is symbiotic — a human being needs a spirit and a soul, just as much as a spirit and soul need a human being."

Molly sat quietly, pondering what Adzullon had just said. "Blimey, so if the human race mucks things up and gets terminated, what happens to us? Where will we go?"

Adzullon smiled again. "Oh now, don't you worry about that, there are thousands of other planets and galaxies which are habitable for Spirit. Earth's not the only planet that Spirit can utilise. You don't think that the great architect of the universe doesn't have a plan, do you? The Divine isn't going to let what he has created meet with some awful demise. You are forgetting that as Spirit, you are pure energy. There are no constraints — you are multi-dimensional, omnipresent and multi-faceted. I think that you need reminding that Spirit originate from a multitude of stars in numerous constellations, for example, Sirius, Arcturus, Vega and of course the Pleiades. These are from where many star seeds originate. Spirit don't require solid mass to exist; it is only when a spirit wishes to incarnate that the need to take on a physical form is sought."

Molly shuffled on the seat as she felt a little disconcerted. "Star seeds? What are they?"

Adzullon smiled. "Why, star seeds are newly-created energy vibrations. They are the naive beginnings of all new spirit who bask in the energies of the Divine, before beginning their development. You have forgotten that humanity is not privy to the magnitude or degree of just how magnificent the universe is. If they were then... well it just doesn't bear thinking about. We know that they wouldn't be able to process or even cope with what is beyond their planet. They can't even discern the numerous dimensions and alternative realms which surround them as it is."

Feeling strangely reassured by what Adzullon had just told her, Molly began to relax.

"Oh, and just for the record," he added, "I noticed that you referred to humans as 'them'; this is good; you are beginning to remember that you are Spirit."

Chapter Thirty-seven: Awakened Knowing

<***>

olly was waiting for Orick to return to the Halls of Learning. He greeted her cheerfully and following him to the library section, she waited while he selected a particular study area. Molly noticed how it felt light and airy and had a totally different ambience to the previous area they had studied in. The energy from the rose quartz crystal benches was softer and much warmer. Molly was eager to start. Sitting next to each other, Orick did that thing of magically making a portal appear.

"You must show me how you do that."

Orick grinned. "When you're a fully-fledged guide you will be able to do lots of things that will totally amaze you."

Once again, a portal opened in front of her brow, and she felt her silver cord connect to the helices again. Her energy became heightened and she was aware of the power surge taking place, as the information download started and her silver cord began to tingle and pulsate again. This time however, her cord had a metallic blue sheen to it. Taking a deep breath, she began to relax.

Focusing on the information which was being downloaded, she suddenly burst out laughing. "What the hell is this all about?" she exclaimed, as she realised that step-by-step instructions were being embedded into her memory, such as *How To Leave Your Memory And Collect It Again On Your Return* and *How To Leave Your Surplus Energy And Collect It On Your Return.*

"You have got to be joking! This is unreal."

Orick smiled. "Yes, I suppose it is. Just wait until you download the programme and instruction manual on *How To Give Healing* — now that will really blow your circuits. Not to mention, *How To Give Protection And Manifest Abundance..*"

Molly began to feel a little overawed. "Okay, so how does this all work? Why do I have to know all this stuff anyway?"

Orick waited for the last piece of information to be downloaded before answering, as he needed her full attention. "As a guide, one of the roles in which you will be expected to be proficient is that of teacher. I'm not completely sure what the Elders have in mind for you — I don't know if they want you to be a life guide or a teacher guide. If it turns out that they want you to be a life guide, and I'm hedging my bets that they will, then you will need to learn everything that you've forgotten, so I'm covering all bases, as it were, and downloading all the knowledge which I think you'll need."

Molly remained still as Orick waved his hand over the crystal bench, detaching her cord. "Okay, so obviously, you're having to re-learn the fundamentals — the bread and butter stuff — before you can get to grips with the more advanced, complex issues, but you also need to know that there are exceptions to the rules."

"Exceptions to the rules? What do you mean?"

"Well, you remember that every spirit who chooses to incarnate knows when their agreed birth and return dates will be as it's all preordained, yes? Well, Spirit even choose the life they want to live, right down to the family dynamics and other relationships."

"Oh…okay. So what happens when there's a major catastrophe or a disaster where a lot of people all die at once — is that all preordained too? Or like if someone dies because of a supposed freak accident or something?"

Orick glanced up. "Yes, it's exactly the same. Whenever and whatever was decided and agreed upon will be fulfilled. Of course, there are events that appear to be freak accidents or tragedies, as they are referred to, but the people who were meant to survive do so. Many people have what we call near misses — those are just lessons. On the other hand, if say, a person has got themselves into a situation which would result in a premature end to their physical life, then their guardian angel or their life guide would intervene."

"Oh, you mean like you did!"

Orick ignored her sarcastic comment. "As I was saying, when their lifetime on the earth is completed, Spirit return on their pre-ordained date, unless of course, like you ..." Orick's voice trailed off.

"Oh yeah, like me being an 'exception to the rules', you mean"

"Yes, you were an exception, because of how, what and who brought about your physical demise. It's the same when a spirit has learned its lessons quicker than anticipated and can see no reason to stay any longer than is necessary. With agreement between the spirit and their soul, together they can exercise freewill and choose to arrange to return home earlier, perhaps by way of a serious accident or illness. These are just some of the circumstances which are exceptions."

Molly suddenly became petulant. "Does what happened to Dolf qualify him as an exception? I mean, he was whinging to me about being back here sooner than he had reckoned on being, and then blamed me for it, the cheeky sod," she seethed.

Orick was taken aback at Molly's retort. "Well yes, I suppose he was an exception. Actually, I don't remember him contracting for a return date, now you mention it."

Molly suddenly lost her temper and flying into an uncontrollable rage, ranted, "That's not fair! He shouldn't just be an 'exception'. He was just downright nasty and it was karma that caught up with him. My mother always said that what goes around, comes around and that nasty people eventually get their comeuppance."

Orick was completely caught out by Molly's outburst and shouting back at her, yelled, "For goodness sake! Does it really matter now?"

"Yes, it does bloody matter, and as far as I'm concerned, Dolf got what he deserved. Good riddance to bad rubbish."

Orick became aware of an uneasy atmosphere between them as Molly sulked. Unsure of how to handle the situation, he was just about to make an excuse to leave, when Molly suddenly apologised. "I'm sorry, Orick, now I've gone and made a complete idiot of myself… again. Just ignore me and carry on. You'd started to tell me something else about Spirit."

Orick reached out and gave her hand a gentle squeeze. "I'm sorry too, I should never have raised my voice like that. I realise how frustrated you are, but you really have to trust me and have faith that all will be well."

Molly pouted. "I know, it's just that… oh never mind, lets carry on."

Orick collected his thoughts again. "Ok, where was I? Oh yes, I was about to tell you that Spirit also know who their parents will be for the forthcoming lifetime. They are usually from the same soul family or group. Unfortunately — or thankfully, depending on how you look at it — once a spirit incarnates, that's when transient amnesia has to be activated and that's where Adzullon comes in. Now Levvinnei, who works with Adzullon, organises an entire workforce of specialist guides who are known as Acclimatisers. It's the Acclimatisers who look after the energy veils which you saw in the Towers. Levvinnei also helps with the energy calculations which Spirit have to make prior to incarnation, and Adzullon also assigns guardian angels and a life guide to a reincarnate who's about to be born."

Molly looked baffled. "Right, so when a spirit returns to earth, they have to leave behind their surplus energy and the memory of being here?"

"Yep, that's the gist of it."

"So why can't we keep our memory of being here, when we go there?"

Orick chuckled. "Because it would be too confusing, and in all probability would mean that Spirit would never fully commit to learning the lessons which they had contracted to learn. I mean, why would they? Most, if not all, have to repeat the same lesson several life times over as it is, so just imagine the mess and confusion that would create."

Molly laughed to herself as she imagined the chaos which would ensue. She sat thinking for a while, trying to make sense of all that she had recently learned, when she felt her energy shift as she had a sudden realisation. "Oh, I get it — when we reincarnate, we store our memory and any unneeded energies in the Towers and then collect them again when we return!"

"Spot on," said Orick, smiling.

"Yeah, but why do we have to leave behind some of our energy in the first place?" she asked, puzzled.

"Well, because a spirit and its soul energy combined are powerful. They have to leave a percentage of their energy behind, because otherwise their energy vibration would be far too powerful for a human baby to cope with. The energy surge would blow its circuits, as it were."

Orick took a moment to organise his thoughts before continuing, "When Spirit reside within the spiritual realm they are — as you are — free to roam the great cosmos and travel to wherever they like. But when Spirit decide that they would like to incarnate, they have a great deal of preparation to do. It takes many different energy calibrations to enable them to be compatible, particularly if they are going to reside in a physical dimension like the earth realm. They must plan the content of their contract with their soul and the life lessons which they are to learn with their life guide and also with the Great Spirit too. Spirit also have to calculate the amount of energy needed to complete the contract and the lessons they have set themselves. Of course, this is dependent on the length of time that they are going to remain on the earth — too little energy and they will have a low reserve and, in all likelihood, won't be able to complete their lessons or contracts. But if they take too much energy, there is a risk of damaging the delicate neural network of the foetus that's been chosen by them."

Molly was aghast at what Orick had just told her. "Wow, this is something else! So if we get it wrong and cause a power surge, as it were, it damages the foetus so that particular spirit won't get to be born? Is that what you're saying?"

"Yes, that's exactly what I'm saying. Very often it's the new, inexperienced incarnates who miscalculate. Being exposed to a physical body's DNA is what we call encodement, it can be overwhelming for some first-timers."

Molly sat pondering for a while. "What about the ones who get to encode but don't stay long enough to be born? Is that pre-ordained too?"

Orick sat down next to her. "Yes Molly, Spirit who encode but who are then stillborn, terminated or miscarried enter their intended physical vessel knowing full well that they will not be born for that particular incarnation. They are usually star seeds — do you remember Adzullon telling you about them? They will have their own agenda or reasons, whether it be as a learning experience or just to become familiar with DNA encodement. You have forgotten Spirits' universal inter-connectedness."

Molly sat quietly, mulling over the whole thing. "So, what happens to them?"

Orick smiled. "Well, having fulfilled that experience, many decide to either stay in the spiritual realm for some time until they feel ready to embark on the process again, or they visit elsewhere."

Molly looked perplexed, but waited for Orick to explain more.

"The thing is Molly, at any one time there are many, many Spirit on earth who have incarnated and contracted with the full intention of allowing other Spirit to undertake encodements. We know them as 'Conceptuals'. As female humans, they allow Spirit who need to encode to have use of their human vessel and its energy vibration."

Molly was doing her best to take it all in, as Orick continued, "A conceptual is highly regarded and very, very loved."

Molly smiled at the realisation of their importance. "So a spirit can choose to encode but then not have a physical existence on the earth realm. Wow, that's amazing."

Orick nodded and frowned at the same time. "Isn't it just! But the paradox of it all, of course, is the amnesia. This beautiful, selfless act of love is forgotten by the human mother involved. Regrettably, most humans see the act of loss as a failing; unaware of why that loss was brought about, the inability to bear a child is seen as imperfection. Some even think that they are being punished, which of course couldn't be further from the truth."

Molly frowned. "That's so sad, yet at the same time so… so… wonderful."

Orick gave a knowing smile. "Yes, it is wonderful but, of course, the downside is that a conceptual will live with the grief and sense of loss until the day she returns to the spiritual realm, not realising that what was thought of as being a loss was, in fact, cosmic correlation and spiritual inter-connectedness — unconditional love at its most powerful, as it were."

Molly began to feel tearful as she realised just what that meant. "Ah… inter-connectedness — the unbreakable, spiritual bond of love. I get it now."

"Good." said Orick, "As you say, that bond is unbreakable and it doesn't matter what the circumstances were — for that particular conceptual mother it's all been agreed, all pre-ordained."

Molly fell quiet as she dwelled on what Orick had just told her. "So if that's encoding, why can't some people ever get pregnant in the first place? I remember one of Mam's friends — Shirley I think her name was — never having kids but always wanting them. How does that work?"

Orick smiled and absentmindedly adjusted his cloak. "Well now, that will just be because they contracted not to have that experience in that particular lifetime. Don't forget Molly, for every experience and lesson which is undergone there's a reverse experience to be had as well."

Molly slumped forwards and her chin fell to her chest. "Arrgh, there is so much to re-learn; this is gonna take me ages," she moaned.

Adzullon had summoned Orick to the Halls of Wisdom, as he wanted to know how much progress Molly was making. As Orick approached him, he sensed that the Overseer of Dates was anxious to hear his news. Adzullon motioned for him to sit, and as Orick joined him on the bench, he knew there was a problem.

"Greetings, Adzullon — why so urgent?" he asked, concerned.

The Elder's expression changed and took on a sombre frown. "Guide Orick, we find ourselves at a critical juncture. I need to know of our Beloved's progress. Is she ready?"

Orick shifted awkwardly. "By ready, I assume you mean, able to take on the next stage of her development?"

"That's exactly what I mean. In your opinion, has she mastered the skills required? Will she be able to assimilate the teachings for the purposes for which they are intended?"

Orick thought long and hard, staring at the wooden acorn which was carved into the top of his staff. He was slow to reply, and chose his words with care. "Yes, I believe that with a few more information transfers, she will be adequately prepared for her undertaking. My only concern is that our Beloved remains tainted with many human flaws — flaws which I do not know how to erase or deactivate. Maybe you have some suggestions?"

Adzullon absentmindedly tapped his stick and playing with the frame of beads which was embedded in its handle, absentmindedly stroked his beard. "Hmmm... human flaws you say. Are they flaws, or character traits — that is the question, Orick. Flaws will need to be erased, as you say, or at the very least, minimised. Character traits, on the other hand, can be overlooked or even embraced. This is a dilemma indeed."

Orick shook his head. "I don't know which one is which. I find myself in somewhat of a quandary, and I don't want to be the one who has to decide."

Later, Molly and Orick met up in the Halls of Wisdom. As Orick greeted her, he noticed how sullen she was. "What's up? You don't look very happy. Who's rattled your cage?"

Molly pouted. "Ha, you're so funny... not! No one as it happens, although you're beginning to. I want to ask you something — I was wondering what's happened to my energy and memory veil? Are they still being stored in one of the towers?"

Orick looked away, avoiding her stare. "No Molly, I'm afraid your veil no longer exists. The Ethereals tried their utmost to avoid its utilisation, but the Healers had to use both the veil and the retained energy to repair the damage which you had sustained. Even then, there wasn't enough to completely repair the damage "

Molly sighed. "Damn! I knew it — that's why I feel empty, isn't it?"

Orick gave a feeble smile, as if to offer reassurance and to demonstrate a degree of understanding. "Yes, probably. Are you okay?" he asked tentatively.

Molly nodded. "Yeah, I suspected as much and it explains a lot. I think I was just hoping to be normal again, but the reality is that I'm not normal, am I?"

"Yes, well you were never that, but it will get easier once you let go of stuff that's no longer important, especially the old earth ways which you're hanging on to. Once you've let all that go, you'll begin to feel a sense of freedom and release. To tell you the truth, I have raised some concerns with Adzullon about it."

"What do you mean concerns, and why the hell have you been talking to Adzullon about me behind my back?"

"As I was saying, it is very clear that you still have numerous human traits and mannerisms which can be quite brash and abrupt, and your apparent lack of respect or deference to highly revered Ethereals is very much in evidence. I'm not saying that you should be all meek and mild or grovel or anything like that, but you could show a little more respect and reverence. You know what I'm saying?"

Molly was taken aback at how forthright Orick had been. She didn't know what to say, but secretly knew that he was right. Normally she would have gone on the defensive and flounced off in a strop but something stopped her. Looking at him in shocked surprise, she caught sight of his aura, and for the first time saw him in a different light, as she suddenly realised how pure of heart he was. She knew that she was becoming fond of him, but in that instant, she suddenly felt her heart light surge with love and her vibration alter as she inextricably released her resentment towards him. Losing her balance, she fell forwards into his energy field, catching him unawares. Orick automatically reached out to steady her and expertly caught her, breaking her fall.

"Whoa, are you all right? What just happened?"

Molly regained her composure, and looking a little coy, replied, "Yes I think so. I'm not sure what happened but I think I've just fallen for you. Oh my God, I'm in love with you! I've fallen in love with you!"

Orick couldn't contain himself. A flash of delight crossed his face, and he whooped loudly with glee, as he realised that Molly had not only regained her love for him but also her love for the spiritual realm.

Molly felt euphoric, as a feeling of contentment and joy swept through her heart light. "Well, that was unexpected. I feel different — is that what's been missing all this time?"

Orick nodded. "Yes, I think it is. You know what? Truth be told, you have never failed to surprise, amaze and confound me. You have always been challenging, as that is your way, but I think that you have just turned a corner. I think that you've just released a massive, negative human trait."

"Really? What trait's that then?"

"Why, ego, of course"

Thinking over what Orick had just said, she realised that she couldn't argue with him now or even feel any animosity or impatience towards him. In fact, she couldn't feel any negative emotion towards him at all. "What does that mean?" she asked tentatively.

"It means that all is equal, and equal is all."

Molly smiled to herself as she realised that what she had just experienced was inextricably linked with how she was going to progress. "Can we carry on now? I have so many questions to ask."

Orick was pleased at Molly's eagerness and nodded encouragingly.

"So, what's the difference between a life guide and a teacher guide?"

Orick smiled and looking affectionately at her, hoped that at long last she stood a good chance of evolving. "Well, firstly there are lots of different guides who all have specialist tasks to perform. There are Inspirers, Healers, Gatekeepers, Enablers, and of course, like you said, Life and teacher guides. The difference is that life guides are just what their name suggests — they stay with their assigned spirit forever, like I have with you. Every spirit and therefore every human, every person if you like, has a primary team of guides and a guardian angel assigned to them from the start, as well as an Ascended Master. Whereas the other guides I mentioned come into a person's life for a reason, and then leave once a particular lesson, skill, or part of an agreed contract has been learned or fulfilled."

Molly contemplated what Orick had just said. "Oh, so when we're in the physical, we're being taught and looked after by different guides, as and when we need them?"

Orick nodded. "Well yes, that's basically it, I suppose. All Spirit inhabiting a physical vessel do so to progress their development and learning. That's why the Earth is known as the 'classroom of teaching'."

Molly looked wistfully into the distance. "Huh, I get it, so it's a double whammy in a way — as kids we go to school to learn and as Spirit we're still in school. So if you don't like school, it's too bad, I guess."

Orick shook his head, struggling to comprehend Molly's way of thinking. "When a person begins to consciously follow their enlightenment or spiritual path, they begin to lose their natal amnesia which means that teacher guides and Inspirers can draw closer — we call it 'unfoldment'. Now when that is achieved, it acts as a catalyst which stirs the memory of what the purpose of their soul is. This is when a person raises their vibration, their level of spiritual consciousness, up into the next dimension. The fact you were denied that is a major catastrophe, for which I and Prenge are to blame. I, for one, cannot apologies enough to you for our oversight."

Molly suddenly realised the implications, not only to herself but also to Orick, Prenge and the entire spiritual realm. Taking his hand in hers she brought it to her lips and gently kissed the back of it. Orick was overcome with emotion as he realised that her love for him was unquestionable, her forgiveness was in its entirety and her trust in him was complete.

Staring into the very depth of his energy she said, "I understand. I accept what can't be changed, and I know that all will be well. You have to carry on — carry on teaching me, nurturing me. Blimey Orick, if I can forgive Dolf for what he did, well it goes without saying that I forgive you, you idiot."

Orick smiled and composing himself, continued with the lesson. "When a person, and therefore their spirit, have learnt all the lessons that they needed to learn and they then honour the soul's essence by living that particular incarnation in a spiritual manner, it triggers the ascension entitlement. It initiates the activation and access that is required for their Ascended Master to draw close, because their spiritual consciousness is now in the fifth dimension. A Master will have already been paired to that particular soul and spirit when they first came into existence."

"Ah, yeah, I remember you mentioning Ascended Masters before — Buddha, Jesus, and the like."

"And the like…!" Orick scowled, shaking his head.

"So what do they do?" Molly asked, shrugging her shoulders and suddenly struggling to suppress a yawn.

"I'm sorry… am I boring you? You're becoming very glib about all of this."

"Sorry, I don't mean to be, it's just hard remembering what I already know, but can't remember, even though I know it. Arrhhh… its infuriating."

Orick inhaled deeply and smiled reassuringly at her. "Hmmm… I know you're struggling with all of this, and I'm sorry to be a hard task master, as it were, but we really need to press on, otherwise we'll be at it all day. An Ascended Master is someone who once lived as a person, but by living in the ethos of love and purity was able to raise their vibration to a level whereby they become free from the cycle of karma, death and rebirth — in other words, they no longer incarnate. Your existence as a spirit means that you are discarnate, but when you reincarnate and develop and evolve towards becoming enlightened, your designated Master works with you, to teach and steer you so that you begin the ascension process too."

Molly looked away lost in thought.

"You paying attention? Now, a healer guide will work with a person who has an overwhelming desire to heal or assist others. Such people will have found themselves on a pathway of being in service, and may have careers which involve the healing of situations, or healing the sick. They are known as 'Light Workers' or 'Earth Angels'. An inspirer guide will help a person make changes in their life to bring about creativity; the person will often experience this as a 'Eureka' moment when they remember their reason for being. They find their calling as it were, and become inspired. An enabler guide brings about a favourable situation which then enables the person to complete whatever has inspired them. See how it works?"

Molly nodded and suddenly broke out into a smile. "It's amazing. Who'd have thought it — we have all this guidance and support around us, all this love! It's like we have a whole team working with us. Although seriously, Orick, I was so angry with you and really thought that you were a rubbish guide. I'm sorry for being a pain in the bum."

Orick grinned. "It's okay, you've had a lot to overcome and you have nothing to apologise for. You were stuck in a kind of limbo. You had retained many of your human traits, so really you were just a human being, being human!"

"Oh yeah, being human — that design fault."

Orick remained silent for what seemed an eternity, and Molly sensed that there was something troubling him.

"What's the matter, what's wrong?"

Orick stared at her, choosing his words carefully. "I was worried that you weren't going to completely let go of some of your more negative human traits, and that they would prove to be a problem. "

"What do you mean... a problem?"

"Well, the thing is Molly, if you were to retain any of those ingrained traits or flaws, they would influence your behaviour and decision-making as a guide and that would probably not be a good thing."

Molly frowned. "Why not?"

"Because there would be a risk that you would project your personality onto whoever you were guiding, and that would never do. The key to being a guide is to remain impartial. We must never influence decisions that our charges make or which would change the course of their destiny. We can only observe and lovingly guide them back to their right path, should they stray from it. Their spirit and soul know what they need to do but the human part, the brain side of things, only works with logic. Thankfully, I think that what just happened has dissolved those retained traits of yours."

Molly grinned like a Cheshire cat. She realised that she felt differently about being back in the spiritual realm. She felt like she belonged and that she was home, and was once again enveloped within the love of the Divine.

"Orick, I need to ask you something else. If I had made the decision to go back — to incarnate again, I mean — would I have been able to?"

Orick shook his head. "Realistically, no, you couldn't have gone back. There just isn't enough of your essence or energy left for you to function in a physical vessel, you being a special case and all."

Molly smiled. "A special case, or a nutcase?" she joked.

Orick laughed and smiled fondly. "You have made tremendous progress, and I think that from now on you will find things a lot easier. However, one of the final filaments which you need to complete is that of insight. Once you regain your insight, everything will become a lot clearer and make sense again."

Molly was perplexed at what Orick had just said. "Insight? Why do I feel like you keep moving the goal posts — just when I feel I've completed my lessons, you come up with something else."

"Insight is the key to acceptance. Insight means being in perfect peace, existing in total joy, being at one again with the spiritual realm. It will be an important part in the completion of the puzzle, as it were. As for moving the goal posts, well I would never do that. It's just that there is a great deal you have to learn or re-learn. You… we… never stop learning."

Molly turned to look at him. "Do you miss it… being able to reincarnate I mean?"

"No, why would I? This way I get the best of both worlds as it were," he replied with a wry smile.

"Now, what do you know about 'walk-ins'?"

Molly frowned, somewhat puzzled at Orick's question. "Haven't the foggiest, but I'm sure that you're about to fill that void."

Orick clapped his hands and rubbed them together. "Well now, walk-ins or as we affectionately call them, 'The News for Olds', are basically two spirits doing a swap. It's when a new spirit takes up residence in a physical body and the original spirit leaves. Instead of having a body die in order to release the original spirit, the new one steps in and picks up where the previous one left off. It's a pre-arranged agreement between the two. The exchange is typically made when the body is unconscious, such as during surgery, a near-death experience, a suicide attempt, or even emotional trauma. It's pretty seamless really. The new walk-in might need to learn how to function in a body again, but by and large the person goes on to recover, however they know that there is something different about themselves. They usually just put it down to the traumatic event."

"Why would any spirit want to do that?" Molly asked, perplexed.

"Why? Well for various reasons. Usually it's because the original spirit has completed its lessons and fulfilled its contract, and so has nothing to gain by staying. They've gone as far as they can in their development and are ready to move on, which means that the new spirit doesn't have to go through all the usual stuff like being born, et cetera. Very often the new spirit is highly advanced, but has incarnated because of its desire to serve the Divine. It's looking to advance quickly for ascension purposes."

"Ascension, huh — don't remind me," said Molly sarcastically.

Chapter Thirty-eight: Case Hearing

<***>

Riizlabll waited patiently for the amassed assembly of Ethereals to settle into their respective places, as a stifled stillness permeated the air. Rising to his full, towering height, he addressed the assembled gathering in a loud, authoritative voice.

"Welcome, light-beings. As you are all aware, we are gathered to discuss a very serious incident, an incident of a type which is becoming all too frequent and is proving to be somewhat of a growing concern. I think it necessary that we hear how this particular situation is developing or resolving, as the case may be."

Riizlabll waited for the numerous 'Ayes' and 'Yays' that rippled round the room to subside before continuing, "As you are all aware, the higher echelons are calling on all light-beings and Ethereal's to utilise their knowledge and experience to assist in the salvaging of a returnee spirit's damaged energy pattern and vibration. The cumulative damage caused by these two detrimental effects, plus other incurred injuries, has caused untold damage to our Beloved's soul. Adzullon, would you like to continue?"

Adzullon stepped into the centre of the room and waited for the assembled gathering to settle again. "Yes indeed, Riizlabll. The Beloved in question has received healing and much love and encouragement. However, sadly there are quite a few essential attributes preventing this spirit from making a full recovery, in as much as there is doubt that she will be able to incarnate again. This begs the question as to whether our Beloved should be entrusted with the responsibility of becoming a guide. And unfortunately, some of her memories have also been lost for all time, which poses the question of what action to take. I should add that Archangel Metatron has been working closely with our Beloved One. Metatron, may I invite you to take the floor?

301

With a flurry of wings, Archangel Metatron swept into the centre of the room, his magnificent, violet aura illuminating the entire space. "My fellow light-beings, yes, it is true that the Beloved known as Brenth, or Molly as she prefers to be called, has experienced difficulties — difficulties which have tested even the most experienced here — but I am delighted to inform you that she is recovering exceedingly well. If anything, she has surpassed all expectations thus far. She has embraced the re-activation of her inherent knowledge, even though up until recently she was still influenced by many retained human traits — traits which have been very, dare I say... challenging. I am however delighted to report that she has begun to embrace her spiritual consciousness once again. Both Archangel Raphael and I are immensely pleased to inform all here that she has taken her leap of faith, as it were, and has fully engaged in her Forgiveness Ceremony. We see no reason therefore why her transition to becoming a guide should not be anything but successful."

Riizlabll stepped forward and nodding graciously, thanked the archangel for his monumental contribution. A silence engulfed the room as the archangel left gracefully, leaving in his wake a trail of glittering, orange stardust. Raising his hands, Riizlabll once again waited for the ripple of hushed voices and nodding heads to subside. Clearing his throat, he stroked his long beard, gathering his thoughts.

"In respect of what has been stated, I acknowledge that the higher dimensions are very much in agreement with what the ethereal realm has proposed. Do we also agree that the only favourable outcome for this spirit's recovery would be for her to become a spirit guide?"

Riizlabll waited for the assembled Elders to cast their votes, while an air of sombre energy filled the chamber. Moments later he addressed the gathering once again, "Our Beloved is currently undertaking teachings and learnings from her life guide, Orick. The proposal to become a guide has been intimated to her and much to her credit, she has agreed. I would therefore welcome views and comments from all who have been overseeing her recovery."

The assembled congress waited expectantly as Kyah and Shelmuthe made their way onto the floor, nodding simultaneously as they addressed the gathering.

"Exultations to all here," said Shelmuthe. "Yes, that is correct. Archangel Metatron and Archangel Raphael have worked tirelessly in their quest to heal and restore our Beloved One's energy and vibration. Indeed, for one whose soul essence was irrevocably damaged, we are very impressed with the progress made thus far."

"Yes, very impressed indeed — Spirit Cloiff, Elder Adzullon and Guide Orick have excelled in their task," enthused Kyah.

Riizlabll addressed the gathering again, "Thank you, light-beings for your positive annotations. Adzullon and Guide Orick, I now entrust this matter entirely to the both of you. I also expect that you will keep me and Council fully informed of this particular Beloved's progress in the coming time."

A murmur of hushed whispers flowed around the room as Riizlabll raised his hand to continue his address. "Which brings me to the matter of the other spirit involved in all of this, Dolf as he is named. Guide Prenge, are you amongst us? He was your charge was he not? "

The room was silenced as Prenge stepped into the middle of the floor and spoke. "Blessings to all here present. You are correct, Riizlabll. Dolf was my charge, and I must inform you that he has undertaken healing and tutorage. He has exhibited regret and instigated his own karmic judgement for his actions. He has already left this realm following the Forgiveness Ceremony, and to his credit, has voluntarily descended. I would like to remind all here present that Dolf was a very juvenile and inexperienced spirit."

Riizlabll frowned and fixed Prenge in his gaze. "I am fully aware of that fact, Guide Prenge, just as I am also fully aware that it was you, along with Guide Orick, who drew up the contracts for Dolf and Brenth's reincarnations. Dolf's inexperience should have been apparent; this unfortunate state of events is clearly down to your misjudgement, is it not?"

Prenge shifted uncomfortably and looked down awkwardly. Suddenly a huge chasm opened overhead, and a figure enveloped in golden light which sparked deep crimson flames, descended down into the centre of the chamber. Effortlessly folding a pair of wings across its face and another pair of wings across its feet, the celestial being expertly folded the third pair neatly into its shoulders and alighted to the floor.

"Holy, Holy, Holy," the Seraph sang with a voice so beautiful it was hypnotic in its dulcet tones. A hushed mumble began to circulate round the chamber as the unexpected arrival had taken everyone by surprise.

The Seraphim unfolded its wings once again, before elevating its position to address the gathering. "Forgive my intrusion, Guide Prenge. I am Chontare, representative of the twelfth dimension's counsel, leader of Seraphims and ambassador to the Divine. I bring tidings to you all, seeded with the love of all that is. It is with much regret that I have need to address all before me, and it is with much trepidation that I do so. We are bearing witness to this catastrophic event, time and time again. What, pray tell, is happening within the earth dimension? The events are unsettling the dynamics of cosmic order. I am sure I do not need to inform you that these, shall we say, unfortunate occurrences have come to the attention of the Divine. It is all too evident that the number of Spirit who are returning with damaged essence in one form or another has substantially increased and as such, the twelfth dimension is becoming seriously concerned."

An uneasy silence filled the room as Kyah, bowing somewhat awkwardly, acknowledged the figure before replying rather curtly, "Yes, yes, Chontare, we are fully aware of that fact and thank you for your expression of interest."

Ignoring the sarcastic comment, Chontare continued, "Through all the eons, we have never had so many souls violated, or so many Beloved Ones return in need of healing. In all of cosmic evolution, I have never before had to report back to the Divine this extent of Spirit requiring succour or curative interventions. I want to know what is being done about it, because in…"

Kyah felt the need to interrupt, as the Seraph was beginning to annoy her. "Yes, thank you, Chontare, you really have no…"

"Thank you, Kyah," interrupted Riizlabll, sensing her growing annoyance. "I fully agree with the points that Chontare has made and I do not need to remind all here that this is a very sensitive and, shall we say, delicate matter, for which I see no point in casting aspersions or indeed discussing culpability."

Riizlabll surreptitiously glanced at Prenge and continued, "A full investigation will take place and as soon as we know why these events are happening, you will all be duly informed. Until then, I ask for your patience, tolerance and, of course, discretion."

Somewhat annoyed by Kyah's attitude, the Seraphim visibly bristled and showed its displeasure by suddenly spewing bright red flames from around its frame. It stared at Riizlabll with a questioning glare, and Riizlabll began to feel uncomfortable as he struggled to release himself from the Seraph's hypnotic spell. Finally, coughing nervously, he turned to address the waiting assembly once again. "Guardian Angel Thumus, do you have anything you wish to add?"

Thumus acknowledged the question with a bow of his head as he alighted to the floor. "Praise be, I can indeed substantiate that Chontare is correct; there is great consternation rippling through the twelfth dimension, just as there is momentous concern within the angelic realm too, all of which is proving to be very disquieting. I am reticent in having to state the obvious but nonetheless, this whole ruinous event has affected every dimension, level and tier within the entire realm."

Riizlabll graciously nodded in Thumus's direction and watched as the convened members muttered amongst themselves and shook their heads in shared disquiet. Raising his hands again, he authoritatively brought the room to silence once more before addressing the gathering. "With grace and honour, all here present are respectfully reminded that solutions are being sought to bring about a conclusion to this problem. As hard as it is for us to come to terms with the reality of what has been, and is still happening, the matter will be rectified and addressed in the same manner as it always has been and always will be. May I remind you all that love is all-powerful, love is all-consuming, love is all there is, and so it is."

Orick and Prenge exchanged glances as the assembly of light-beings and Ethereals solemnly filed out of the room.

Chapter Thirty-nine: Making Sense

<***>

Molly and Orick had met up in the Gardens again, and were huddled under the old cedar tree. "So, what's going on?" Molly asked. I waited for you to show up but when you didn't, I began to wonder."

Orick looked around, making sure no one was near enough to over hear what they were saying. "Shush, let's go somewhere a bit more private," he whispered.

"Oh, I love intrigue," Molly whispered back, playing along with him.

"Things are happening. There's stuff we need to discuss."

"What stuff?"

"Hush-hush stuff."

They made their way to the library, and finding an unoccupied bench on the far side of one of the rooms, Orick sat down and eagerly motioned for Molly to join him.

"So, what's happened — why were you gone so long, and why are you being all weird?" Molly asked, intrigued.

Orick looked around furtively, making sure that they couldn't be overheard. "I'm not being 'all weird'. I was called to an assembly, as was every light-being and Ethereal who is involved with your predicament — and I mean every one of them. And judging from the response of the light-beings, they're all really twitched. I don't know for sure exactly why that is, to be honest, but even one of the Seraphims from the twelfth dimension made an entrance, wanting answers, which suggests it's something really serious. And judging by the look which Prenge gave me, I'd say he knows it too."

"Sorry, what's the twelfth dimension got to do with anything?"

"Molly, the twelfth dimension is the equivalent of the Head Office. It's the top of the organisation; you don't get any higher.

You know — Source… God… The Man Upstairs… The Great Spirit."

"No way! The twelfth dimension, eh? Blimey, then it must be serious. Who'd have thought that little old me could cause so much bother."

"That's what I mean — this has gone straight to the top. And I'll tell you another thing, you could feel the tension between the Seraphim and the Elders. Kyah was really annoyed that the Seraph had made an appearance. I think she's taking it personally though, and I thought they were going to have a row at one point, but Riizlabll, ever the diplomat, stepped in and calmed things down. And by all accounts, I think it was a good job that he did."

"Yeah well, I wouldn't be surprised if it's all to do with 'you-know-who', the proverbial 'bad apple'." Molly gesticulated the inverted commas in mid-air.

"Oh, there's no doubt about that, no doubt at all," sighed Orick. "The question is, why was he such a bad apple? In fact, why are there so many bad apples, particularly the kind of bad apples who have no qualms about damaging fellow spirits to the point of rendering their souls totally and sometimes permanently shattered. By all accounts, you were one of the luckier ones."

"What do you mean, one of the luckier ones? Is what happened to me more common than anyone is letting on?"

Orick didn't answer but just nodded his head.

"Well, what do you think is happening?"

"I think there's a power struggle going on again. I think a particular entity is trying to throw his weight around and is having a go at challenging the order of things by challenging the Great Spirit."

"What do you mean, challenging things? Who would do such a thing?"

"Oh, probably that bad boy, Lucifer, again. He's a right one — trouble with a capital T. Every so often, usually when he's bored, he likes to chuck his weight around and tries to give the Great Spirit the run around. Of course, things go so far before Lucifer is put in his place again. Yes, I get the feeling that Lucifer is up to his old tricks. It sounds like it's not enough just to dole out temptation. No, this is a whole new ball game, even by his standards."

Molly felt a little uneasy. "Can I ask you a couple of things?"

"Sure, ask away."

Molly swivelled round to face him. "Going back to what happened to me, why didn't you save me? Why couldn't you intervene? Why didn't Thumus see what was coming? Why didn't anyone else see what was about to happen?"

Orick was taken aback by Molly's candour. "That's a lot of why's, Molly, and truth be told, I don't know the answers — nobody seems to know and no one anticipated what would happen to you. That's one of the things which the Elders are still trying to figure out, and if it's any consolation, both Thumus and myself are dismayed that we failed to protect you in the way you needed."

Molly gave a weak smile. "I know that my physical vessel was supposed to die at Dolf's hands. I know that's what I contracted for — I get that — but why did he overplay the power and trust card? Why go for the total soul decimation bit? That's the part I don't get"

"Like I said, I think Lucifer is up to his old tricks, but this is something else, even by his standards. This is so impure, and as much as I hope I'm wrong, it wouldn't surprise me in the least if he's behind it. I think he's trying his hand at really hitting the Divine where it hurts, so as to speak. I think he's actually trying to destroy souls, and that is a whole new ball game."

Molly sat dumbfounded. "Yeah, but it didn't work, well not fully I mean. I'm still here after all."

"Yes, but only just. Don't forget, you're only still here because you were rescued and healed… well sort of. You're damaged — there's no doubt about that — but I think the fact that you are very advanced and left a substantial energy veil behind is probably what saved you. But as you know, the same can't be said for your soul essence, and therein lies the problem."

"What do you think's going to happen, if this is his plan and it works? What if Lucifer wins?" she asked, concerned.

"Well, obviously he mustn't win, and I think that a strategy is being drawn up to make sure he doesn't. I mean, can you imagine what that would mean? Can you even comprehend such a thing?"

Molly took a deep breath and sighed as she suddenly became aware of an almost tangible silence hanging between them. She sensed that their conversation had drawn to a close and that Orick, now lost in his own thoughts, was one very troubled guide.

The following dawn, Molly met Orick in the Halls of Learning. Sitting together at one of the long, crystal benches, Orick was just about to wave his hand over its surface to activate a portal when she put her hand out to stop him.

"So... any developments?" she asked in a whisper.

Orick shook his head. "Not as yet, although I did see a gathering of Elders and guides going into one of the chambers over in the Halls of Wisdom earlier."

Molly shrugged her shoulders. "Oh well, I'm sure they'll let us know when they've sorted something. I have every confidence."

Orick was looking far off into the distance, seemingly distracted. He was watching a very large, red cloud which was beginning to form and was swirling and spinning, almost in the guise of a tornado. Molly followed his gaze and was just in time to see the cloud suddenly expand to fill the entire horizon. Transfixed by the spectacle, they watched the unfolding event in silence. Orick was the first to notice the black forms which leapt from the cloud, and with mounting apprehension, he abruptly grabbed Molly's arm while simultaneously changing his energy into an orb. Spinning her around, he propelled her in the opposite direction and pushed her forwards into a linear dimension.

Molly was startled by Orick's actions and feeling somewhat disorientated, looked at him, stunned. "What on earth was that all about?" she asked, somewhat affronted.

"Are you all right? Sorry I dragged you off like that, but they were coming our way and I thought it best to get us out of there."

"Who were coming our way? I don't understand. What just happened?" Molly asked, alarmed.

Orick sat down next to her. "That was Lucifer and his nasties being put in their place. I've only ever seen that twice before, and it's something that you don't want to hang around to witness if it can be avoided — gets a bit messy."

"Well, you whisked me off before I had a chance to see what was going on, anyway."

"Huh, yes, well it was for your own good. I presumed you'd seen the red cloud beginning to gather, but what you probably didn't see were the shape shifters, the Lessers from the lower astral dimensions. I had to get you away before the Dominions and Powers — formidable ranks of angels — had started to resonate their vibrations to bring them under control."

"You mean there was a battle... a fight?" exclaimed Molly, disappointed that she had missed it.

Orick nodded. "Oh yes, there would have been a fight all right, but not the blood bath that you think. No, this was a fight where the only weapon used was that of love. Because love is a pure, positive energy, evil cannot match it. Love cannot be defeated and evil will never prevail. Lucifer and his minions would have been overcome — of that I have no doubt — and would have been banished back to where they came from."

"Blimey, so that's that then. Good triumphs over bad... over evil."

"Always, but I should imagine that steps will have been taken to find out how and why all this started again and what they're going to do about it. The big question though, is what it is it that Lucifer hopes to gain. I don't know if anyone knows, but I'm sure that the Great Spirit will be doing everything in his power to find out."

Orick connected to Molly's energy again and propelled her back into the dimension they had just left. Molly looked around, and a wave of relief washed over her. There was no sign of any red cloud or that anything untoward had even happened. Everything was calm and tranquil again, just as it should be. Beginning to relax again, a rising sense of gratitude overawed her. Reaching out to Orick, she grasped his hand and placed it over her heart vortex while they were both lost in the moment of having experienced what had been an extraordinary encounter.

The following dawn they resumed the teaching session and Molly was full of questions. "I wanted to ask you more about suicide. You said something before about not taking enough energy or something, and I vaguely remember my grandpa calling them 'strugglers' and that they needed a lot of love and care."

Orick gave her a sideways glance and shuffled along the bench to get nearer to her. "Well now, let's see. Anyone who crosses themselves over, by whatever means, makes the decision to do so while they are earth-side. They make that choice through free will — it's not something that's made within their contract. Usually, like I said before, it's because when they were calibrating their energy requirement, they underestimated the amount they'd need. Sometimes spirits take too little energy with them, only to find that they can't cope with all the traumatic events or incidents which happen to them. Effectively they burn out; they lose all sense of purpose or self-belief and think that the only solution is to self-impair."

"Self-impair — is that what you call it?

"Well yes, that is effectively what they do; they render themselves impaired of power and then lack the energy reserves to fulfil their agreed contracts."

"That's awful. Imagine incarnating, then trying to live your life but not having the energy to do so."

"Yes, it is pretty tough, but whatever the reasons were as to why they couldn't cope, when they come back to the spiritual realm, they have to re-activate their contract. By the time they get to reincarnate again they will have learned how to manage their energy better, and how to do things differently. See, it's all a learning curve."

Molly frowned. "I suppose it's because when we go back earth-side, we forget."

Orick nodded. "Yeah, that's the thing, Molly, and unfortunately there's no other way — like I said, it's a learning curve. Everything that Spirit does is about learning, and most of the lessons to be learned on earth are to do with emotions and limitations."

"Well, what about the archangels and angels? Do they have free will and choice, like us?"

"What? Goodness no! They are in service — they oversee the Great Spirit's creation. They have never endured earth or imprinted the human vibration, and they have never been mortal. They only know pure love and want nothing more than to help humanity, because by helping a human being — a person — they are helping the resident spirit and soul essence. There are multitudes of angels and they have ranks and structure, and all have different purposes. For instance, the Cherubims and Seraphims are the highest-ranking angels because they work very closely with the Great Spirit. Then there's the Powers, the

Virtues, the Princes and Dominions, there's the Principalities, Archangels and, of course, guardian angels."

Molly let a smile cross her lips as she suddenly felt a wave of love engulf her. She surmised it was because the memory of inherent knowing had been triggered again. She continuing to half listen to Orick going on with his explanation, as she didn't have the heart to tell him that she now remembered it all.

Orick continued, "Now, Adzullon assigns a guardian angel to every new-born baby — incidentally, twins or similar get one each. guardian angels are mainly protectors who endeavour to keep their human safe, although they do guide as well. Whereas we guides do just that — we guide. Although a guardian angel is assigned at birth, they have to wait to be invited to help before they can do so. The human they are working with has to ask for their angel's help. That usually happens when the human perceives themselves to be in danger or undergoes enlightenment and learns to invite their angel into their consciousness. The angels are then enabled to serve for the greatest good and highest joy for that particular human being."

Molly sat quietly and thought about what Orick had just told her. "Okay, so we're back to free will — I sort of get that — but what happens when we come home, seeing as how I missed out on all that. What do we do? What happens to us?"

Orick smiled at her as he remembered the joy that those occasions brought. "Well you know about stepping into the light, don't you? That's a direct route back to the spiritual realm and the one which most spirit take. Fortunately, it avoids having to go through the astral plane — it's a short cut, if you like."

Molly nodded. "Oh yeah, I remember Grandpa coming to get me from the astral plane."

"Yes, he did, because you were incapable of finding your own way back, and he had good reason — there are all kinds of lower entities and nasties lurking there."

"What do you mean, all kinds of nasties? I didn't see any ghouls or ghosts! Actually, now I come to think about it, I didn't see much of anything."

"Well, I'm presuming you couldn't see them because you weren't sensitive to their vibration. The astral plane is a place much like the earth realm with lots of layers and tiers and many dimensions. Each of the astral levels has various entities residing within it — entities such as demons, and other lower dark energy forms. The list is endless, and like I said, there's nothing nice about any of them. Your grandpa was right to get you away as fast as he could."

"So why are they there then?"

"Well, the really nasty ones are there because they are from the dark. They're the Astrals and they've never known love and light. Then there are spirits who were too afraid to cross over into the light when they left the physical vessel that they were in. If they were really impure as a human being and didn't have a life review or weren't able to reconcile their karma, they'll stay there because they've imposed their own containment; in effect, they've instigated their own retribution. They are too afraid to face the music, as it were. Oh, and as for ghouls and ghosts, they aren't the same. They're an energy imprint or energy memory that's left behind in a given tier or dimension. Usually it's because, like Jenny, they have unfinished business or they can't move beyond their past, so they haunt a place. They're locked in, if you want to think of it that way. Their essence and soul vibration have gone home but their residual energy remains as a memory shadow."

Molly nodded her understanding as she remembered the conversation she'd had with her grandpa when she had been in the pub with him and Jenny. A smile crossed her face as she recalled how he had come to rescue her. Orick noticed that she had gone into a daze and clicked his fingers in front of her face to snap her out of it.

Pursing her lips, she tutted. "You didn't have to do that, you know, I was just remembering my grandpa. I haven't seen him for a while. Anyway, how would you like it if I poked you in the eye?"

"I didn't poke you in the eye."

"No, but you might as well have done. How rude!"

"Oh, shut up — we've got a lot to get through."

"Like I said, rude!"

Exasperated, but having secretly enjoyed their little spat, Orick continued, "Pay attention! Now, the dimension which we reside in — the spiritual realm — is also very similar to the astral plane in that there are levels which are below, above and beyond this one. Obviously, this particular dimension is full of goodness, light and love, but there are other dimensions which house the healing altars where Spirit can go for succour while their physical body is asleep. There are also tiers that Spirit can go to if the physical body that they are inhabiting lapses into a coma or becomes deeply unconscious, for whatever reason. There's all manner of things happening. Some Spirit are even able to astral travel to other dimensions and realms when the physical body is asleep, even though the human doesn't know or even remember it most of the time. Then there are people who have an 'out-of-body experience'; they get as far as the light at the end of the tunnel before they turn back. And why do you think babies sleep such a lot? It's because the new resident spirit likes to keep checking in back here all the time."

Molly shifted her position. "So how does that astral travel thing work? Blimey Orick, there's so much I've forgotten."

Orick reached out to comfort her. "It's okay Molly, don't worry about it — things will fall into place again. Do you remember your grandpa talking to you about the three cords of attachment?"

Molly nodded as she vaguely remembered.

"Well, anytime a spirit leaves the physical body, that's when the silver cord comes into play. The silver cord anchors the spirit to the physical body as it is attached to the pineal gland, making sure that the spirit can find its way back into the body again."

Molly was suddenly overcome with a fit of the giggles as she imagined of millions of spirts on lengths of elastic bungee ropes, bouncing and twanging all over the place.

"Honestly Molly, control yourself! It's not that funny. Right, what's next? Oh yes, assuming that a human vessel has an uneventful and straightforward death, the returning spirit will head for the white light and a designated family member will meet them and show them the way back to the Halls of Wisdom, where they check in, as it were. That's when the returnee spirit meets Archangel Azrael and Elder Hamneth."

Molly stretched and yawned. "Guess I missed out on that particular party then."

Orick frowned. "Hmmm, you missed out on a lot of things, unfortunately. Anyway, Elder Hamneth, the Chief Adjuster, oversees a vast council of adjusters. Sometimes returnees are disorientated when they return, and it's the adjusters who help them to well… adjust. Then their life guide takes them to the Towers so that they can collect and reconnect to their veils and energy vessels. Oh, and they also reactivate their memories of spiritual consciousness at the same time, after which they get to reunite with other family members and loved ones. It's very moving to watch, as the amount of love being exchanged is a beautiful sight to behold. It can be quite overwhelming sometimes."

Molly smiled to herself, as at that exact moment she felt something stir deep within her. She felt her heart light swell with the vibration of love, and realised that her love for her fellow Spirit was becoming stronger. She felt elated and euphoric, as a deep emotional connection surged through her.

Orick carried on talking, oblivious as to what had just happened. "Some returnees go to bathe in the Waters of Purity, just as you did, because quite often their energies are tainted or soiled and they have a need to wash away any karmic dross.

Some returnees even have to go to the healing altars to rejuvenate and recuperate, because they are weak or tired on their return. Following that, every returnee spirit goes to the Temple of Deeds to access their Akashic records, followed by a reunion with their soul group."

"Oh yeah, I remember the healing altars. Gosh, busy aren't we," she said, smiling. "Seriously though, how many others do you know of who have done what I'm having to do — you know, learning to become a spirit guide before we normally would?"

Orick thought for a while. "Well, not many to my knowledge, but judging by what Riizlabll was saying at the assembly, it's becoming a worrying trend, I think. Usually Spirit progress to becoming guides once they have completed the majority of their lessons and graduated, as it were."

Molly thought for a while. "Adzullon told me there are more Spirit reincarnating back to earth than there's ever been, so is it possible that the newer, less experienced ones are slipping through, like Dolf did?"

Orick looked surprised. "You know what, you could be right. Dolf was an inexperienced spirit and from what Prenge told me, he made a terrible human being as well so if that were the case, a lot of it would make sense, particularly if Lucifer had turned him. And knowing Lucifer, he would probably have promised him the earth, excuse the pun. But seriously, I do think it seems like Lucifer is having a bit of a recruitment drive."

Molly pouted. "I was just thinking... did Dolf have a guardian angel? I know that Prenge was his life guide but no one's mentioned him having his own angel."

Orick suddenly lapsed into silence as he thought about what Molly had just said.

"Are you all right? You look like you've just seen a ghost, as they say — no pun intended," she said grinning.

"Hmmm... yes, I'm fine. Actually, I think you're onto something — I don't recall an angel ever being mentioned. I'm surprised that Thumus and Prenge didn't pick up on that. Tell you what, keep this to yourself for now... I need to go."

"Go where?"

"To find Riizlabll, of course."

Chapter Forty: Hatches, Matches and Despatches

<***>

Adzullon was pacing backward and forwards, eager that his schedule should go to plan. He was becoming increasingly impatient, as Molly hadn't yet show up for a pre-arranged visit. "Come on! Hurry up… we haven't got all day. I need to get this lot matched up with their physical vessels and assign the right guides and the correct angels. What have you been doing? Why are you so late?"

"I'm really, really sorry," apologised Molly, "But I had to go and see someone"

Adzullon tutted and continued to mutter under his breath. "See someone, she says — what are the heavens coming to! Now, you stay here and watch what's going on. There's a lot to be done." He shuffled to the front of the hall to address the gathering spirits who were waiting to reincarnate.

"Now, can I have everyone's attention. I know you are excited and eager to get going, but we have to follow procedure and… BE QUIET!" he suddenly bellowed above the noise. "Goodness, I can't hear myself think." A silence swiftly descended over the hall. "That's better. As you all know, today is the forty-ninth day of conception for your chosen birth mothers and this is when you and your soul essence take up residence in your assigned vessel. When your name is called, please make your way to the front of the hall. Levvinnei, have all the angels and guides arrived yet?"

Levvinnei looked over to where the assembled angels and guides were waiting and nodded his confirmation, after scanning down a list which was attached to a clipboard. Gripping it tightly, he made his way over to the front of the gathering.

Adzullon continued, "Right, listen carefully! Twins and multiples move to the left, everyone else should have been given a spark with a geometric symbol embedded in it. The symbol should match both the date and time of delivery and the date and time of return, as scribed on the white light boards over there, along with your soul name. Is everyone clear? Once you've done that, please take the opportunity to re-acquaint yourselves with your life guide, Ascended Master and guardian angel again — as you know, they will re-join you as you are being born."

An excited murmur began to rise in volume as the waiting spirits jostled to take up their order of position.

"Just to remind you all, the amnesia sprites are waiting to whisk your memory and energy veils away, along with any energy which is surplus to requirements. Now don't forget, you'll all have natal amnesia once you're born. I don't know why I have to say this every time, seeing as how you all still have your memory, for goodness sake… well, at least for the time being that is." Adzullon chuckled at his own joke. "And have you all selected your correct birth mother and checked the final calculations for your energy requirements?"

A low murmur rumbled around the hall as some of the spirits realised that with Levvinnei's help, they still needed to recalculate their energy needs. Molly watched in amazement and awe as what appeared to be organised chaos began to gather momentum. Adzullon was calling out names and making sure that each spirit and its soul essence were paired accordingly. Molly watched as each pair melded their energies into one huge orb before they floated towards a tunnel. Molly could see that just as they entered the tunnel it became illuminated by their brilliant white light essence, just before they disappeared out of sight. Suddenly her attention was caught by movement through a window on the far side of the hall. Going over to the window, she could see row upon row of shimmering and glistening veils which were being carefully transported back to the Towers.

She was just about to leave, when she bumped into Orick. "Ah, thought I'd find you here. How's it going with Adzullon?" he asked, pensively.

"Oh, it's okay, thanks. Actually, it's brilliant… chaotic but brilliant. Well that's how it seems anyhow, but I'm sure everything is in perfect and divine order, as they say. Adzullon can be a bit of a stickler, but he really is something else."

Orick rested his hand on her shoulder. "Good, you are progressing really well. It won't be long before you have your first assignment. All that's left is for you to work with Archangels Azrael and Hamneth, meet the Ascended Masters, and have your inauguration ceremony as a qualified life guide."

Molly smiled surreptitiously to herself. "Actually, I've already met one of the Masters."

Orick spluttered. "What, you've already met an Ascended Master? Tell me, who?"

Molly had a mischievous look in her eye. "Well if you must know, I went to see Master Jesus."

"What! You went to see Jesus? Are you mad? I can't believe it. No way! Don't you realise how special that is? We do it all the time, but I'm not sure that you should have that sort of access — well, not yet anyway."

"Well, believe it! I did, and it's done and he was very kind. I think I'm in love with him."

Orick was dumb struck. "How on earth did you manage that?"

"How in Heaven, don't you mean?"

"Oh, stop splitting hairs, — you are unbelievable! I'm so… so… I just can't believe it."

"Oh, for goodness sake, Orick, get a grip! It's okay, and anyway, the Elders said that I could."

Orick looked sheepish as he realised that she was right. "So, what happened? What did you talk about?"

"Well first of all, he knew exactly who I was and what had happened to me, and we chatted for a while. Then anyways, I kind of said that I had a theory about what had happened to me and why. I told him that maybe inexperienced spirits might be causing all this mayhem — you know, what we talked about before. And I mentioned that what's-his-face, Lucifer, might be up to his old tricks."

"You told him all that!"

"Yep, and — get this — Jesus said that he knew all about Lucifer's little antics and that — you're not going to believe this — that Dolf was in fact a soul saboteur! I mean, can you believe that?"

"He said that?"

"Yep — knew everything."

"What did you do?"

"Smiled and thanked him for hearing me out. Then he thanked me for my interest and said that I wasn't to worry because it was all in hand. Just like that — cool as a cucumber."

"Wow! A soul saboteur, eh? Did he say anything else?"

"Well no… not exactly…"

"Right… not exactly…?"

"Well, he just mentioned that he was glad that things were turning out okay, and he made some comment about forgiveness being as important as love, or something like that."

"You are unbelievable!"

"Yeah, I know — you said. Anyway, what did Riizlabll have to say about Dolf not having a guardian angel?"

"Ah well, from what I can gather, Adzullon and Riizlabll had already noticed that when Dolf returned to the spiritual realm. Evidently his energy veil was missing, and — get this — his gold cord had been severed too."

Molly was shocked. "Oh well, that explains a lot, doesn't it? If his gold cord had been severed, that means that he no longer has a connection to God — I mean the Great Spirit — doesn't it?

"Yes, exactly that Molly, exactly that"

Chapter Forty-one: Running Totals

<***>

Archangel Azrael and Elder Hamneth were in the Returns Office situated in the Halls of Wisdom, where they were adding up the totals for the number of spirits who had returned that day. Azrael scratched his head. "No, these figures aren't right — we should have had 129,897 returnees according to my calculations, there's three missing."

Hamneth took the clip board from Azrael and started to tot up the totals again. "Well, I don't know how three have come to be missing. Are you sure they were originally logged out?"

Azrael scowled. "Of course, they were logged out — what do you take me for? They're logged when they leave and logged again when they come back."

Hamneth shook his head. "Well, maybe Adzullon has got it wrong. There's a first time for everything, as you well know."

Just then there was a commotion coming from down the hallway. "Oh, wait a minute, here's the stragglers arriving now by the sounds of it."

Going over to the Returns window, Hamneth poked his head through the opening. "Hello there, welcome home. What kept you all? We were expecting you ages ago. You've had Azrael in a right old tizzy," he said benignly, "Could you all just confirm your names for me, please."

The three returnees stepped up to the window and gave their names in turn. Archangel Azrael scanned down the list on the clipboard and ticked them off with a flourish. As he did so, each name changed colour from a pale, creamy yellow to either a silver or a gold, depending on how advanced each of them were.

"Well, everything seems to be in order. Right then, we have Kenneth Alan Murray, Stanley Brown, and last but not least, Josephine Louise Carmichael. Good... lovely to see you all again" Azrael smiled to himself. He had always taken pride in making sure that every returning spirit was personally greeted and welcomed home.

Hamneth asked them what had delayed their return. In response, Ken shrugged his shoulders and explained, "Hah now see, we'd have been on time, but it's all the technology malarkey that's down there now. You can't just die of a heart attack anymore. Oh no, at least not without some bloody do-gooder trying to keep you alive. What with all this CPR nonsense, and the latest drugs for this, and new drugs for that and what not, it's a right bloody carry on, I can tell you. Josephine, here, was a drowning but they kept her back for a full nine hours, and Stan, here, was revived several times after he got electrocuted. I'm telling you, it's different now — you're trying to come home and they keep bringing you back! It plays havoc with your bloody vibration; I can tell you. One minute you're going, then you're jolted back, then you're going again! It's a right game of soldiers, talk about having an OBE."

"You never said anything about having a medal!" said Stanley surprised."

"What! what are you talking about?" replied Ken, somewhat confounded. "I didn't mean 'OBE' as in a medal, I meant an out of body experience, you idiot."

"Oh, well excuse me for breathing."

Ken and Josephine looked at one another, and shaking her head in exasperation Josephine said, "Eee, it's good to be home at long last though — I've kind of missed the place."

Ken and Stanley nodded in agreement. "Right, chief — where do you want us?" enquired Stan.

Archangel Azrael came out of the office and extended his arm as if to shepherd them towards a number of doors on the far side of the room. "I'm sorry, forgive me. As I was saying… Welcome home, it's nice to see you all again. Now if you just follow the signs over there and select the door which has your name on it, one of the Adjusters will see to you before you go through to see your loved ones."

The three returnees floated over to the doors which Azrael had indicated. Shaking hands with one another, and giving a cheery wave to Hamneth and Azrael, they each went through their respective door and disappeared from view.

Hamneth shook his head. "Right, you're sure you've ticked them off on the checklist? You know that Adzullon is a stickler for numbers. I'll have to have a word with Council about all these delays. They need to know what's going on. All these technical breakthroughs being made down there — well it just isn't right. This is becoming much too regular now, and we can't be waiting round here all day and night. We've a schedule to follow."

Azrael nodded in agreement. "Yes, I think you should mention it; dying used to be so straight forward."

Orick had arranged for Molly to go to the Halls of Wisdom so that she could observe what Archangel Azrael and Elder Hamneth did. Jokingly calling them the 'Meeter and Greeter Service', Orick felt that he should at least warn Molly not to be put off by Azrael, who could be a bit stern at times. Orick reassured her that his bark was worse than his bite. After all, this was a serious business and he wasn't one to shirk his duty, he explained. He was in a position of great responsibility, and she shouldn't forget that.

Entering through the door at the top of the stairs, Molly was just in time to see a new group of returnees being welcomed home. She watched as the creamy white aura which surrounded Archangel Azrael ebbed and flowed around and through him, as he ceremoniously welcomed each of them back, while Elder Hamneth was busy going through the process of logging the returnees in. Molly noticed how serene and composed the returnees were, and she could feel a beautiful, shimmering aura of yellow and green energy emanating from each of them. Waiting until the last of the returnees had gone through a door marked 'Arrivals', she wandered over to where Archangel Azrael was standing and held out her hand to offer a handshake. Azrael frowned and ignoring her gesture, continued to look down the list which he held in his hand. Molly shifted uncomfortably and flashed a questioning look at Hamneth.

"Oh, take no notice of him," scoffed Hamneth as he came to her side. "He's got his reputation to think of, him being the Angel of Death and all."

Azrael glared at Hamneth.

"Well, if looks could kill," Hamneth chuckled.

Azrael looked Molly up and down, "So you're the one that's causing all the kerfuffle round here! Guide Orick has filled me in on the details. Go and sit somewhere and don't move — we're due another batch of returnees soon, and I really could do without the distraction."

Doing as she'd been told, Molly found a bench to sit on in the farthest corner of the room. Curiously looking around her, she could sense that the room was cavernous and realised that there were numerous doors, all of which were firmly closed. Each of the doors had a geometric symbol above it, like she'd seen when she'd been with the Archangel Metatron. Molly noticed that some of them were flashing in different colours.

Hamneth smiled as he came over and sat with her. "Don't mind old grumpy-drawers, he's just a bit touchy of late, probably because he's not getting job satisfaction any more. I'll tell you what, why don't you go and have a chat with the guides who have just returned with the last intake. I'm sure you've got lots of questions to ask. I'll see you later if you like, and fill you in on a couple of things, and explain anything you don't understand."

Molly was relieved and happy to get away for a while. She followed Hamneth's instructions and floating down the corridor, looked for the third door on the right. Hearing voices and banter, she pushed the door open and peeped into the room beyond. She was taken aback at how many guides were congregating together. Most were sitting down, relaxing in what looked like enormous bean bags floating in mid-air. Others were standing around the room, engaged in deep conversation; she eavesdropped on a few of the discussions as the guides recounted the lives that their last charges had experienced. Looking around, she noticed a group of teacher guides, chatting amongst themselves. Standing nervously in the doorway, she tried to catch the attention of one of them, hoping that she might be able to ask a couple of questions and pick up a few tips, but no one seemed to be paying any attention to her.

Just then, she felt a presence standing behind her and turning around, came face to face with a beautiful archangel. She stepped aside to allow the angel access. The room was instantly illuminated in a brilliant white light, and conversations stopped mid-sentence. The guides looked towards the figure and greeted the archangel with a hearty, welcoming cheer and lots of laughter and congratulations.

Molly shuffled nervously. "Who's that?" she asked a guide who was standing next to her.

"Why, that Archangel Gabriel, of course."

Molly was taken aback. "Oh, thanks… erm… does she come in here often? Like this, I mean"

"Why, of course! Gabriel is the angel of conception and birth, and of communication and protection, so she oversees all Spirit incarnations. We always have a meeting with her — it's part of our preparation before we return to the earth realm with our charges. We meet her again when our charges return home; she likes to know how they fared, as it were."

Molly couldn't take her eyes of the beautiful archangel. She studied her features and the way the light-being moved. Molly was mesmerised by the soft, gentle voice which had a hypnotic, melodic tone, and before long she was completely captivated and enthralled by the angel's gentle, loving energy. She observed how the angel interacted with each guide in turn as they discussed their charges' achievements and accomplishments. The angel smiled knowingly as she gave encouragement and praise to each of the guides and congratulated them on their diligence and care.

It was some time before Molly realised that the room was slowly emptying as the guides gradually left to go about their business. Molly was contemplating what to do next when Archangel Gabriel turned to leave the room. Noticing Molly's energy as she did so, she stopped, smiled at her and stooping forwards, gently kissed Molly on the forehead. Molly was rooted to the spot as the angel spread and stretched her wings, before disappearing in a twinkle of brilliant white light, leaving behind a single white feather which fluttered and swirled around Molly's head. Feeling overcome with emotion, Molly was completely taken aback and dazed at the interaction which she had just experienced.

She hurriedly made her way back along the corridor to where Azrael and Hamneth had been. She felt like she would burst with excitement, and she couldn't wait to share her experience with Hamneth. Excitedly pushing the door open, she expected to find the two of them busy with their tasks, but the room was empty. Glancing around, she called out, "Hello, anybody here?" but there was no answer. She decided to sit down on one of the chairs to wait. Looking idly around the room, she noticed that the walls were covered with huge graphs and charts, displaying a multitude of different numbers and calculations. Glancing at some papers which were on top of the desk, she noticed a blue folder buried under a box-file. Curiously, she moved the box-file out of the way and turned the folder over to have a better look. The folder had silver and magenta-coloured binding running along its edges and a silver inlay on its front. Staring at the inlay, she recognised the word which was written there in ancient Sanskrit; it was her name, etched in gold lettering. Her curiosity got the better of her and nervously picking the folder up, she opened it and started to read the beautiful lettering inside. The words were written in a glorious colour, although she couldn't for the life of her put a name to it, and she suddenly realised that she had never seen that colour before. Carefully turning over each page, she slowly read the text. After turning a few of the pages over, she realised that as soon as she had read a line the words started to become illegible. She looked back over the words which she had already read, and saw them slowly fade away before they disappeared completely. She gasped and hurriedly closed the folder, quickly putting it back where she had found it.

Continuing to look around the room, she noticed an array of boxes and files of various sizes and colours stacked from floor to ceiling in one corner. They all had writing on the spines but most of it was illegible. Leaning back in the chair, she resisted the temptation to snoop, and drummed the table with her fingers, wondering where Hamneth and Azrael had got to. Unable to resist the soporific feeling which was rapidly sweeping over her, she relaxed and surrendered to the invitation of slumber.

Soon afterwards, Azrael and Hamneth returned to find her fast asleep. Having been called to one of the other vestibules in the Towers to help with a recount, they were surprised to find her there. Molly woke with a start as Azrael leant over and gently shook her awake. She was embarrassed to have been caught napping.

Hamneth smiled as she sat up. "You okay?" he asked softly.

"Yes thanks, I'm fine. Just got a little too comfortable. Sorry I missed whatever it is I missed. Ermm… so what have I missed, actually?"

Hamneth busied himself with filing some of the folders away. "Oh, nothing much and nothing to concern you. We've just had an intake of returnees following some sort of catastrophe. So how did it go with the guides?"

"The guides…" she said, suddenly gathering her thoughts, "…Oh yes, the guides. It was really great, especially as I got to meet Archangel Gabriel as well. To tell you the truth Hamneth, I can't wait to qualify as a guide; it's all very exciting."

Azrael reached over and picked something up off the desk. "Exciting, eh? Here… you can help us count the next intake of returnees," he said as he held out a pen to her. "They'll be due any time soon. Just ask them their name, tick them off the list and direct them to whichever door has a flashing symbol over it."

Molly stretched and yawned and smiling, reached for the pen. Studying it, she realised that the pen was a beautiful, solid crystal wand which glinted in her hand and began to gently pulsate.

"Well you didn't honestly think that it would just be any old pen, did you?" Azrael said somewhat haughtily.

Molly and Hamneth were working together in the office. They were nearing the end of what had been a very busy couple of days, and this was the first chance that they'd had to talk properly.

"This place is amazing… I mean, the whole setup. Everything is just so… so… well… amazing! Everyone is so happy to be here, and seeing all the returning spirits coming through and then meeting their loved ones… well, amazing is the only word for it!"

Hamneth smiled. "I hadn't thought that what we do is particularly special but you know what, now you come to mention it, yes I would agree with you, it is amazing — absolutely amazingly marvellous!"

Molly blushed. "Are you teasing me?"

Hamneth winked. "Yes, just a little."

"Can I ask you something? What's the matter with Azrael? Why is he so stern all the time?"

Hamneth grinned. "I suppose he does come over as being like that but it's hardly surprising really, especially when he's been given such a bad press all this time — you know, him being the Grim Reaper, the Angel of Death and all that. But actually, he's very conscientious and just wants the best for Spirit. He's a pussy cat, really."

Molly smiled to herself, as she continued to tidy away some of the folders. She felt comfortable in Hamneth's company. "A pussy cat, eh? I'll remember that next time he's growling at me"

Looking around the office, her attention was suddenly drawn to the table, as if a magnet had hold of her stare. She couldn't stop herself from staring at the folder which was exactly where she had left it, peeking out from under the box file on the desk.

Hamneth followed her gaze. "You've seen it, haven't you? You've seen your element?"

Molly shifted awkwardly. "I didn't mean to… it just sort of appeared like it wanted me to find it, but when I opened it and started to read, the words faded and disappeared, so I quickly closed it again. I couldn't understand the writing anyway. I'm sorry, I know it was wrong of me, but I just couldn't seem to help myself."

Molly couldn't stop staring at the folder. It was pulling her energy towards it and she was struggling to suppress an overwhelming desire to reach for it and open it again.

Hamneth let out a deep sigh. "Well, no matter, what's done is done. We shouldn't have left it there in the first place. It's just that we needed to know what had befallen you, as Orick had asked us to show you things which Spirit usually don't concern themselves with. This, is what is known as an element. It's like a condensed dossier, recording every life trial which you experienced during your previous life lived. Eventually it will be added to your overall Akashic record. Of course, you now know you shouldn't have seen it, let alone have read it — well, certainly not in its present format."

Molly looked puzzled. "Yes, I know what it is, I've seen something similar already, but why shouldn't I have seen it and why didn't any of it make sense? And I don't understand why the words disappeared as I was reading them."

"You couldn't make sense of it because you are incomplete, and so the story within — your story — is therefore also incomplete. It caused you much confusion because the experiences of your past life still don't make any sense to you. Sadly, you are a spirit with a shattered soul — you're fragmented — which means that for now you are unable to relate to the element's content."

Hamneth reached for the element and opening it, stared at the first page before turning it over. He turned the second, then the third and then several more; it was worse than he had first thought — they were all blank.

Molly noticed his concerned expression. "Well, what's the verdict?" she asked nervously.

Hamneth continued to turn the pages. "Well, as far as I can see, sixteen pages are completely blank, which means that sixteen life trials which you've experienced have been erased. I'm sorry Molly, but you've unwittingly erased some of your last life experiences... well the first sixteen anyway. You will have to go back to the Akashic library to find out how that will affect your overall Akasha. Hopefully there will be minimal problems, but you must seek guidance from Kyah — she will know what to do."

Molly put her head in her hands, crying out, "Oh, how could I have been so stupid? Sixteen experiences... how am I going to make that right? What if those sixteen were really important? This could really screw up my chances of becoming a guide. Why did I have to be so damned nosey?"

Hamneth closed the element and returned it to the desk. "I'm sorry, but I really don't know what happens now. Like I said, that's for Kyah and the Elders to decide. I just hope that it's only the content of this element which was erased. Hopefully the collective total of your Akashic record will still be intact."

Chapter Forty-two: Good To Be Home

<***>

It was time! Ged waited patiently in the corner of the hospice room, ready to help Nan make her transition. It had been eight months since she had been diagnosed with inoperable lung cancer, and now she was on her death bed. Her breathing had become shallow and guttural, and although her eyes were open, they were unseeing. A single tear rolled down her right cheek.

Annie was sitting by the side of the bed, holding and gently stroking the back of Nan's hand. She noticed the brown liver spots and arthritic finger joints which were gnarled and stiff. Annie studied her mother's face, as though seeing for the first time the deeply etched, furrowed lines of a brow filled with a lifetime of worry, and in the harshness of the single overhead bed light she brushed the single falling tear away. Noticing the sallow, pale complexion and shallow breathing, she leaned forwards, as if by doing so would make Nan's struggle less of a burden. Annie thought to herself how Nan's small frame looked lost in a bed which was seemed to be too big for her.

"Can I get you anything — cup of tea, maybe?" whispered the nurse as she straightened the cotton bed sheets and gently plumped the pillows under Nan's head.

Annie shook her head and forced a numb smile. "No, I'm fine, thanks. She looks quite peaceful, doesn't she?"

The nurse nodded. "Yes, I've made her comfortable. It's just a matter of time now."

Ged knew that it wouldn't be much longer before Nan drew her last breath. Periodically he whispered into her ear, reassuring her that everything was as it should be and that there was nothing to fear, as he was waiting for her.

It was during the early hours of that dark winter's morning that Nan surrendered her frail body and exhaled her last breath. Ged waited for her spirit to rise above her now lifeless vessel, and gently pulled the silver cord free from her brow chakra. He looked on as her guardian angel and life guide released her gold cord and gathered up her soul vibration before they crossed back into the spiritual realm.

"What kept you? I've been hanging around for what seemed like an eternity. I thought you were never coming, but then you always did like to keep me waiting!"

Nan flung her arms around Ged's neck. "Oh Ged, is it really you?" she said ecstatically, "I had hoped that you'd be the one to meet me."

Smiling and grinning, Ged held Nan in his arms, hugging her tightly. "I can't tell you how long I've waited for this moment, for you to come back to me. And now I can take you home."

Nan quickly glanced around the room. "Just give us a minute, love. I want to tell Annie something."

Annie was standing by the window, peering out into the pervading nothingness. Putting his stethoscope back into the pocket of his white coat, the doctor turned to Annie with a look of anguish across his tired, drawn face. In a soft but reassuring voice he said, "I'm so sorry, but she's gone. Is there anything I can get for you?"

Annie felt the tears begin to roll unchecked down her face, and in a controlled whisper replied, "No, I'm fine. Thank you, doctor, you're very kind." Forlornly she returned to the single chair by the bedside and taking hold of Nan's hand again, gently caressed it as she silently wept in the semi-darkness. She didn't notice the fleeting shadows caught by the overhead bed light dancing around her, nor see the portal of white light which had opened in the farthest corner of the room.

Nan placed her hands gently on Annie's shoulders and bending forwards, kissed her cheek. Annie swept her hand across her face, brushing away the tickling sensation caused by Nan's energy. Whispering into her ear she said, "My darling Annie, don't be upset. I'm perfectly fine — your dad's here to take me home. Everything will be okay."

Ged smiled, as Nan turned to face him. "Ready?" he asked.

"Ready as I'll ever be," Nan replied, expectantly.

Taking her hand in his, they floated upwards towards the light portal, and with a backwards glance, Nan blew Annie a kiss.

Ged had arranged to meet Molly in the Gardens. It had been a while since they had been together, and as she approached him, she realised just how much she had missed him. Flinging her arms around his neck, they embraced.

"Oh Grandpa, I've missed you so much. It's been ages since we've chatted. I've been so busy with all this guide business. How's things with you? What have you been up to?"

Holding her at arm's length, Ged stood back a little and let a broad smile cross his face. "Actually, I have someone who wants to say hello to you."

Molly clapped her hands in excitement. "Who is it?" she asked, looking round excitedly. "Who, Grandpa? Who?"

Ged stepped to one side as a figure of spirit energy appeared. Molly instantly recognised Nan and rushed forwards to meet her. Throwing their arms around each other, they merged their energies with love and happiness.

"Oh Nan, it's you! When did you get back? I can't believe that you're here at last! What happened to you? How's Mam? So much has happened! Oh, I've got so much to tell you and ask you, and I'm so excited to see you."

"Calm down, Molly! Blimey, I haven't seen you this excited in a long time," Ged said smiling.

They all walked hand in hand towards the Tree of Wisdom and sat together beneath it. Ged couldn't quite believe that Nan was back with him — back by his side.

"Well now, where to start! We all have a lot of catching up to do and I'm sure Nan is eager to hear all about it," he said excitedly. "Molly, why don't you start first."

Nan listened intently and tutted and gasped and shook her head disparagingly as Molly recounted what had happened to her.

"Unbelievable! My poor, poor, Molly. What an ordeal you've been through, but at least the little bastard got his comeuppance after all. Sounds like karma really did bite him on the arse."

"Nan, you're not supposed to say things like that here!" exclaimed Molly in surprise.

"What! Why ever not? It's true, isn't it?"

Ged laughed out loud. "Well, you always did speak your mind."

"Yes, I did, and not always as kindly as I should have, I might add. I owe you an apology Molly, I'm really sorry for how I treated you. I had no reason for being so horrible to you. I hope you can forgive me."

Molly spluttered and trying to suppress a rising laugh giggled. "Forgive you, ha-ha-ha, haven't you heard? I'm a dab hand at forgiveness. Why, forgiveness is my middle name."

Nan frowned and glanced over at Ged. "Have I missed something?"

Ged smiled and mouthed, "I'll tell you later."

"So, when do you think you'll be going back? Have they told you yet?" asked Nan.

"Hmm... no, I'm not too sure. Orick hasn't said anything, but I don't think it will be long now. I think I'm ready and I'm quite excited at the prospect. It's a huge responsibility I know, but it's not like I'm going to be on my own — at least I'll be with an angel, I expect."

"Well, we're very proud of you; we know you'll do really well."

Molly beamed with pride, and feigning sarcasm and laughing playfully, joked, "Nan, good grief, you almost sound like a doting grandmother, which I'll remind you, you never were."

"Why, you cheeky monkey! Yes well, I suppose I'll have my own karma to sort out, but I think I've learned a thing or two, eh Ged?"

Molly was relaxing in the Gardens when she was unexpectantly summoned by Kyah. They met in the Towers. and feeling a little nervous, Molly fidgeted as they sat opposite each other. Kyah placed what looked like a small booklet on the table between them. Molly shifted awkwardly. Opening the booklet, Kyah ran her fingers over the gold lettering and fixed Molly in an austere stare.

"Well, Beloved, I have asked you here to inform you that the Council of Wise Ones have decided it is time for you to return to the earth realm with an incarnate. Do you feel ready?"

Molly laughed out loud. and a huge smile crossed her face. "Ready? Oh yes, I'm more than ready — I can't wait to be a guide."

Kyah smiled, delighted that Molly was so eager. "A great deal of collective wisdom has been sought and gathered in bringing about this monumental decision. It has been decreed that you shall be a life guide. That is what you were hoping for, isn't it?"

Molly forgot herself and jumping up, made to hug the great Elder. "No way… really? I'm going to be a life guide? I can't believe it! Yes, that's what I've been hoping for. Me… a life guide… oh my gosh, who'd have thought? I can't wait to tell everyone! Me… a life guide! I can hardly believe it."

Kyah was surprised by Molly's spontaneity as it caught her off guard. Austerely she gestured for Molly to compose herself. "Now, now, you must restrain yourself, Beloved; outbursts of such emotion are not to be so readily displayed. You must not demonstrate such impulsiveness, especially when you have a charge to take care of. Do I make myself clear?"

Feeling awkward, Molly composed herself again. "Yes, of course. I'm sorry — guess I forgot myself. It won't happen again, sorry."

"Very well. I'm not saying that you can't display actions of love and joy and such like, but you have a responsibility to be measured in your actions — you must remember that. Now, there are a few matters which need to be discussed, namely your little escapade in going to see Master Jesus, and not forgetting the matter of the sixteen life lessons you unwittingly erased."

Molly fidgeted nervously, aware that to all intents and purposes she had overstepped the mark and had probably made a fool of herself in the process.

"Yeah, sorry, forgot myself a bit there. And about me trying to sort things out — I thought I was showing initiative by going to see him. After all, Riizlabll did say I was to work with the Ascended Masters, and I couldn't think of a better one to go and see. I just figured that he'd be the best Master to ask, as I reckoned he'd know what was going on. I also wanted to tell him my take on things. And I went to the library to… well…speed things up a bit and as it turned out, my records were intact after all, so no harm done, eh?"

Kyah fell quiet for a while as she considered Molly's response, and then replied. "Yes, that's as maybe, although I think you should consider yourself more than just a little fortunate. Nevertheless, you should have consulted me before acting so impulsively. Now, against my better judgement, I am in receipt of a message which Master Jesus has asked me to pass on to you."

Molly was elated and clapping her hands excitedly, begged Kyah to tell her what Jesus had said. She was overjoyed at the thought that he actually wanted to pass on a message to her.

"Jesus wishes you much love and every success as a life guide and says he will be on hand to assist you as and when you need it. Likewise, if you have any problems or difficulties at all in the future, he will be with you to assist. All you'll need to do is send out a thought to him"

As Kyah looked on, somewhat bemused, Molly began to do a silly dance, and forgetting herself again, started chanting, "Jesus loves me, Jesus loves me," in time to her dance. "Oh, I'm so happy… no, ecstatic… yes, ecstatic. I can't believe it. Jesus loves me," she exclaimed as she continued to dance around Kyah.

Kyah drew in a deep breath, clearly exasperated by Molly's behaviour and remarked, "Jesus loves everybody, for goodness sake."

Molly pouted, somewhat deflated by Kyah's comment. Suddenly changing the subject, she asked, "Anyway, what did happen to 'Loser-of-the-century'?" while doing the inverted commas in the air gesture.

"'Loser-of-the-century'? Oh, I presume you're referring to Dolf? Well, as it turns out he has demonstrated remorse and has been transferred back to Vega, the place from where he originated. He will receive additional teachings and support for his violent tendencies, his anger, and his addiction traits, amongst other things."

"Whoa, Vega! That's like being sent to rehab, isn't it? Oh well, whatever… And what's the low-down on Lucifer?"

"Lucifer is a different matter and is no concern of yours."

Molly let a beaming smile cross her face. "I can't believe he got back to me. Who'd have thought it? Me and Jesus! We had kind of a thing going there, I think."

Kyah gave Molly a stern look. "Seriously? I very much doubt that. Being in the presence of an Ascended Master is one of the most emotional experiences Spirit will ever have; few remain unaffected. You were probably able to communicate with him because of your lowered vibration."

Molly pouted again, as she realised that Kyah was being dismissive and even chastising her, but she didn't really care.

"Now I think you should prepare yourself. You need to say your goodbyes and start planning for your departure, as once you are assigned, there will be no time for any distractions or further interactions."

Molly could hardly contain herself as she rushed to tell Ged and Nan her good news. She told them what Kyah had said about Jesus and how Dolf wasn't even in the same constellation as her anymore.

Ged beamed with pride as Molly's excitement was infectious. "We'll miss you, Molly girl. Don't forget to think about us occasionally though, will you?"

"Of course, I'll think about you. I'll think about you both all the time and when I do, I'll know that you are thinking about me too. We'll still have our interconnectedness and telepathy, won't we? And you will look after Mam as well, won't you? Send her some good luck and happiness for a change."

"Aww, don't worry. Of course, we'll keep an eye out, won't we Ged? Don't you worry Molly, she'll be fine. Actually, I've got my sights set on a rather nice gentlemen friend for her. I'm arranging for one of those chance meetings to happen. Who knows, there could be the sound of wedding bells for her yet!" Nan said, as a smile crossed her lips.

Molly gave them extra hugs before she returned to the Gardens to see her soul group again. Embracing Braugh, she momentarily felt sad and a deep sense of melancholy sweep over her. She felt bereft.

"Why the long face?" Braugh asked.

"Oh, I don't know. I suppose I'll miss you, but truth be told, actually I think I'm a little envious since you're going to be ascending very soon."

"Well that's as maybe, but just think of the adventures that you're going to have. I'm somewhat envious of you too, as it happens."

Molly laughed as she looked around her. "Where's Vimprn? I can't see her."

"Haven't you heard? She's just having some final teachings before she reincarnates. Looks like we're all going our separate ways. I shall miss her too."

Molly smiled ruefully and corrected her, "No, not separate ways, just different ways. We'll always be connected, which means we'll never be apart."

Wandering over to the Towers again, Molly observed Adzullon organising another group of spirit who were getting ready for their incarnations. Idly glancing around, she suddenly saw a familiar light on the far side of the hall and recognised it as Vimprn. Molly shouted and waved to get her attention, and they met in the middle of the vast space.

"Hi! Braugh said you were getting ready to leave," Molly shouted above the noise

"Yes, today's the day," Vimprn replied, beaming.

"Fantastic! I wanted to catch you before you left. Have you heard my good news?"

Vimprn shook her head. "No, what news?

"I'm definitely going to be a life guide. They haven't said when though. I can still hardly believe it."

Vimprn beamed and embraced Molly. "Wow, that's fabulous news. Oh Molly, I'm so happy for you. You'll love it, I just know you will, and you'll be a fantastic guide for some lucky spirit."

"Well, I hope so! I guess I'll see you around then, though who knows when we'll get to meet up again."

Embracing one last time, they said their goodbyes. Molly watched Vimprn disappear into the twinkling crowd of Spirit lights, before she returned to the Gardens. It was here that she felt nurtured and happy, and she wanted to see as much of Braugh as possible before she left. Molly found him sitting under the cedar tree.

"You okay? You look a bit down," he asked, concerned.

"Yeah, I'm fine. I've just been to see Vimprn before she left. I feel like I'm missing her already. I wanted to see as much of you as possible before I go… or you go. Well, who knows which of us is going first."

Braugh motioned for her to sit next to him and replied, "I know, I'm really gonna miss her, as well as you."

"I hadn't realised that this changes so much. We can still keep in touch, though. You won't forget to think about me, will you, cos I'll be thinking about you. If we can both think about each other, we will always be connected," she said, smiling.

Chapter Forty-three: Inauguration

<***>

Many dawns had come and gone when Molly suddenly became aware of Orick telepathically asking her to meet him in the Halls of Wisdom. Instantly appearing at his side, she was surprised to see Prenge there as well.

"What's up? Molly asked nonchalantly.

Orick and Prenge smiled simultaneously. "Oh good, you're here. Well, nothing's up as such, it's just that it's been decided that today is the day for your inauguration. It's today that you become a fully-fledged life guide."

"What, now?"

"Yes, now."

Molly laughed nervously. "You have got to be joking. I'm not ready… I don't know what to do or what to say, even. It can't be today."

Prenge came to her side. "Don't worry, it'll be fine. You're more than ready. Just follow us and do whatever they ask you to do," he said, reassuringly.

Nervously following the two guides, Molly realised that they were entering the Temple of Deeds. They all floated silently down a long corridor, but Molly's apprehensiveness was evident as she began to slow her pace.

"Hold on, will you — you're moving too fast."

Orick and Prenge stopped and waited for her to catch them up. "It's okay, we know you're nervous," Prenge said reassuringly, "but have faith and trust us. Honestly, you will be absolutely fine,"

"Look, we're here," said Orick.

Molly stood transfixed, staring at the door in front of them. Pushing the door open, Orick encouraged her to cross the portal, and after doing so, she found herself in front of a gathering of Elders and Wise Ones. Scanning the energies before her, she recognised Shelmuthe, Kyah and Riizlabll. Smiling they nodded their acknowledgment, as Orick whispered to her, "See the podium over there? Go over to it."

Molly did as he asked and turning to the audience, suddenly recognised many other familiar faces. A silence descended over the vast hall as suddenly a silver beam of light appeared above her and illuminated her energy.

Orick approached the podium and hovering at her side, welcomed the assembled mass of Ethereals and Spirit. "With love, grace and joy, I am delighted to oversee our Beloved's transition to becoming a life guide. As you are all aware, getting to this moment hasn't been without its challenges and difficulties, but standing here before us now is a spirit who has excelled in her recovery and achievements."

Molly could sense the love being sent to her and began to feel a little heady and dazed.

Orick turned to face her before continuing, "Molly, as you were known in your previous incarnation, with reverence and fulfilment you willingly now retake your own divine name and from this moment you shall once again be loved as Brenth."

A wave of excitement and loving energy suddenly washed over and through her and she found that she couldn't take her eyes of Orick. The connecting pull of energy was overpowering as she found herself absorbing what Orick was saying.

"Brenth, I ask that you repeat after me the Guide Guild's Code of Conduct."

She cleared her throat in readiness as Orick began, "As you all bear witness, I, Brenth, shall always follow the path of divine love and light as gifted to me by the Great Spirit. I shall unconditionally follow that light, and endeavour to serve with love, integrity and grace. In my role as a life guide, I will never intervene, interpose or interfere with my charge's free will and overall life contracts, nor shall I preclude any opportunity for my charge to learn additional valuable life lessons. And so it is."

Repeating the oath word for word, she looked towards the rear of the chamber and recognised her grandpa's light. Next to him was Nan and Great Grandma Hilda.

A feeling of elation passed through her as Orick spoke once again. "Brenth, it has been decreed that you shall receive your guiding light from Joshua, your assigned Ascended Master. Joshua is of the first ray — the ray of the Great Spirit's will. Joshua was assigned to be with you in your last life lived, in preparation for your eventual ascension, which sadly did not come to fruition."

An excited murmur filled the chamber as a light-being made his way to the front of the gathering. He appeared to glow with a luminescent, silver flicker and was almost translucent. Surrounding his energy was a silvery-blue aura. Brenth watched, entranced, as the light-being shifted his energy form so that she could recognise him. He was tall and of slim build, with Negro features. His jaw was so firmly set that it looked like it would break were a smile to cross it and his dark brown eyes bore into hers, as if searching for something which was no longer there. Without breaking eye contact, he reached out, took hold of her right hand, and placed a glint of light into it.

"Brenth, this is your guiding light which I, Joshua, gift unto you with blessings and reverence. Nurture and cherish it for all eternity; it means to serve you well."

Brenth looked down at her hand and watched as the guiding light rose and hovered above her, before suddenly dropping into what would have been her crown chakra. Instantly she felt a surge of energy shift into the core of her being as it sought to bring into alignment her energy force of vigour and resilience. Looking towards her grandpa and Nan, she blew them a kiss and waved goodbye while she watched their spirit lights fade into the distance.

"You okay, Brenth?" asked Orick and Prenge simultaneously.

"Err… yes… I think so. Wow, I'm a fully-fledged guide now, aren't I? It's strange though, how I recognised Joshua and I feel as if I've known him for all eternity. I'm sure he used to be in my dreams too. Anyway, what happens now?"

Orick grinned. "Well my dear Brenth, we are going to take you to meet some of the other guides who have just had their inauguration too. I think you might want to have a bit of a celebration and I believe that a certain soulmate is waiting to see you, too."

Chapter Forty-four: New Beginnings

<***>

When she met Braugh in the Gardens, Brenth knew it would be for the last time. She was overcome with mixed emotion and couldn't stop herself from feeling sad one minute then elated the next, as she realised that he was eager and more than ready for his ascension. He talked excitedly about what was going to happen and how much he was looking forward to his new role as a teacher guide.

"So… I guess this is it. A part of me wishes I was coming with you. In fact, had things not turned out the way they have, I would have been. You will stay in touch, won't you?"

"Of course, I'll stay in touch — you're not going to get rid of me that easily — and anyway, you're going on to new beginnings too, don't forget"

"You being funny? 'Forget' … that's my middle name, don't you know."

Braugh laughed out loud and reassuringly reached out and drew her close to him. "You're funny, and I'm glad that you've kept your sense of humour. You'll be okay, you know, Orick will see to that. Whatever happens, he'll look after you — he always has and he always will."

"Yeah, I'm sure he will. It's odd how things have turned out, when you think about it. I mean, you don't ever have to incarnate again, and I can't."

Braugh smiled. "Well you know what they say…?"

"No… what do they say?"

"Reach for the stars, embrace change and never go back."

Shaking her head, she tutted. "Whatever. See you around, maybe."

The following dawn, Brenth received a message from Adzullon asking her to meet him over in the Towers. Pushing her way through the crowd of assembled spirits, she headed towards him, waving to catch his attention.

His eyes lit up and shone brightly as he caught sight of her. He greeted her excitedly, "Ah, good to see you. Here, hold this… don't lose it," he said and thrust something into her hand. "I won't be long… I'll be with you after I've finished organising this lot."

Nodding and smiling, she decided to explore more of the Towers whilst she waited. Drifting down a corridor, she was drawn to a brilliant light which was shining into the corridor from one of the rooms. She peeped round the open door it was coming from and was surprised to find it a hub of activity, as multitudes of guardian angels and life guides were assembled in readiness to join their charges who were about to be born.

Looking around, she realised that Archangel Gabriel was there. Brenth watched from a distance as Gabriel bestowed blessings on each of the angels and guides. She could see that the archangel was holding a gold-coloured purse which contained a mixture of angel tears and star dust. As each angel or guide filed past her, she sprinkled the dust over them before they exited through a tunnel of white light. When the last of them had left, the archangel floated over to where Brenth was.

"Welcome, Beloved… Brenth isn't it, I thought I recognised your spirit light. I've been hearing good things about you. I believe your development has gone exceedingly well."

"Oh, erm… yes, thanks, I think so. I'm actually waiting for Adzullon — he's busy over in the Departures Lounge, as it were."

Gabriel smiled. "Yes, I know. He's been held up unfortunately, and has asked me to prepare you instead."

Feeling a little awkward, Brenth fidgeted as she didn't quite know what else to say or do. Out of the blue, the archangel blessed her and threw a handful of stardust over her energy.

Brenth was momentarily distracted as the stardust seeped into her vibration and then Gabriel reached for the ticket which was crumpled in her hand. Carefully unfolding it, the archangel read the symbols which were written on it, smiled, and instructed Brenth to go and wait by a large, imposing doorway.

Drifting over to the door which Gabriel had pointed out, she nonchalantly leaned against it, assuming that Adzullon would be joining her soon. Without warning, the door swung open, revealing a portal and Brenth lost her balance and tumbled backwards through it. Regaining her equilibrium, she was momentarily blinded by a brilliant white light. Becoming accustomed to what she was feeling and sensing, she realised that she was being enveloped in a swirling, purple mist which felt moist and warm. She wanted to languish and enjoy the wonderful feeling of being cocooned in its loving energy, and to relish the sensation of floating weightless, with a sense of limitless space.

Suddenly she realised that she could hear a familiar noise, a noise which she instinctively recognised as the unmistakable 'lub-dub' rhythm of life. Listening to the audible beats, she realised that she was actually hearing the beats of two hearts, one of a mother and the other of her baby.

"Brenth... Brenth... is that you? I can't see you, but I can sense you. Where are you?" asked a voice in surprise.

"Vimprn... is that you? I can't see you, either. Yes, I'm here. What's going on? What's happening?"

"I'm about to be born. Hang on a minute... what's this I can feel! Brenth, you're not gonna believe this — I've got dangly bits! Oh, good grief... no way! I'm a boy!"

Suddenly Brenth was aware that she was in a brightly lit maternity delivery room, looking down on a new-born baby boy.

"Vimprn... Vimprn... can you still hear me?"

"It's okay, Brenth, you're doing great. Just relax... enjoy the moment."

Brenth swung round in surprise to locate where the familiar voice had come from. "Orick, what the heck are you doing here?"

"I'm here to assist you," he said, as a beaming smile crossed his face. "Thumus will be here any minute as well. The Elders aren't leaving anything to chance. Guess what! You and I have both been assigned to be Vimprn's guides. She can't hear you anymore, by the way — her natal amnesia has just been activated."

25871588R00203

Printed in Great Britain
by Amazon